W9-AWX-055

WHITE BIRD

A WONDER STORY

Written and illustrated by R. J. PALACIO

INKED BY KEVIN CZAP

ALFRED A. KNOPF • NEW YORK

For Mollie, her ancestors,
and her descendants
—R.J.P.

THIS IS A BORZOI BOOK PUBLISHED BY ALFRED A. KNOPF

This is a work of fiction. Names, characters, places, and incidents either are the product of the author's imagination or are used fictitiously. Any resemblance to actual persons, living or dead, events, or locales is entirely coincidental.

Text and illustrations copyright © 2019 by R. J. Palacio
Afterword copyright © 2019 by Ruth Franklin
Inking by Kevin Czap

All rights reserved. Published in the United States by Alfred A. Knopf, an imprint of Random House Children's Books, a division of Penguin Random House LLC, New York. Originally published in hardcover in the United States by Alfred A. Knopf, an imprint of Random House Children's Books, a division of Penguin Random House LLC, New York, in 2019.

Knopf, Borzoi Books, and the colophon are registered trademarks of Penguin Random House LLC.

Image credits are located on page 219.

"Fourth Elegy: The Refugees," from *The Collected Poems of Muriel Rukeyser.*
Copyright © 2005 by Muriel Rukeyser. Reprinted by permission of ICM Partners.

Visit us on the Web! rhcbooks.com
Educators and librarians, for a variety of teaching tools, visit us at RHTeachersLibrarians.com

Library of Congress Cataloging-in-Publication Data is available upon request.
ISBN 978-0-525-64553-5 (trade) — ISBN 978-0-525-64554-2 (lib. bdg.) — ISBN 978-0-525-64555-9 (ebook) — ISBN 978-0-593-48778-5 (pbk.)

The text of this book is set in RJ, a font especially created for this book.
The illustrations were created digitally.

MANUFACTURED IN ITALY
10 9 8 7 6 5 4 3 2 1
First Paperback Edition 2021

Random House Children's Books supports the First Amendment and celebrates the right to read.

They are the children.   They have their games.

They made a circle on a map of time,

skipping they entered it, laughing lifted the agate.

I will get you an orange cat, and a pig called Tangerine.

The gladness-bird beats wings against an opaque glass.

There is a white bird in the top of the tree.

They leave their games, and pass.

       —Muriel Rukeyser, "Fourth Elegy: The Refugees"

PROLOGUE

Those who cannot remember the past are
condemned to repeat it.
-George Santayana

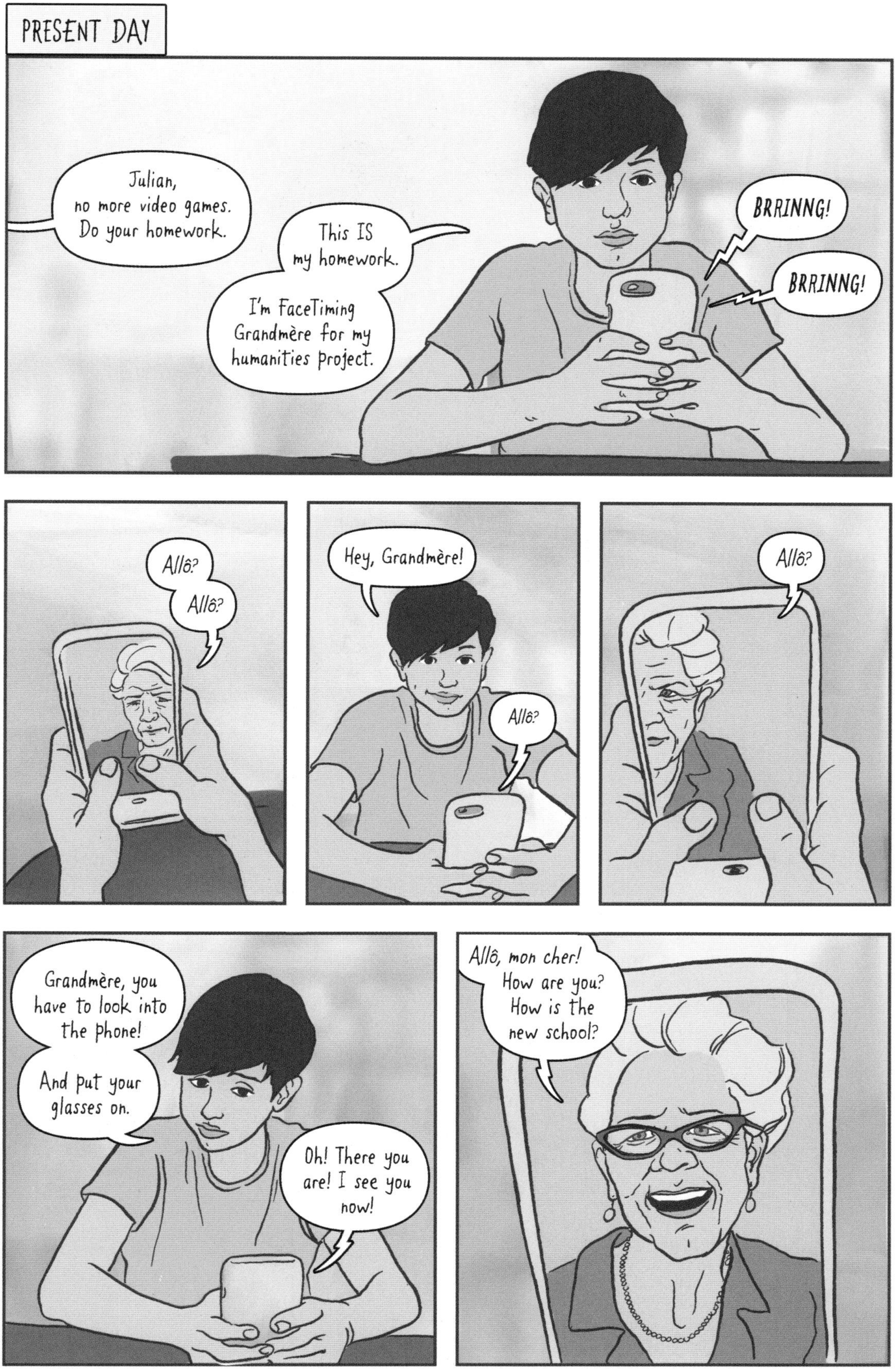
PRESENT DAY
Julian, no more video games. Do your homework.
This IS my homework.
I'm FaceTiming Grandmère for my humanities project.
BRRINNG!
BRRINNG!
Allô?
Allô?
Hey, Grandmère!
Allô?
Allô?
Grandmère, you have to look into the phone!
And put your glasses on.
Oh! There you are! I see you now!
Allô, mon cher! How are you? How is the new school?

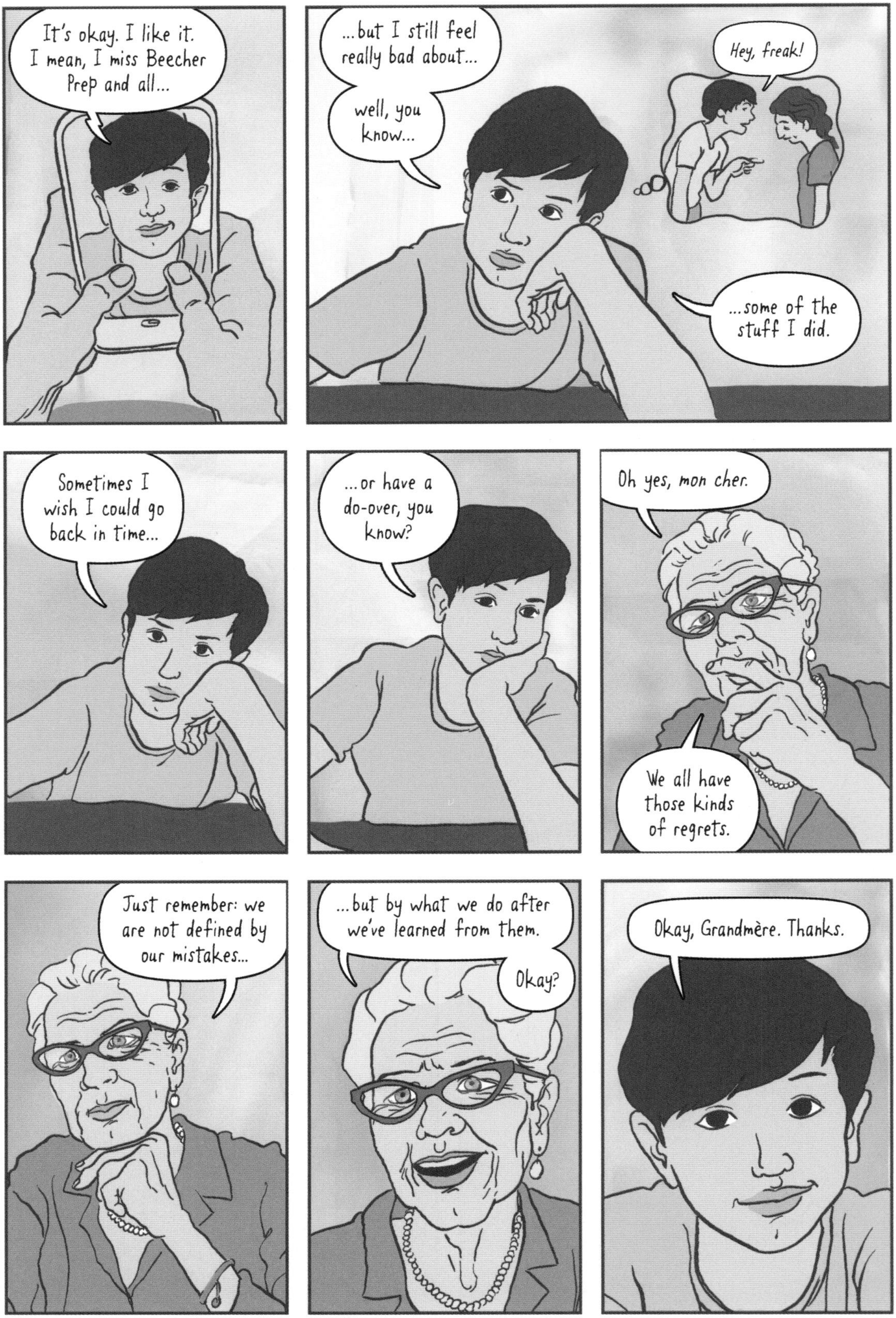
It's okay. I like it. I mean, I miss Beecher Prep and all...
...but I still feel really bad about...
well, you know...
Hey, freak!
...some of the stuff I did.
Sometimes I wish I could go back in time...
...or have a do-over, you know?
Oh yes, mon cher.
We all have those kinds of regrets.
Just remember: we are not defined by our mistakes...
...but by what we do after we've learned from them.
Okay?
Okay, Grandmère. Thanks.

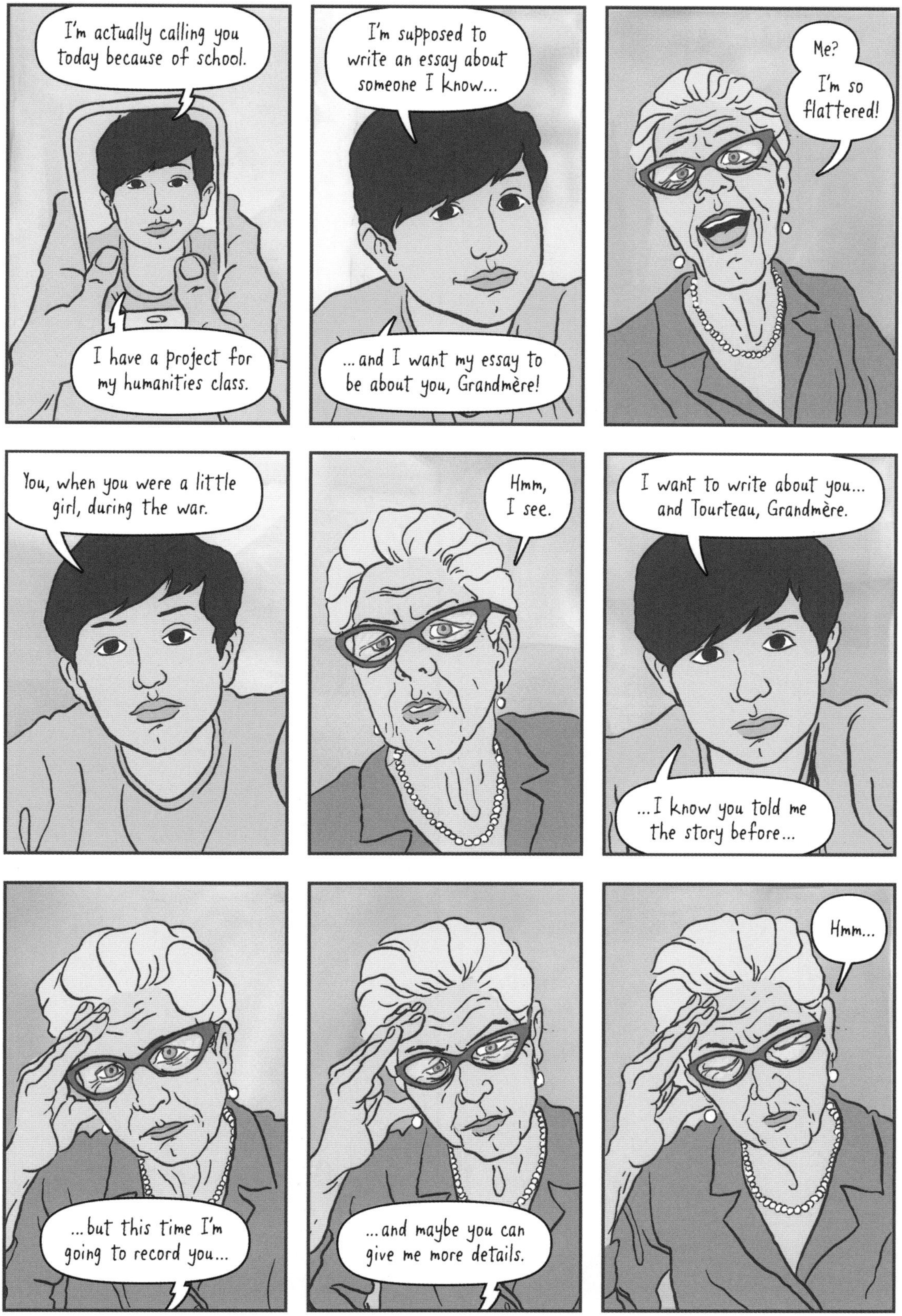

I'm actually calling you today because of school.
I have a project for my humanities class.
I'm supposed to write an essay about someone I know...
...and I want my essay to be about you, Grandmère!
Me?
I'm so flattered!
You, when you were a little girl, during the war.
Hmm, I see.
I want to write about you... and Tourteau, Grandmère.
...I know you told me the story before...
...but this time I'm going to record you...
...and maybe you can give me more details.
Hmm...

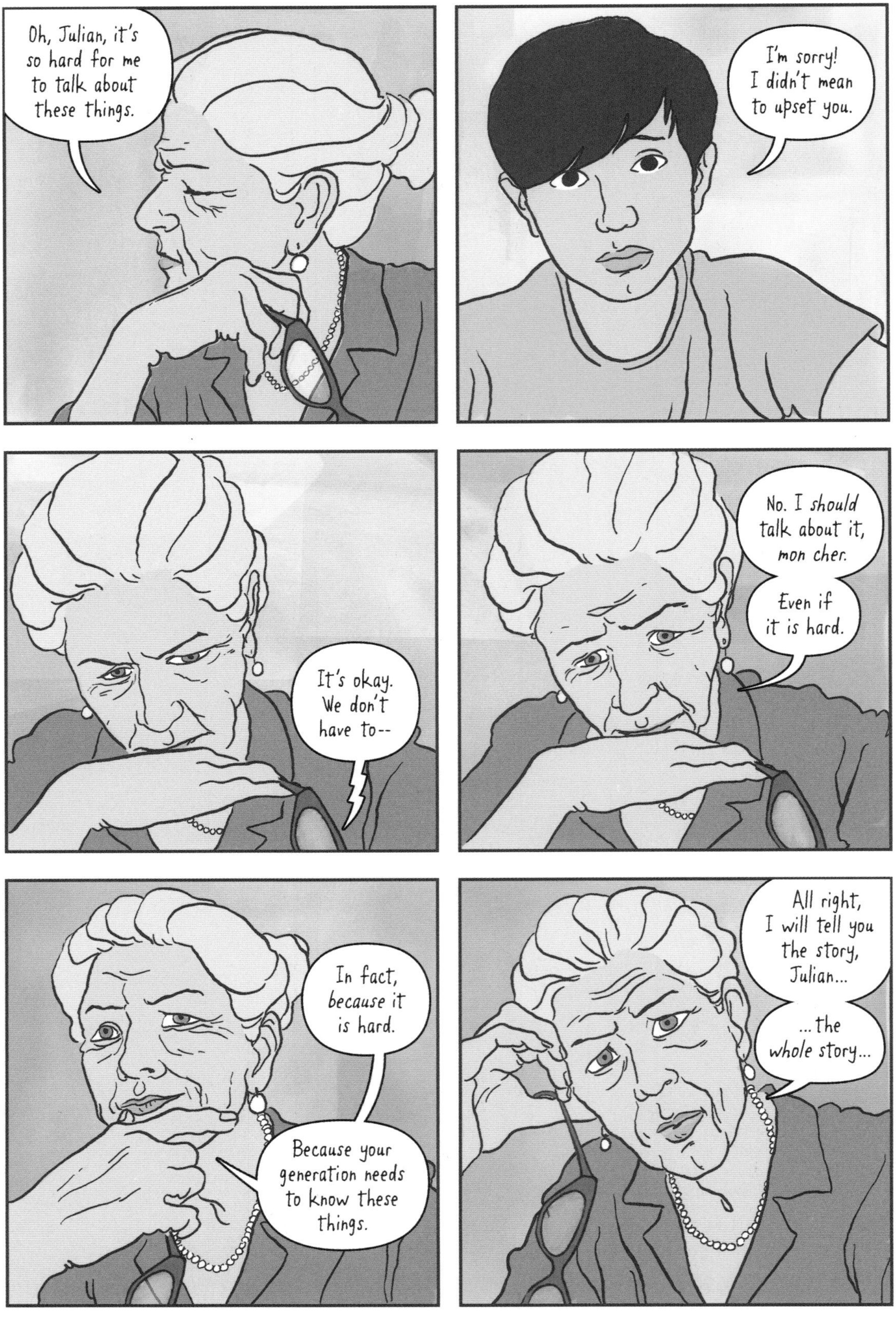
Oh, Julian, it's so hard for me to talk about these things.
I'm sorry! I didn't mean to upset you.
It's okay. We don't have to--
No. I *should* talk about it, *mon cher.*
Even if it is hard.
In fact, *because* it is hard.
Because your generation needs to know these things.
All right, I will tell you the story, Julian...
...the *whole story...*

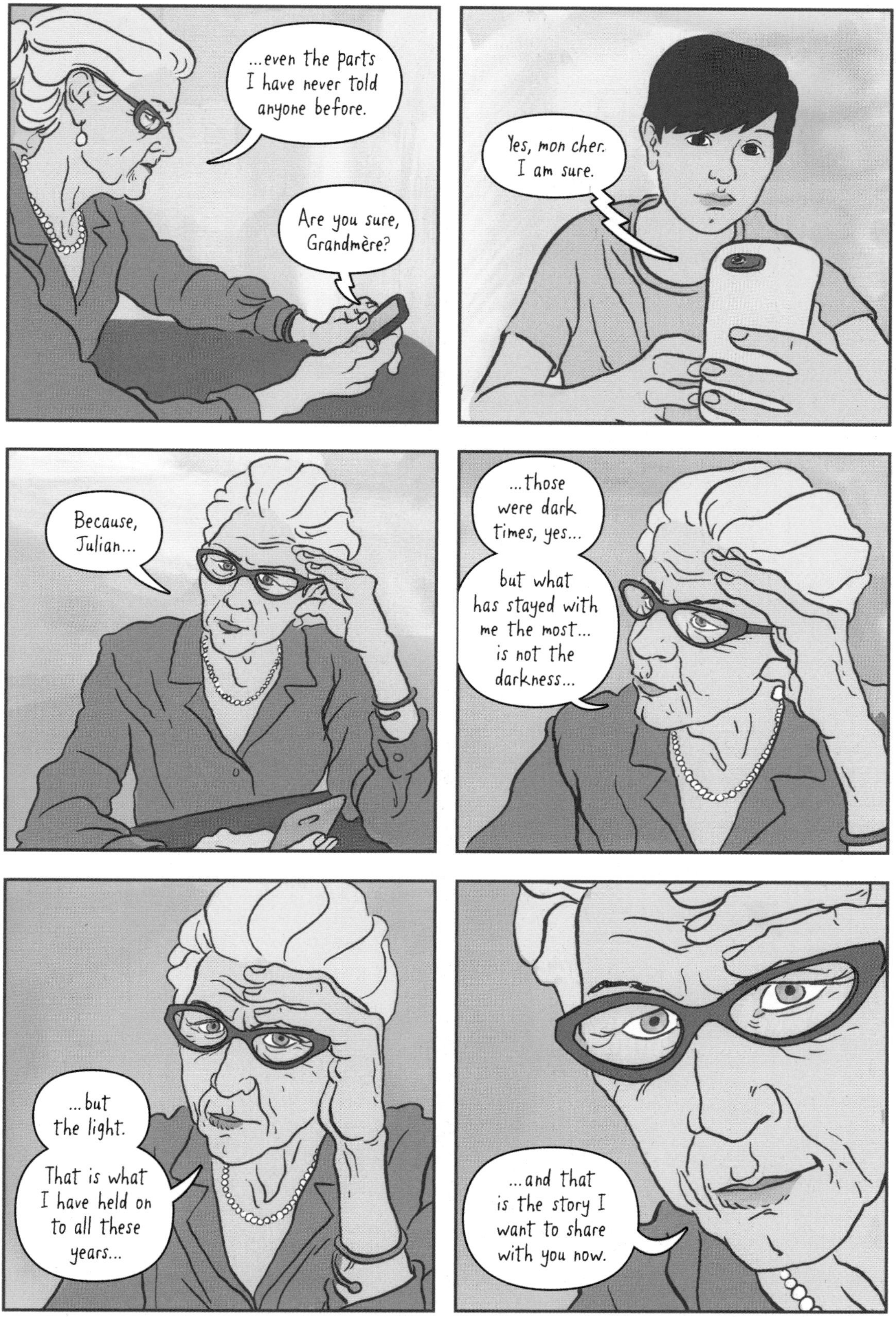
...even the parts I have never told anyone before.
Are you sure, Grandmère?
Yes, mon cher. I am sure.
Because, Julian...
...those were dark times, yes...
but what has stayed with me the most... is not the darkness...
...but the light.
That is what I have held on to all these years...
...and that is the story I want to share with you now.

PART ONE

The birds know mountains that we have not dreamed...

-Muriel Rukeyser, "Fifth Elegy: A Turning Wind"

CHAPTER 1

"ONCE UPON A TIME" IS HOW MOST FAIRY TALES BEGIN. THAT IS HOW I WILL START MY STORY, TOO, BECAUSE MY LIFE TRULY BEGAN AS A FAIRY TALE.

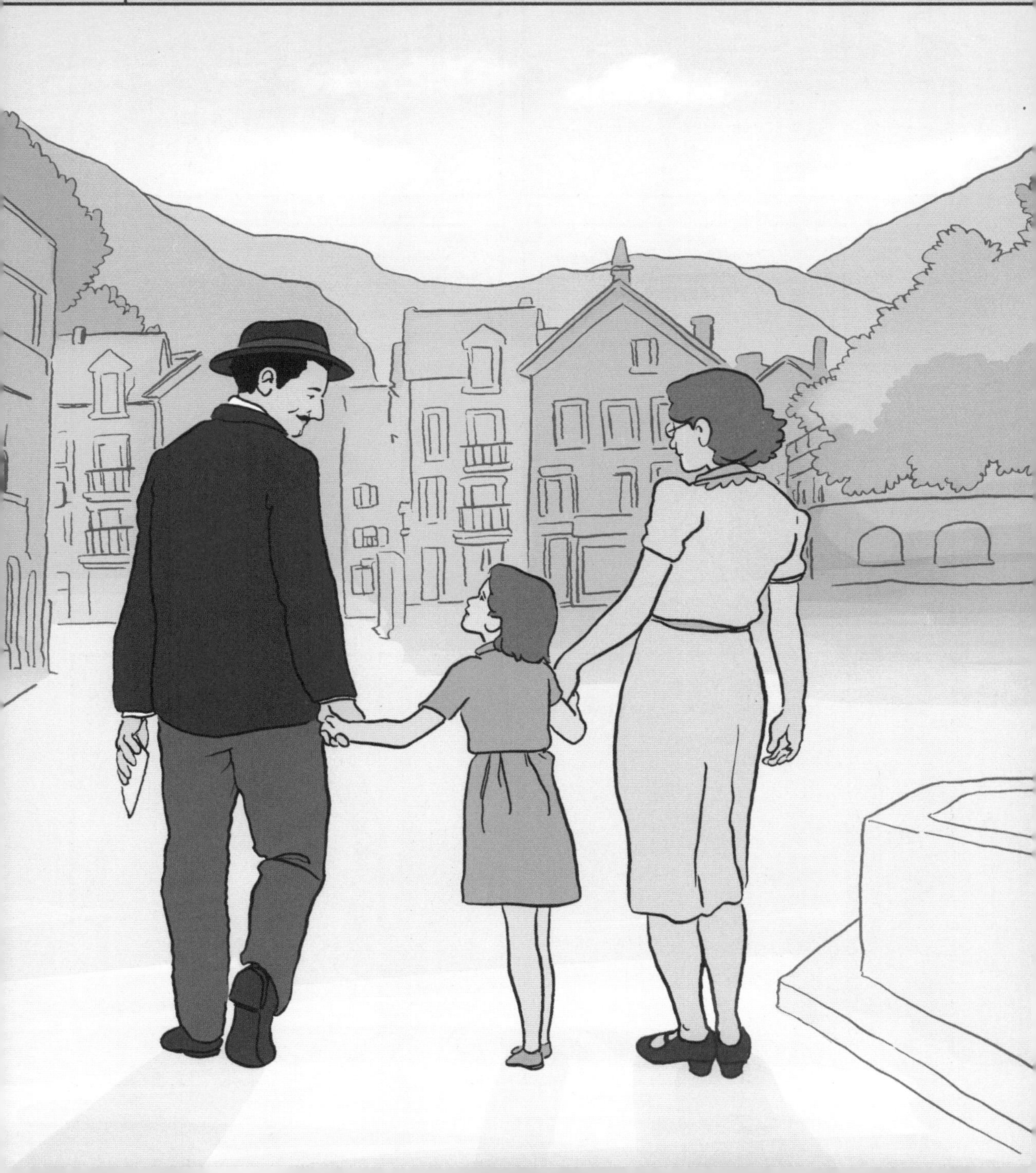

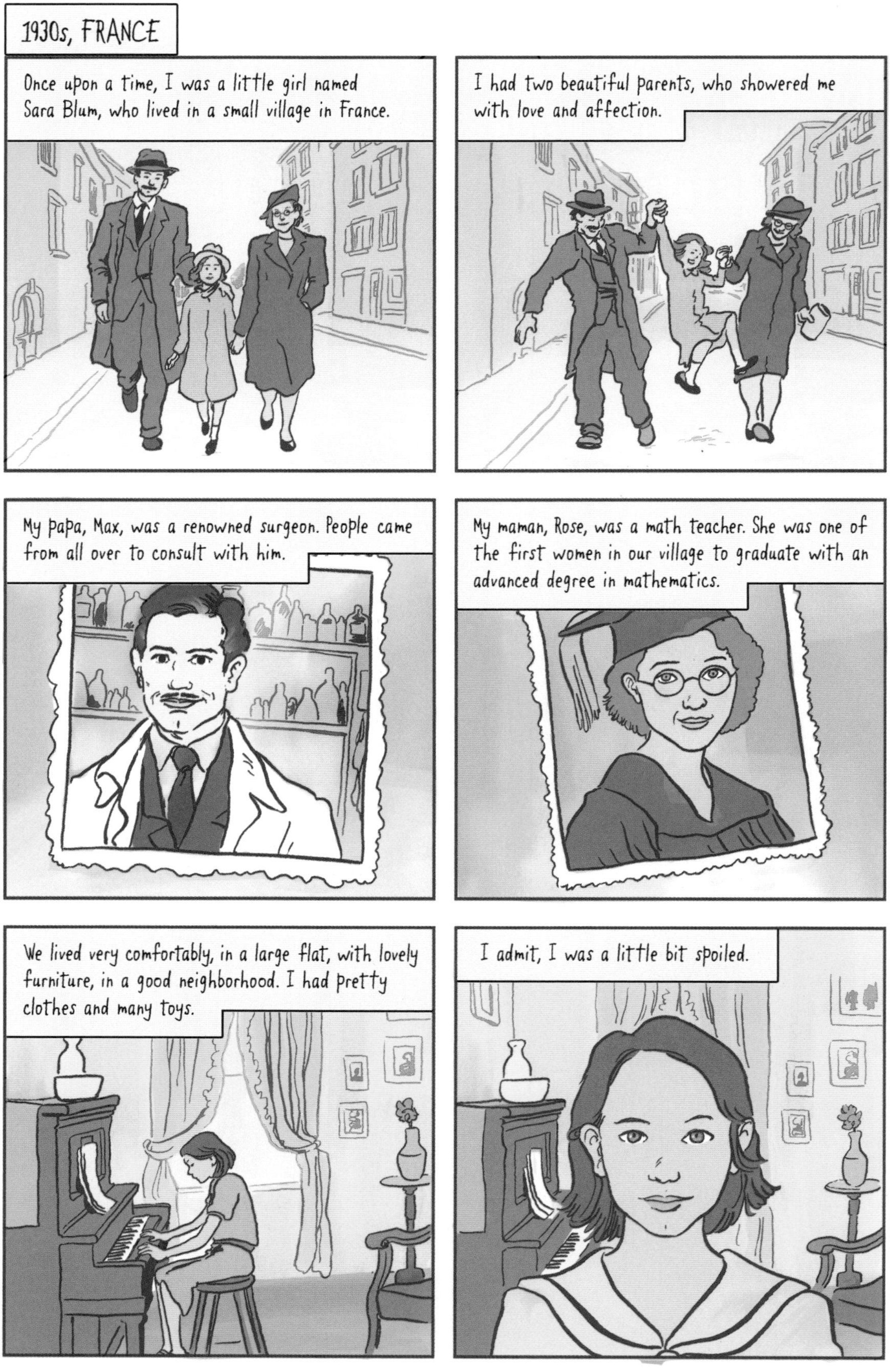
1930s, FRANCE
Once upon a time, I was a little girl named Sara Blum, who lived in a small village in France.
I had two beautiful parents, who showered me with love and affection.
My papa, Max, was a renowned surgeon. People came from all over to consult with him.
My maman, Rose, was a math teacher. She was one of the first women in our village to graduate with an advanced degree in mathematics.
We lived very comfortably, in a large flat, with lovely furniture, in a good neighborhood. I had pretty clothes and many toys.
I admit, I was a little bit spoiled.

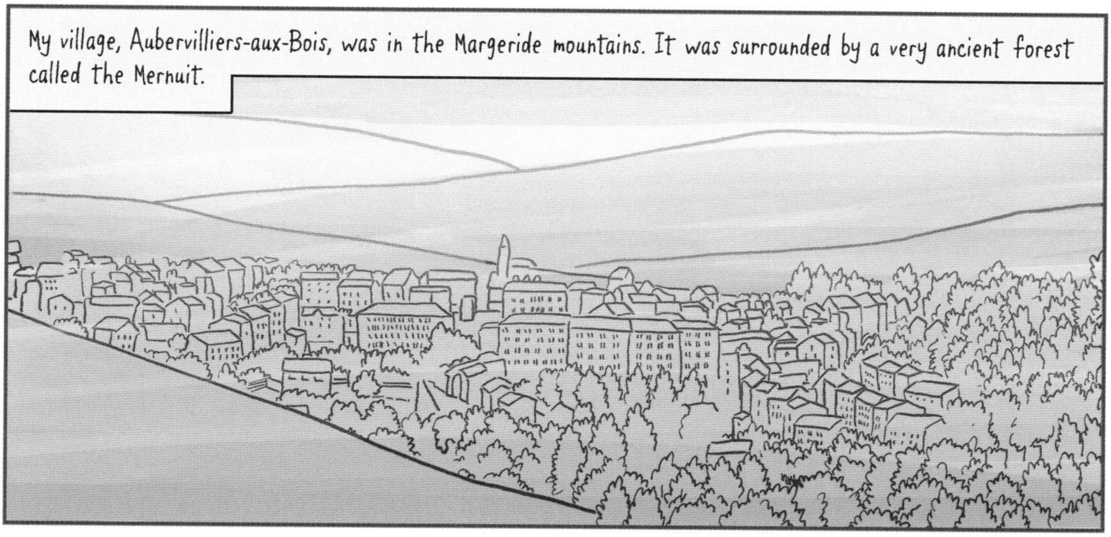
My village, Aubervilliers-aux-Bois, was in the Margeride mountains. It was surrounded by a very ancient forest called the Mernuit.

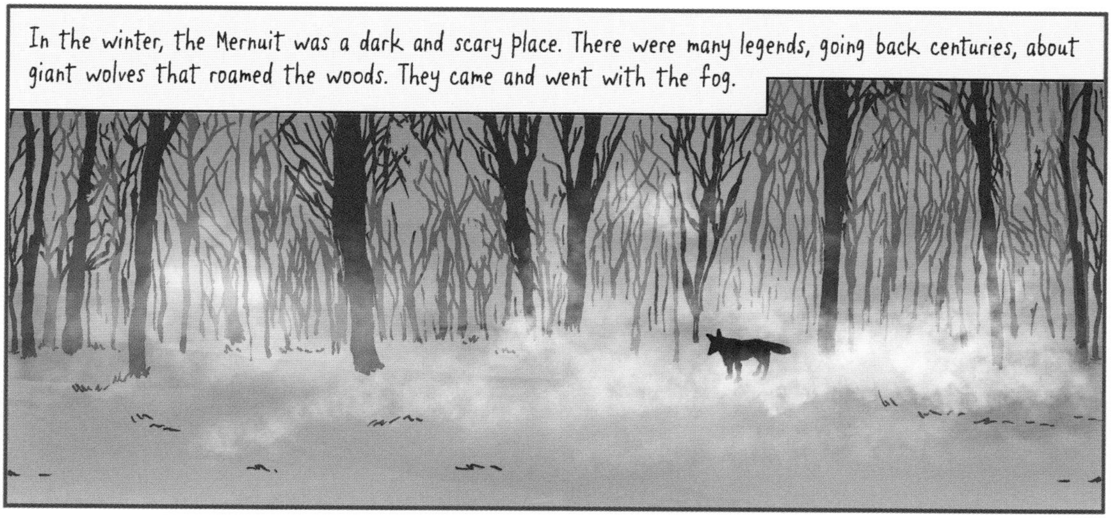
In the winter, the Mernuit was a dark and scary place. There were many legends, going back centuries, about giant wolves that roamed the woods. They came and went with the fog.

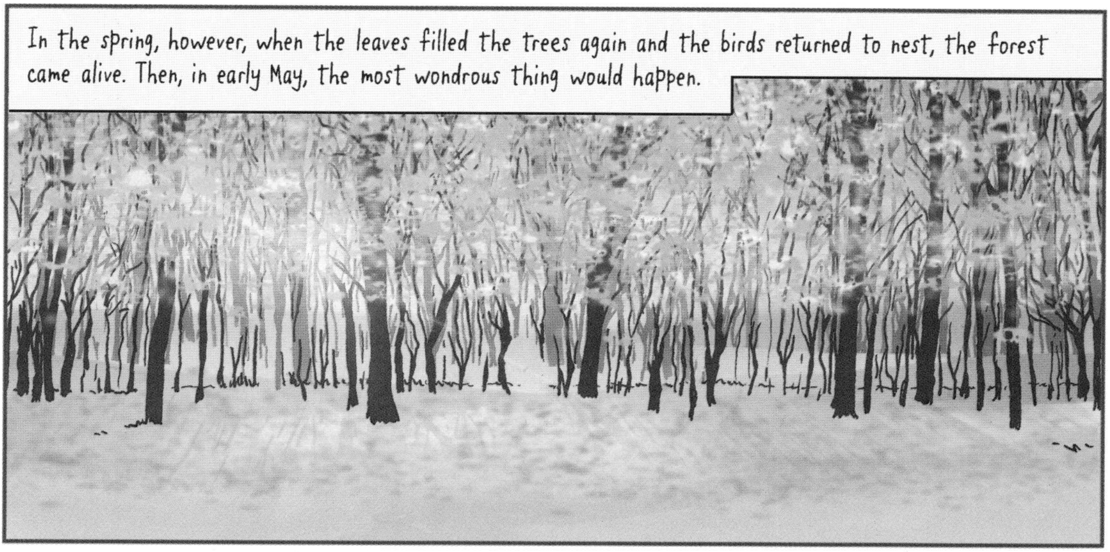
In the spring, however, when the leaves filled the trees again and the birds returned to nest, the forest came alive. Then, in early May, the most wondrous thing would happen.

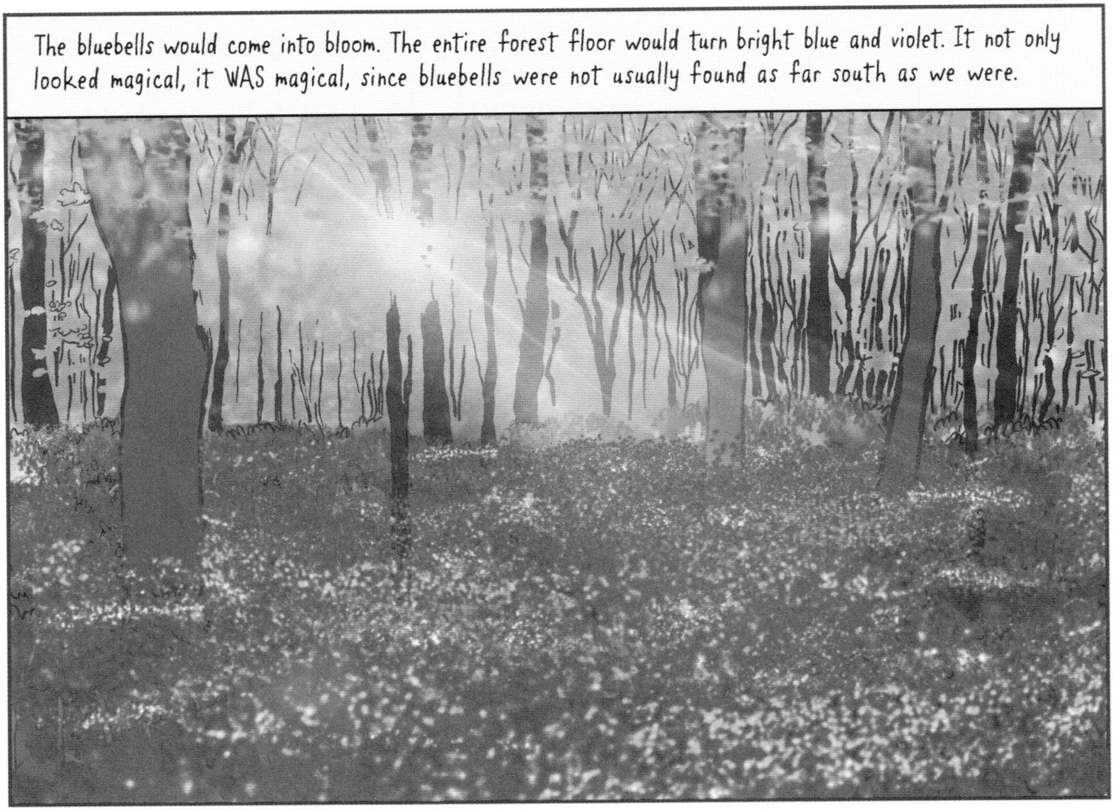
The bluebells would come into bloom. The entire forest floor would turn bright blue and violet. It not only looked magical, it WAS magical, since bluebells were not usually found as far south as we were.

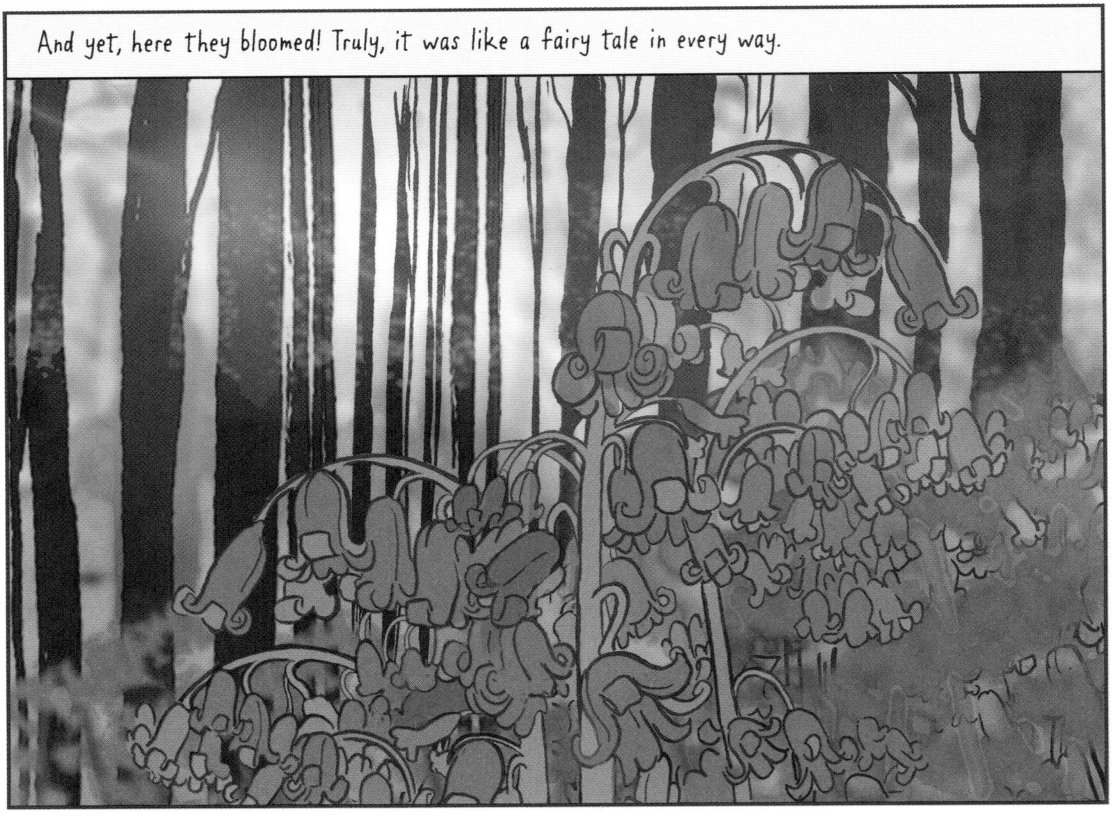
And yet, here they bloomed! Truly, it was like a fairy tale in every way.

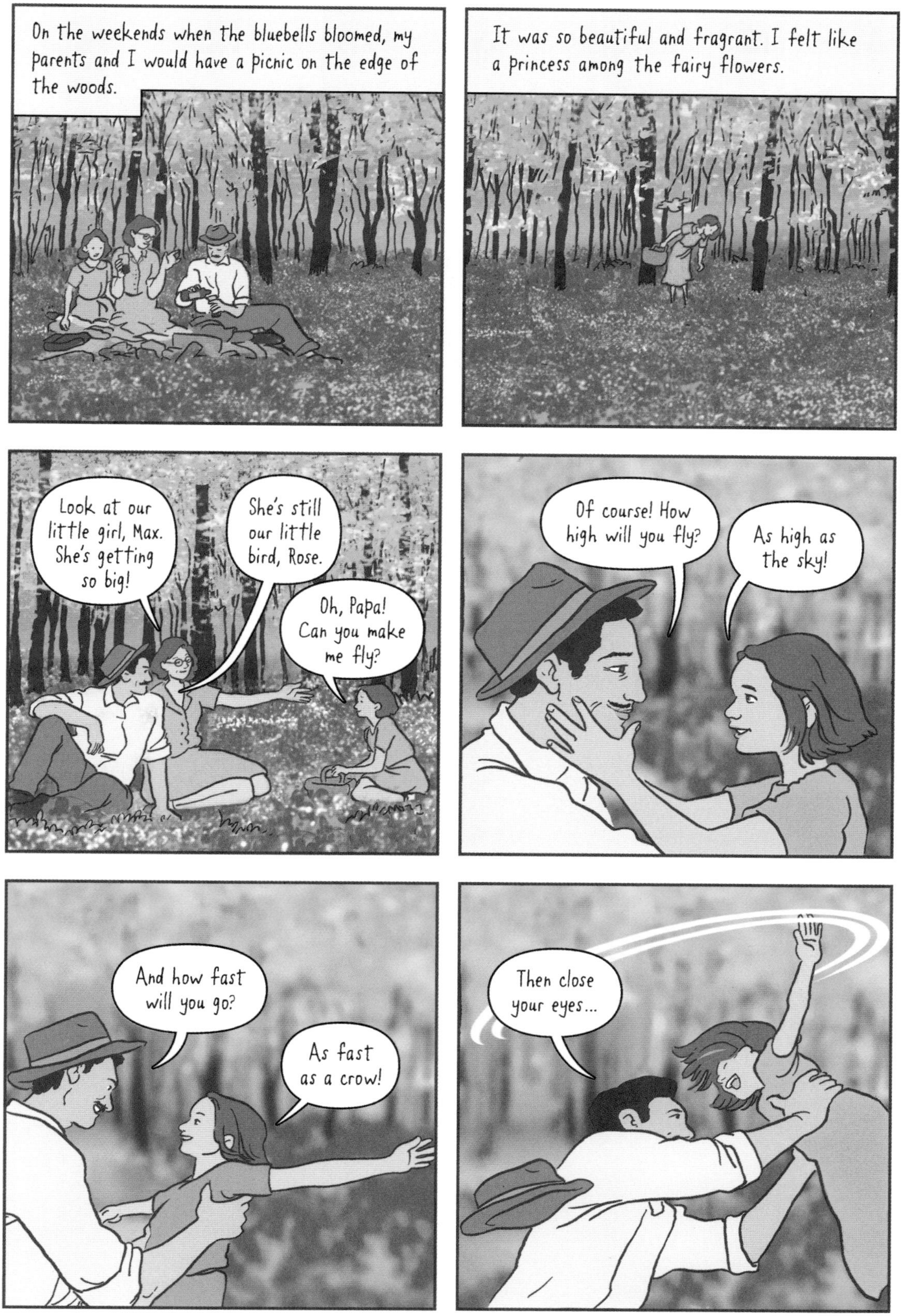
On the weekends when the bluebells bloomed, my parents and I would have a picnic on the edge of the woods.
It was so beautiful and fragrant. I felt like a princess among the fairy flowers.
Look at our little girl, Max. She's getting so big!
She's still our little bird, Rose.
Oh, Papa! Can you make me fly?
Of course! How high will you fly?
As high as the sky!
And how fast will you go?
As fast as a crow!
Then close your eyes...

...time to rise!

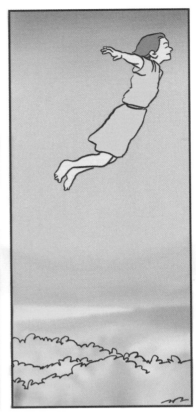

Yes, in those days, I was as happy and carefree as a bird. But the world was changing.

CHAPTER 2

FRANCE SURRENDERED TO GERMANY IN JUNE 1940. AS A RESULT, THE COUNTRY WAS SPLIT INTO TWO ZONES: THE OCCUPIED ZONE AND THE FREE ZONE.

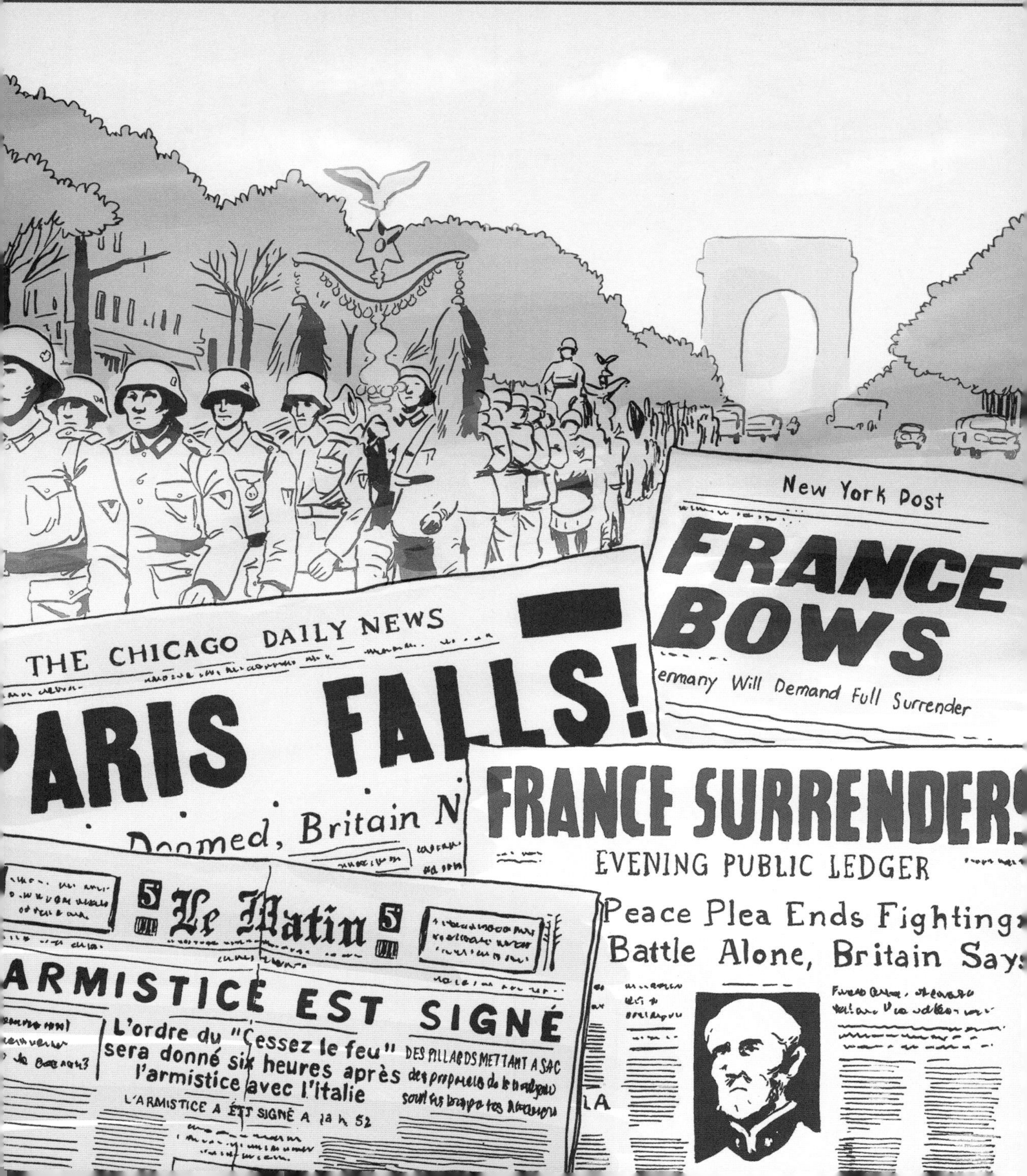

New York Post
FRANCE BOWS
ermany Will Demand Full Surrender
THE CHICAGO DAILY NEWS
PARIS FALLS!
Doomed, Britain N
FRANCE SURRENDERS
EVENING PUBLIC LEDGER
Peace Plea Ends Fighting
Battle Alone, Britain Says
Le Matin
ARMISTICE EST SIGNÉ
L'ordre du "Cessez le feu" sera donné six heures après l'armistice avec l'Italie
L'ARMISTICE A ÉTÉ SIGNÉ A 18 h. 52

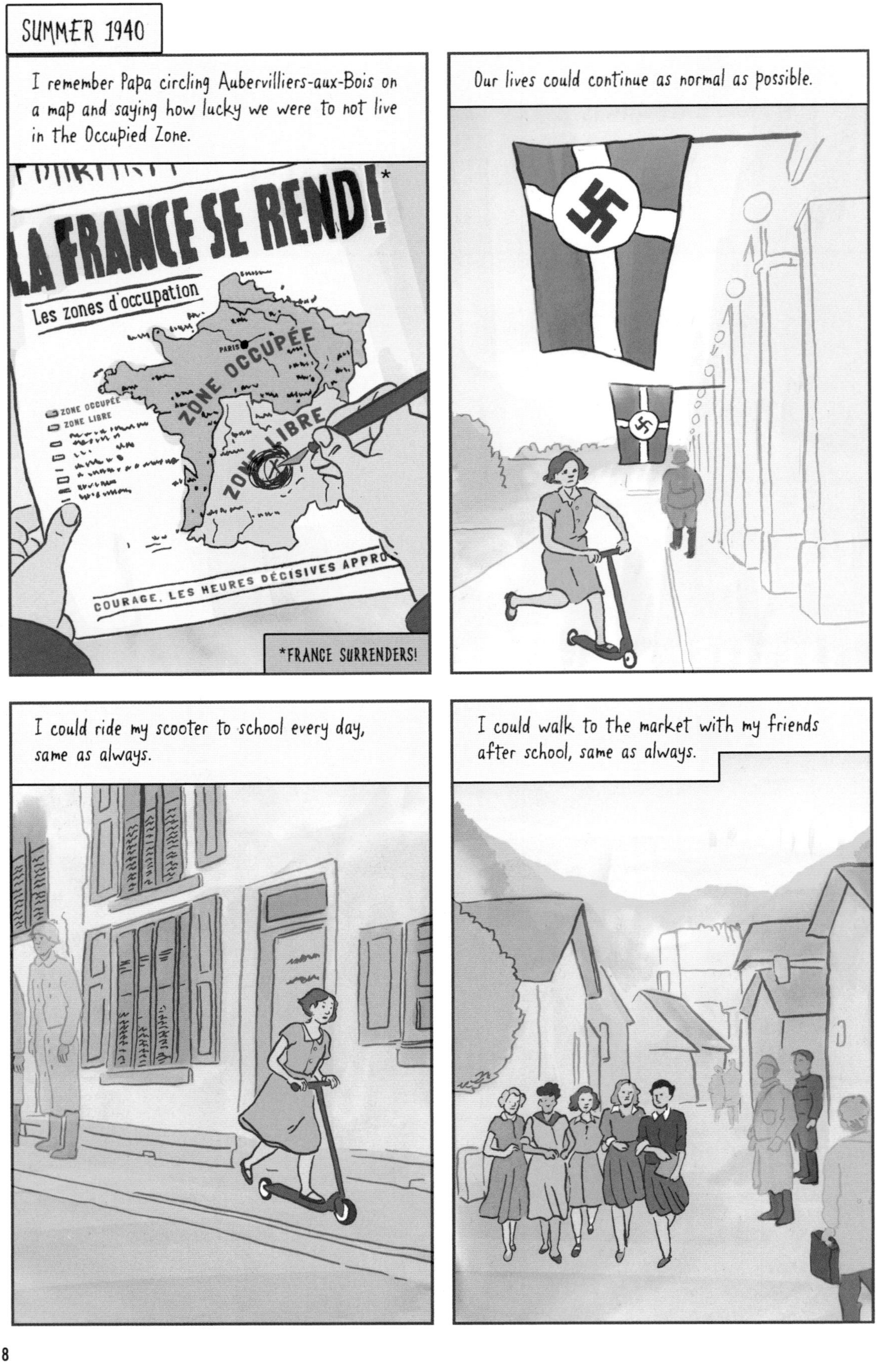
SUMMER 1940
I remember Papa circling Aubervilliers-aux-Bois on a map and saying how lucky we were to not live in the Occupied Zone.
LA FRANCE SE REND!*
Les zones d'occupation
PARIS
ZONE OCCUPÉE
ZONE LIBRE
ZONE OCCUPÉE
ZONE LIBRE
COURAGE, LES HEURES DÉCISIVES APPRO
*FRANCE SURRENDERS!
Our lives could continue as normal as possible.
I could ride my scooter to school every day, same as always.
I could walk to the market with my friends after school, same as always.

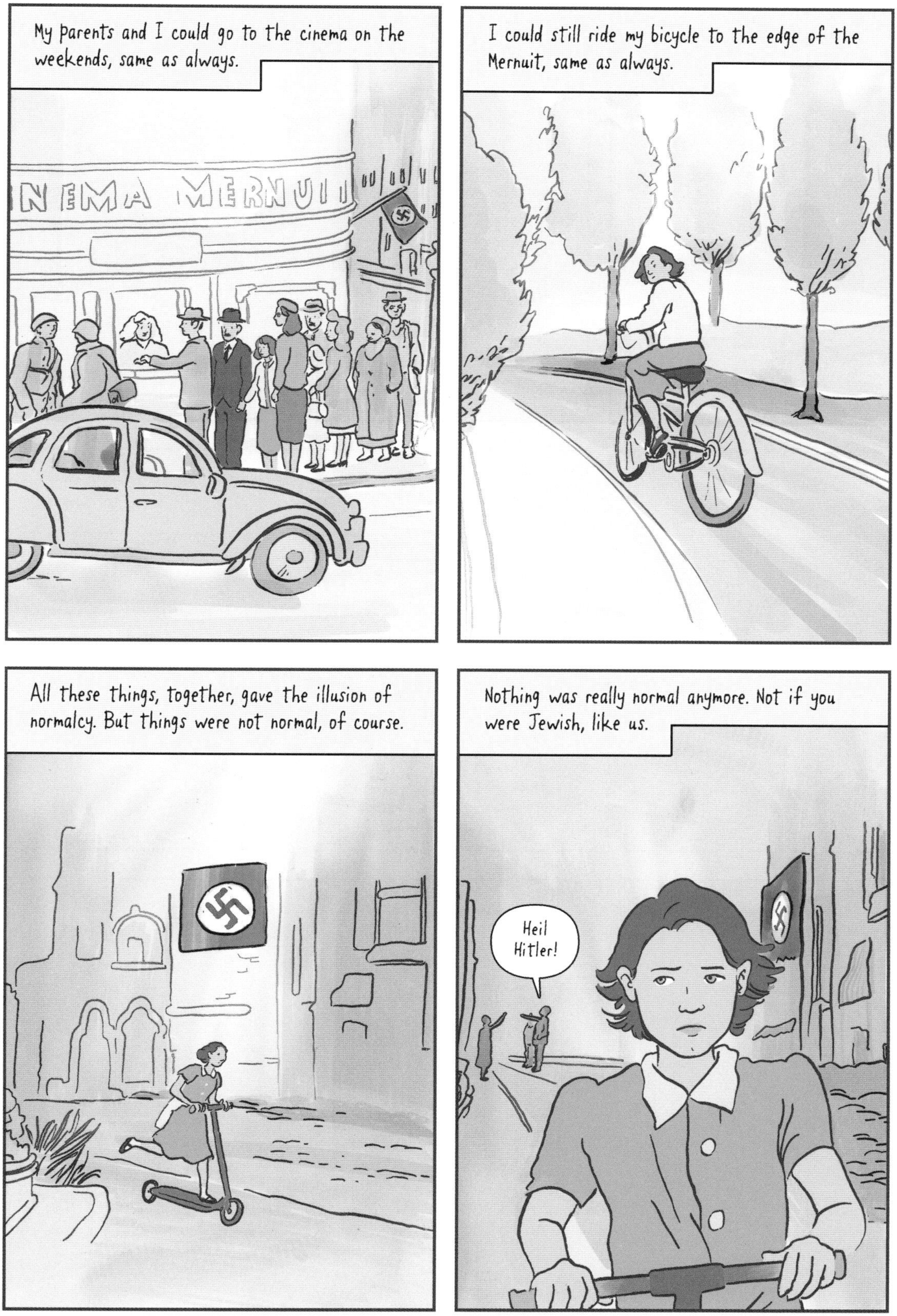
My parents and I could go to the cinema on the weekends, same as always.
I could still ride my bicycle to the edge of the Mernuit, same as always.
All these things, together, gave the illusion of normalcy. But things were not normal, of course.
Nothing was really normal anymore. Not if you were Jewish, like us.
Heil Hitler!

The illusion of normalcy did not last very long, anyway.

The Vichy government passed a series of anti-Jewish laws.

*STATUT DES JUIFS

*STATUTE ON JEWS

They banned Jews from going to certain public places.

*PARC AUX ENFANTS
INTERDIT AUX JUIFS

*PARK FOR CHILDREN FORBIDDEN TO JEWS

They kept lists of Jewish people and where they lived.

9	COHEN	Abraham	Bul...
0	COHEN	Meer	Aron
11	BLUM	Rem	Arke
12	BLUM	Sara	Ayla
13	BLUM	Samuel	Em...
14	MOSCOWITZ	Frances	Jh...
15	NEILL	Solomon	Jh...
116	WEILL	Daniel	Ar...
117	LEVY	Abram	g...
118	MAHLER	Zelik	...
119	FEINBERG	Anya	...
120	BLOCH	Jacob	...
	MEYER	Rachel	...

They stamped the word *Juif* or *Juive* on our identity cards. "Jew." They would not let Jews work in certain jobs. Maman lost her job at the university.

Sara Blum

JUIVE

There began a very systemized campaign of anti-Jewish propaganda, blaming Jews for all the troubles in France.

BOULANGERIE PATISSERIE

DER EWIGE JUDE

Posters, movies, and even radio programs sought to dehumanize us, turn us into hideous stereotypes.

DER EWIGE JUDE

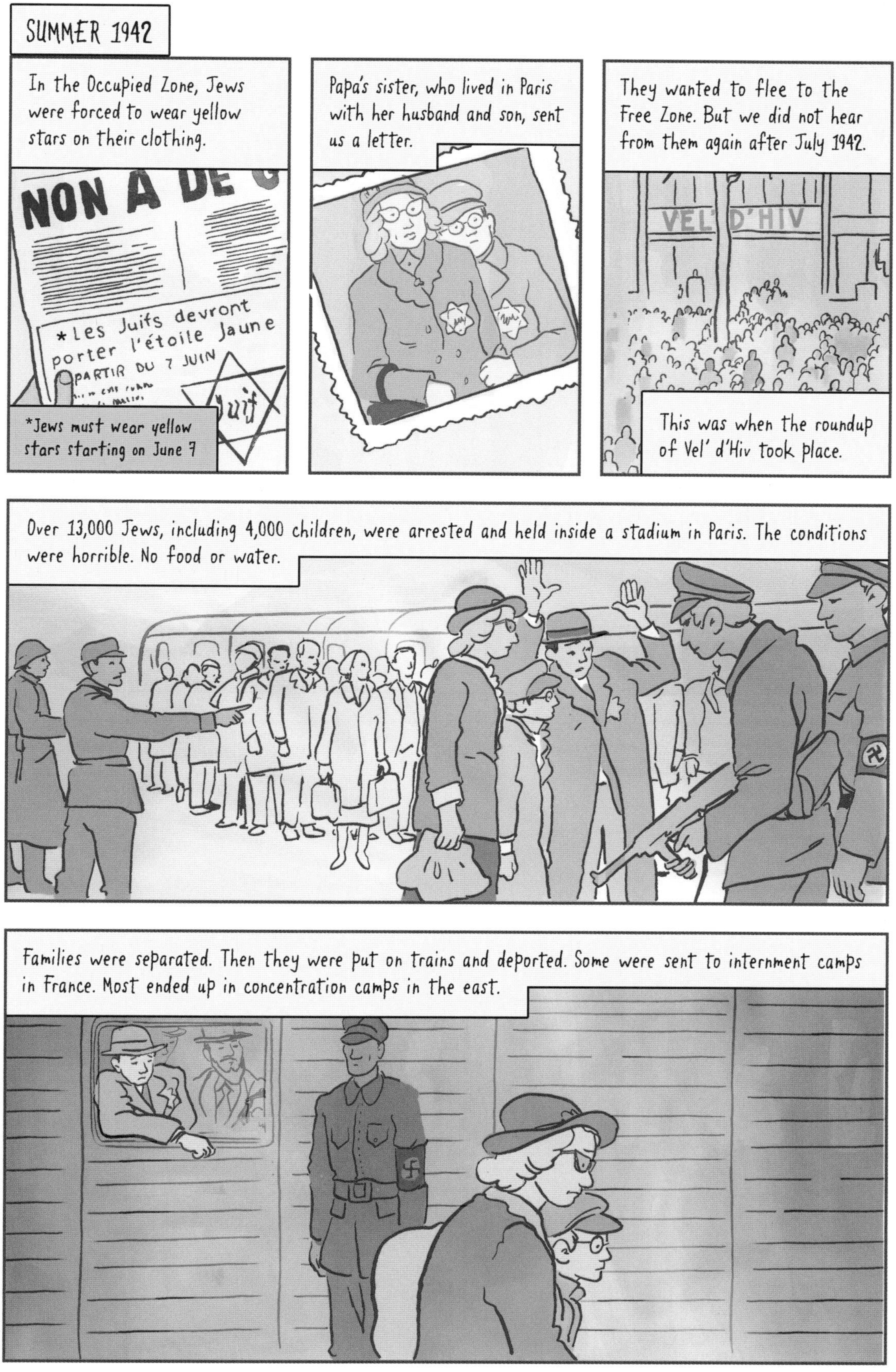
SUMMER 1942
In the Occupied Zone, Jews were forced to wear yellow stars on their clothing.
NON A DE G
*Les Juifs devront porter l'étoile Jaune
PARTIR DU 7 JUIN
Juif
*Jews must wear yellow stars starting on June 7
Papa's sister, who lived in Paris with her husband and son, sent us a letter.
They wanted to flee to the Free Zone. But we did not hear from them again after July 1942.
VEL' D'HIV
This was when the roundup of Vel' d'Hiv took place.
Over 13,000 Jews, including 4,000 children, were arrested and held inside a stadium in Paris. The conditions were horrible. No food or water.
Families were separated. Then they were put on trains and deported. Some were sent to internment camps in France. Most ended up in concentration camps in the east.

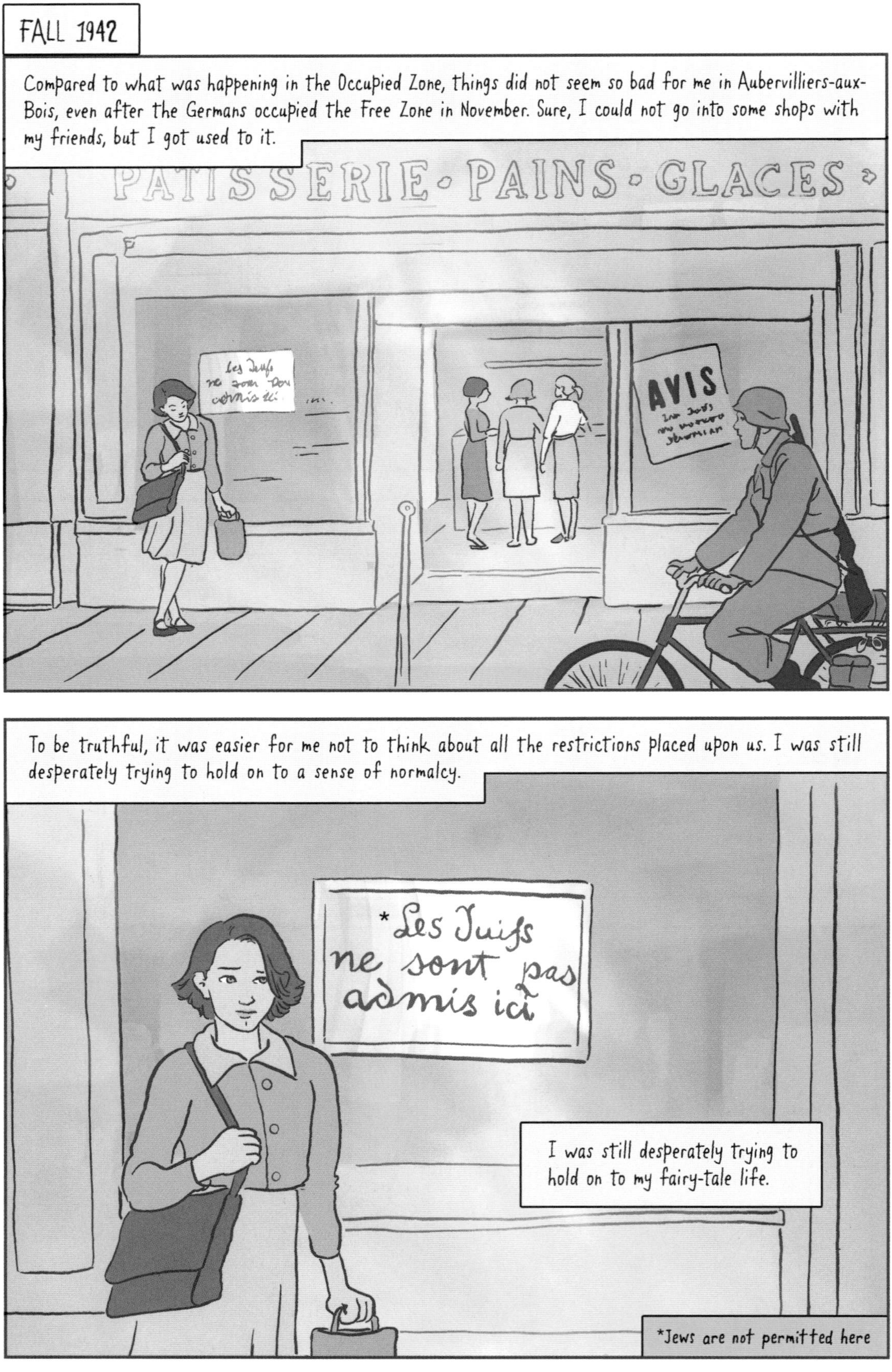

FALL 1942
Compared to what was happening in the Occupied Zone, things did not seem so bad for me in Aubervilliers-aux-Bois, even after the Germans occupied the Free Zone in November. Sure, I could not go into some shops with my friends, but I got used to it.
PATISSERIE • PAINS • GLACES
AVIS
To be truthful, it was easier for me not to think about all the restrictions placed upon us. I was still desperately trying to hold on to a sense of normalcy.
*Les Juifs ne sont pas admis ici
I was still desperately trying to hold on to my fairy-tale life.
*Jews are not permitted here

CHAPTER 3

MY SCHOOL, LUCKILY, WAS A HAVEN FOR ME. THE ÉCOLE LAFAYETTE WAS FOUNDED ON THE PRINCIPLES OF THE ENLIGHTENMENT. IT WELCOMED CHILDREN OF ALL FAITHS.

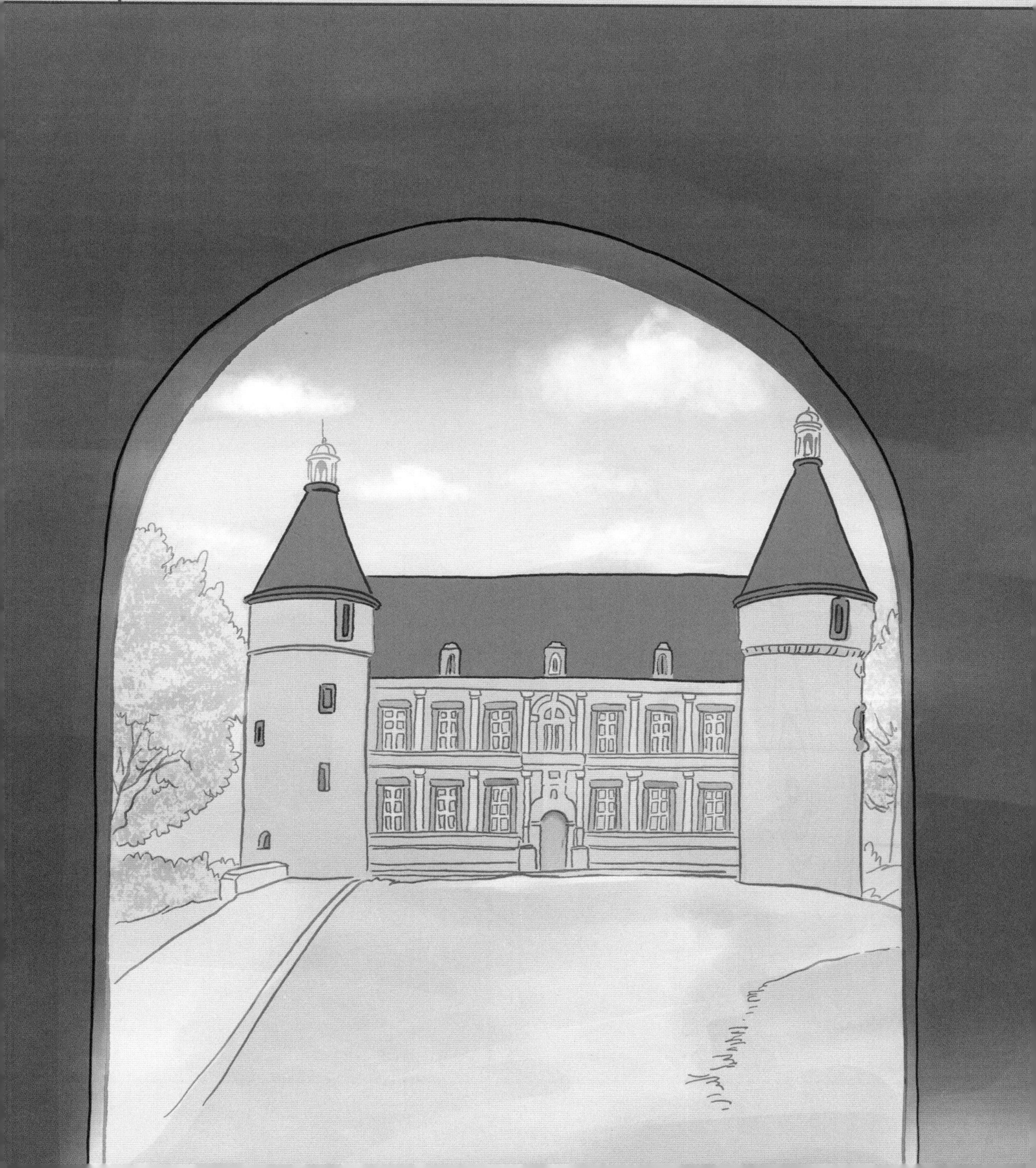

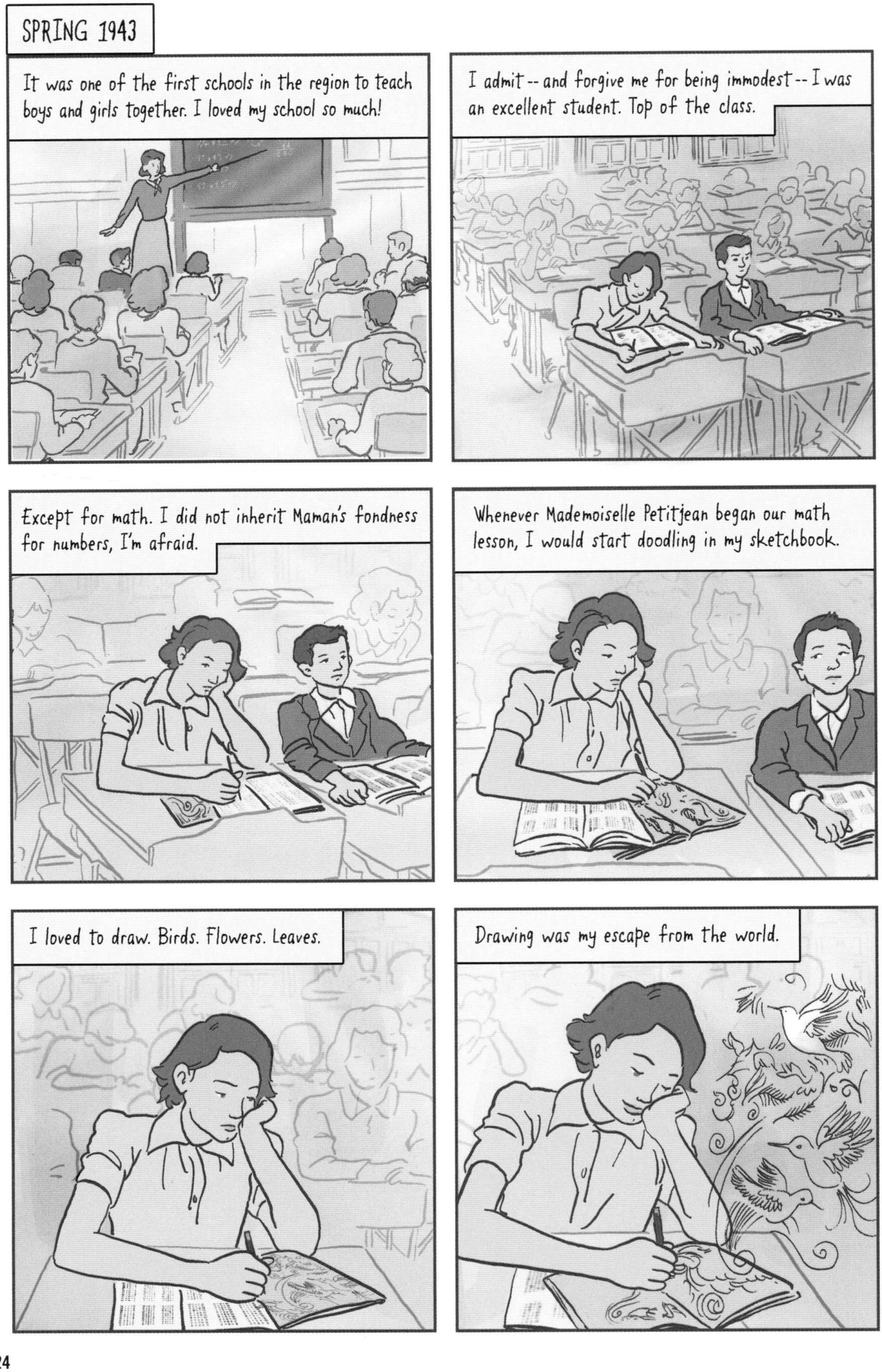
SPRING 1943
It was one of the first schools in the region to teach boys and girls together. I loved my school so much!
I admit -- and forgive me for being immodest -- I was an excellent student. Top of the class.
Except for math. I did not inherit Maman's fondness for numbers, I'm afraid.
Whenever Mademoiselle Petitjean began our math lesson, I would start doodling in my sketchbook.
I loved to draw. Birds. Flowers. Leaves.
Drawing was my escape from the world.

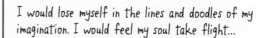

When I drew, I would forget about the war, the Nazis, and everything that was going on around me.

Sara?

I would lose myself in the lines and doodles of my imagination. I would feel my soul take flight...

Sara!

Sara!

Huh? Yes?

Would you like to share your drawing with the rest of the class?

No, Mademoiselle Petitjean!

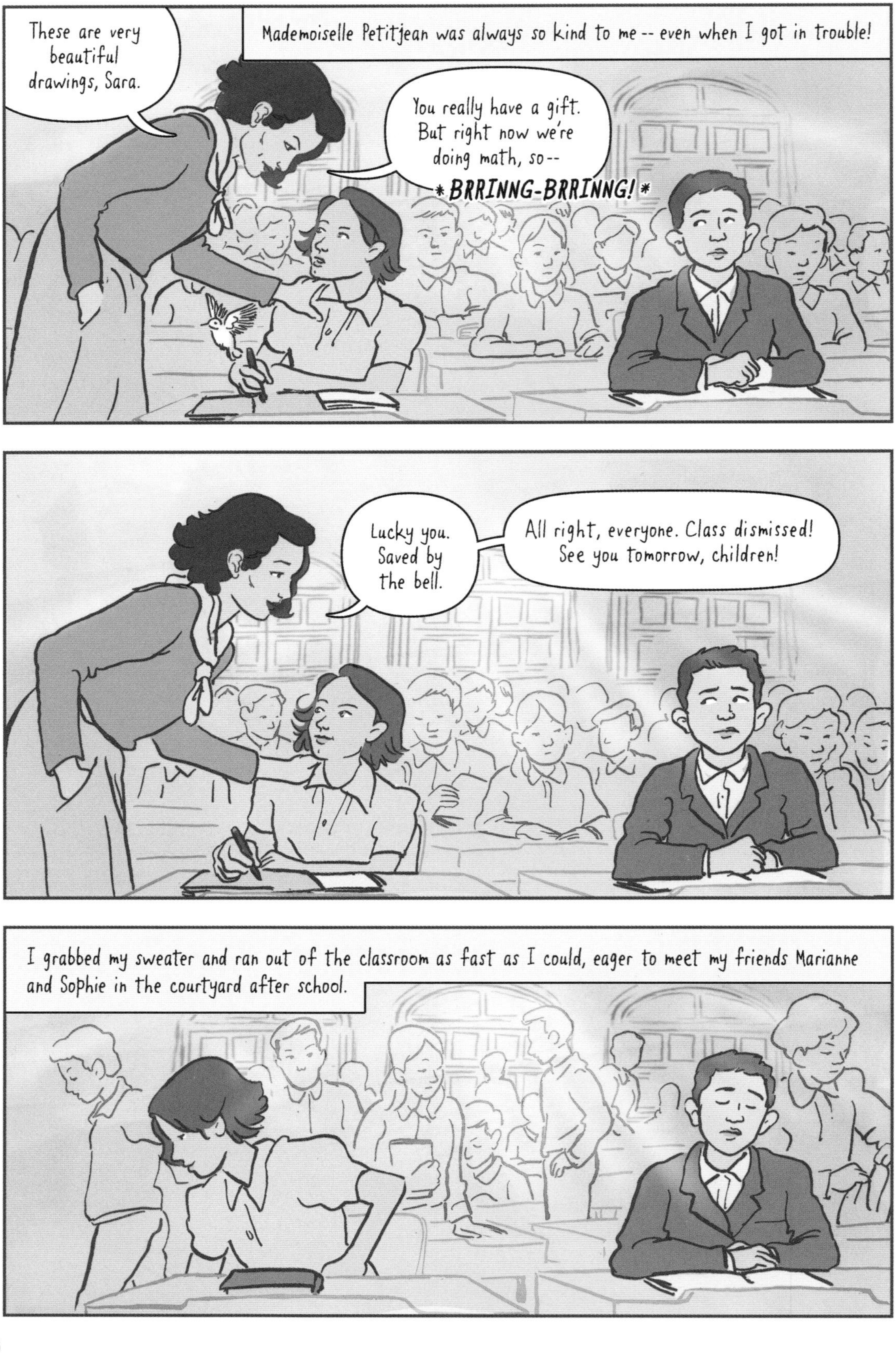
These are very beautiful drawings, Sara.
Mademoiselle Petitjean was always so kind to me -- even when I got in trouble!
You really have a gift. But right now we're doing math, so--
BRRINNG-BRRINNG!
Lucky you. Saved by the bell.
All right, everyone. Class dismissed! See you tomorrow, children!
I grabbed my sweater and ran out of the classroom as fast as I could, eager to meet my friends Marianne and Sophie in the courtyard after school.

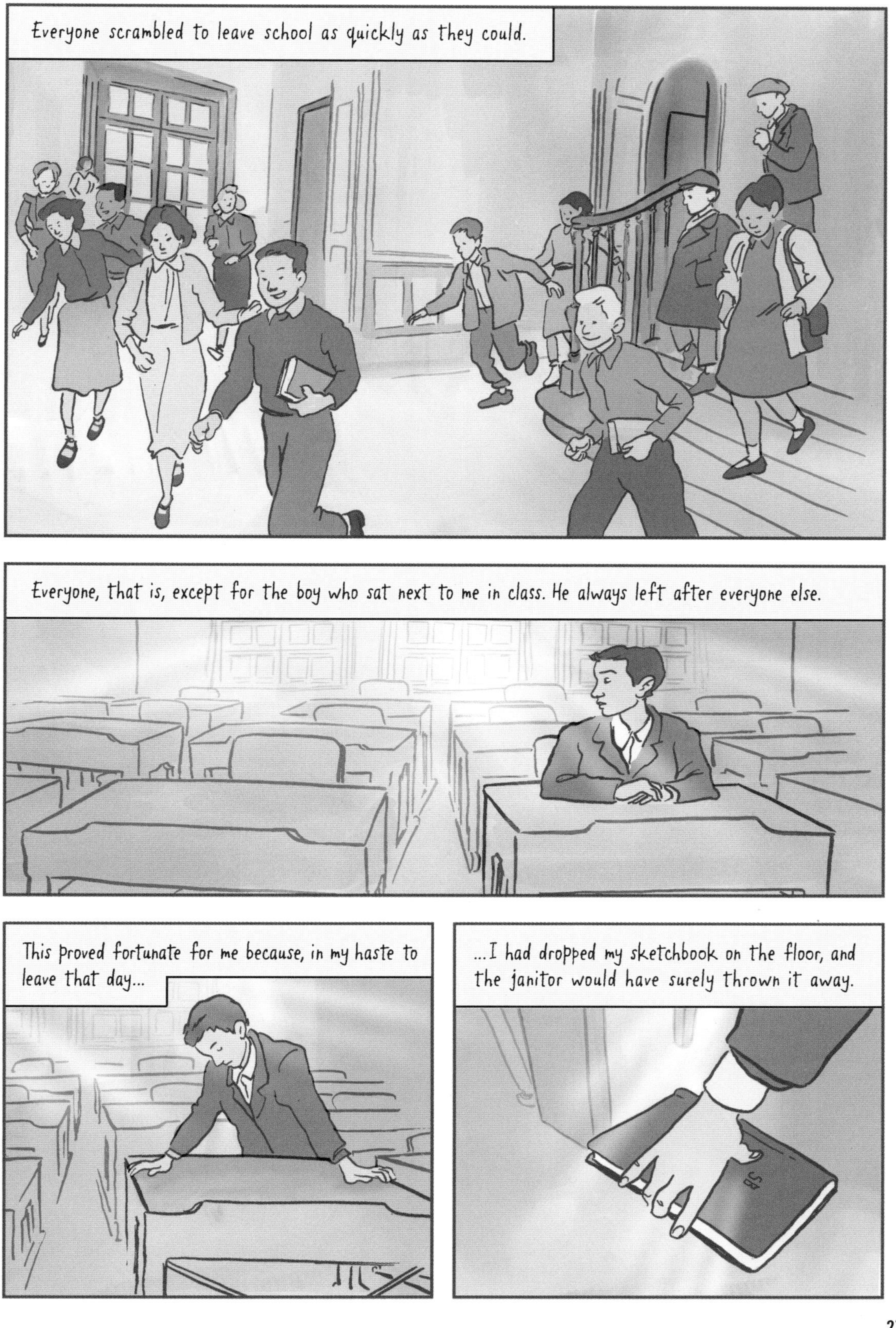
Everyone scrambled to leave school as quickly as they could.
Everyone, that is, except for the boy who sat next to me in class. He always left after everyone else.
This proved fortunate for me because, in my haste to leave that day...
...I had dropped my sketchbook on the floor, and the janitor would have surely thrown it away.

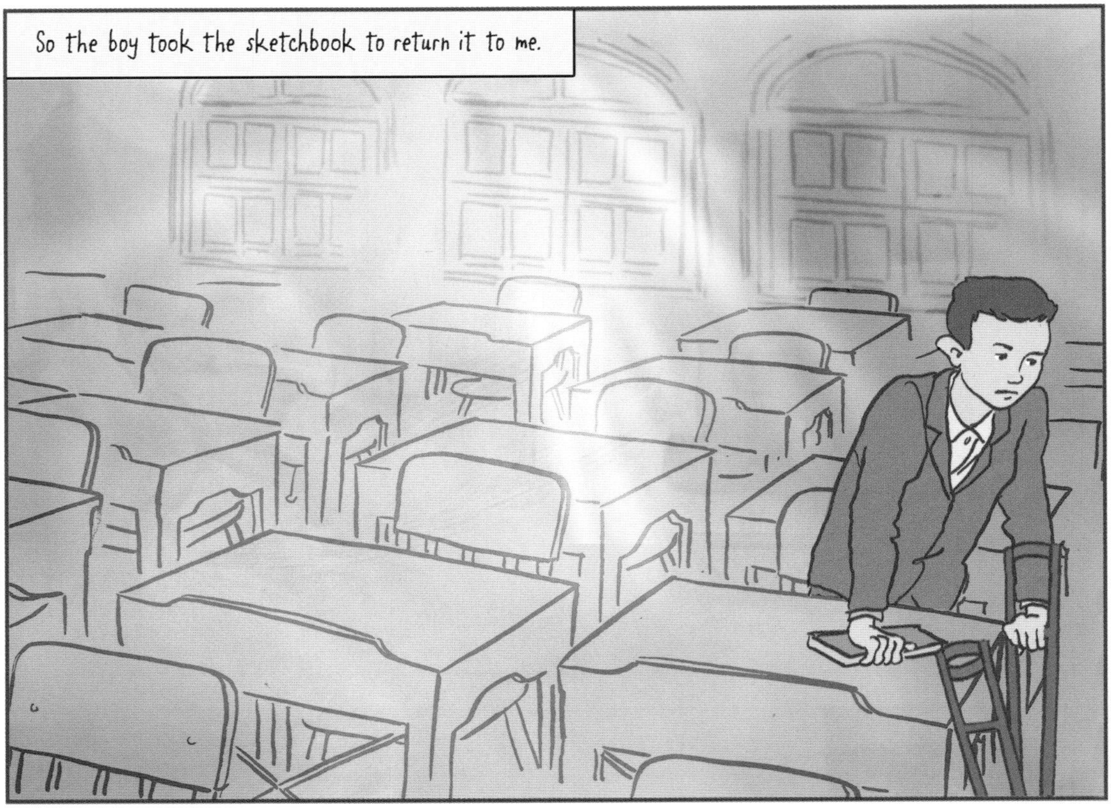
So the boy took the sketchbook to return it to me.

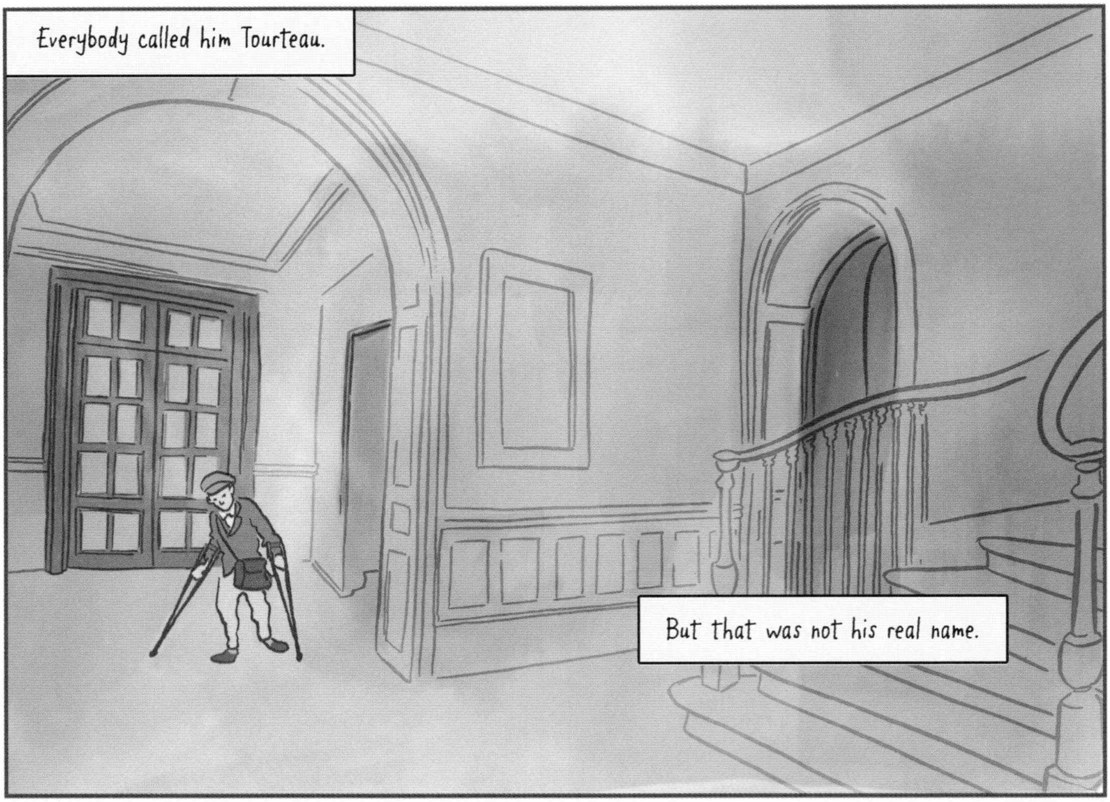
Everybody called him Tourteau.
But that was not his real name.

CHAPTER 4

TOURTEAU MEANS "CRAB" IN FRENCH. IT WAS A CRUEL NICKNAME FOR A BOY WHOSE ONLY "CRIME" WAS CONTRACTING POLIO AS A YOUNG CHILD.

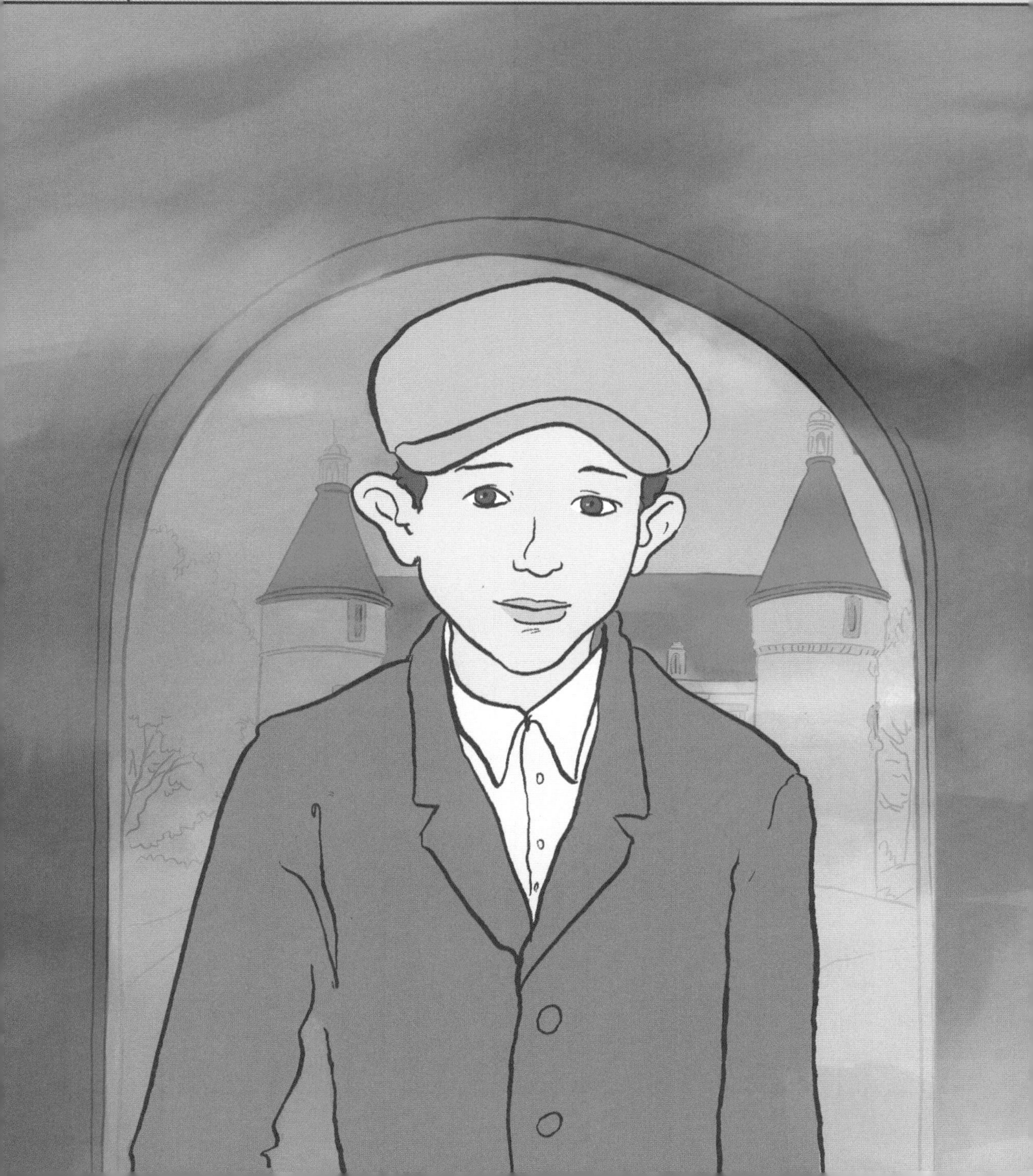

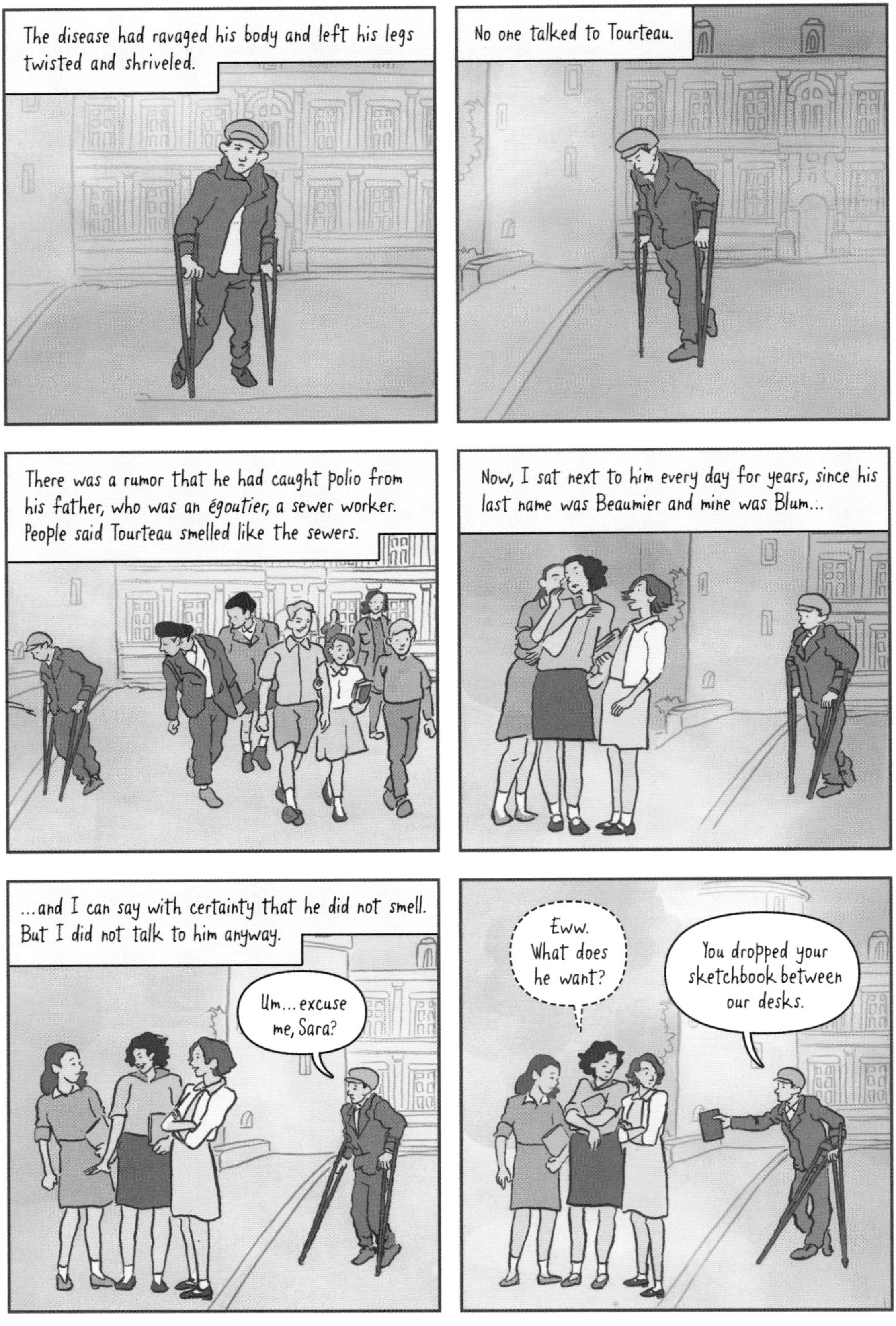

The disease had ravaged his body and left his legs twisted and shriveled.
No one talked to Tourteau.
There was a rumor that he had caught polio from his father, who was an *égoutier*, a sewer worker. People said Tourteau smelled like the sewers.
Now, I sat next to him every day for years, since his last name was Beaumier and mine was Blum...
...and I can say with certainty that he did not smell. But I did not talk to him anyway.
Um... excuse me, Sara?
Eww. What does he want?
You dropped your sketchbook between our desks.

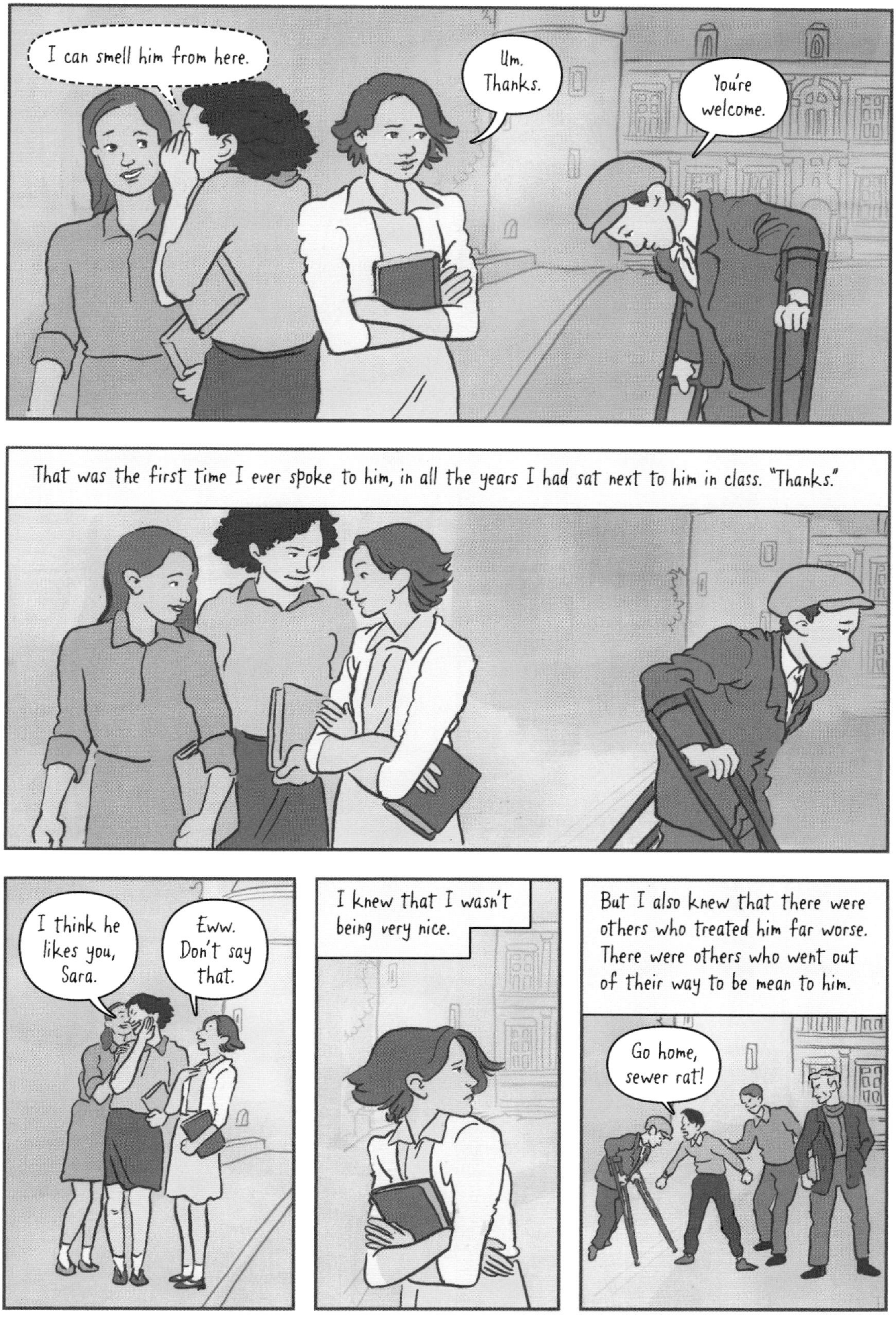
I can smell him from here.
Um. Thanks.
You're welcome.
That was the first time I ever spoke to him, in all the years I had sat next to him in class. "Thanks."
I think he likes you, Sara.
Eww. Don't say that.
I knew that I wasn't being very nice.
But I also knew that there were others who treated him far worse. There were others who went out of their way to be mean to him.
Go home, sewer rat!

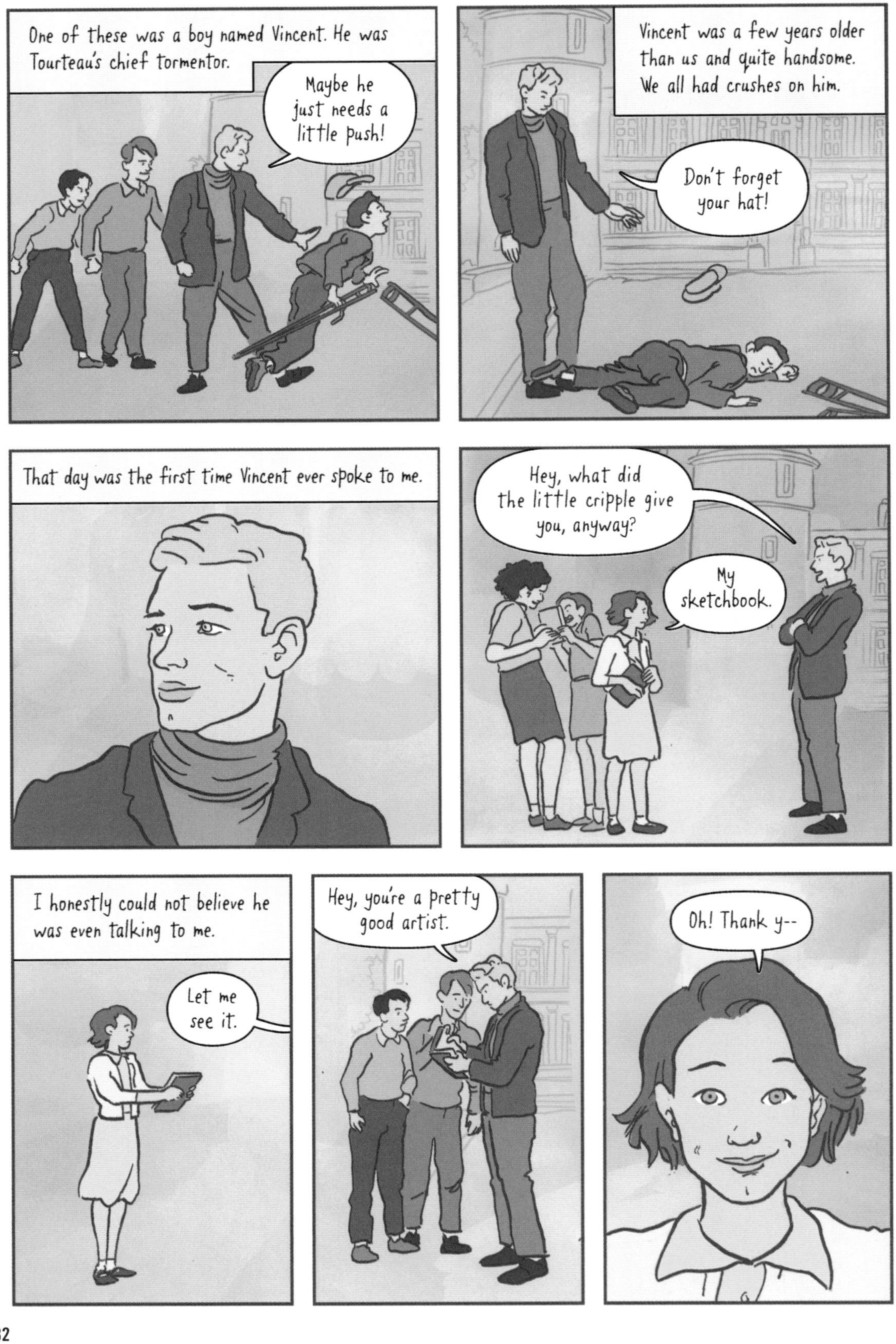
One of these was a boy named Vincent. He was Tourteau's chief tormentor.
Maybe he just needs a little push!
Vincent was a few years older than us and quite handsome. We all had crushes on him.
Don't forget your hat!
That day was the first time Vincent ever spoke to me.
Hey, what did the little cripple give you, anyway?
My sketchbook.
I honestly could not believe he was even talking to me.
Let me see it.
Hey, you're a pretty good artist.
Oh! Thank y--

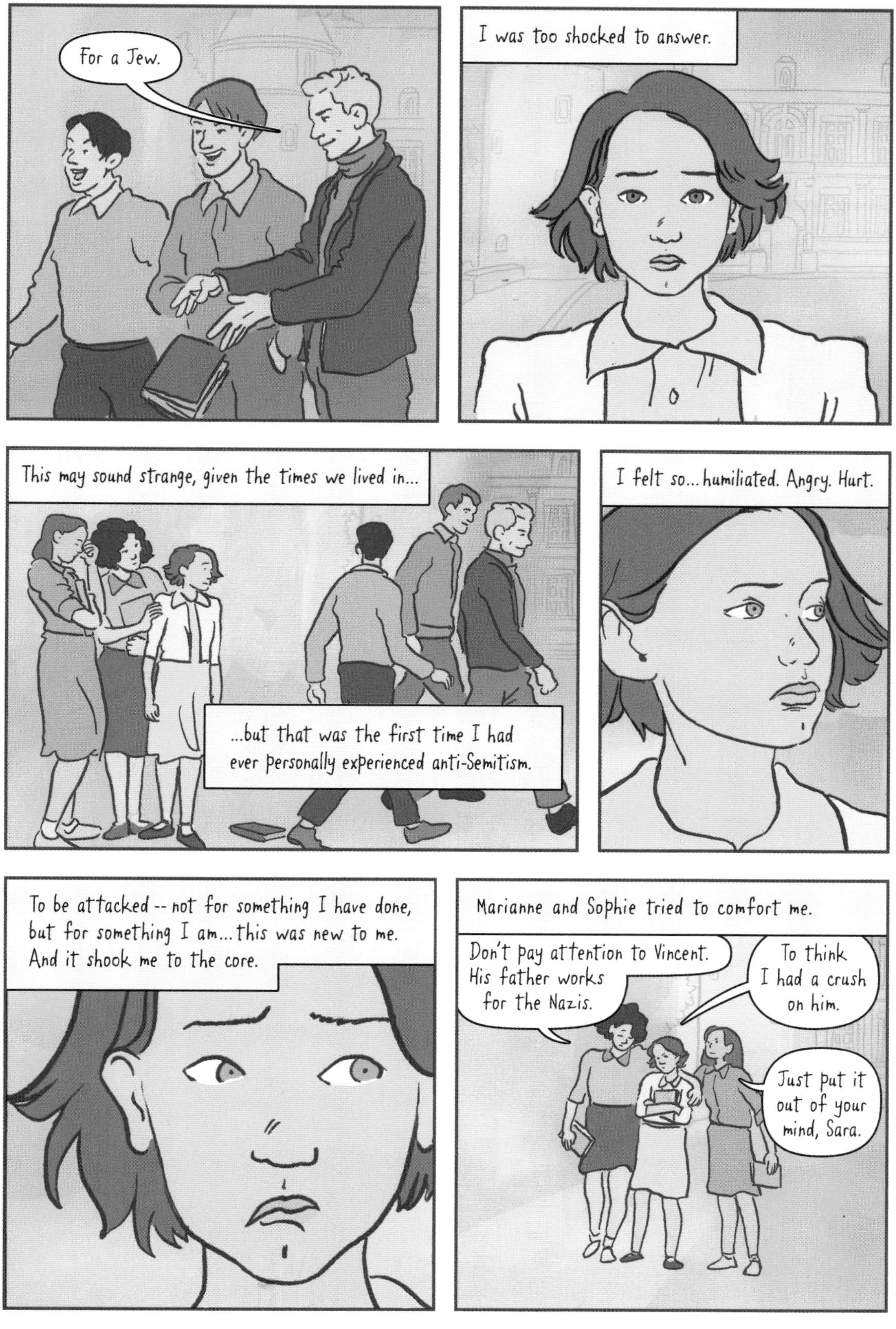
For a Jew.
I was too shocked to answer.
This may sound strange, given the times we lived in...
...but that was the first time I had ever personally experienced anti-Semitism.
I felt so... humiliated. Angry. Hurt.
To be attacked -- not for something I have done, but for something I am... this was new to me. And it shook me to the core.
Marianne and Sophie tried to comfort me.
Don't pay attention to Vincent. His father works for the Nazis.
To think I had a crush on him.
Just put it out of your mind, Sara.

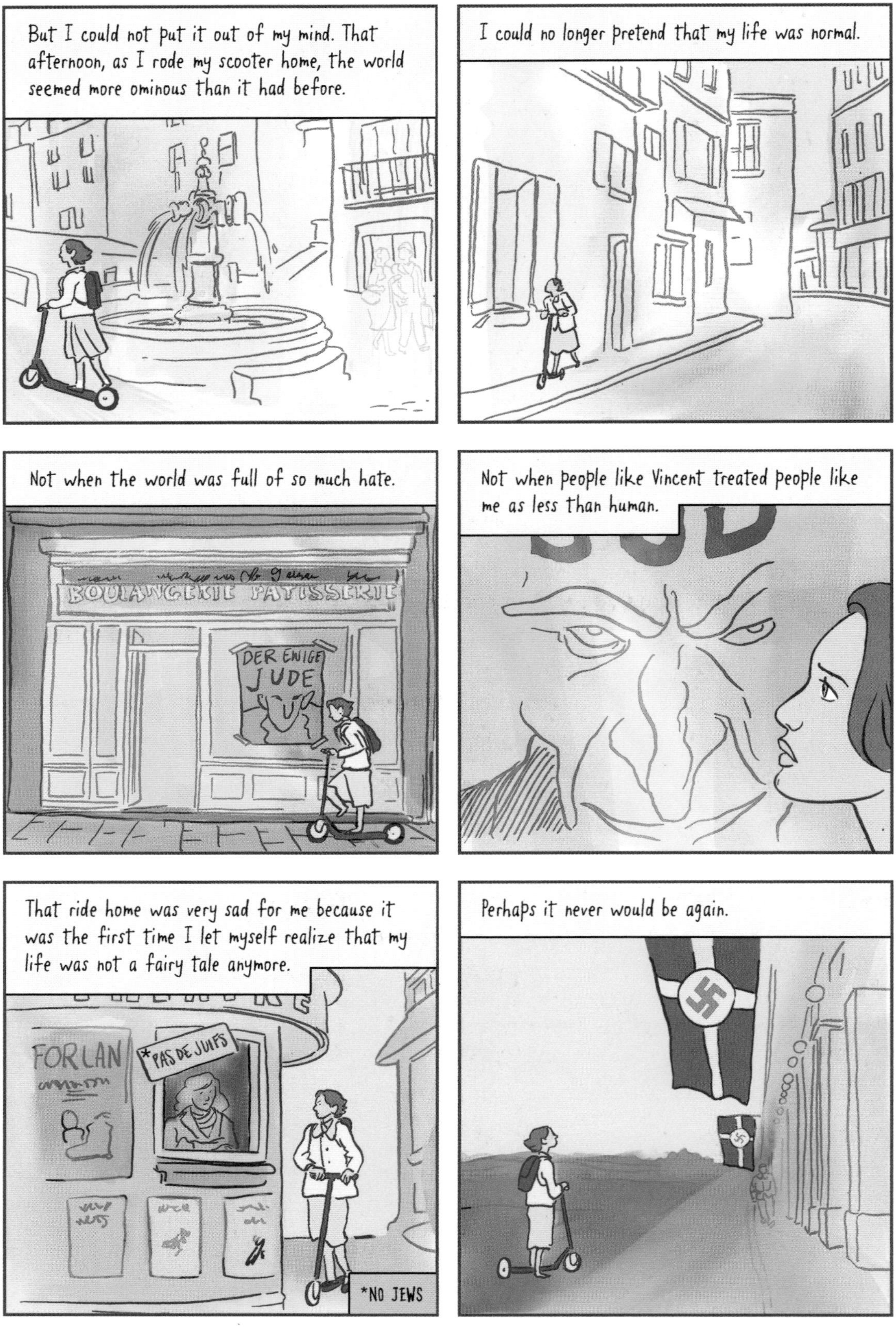
But I could not put it out of my mind. That afternoon, as I rode my scooter home, the world seemed more ominous than it had before.
I could no longer pretend that my life was normal.
Not when the world was full of so much hate.
BOULANGERIE PATISSERIE
DER EWIGE JUDE
Not when people like Vincent treated people like me as less than human.
That ride home was very sad for me because it was the first time I let myself realize that my life was not a fairy tale anymore.
FORLAN
*PAS DE JUIFS
*NO JEWS
Perhaps it never would be again.

CHAPTER 5

I TOLD MY PARENTS ABOUT WHAT HAPPENED WITH VINCENT. IT REIGNITED AN ARGUMENT THEY HAD BEEN HAVING FOR MONTHS. PAPA WANTED TO LEAVE FRANCE. MAMAN DID NOT.

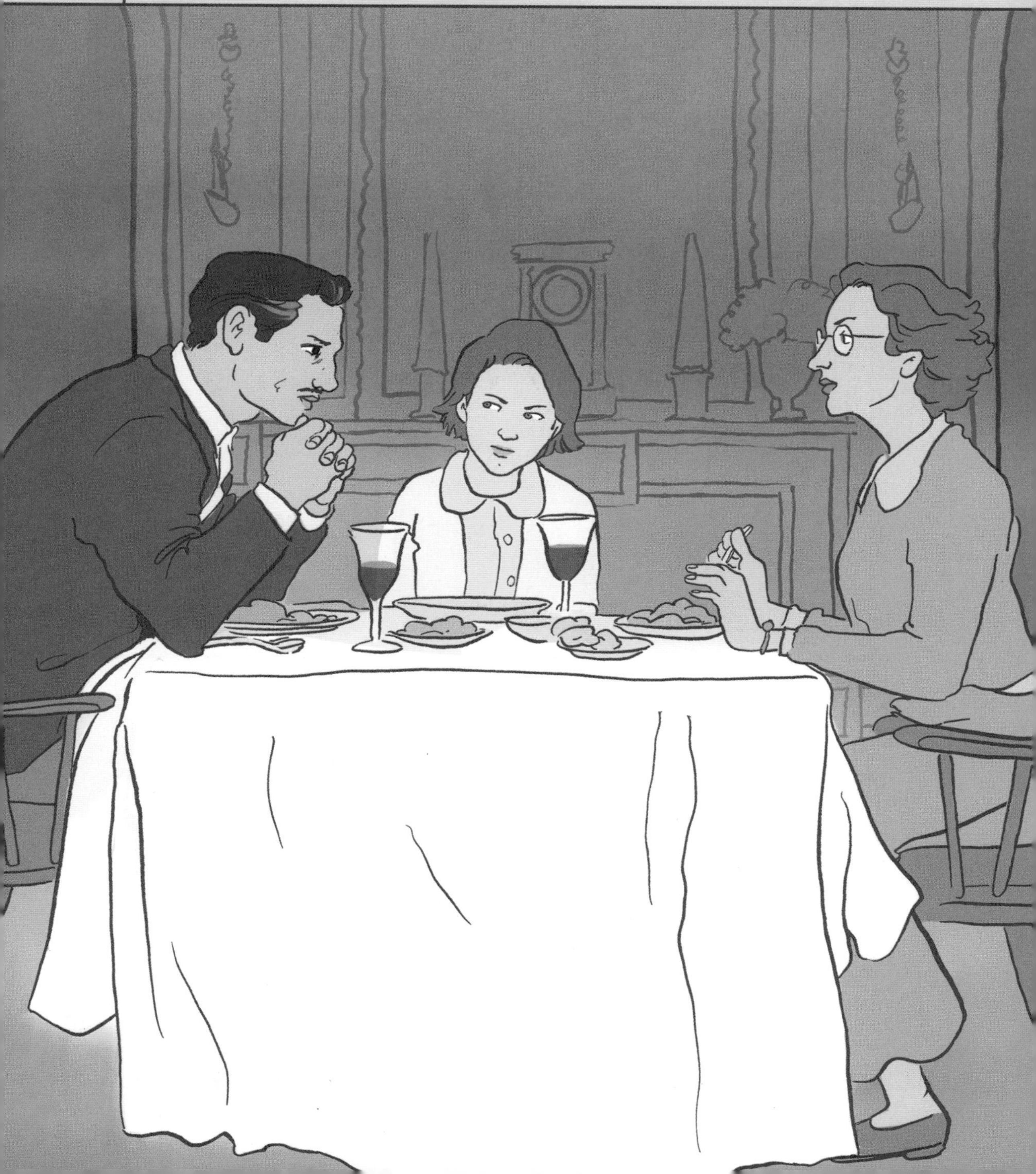

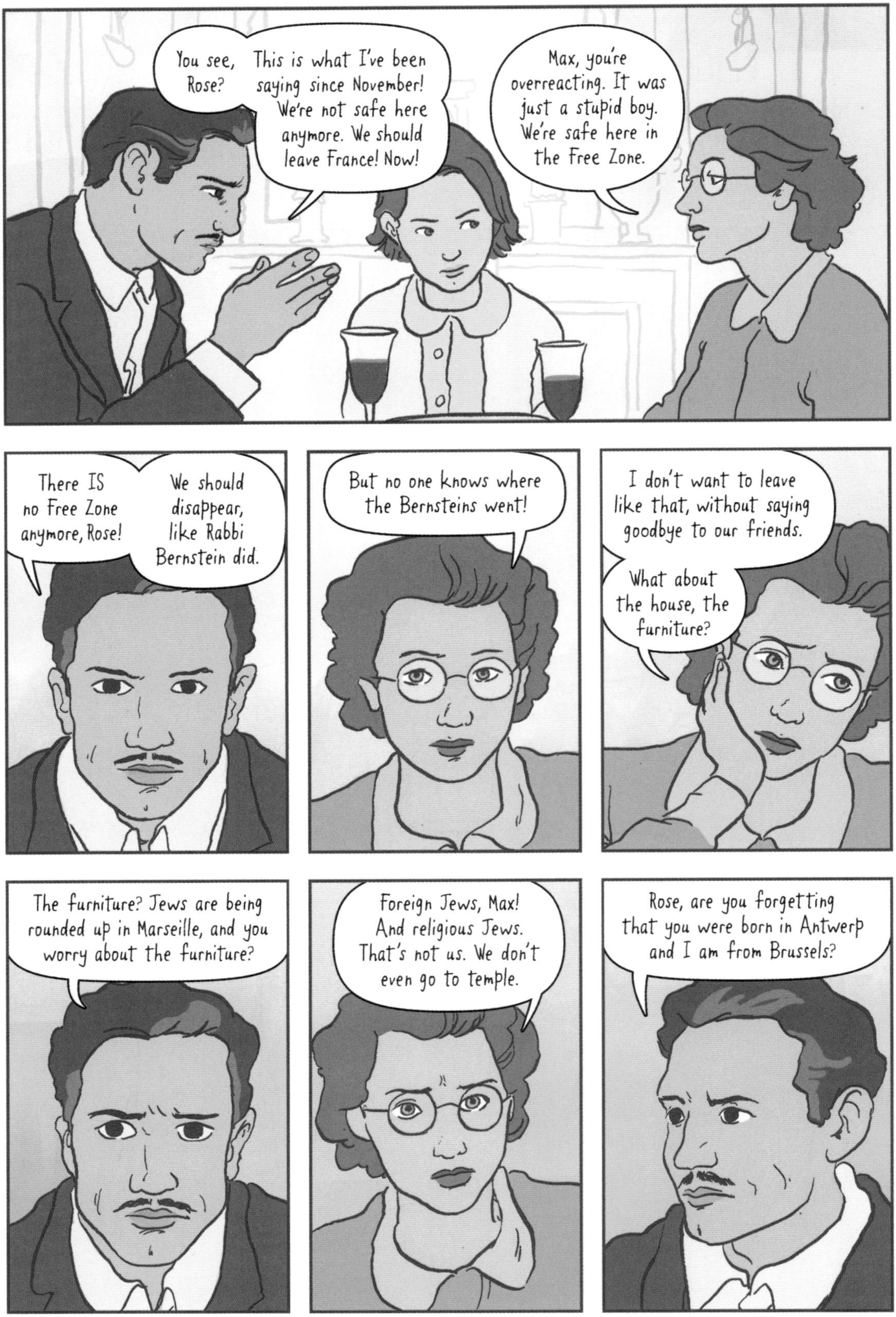
You see, Rose?
This is what I've been saying since November! We're not safe here anymore. We should leave France! Now!
Max, you're overreacting. It was just a stupid boy. We're safe here in the Free Zone.
There IS no Free Zone anymore, Rose!
We should disappear, like Rabbi Bernstein did.
But no one knows where the Bernsteins went!
I don't want to leave like that, without saying goodbye to our friends.
What about the house, the furniture?
The furniture? Jews are being rounded up in Marseille, and you worry about the furniture?
Foreign Jews, Max! And religious Jews. That's not us. We don't even go to temple.
Rose, are you forgetting that you were born in Antwerp and I am from Brussels?

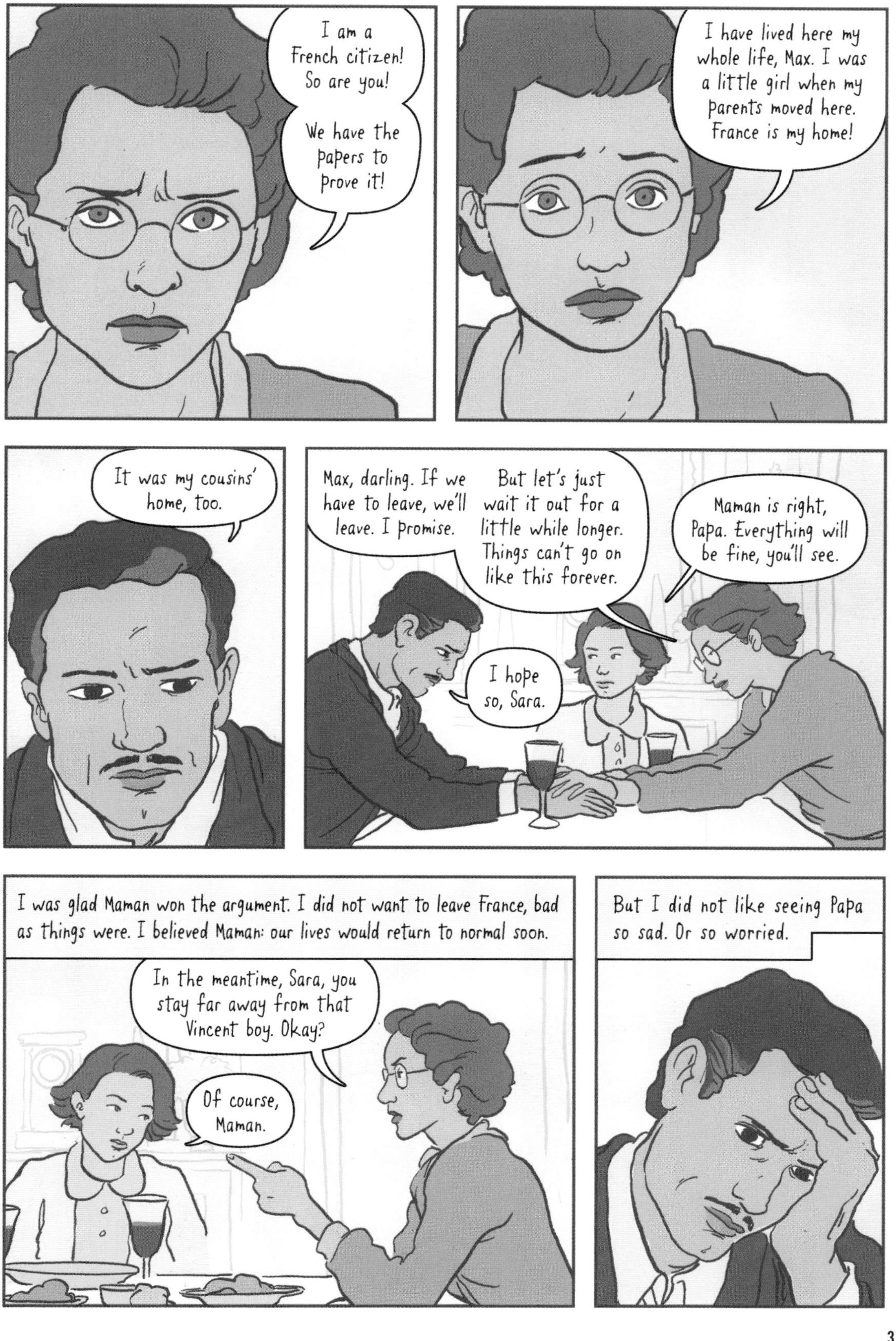
I am a French citizen! So are you!
We have the papers to prove it!
I have lived here my whole life, Max. I was a little girl when my parents moved here. France is my home!
It was my cousins' home, too.
Max, darling. If we have to leave, we'll leave. I promise.
But let's just wait it out for a little while longer. Things can't go on like this forever.
Maman is right, Papa. Everything will be fine, you'll see.
I hope so, Sara.
I was glad Maman won the argument. I did not want to leave France, bad as things were. I believed Maman: our lives would return to normal soon.
In the meantime, Sara, you stay far away from that Vincent boy. Okay?
Of course, Maman.
But I did not like seeing Papa so sad. Or so worried.

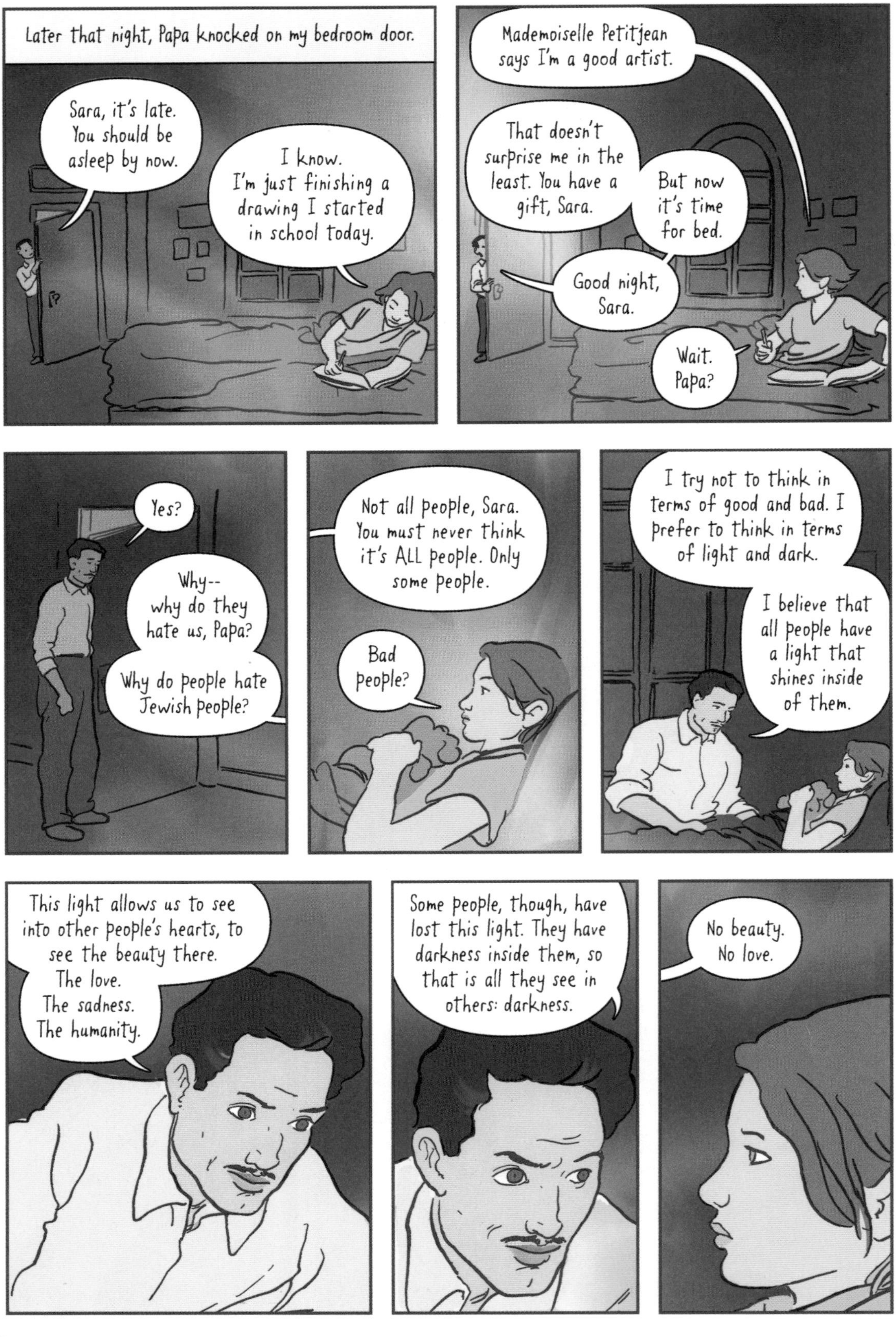
Later that night, Papa knocked on my bedroom door.
Sara, it's late. You should be asleep by now.
I know. I'm just finishing a drawing I started in school today.
Mademoiselle Petitjean says I'm a good artist.
That doesn't surprise me in the least. You have a gift, Sara.
But now it's time for bed.
Good night, Sara.
Wait. Papa?
Yes?
Why-- why do they hate us, Papa?
Why do people hate Jewish people?
Not all people, Sara. You must never think it's ALL people. Only some people.
Bad people?
I try not to think in terms of good and bad. I prefer to think in terms of light and dark.
I believe that all people have a light that shines inside of them.
This light allows us to see into other people's hearts, to see the beauty there. The love. The sadness. The humanity.
Some people, though, have lost this light. They have darkness inside them, so that is all they see in others: darkness.
No beauty. No love.

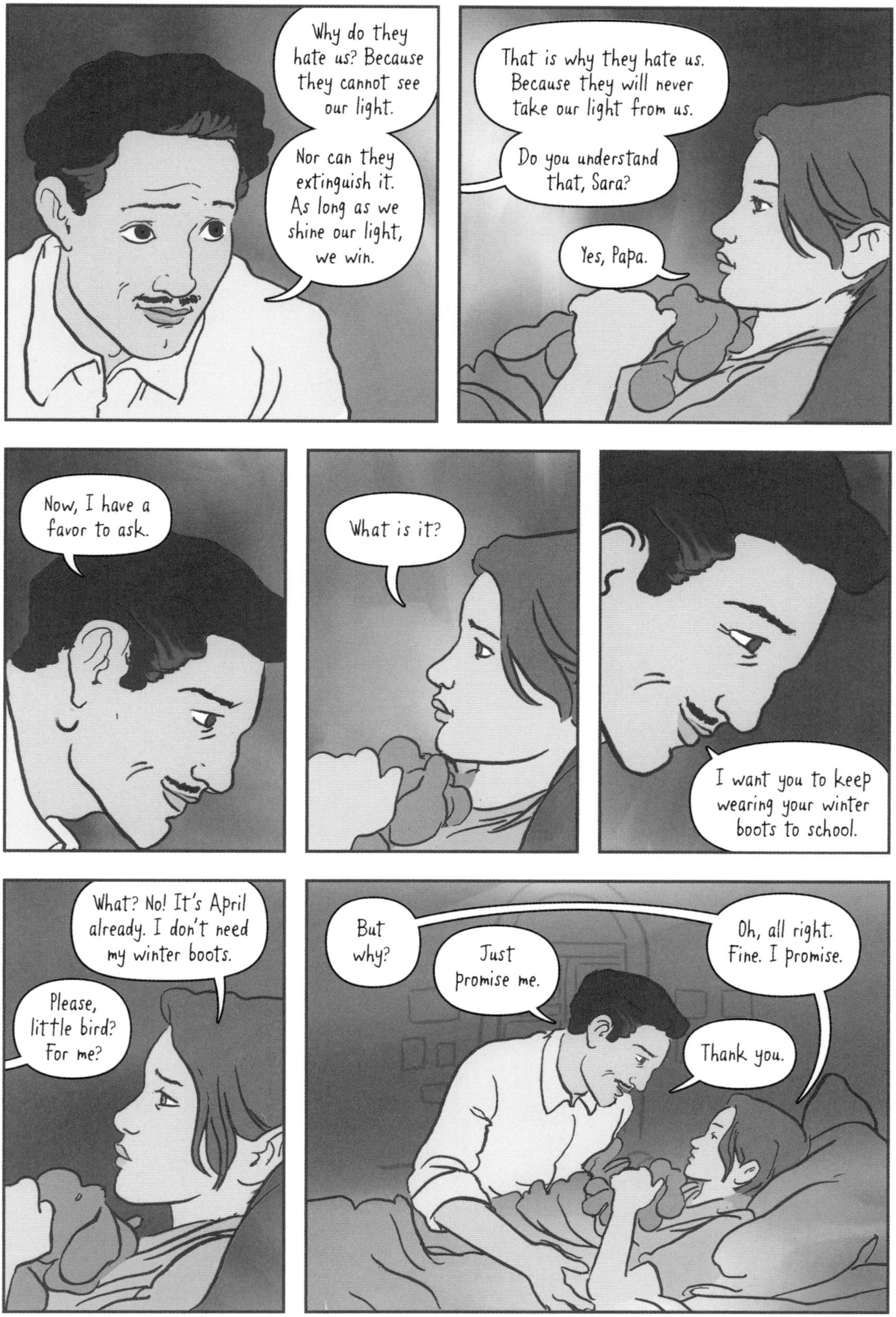
Why do they hate us? Because they cannot see our light.
Nor can they extinguish it. As long as we shine our light, we win.
That is why they hate us. Because they will never take our light from us.
Do you understand that, Sara?
Yes, Papa.
Now, I have a favor to ask.
What is it?
I want you to keep wearing your winter boots to school.
What? No! It's April already. I don't need my winter boots.
Please, little bird? For me?
But why?
Just promise me.
Oh, all right. Fine. I promise.
Thank you.

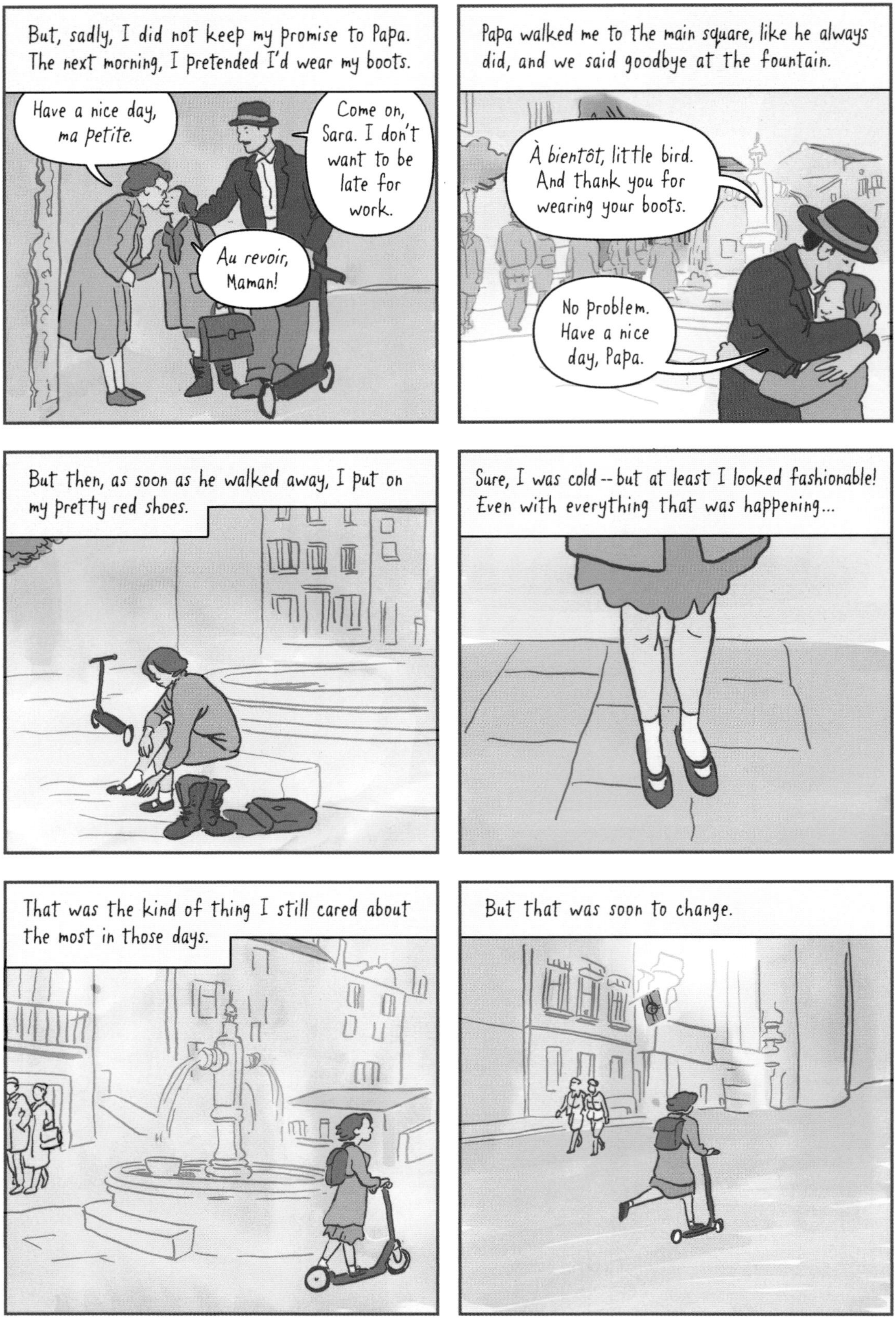

But, sadly, I did not keep my promise to Papa. The next morning, I pretended I'd wear my boots.
Have a nice day, *ma petite.*
Come on, Sara. I don't want to be late for work.
Au revoir, Maman!
Papa walked me to the main square, like he always did, and we said goodbye at the fountain.
À bientôt, little bird. And thank you for wearing your boots.
No problem. Have a nice day, Papa.
But then, as soon as he walked away, I put on my pretty red shoes.
Sure, I was cold--but at least I looked fashionable! Even with everything that was happening...
That was the kind of thing I still cared about the most in those days.
But that was soon to change.

CHAPTER 6

THE DAY STARTED LIKE ANY OTHER DAY. IT WAS A WEDNESDAY. THERE WAS A CHILL IN THE AIR. ALTHOUGH SPRING HAD OFFICIALLY STARTED, IT STILL FELT LIKE WINTER.

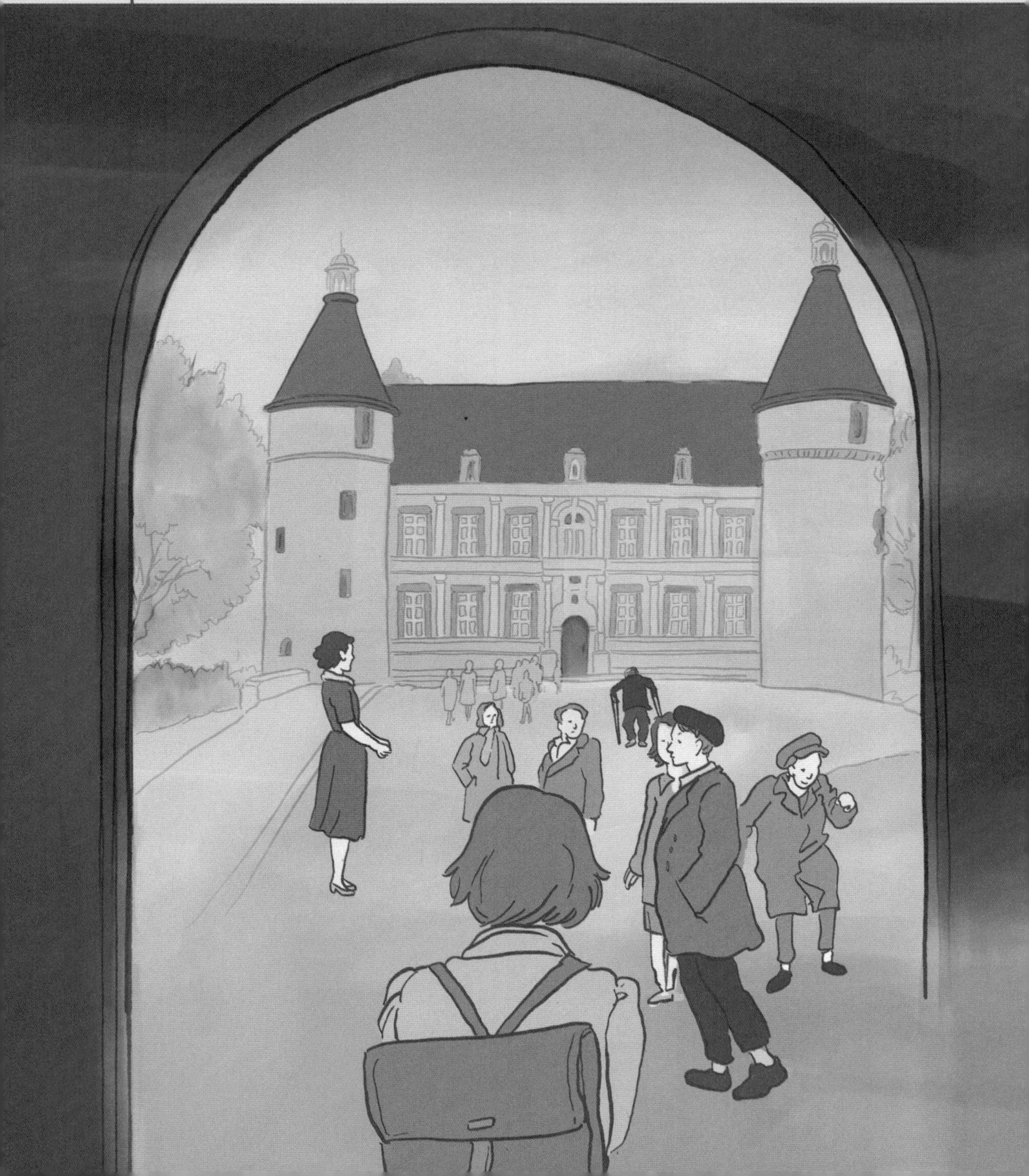

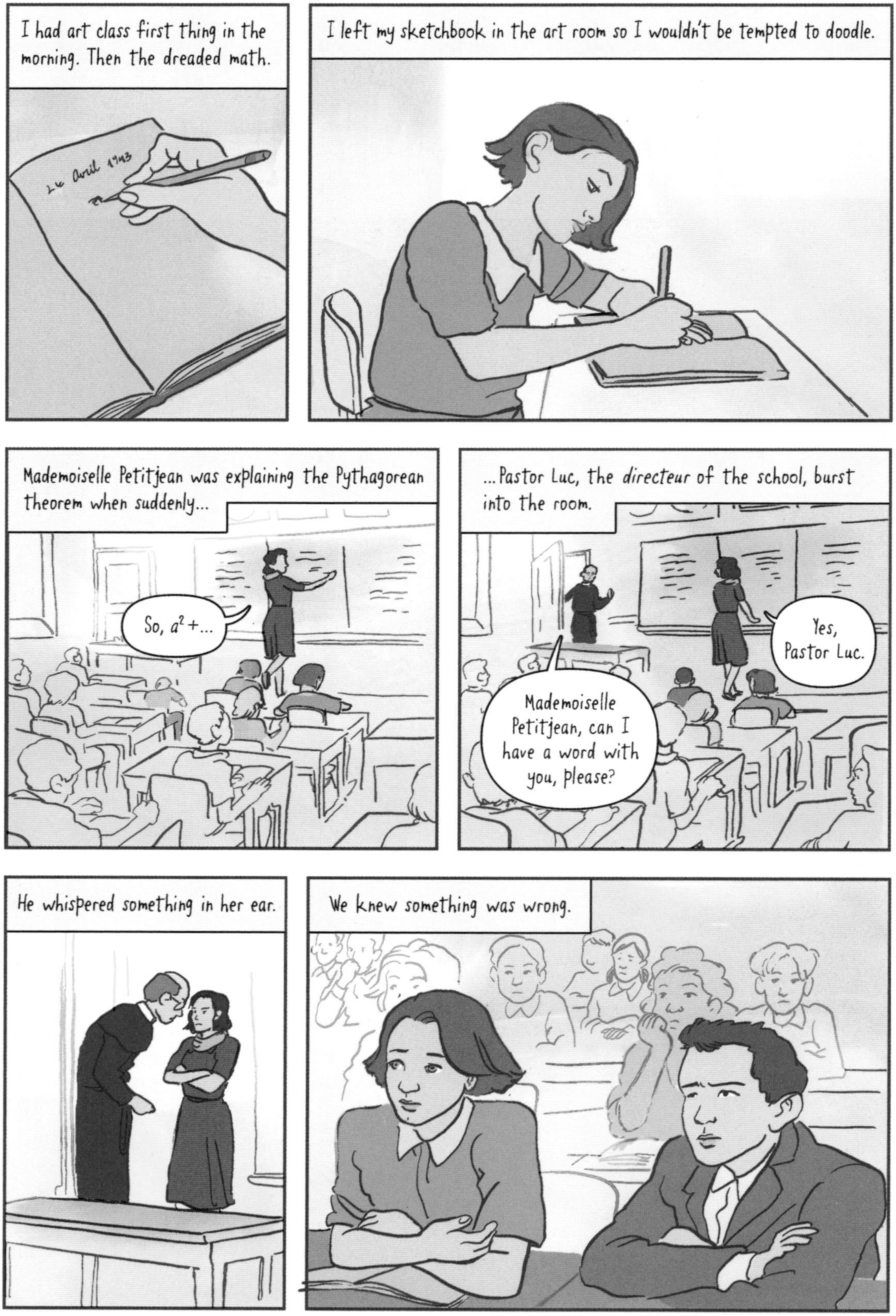
I had art class first thing in the morning. Then the dreaded math.
I left my sketchbook in the art room so I wouldn't be tempted to doodle.
Mademoiselle Petitjean was explaining the Pythagorean theorem when suddenly...
So, a^2+...
...Pastor Luc, the *directeur* of the school, burst into the room.
Mademoiselle Petitjean, can I have a word with you, please?
Yes, Pastor Luc.
He whispered something in her ear.
We knew something was wrong.

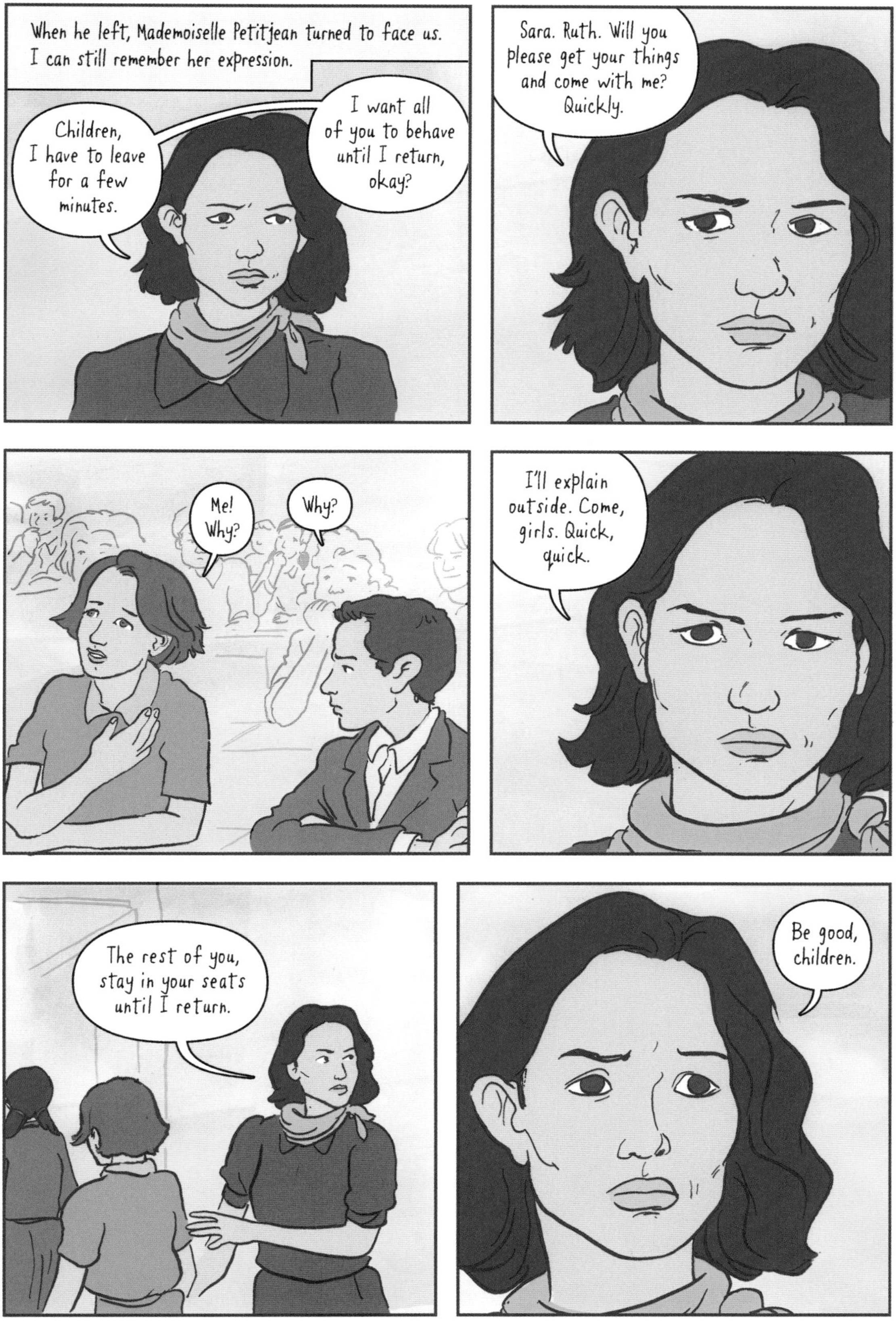
When he left, Mademoiselle Petitjean turned to face us. I can still remember her expression.
Children, I have to leave for a few minutes.
I want all of you to behave until I return, okay?
Sara. Ruth. Will you please get your things and come with me? Quickly.
Me! Why?
Why?
I'll explain outside. Come, girls. Quick, quick.
The rest of you, stay in your seats until I return.
Be good, children.

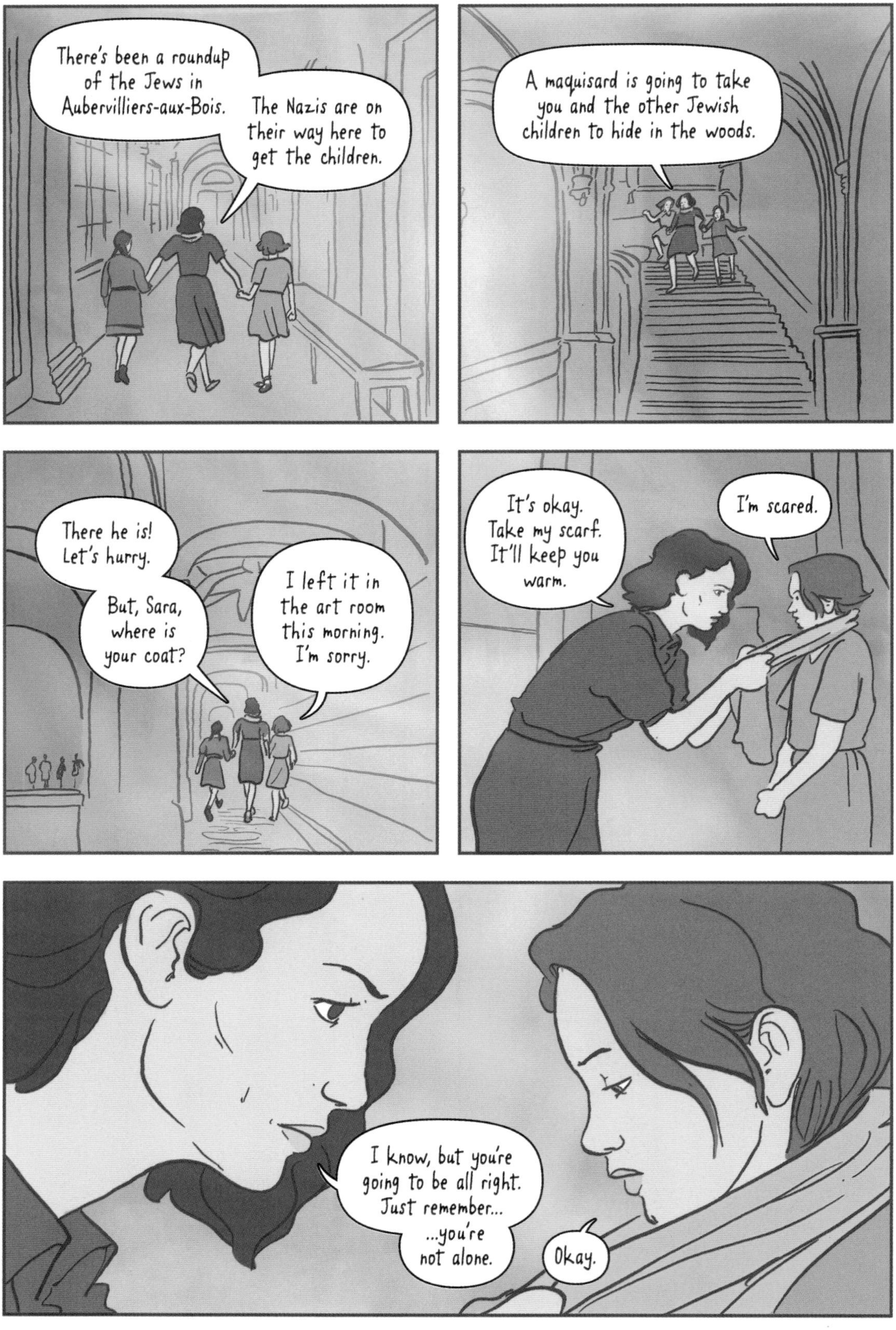
There's been a roundup of the Jews in Aubervilliers-aux-Bois.
The Nazis are on their way here to get the children.
A maquisard is going to take you and the other Jewish children to hide in the woods.
There he is! Let's hurry.
But, Sara, where is your coat?
I left it in the art room this morning. I'm sorry.
It's okay. Take my scarf. It'll keep you warm.
I'm scared.
I know, but you're going to be all right. Just remember...
...you're not alone.
Okay.

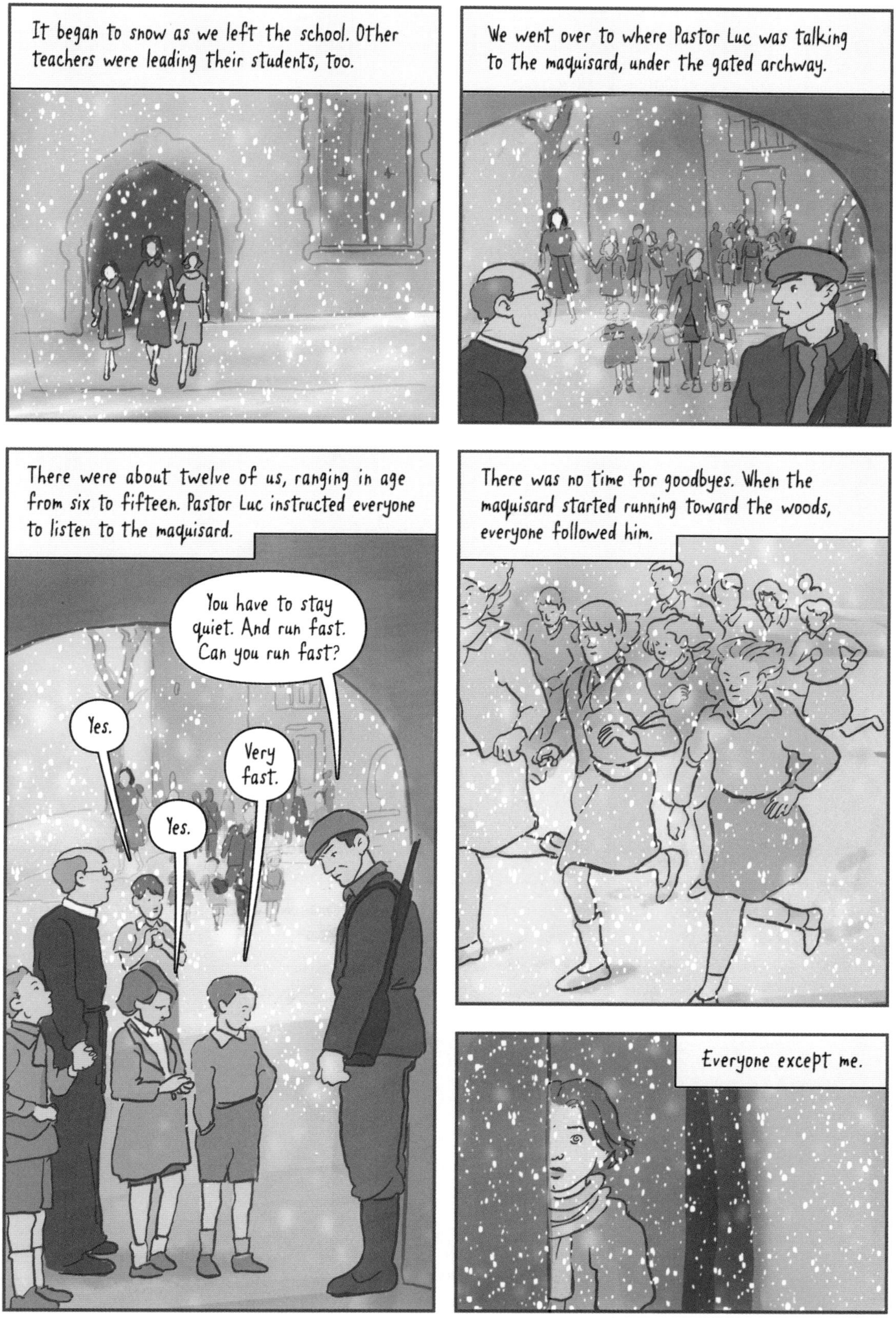
It began to snow as we left the school. Other teachers were leading their students, too.
We went over to where Pastor Luc was talking to the maquisard, under the gated archway.
There were about twelve of us, ranging in age from six to fifteen. Pastor Luc instructed everyone to listen to the maquisard.
You have to stay quiet. And run fast. Can you run fast?
Yes.
Very fast.
Yes.
There was no time for goodbyes. When the maquisard started running toward the woods, everyone followed him.
Everyone except me.

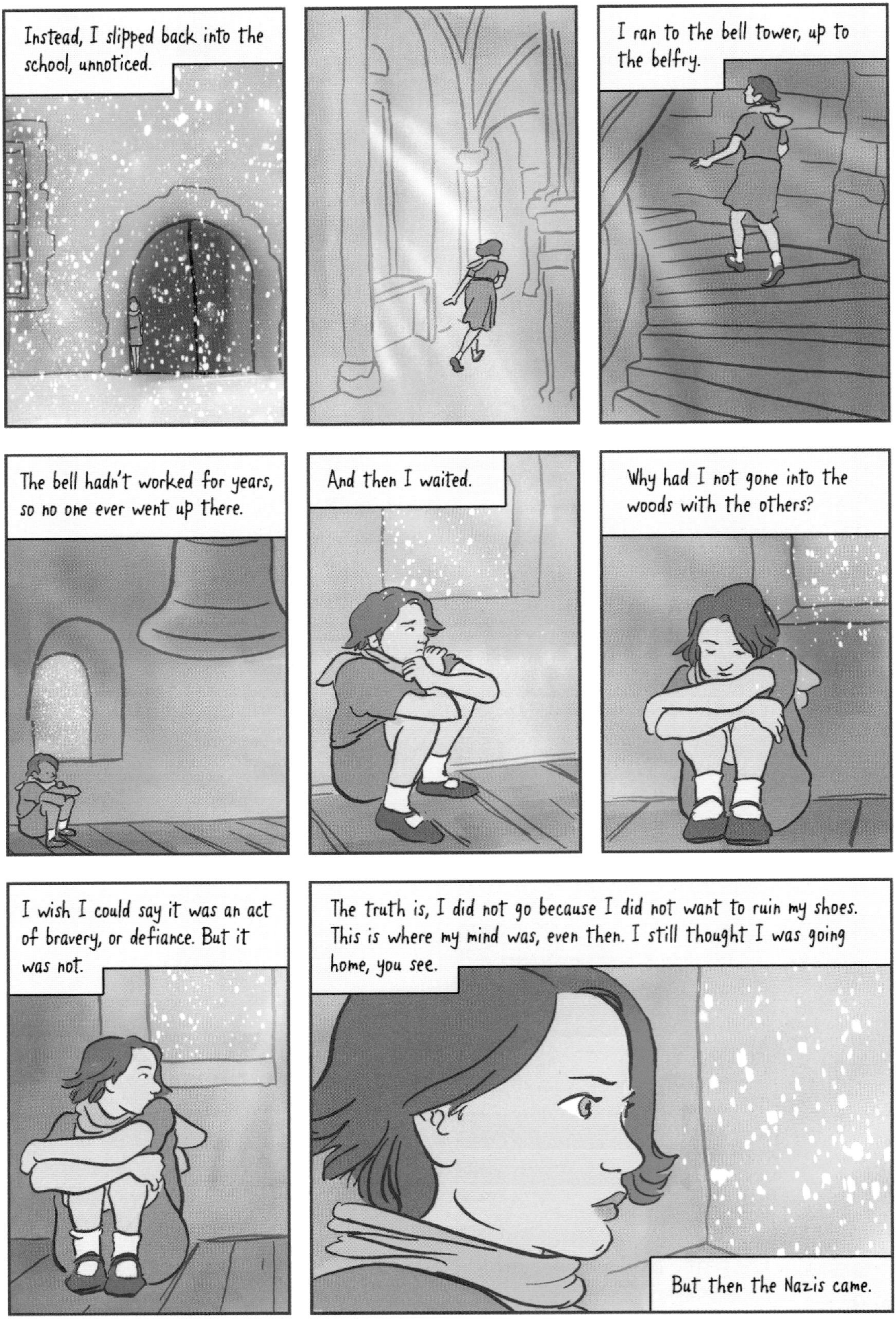
Instead, I slipped back into the school, unnoticed.
I ran to the bell tower, up to the belfry.
The bell hadn't worked for years, so no one ever went up there.
And then I waited.
Why had I not gone into the woods with the others?
I wish I could say it was an act of bravery, or defiance. But it was not.
The truth is, I did not go because I did not want to ruin my shoes. This is where my mind was, even then. I still thought I was going home, you see.
But then the Nazis came.

CHAPTER 7

IT WAS ONLY WHEN THE NAZIS PULLED UP IN A TRUCK, FOLLOWED BY THE GENDARMES IN ANOTHER TRUCK, THAT I FINALLY UNDERSTOOD: I WAS NOT GOING HOME TODAY.

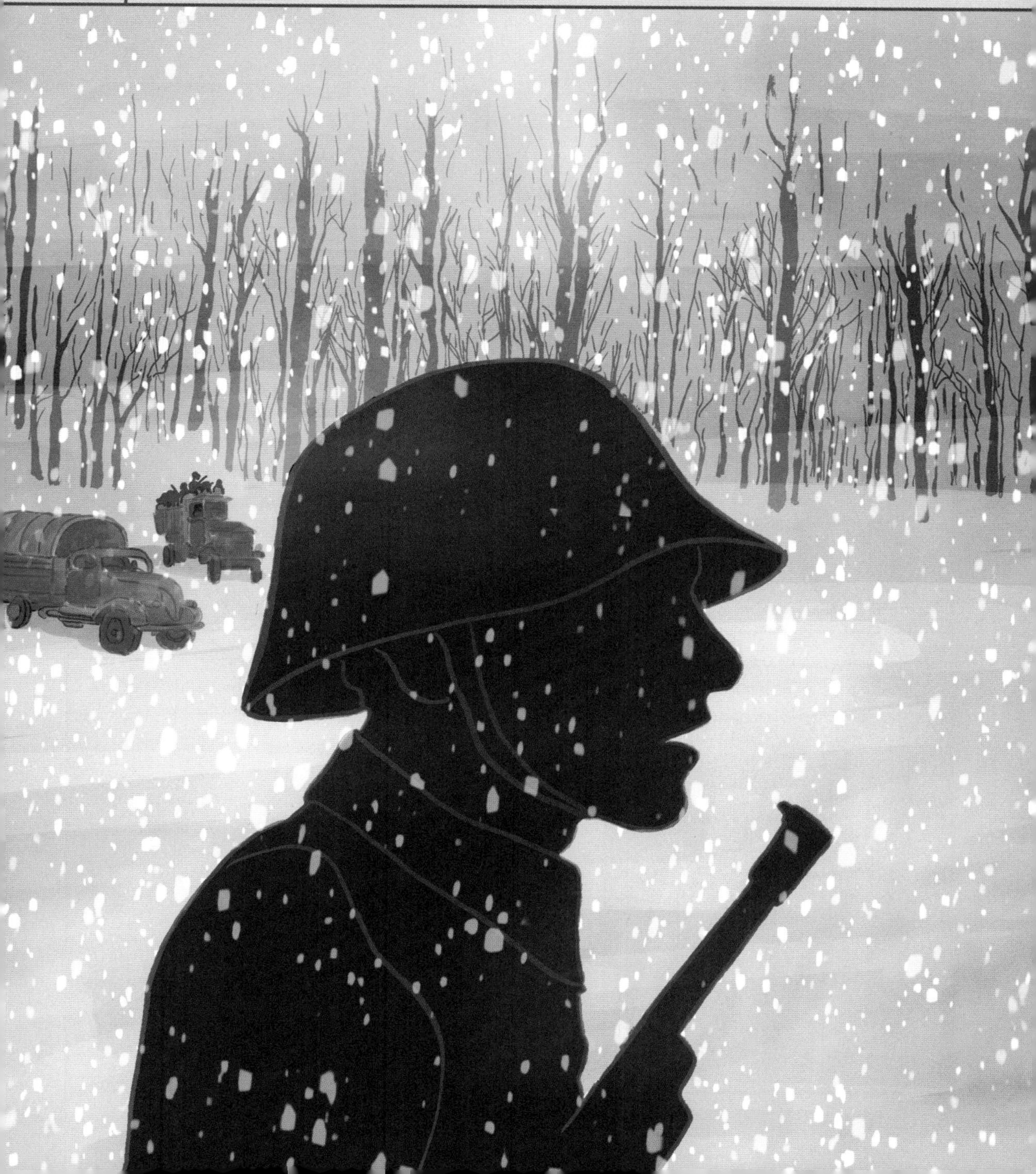

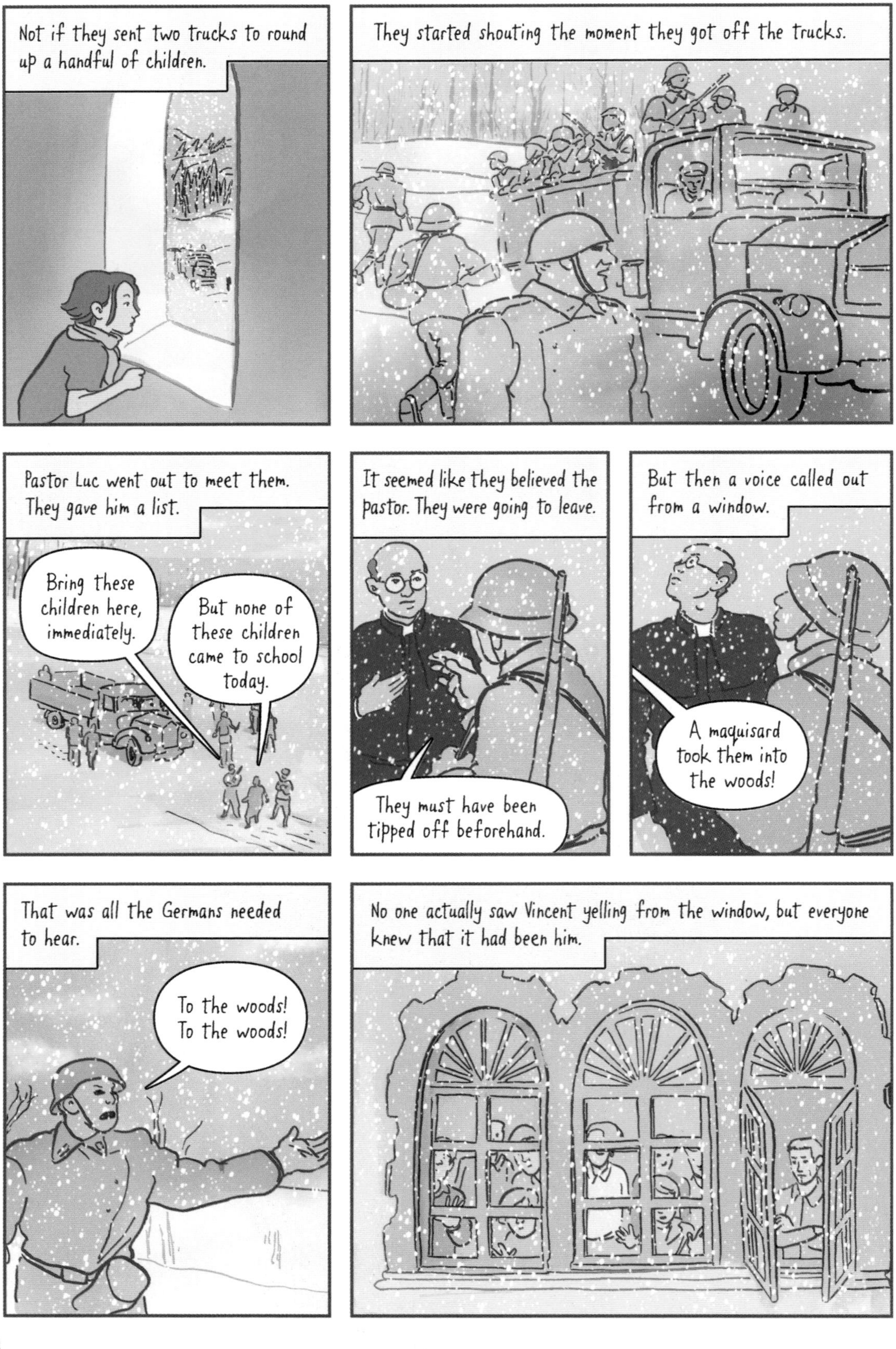
Not if they sent two trucks to round up a handful of children.
They started shouting the moment they got off the trucks.
Pastor Luc went out to meet them. They gave him a list.
Bring these children here, immediately.
But none of these children came to school today.
It seemed like they believed the pastor. They were going to leave.
They must have been tipped off beforehand.
But then a voice called out from a window.
A maquisard took them into the woods!
That was all the Germans needed to hear.
To the woods! To the woods!
No one actually saw Vincent yelling from the window, but everyone knew that it had been him.

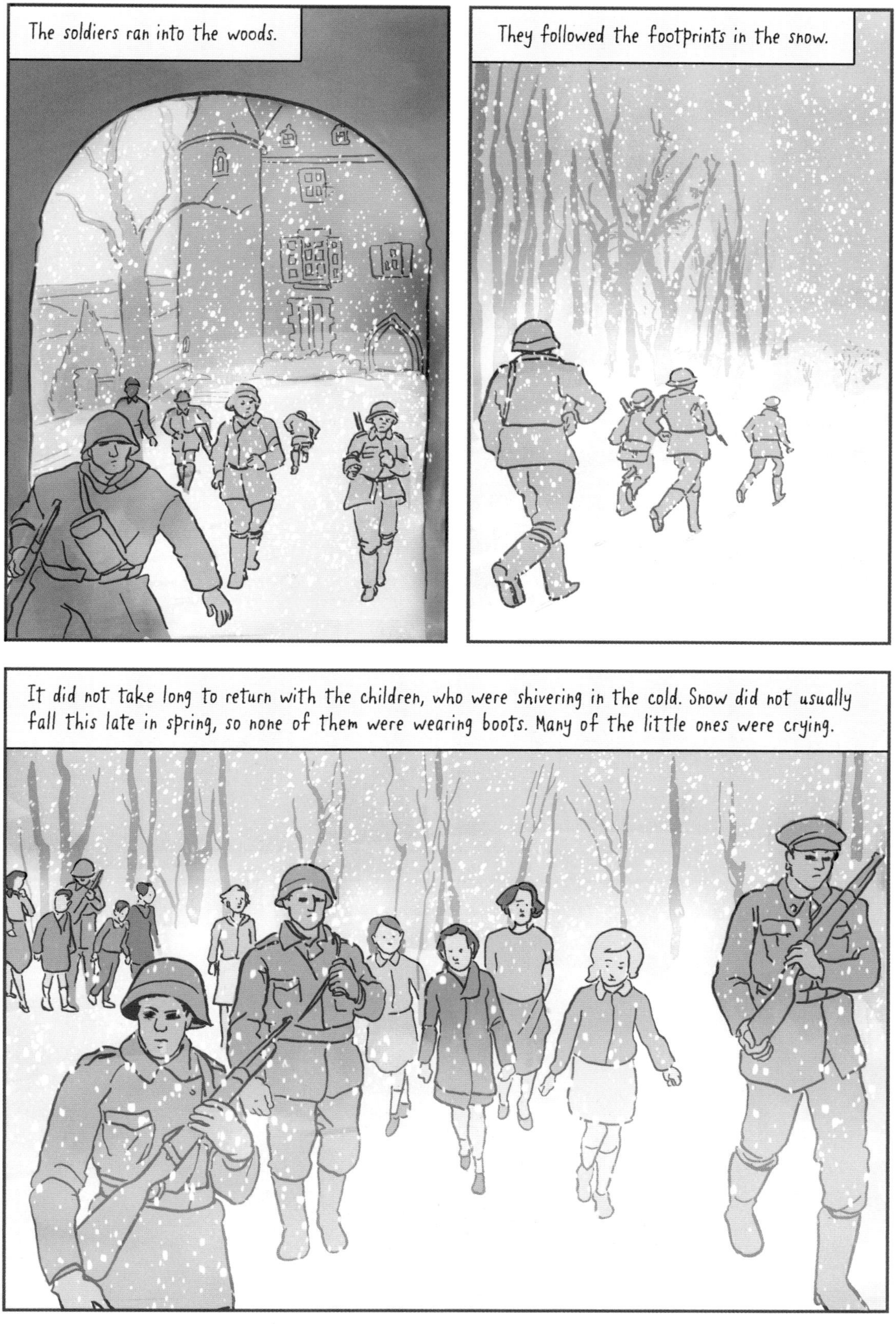
The soldiers ran into the woods.
They followed the footprints in the snow.
It did not take long to return with the children, who were shivering in the cold. Snow did not usually fall this late in spring, so none of them were wearing boots. Many of the little ones were crying.

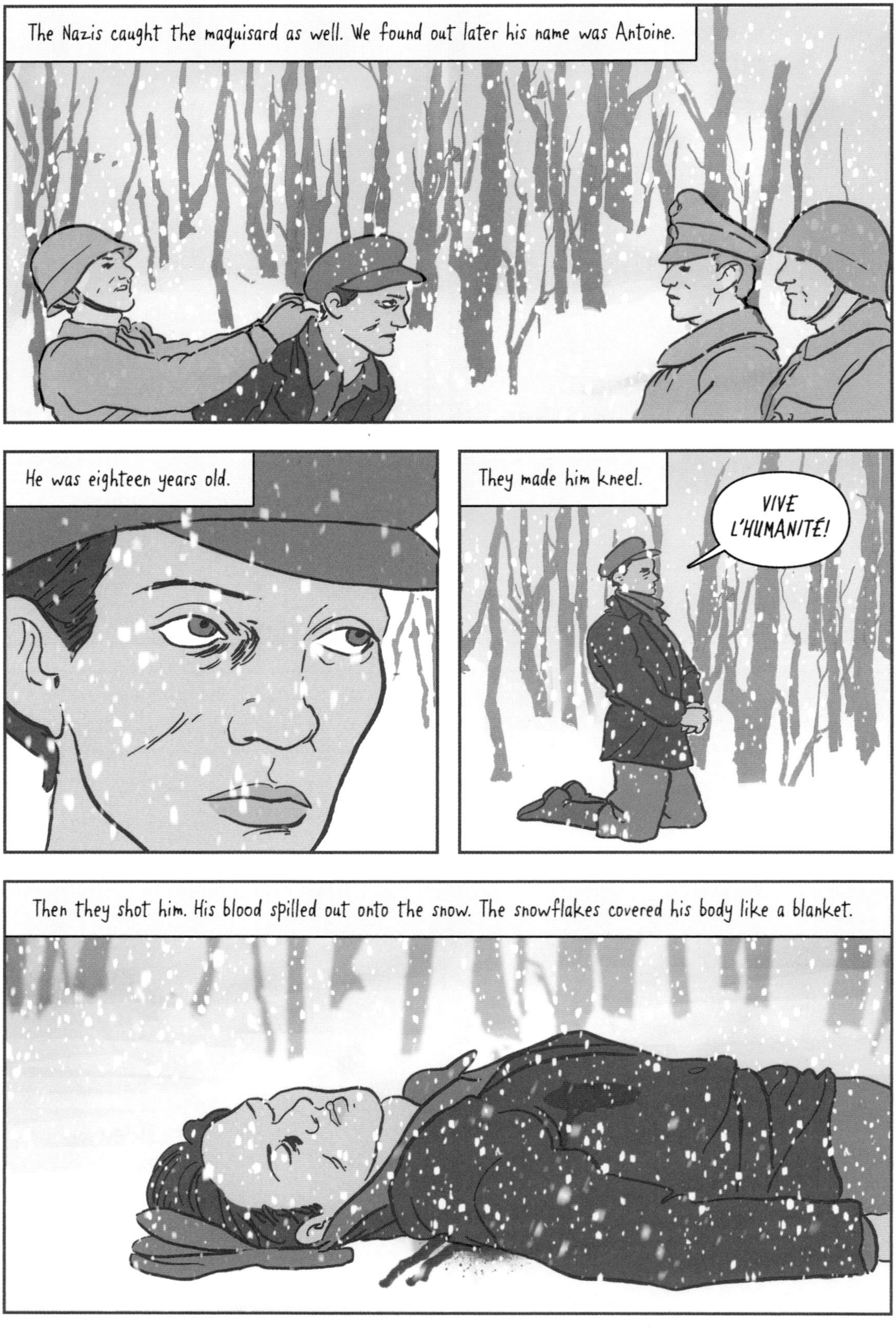
The Nazis caught the maquisard as well. We found out later his name was Antoine.
He was eighteen years old.
They made him kneel.
VIVE L'HUMANITÉ!
Then they shot him. His blood spilled out onto the snow. The snowflakes covered his body like a blanket.

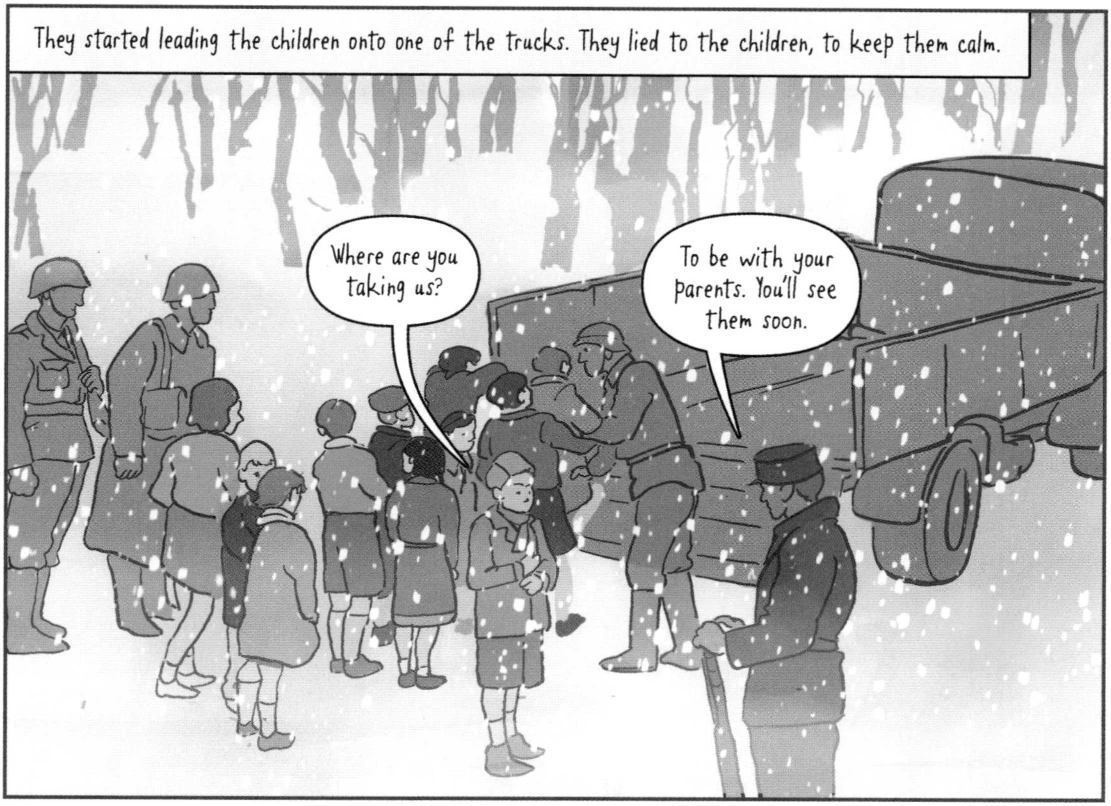
They started leading the children onto one of the trucks. They lied to the children, to keep them calm.
Where are you taking us?
To be with your parents. You'll see them soon.

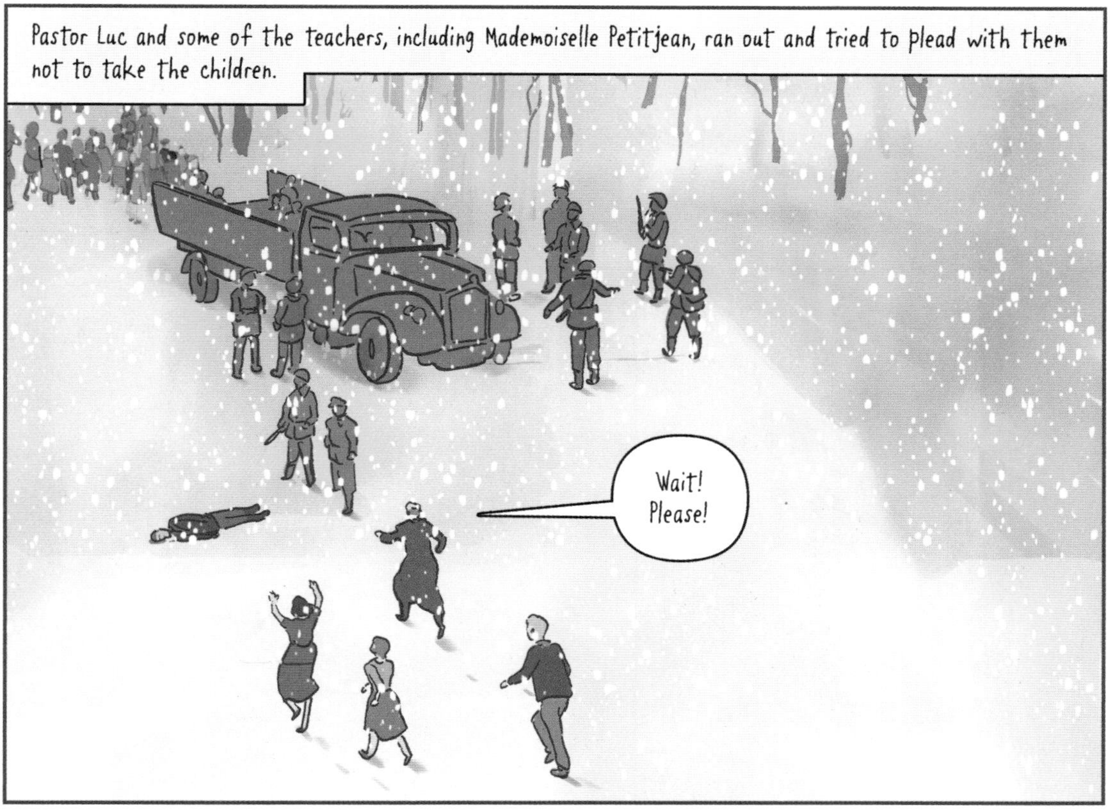
Pastor Luc and some of the teachers, including Mademoiselle Petitjean, ran out and tried to plead with them not to take the children.
Wait! Please!

I implore you, for the love of God, let these children go.

I should shoot you for lying to us.

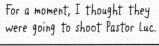

For a moment, I thought they were going to shoot Pastor Luc.

I suggest you and your teachers go back inside and mind your own business.

The children ARE our business.

Go inside, or I'll shoot one of your teachers right in front of you.

Okay.

Marie, there is nothing more we can do here. Let's go inside.

But the children--

Come inside. Now!

No.

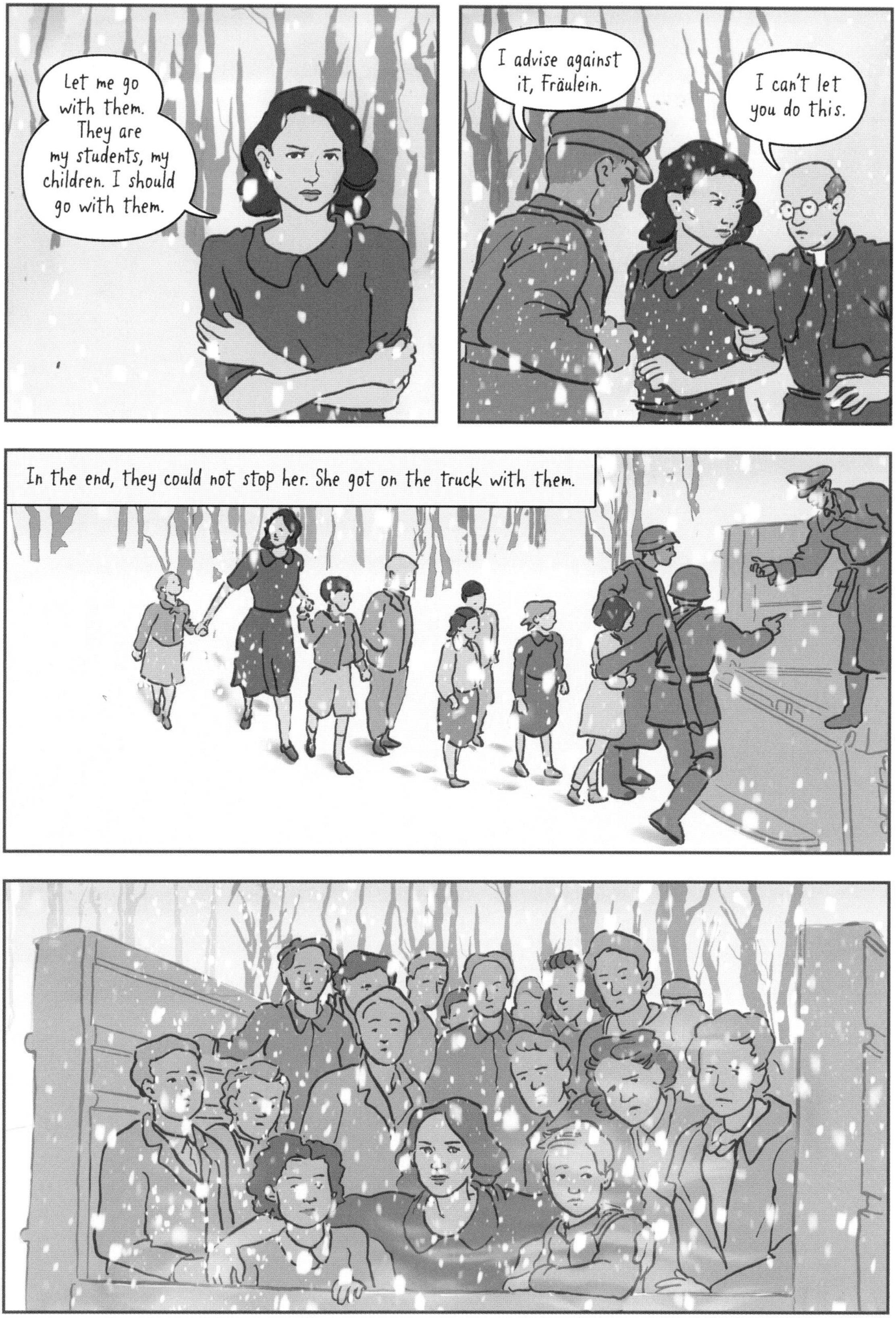
Let me go with them. They are my students, my children. I should go with them.
I advise against it, Fräulein.
I can't let you do this.
In the end, they could not stop her. She got on the truck with them.

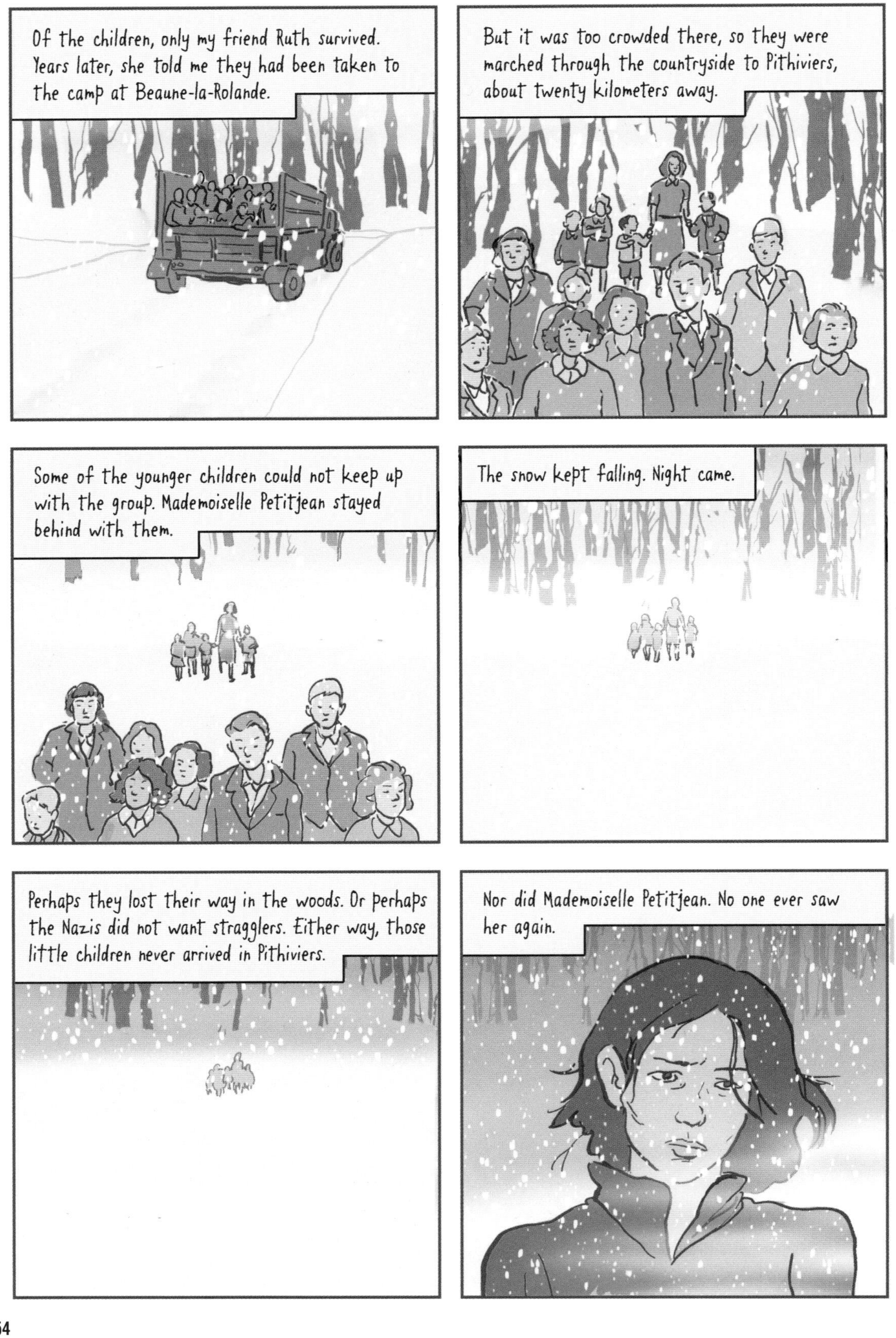
Of the children, only my friend Ruth survived. Years later, she told me they had been taken to the camp at Beaune-la-Rolande.
But it was too crowded there, so they were marched through the countryside to Pithiviers, about twenty kilometers away.
Some of the younger children could not keep up with the group. Mademoiselle Petitjean stayed behind with them.
The snow kept falling. Night came.
Perhaps they lost their way in the woods. Or perhaps the Nazis did not want stragglers. Either way, those little children never arrived in Pithiviers.
Nor did Mademoiselle Petitjean. No one ever saw her again.

CHAPTER 8

BY NOW, NEEDLESS TO SAY, I WAS NO LONGER WORRIED ABOUT MY STUPID RED SHOES. ALL I COULD THINK ABOUT WAS THE MAQUISARD LYING DEAD IN THE SNOW...

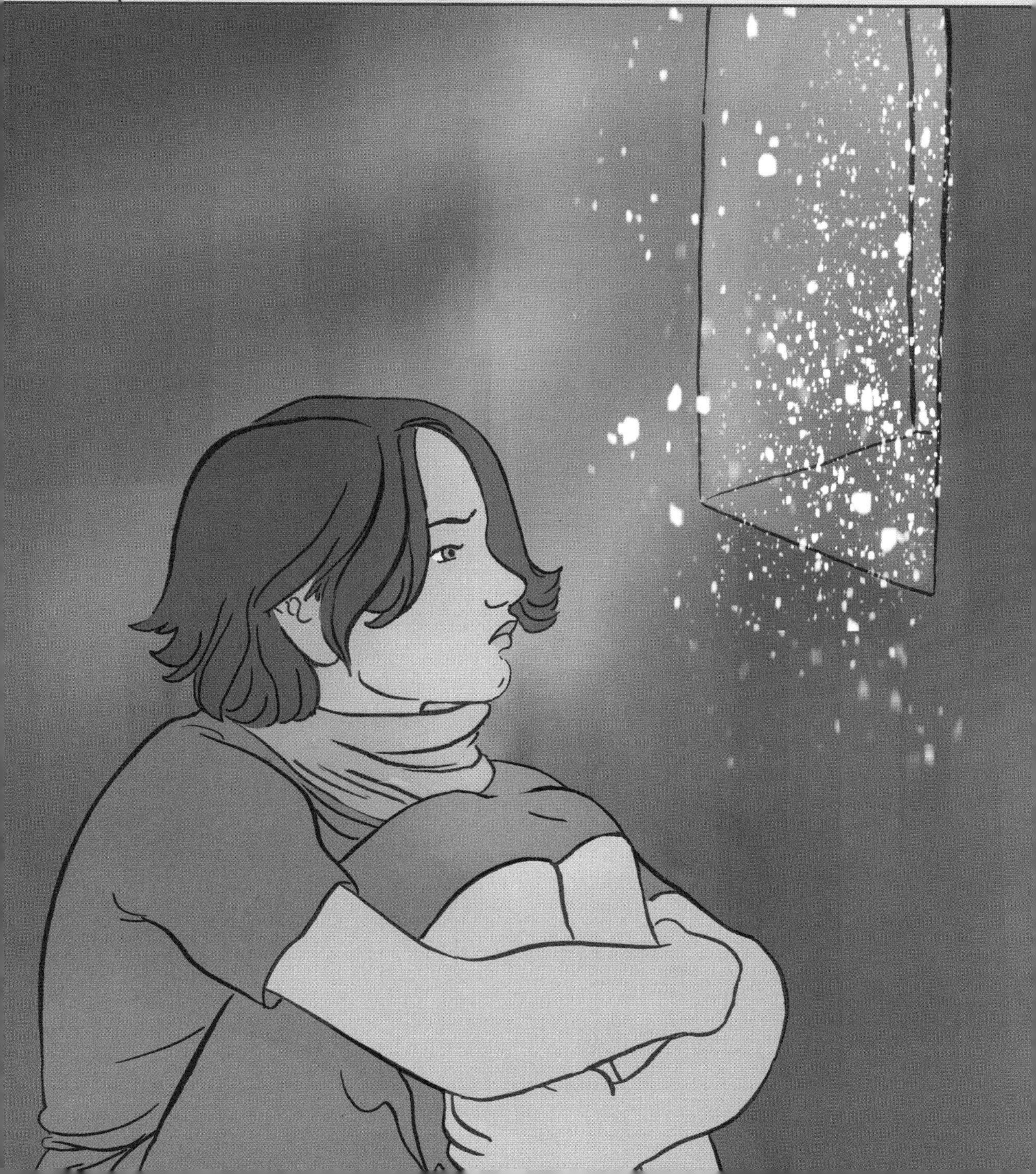

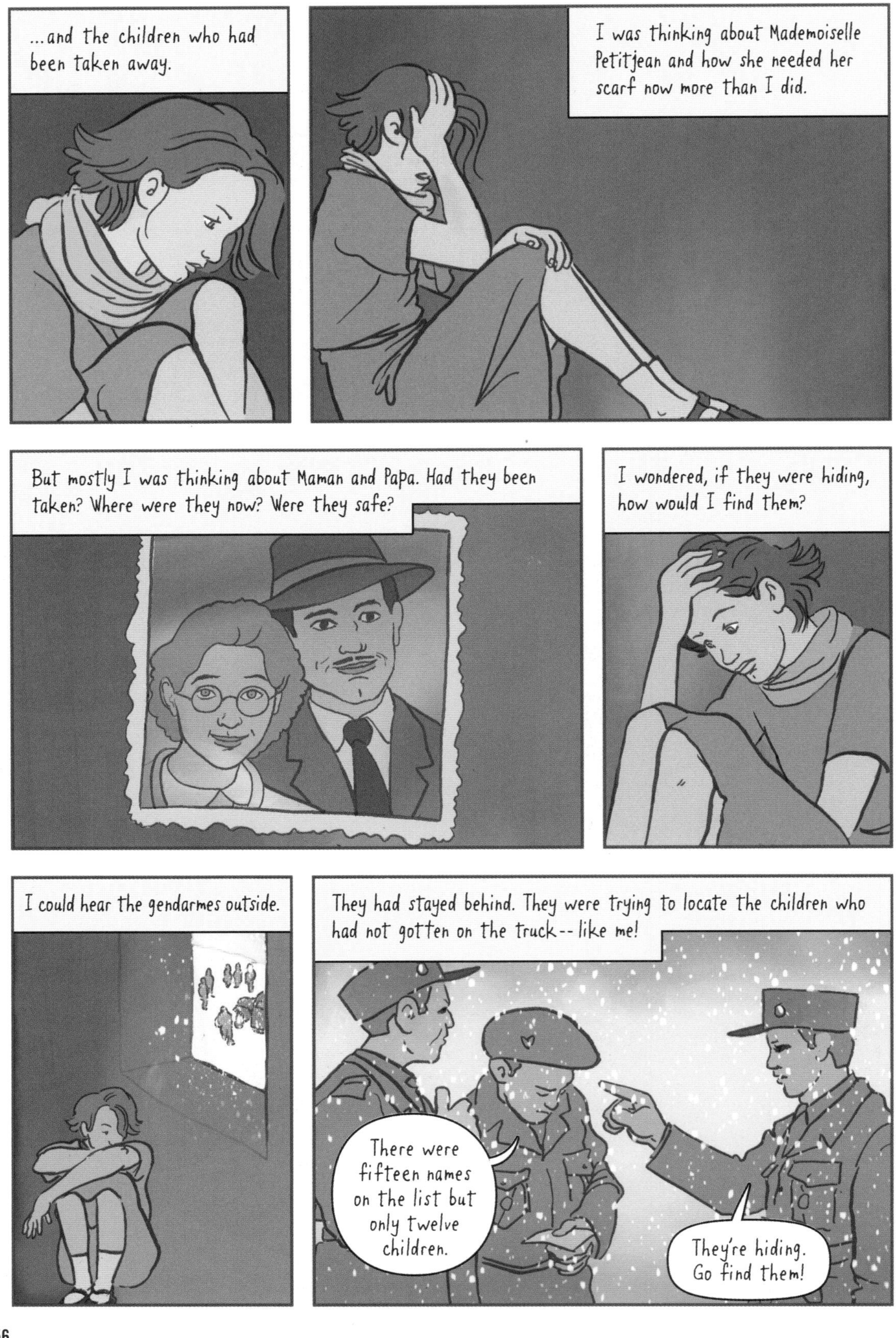
...and the children who had been taken away.
I was thinking about Mademoiselle Petitjean and how she needed her scarf now more than I did.
But mostly I was thinking about Maman and Papa. Had they been taken? Where were they now? Were they safe?
I wondered, if they were hiding, how would I find them?
I could hear the gendarmes outside.
They had stayed behind. They were trying to locate the children who had not gotten on the truck--like me!
There were fifteen names on the list but only twelve children.
They're hiding. Go find them!

I knew that it was just a matter of time before they found me.

When I heard footsteps on the stairs, I thought my time had come.

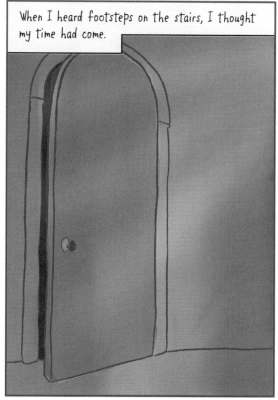

I watched the door slowly open. My heart was beating wildly.

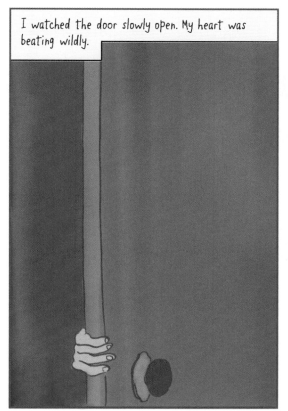

I closed my eyes, too afraid to look. The last thing I expected to see was...

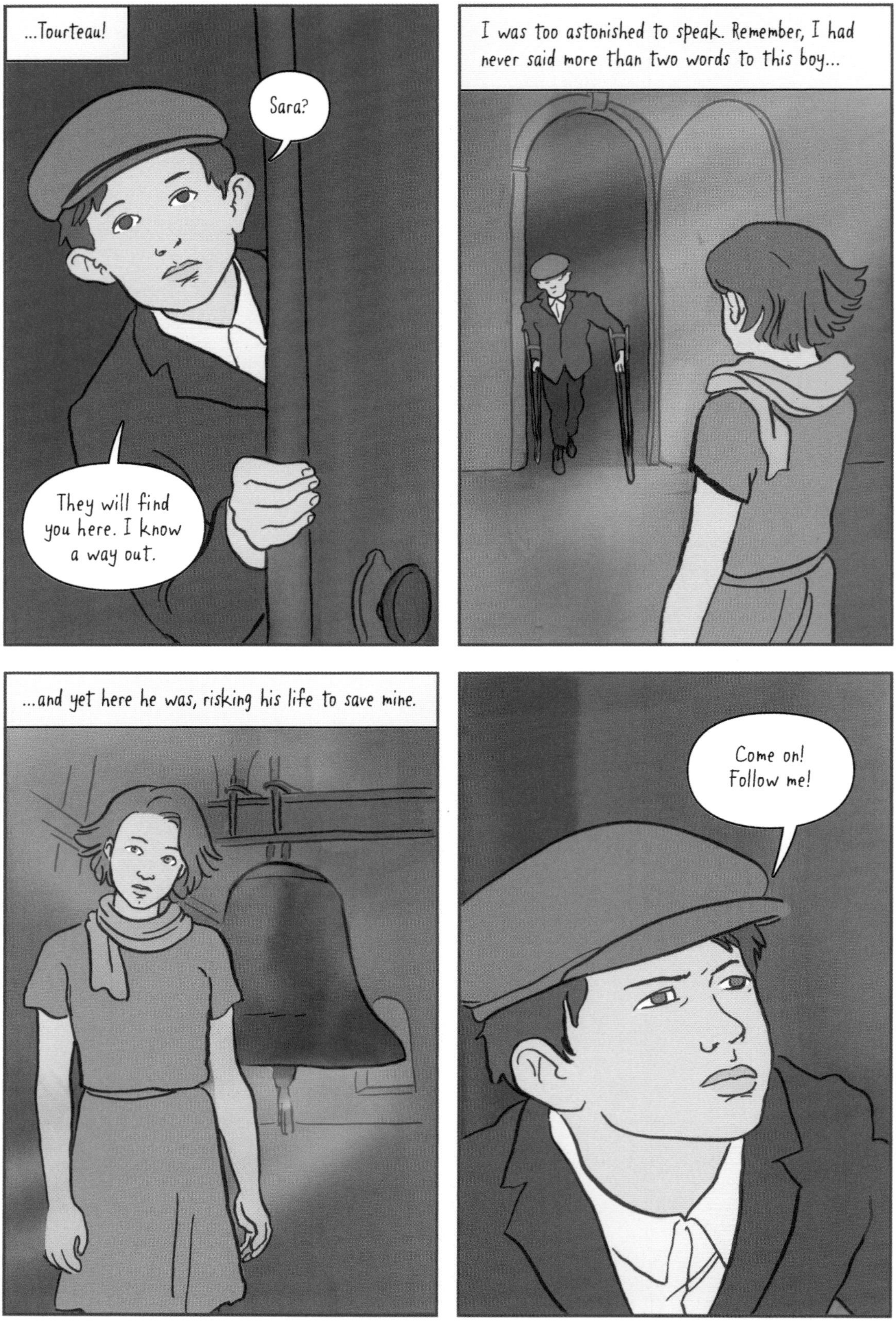
...Tourteau!
Sara?
They will find you here. I know a way out.
I was too astonished to speak. Remember, I had never said more than two words to this boy...
...and yet here he was, risking his life to save mine.
Come on! Follow me!

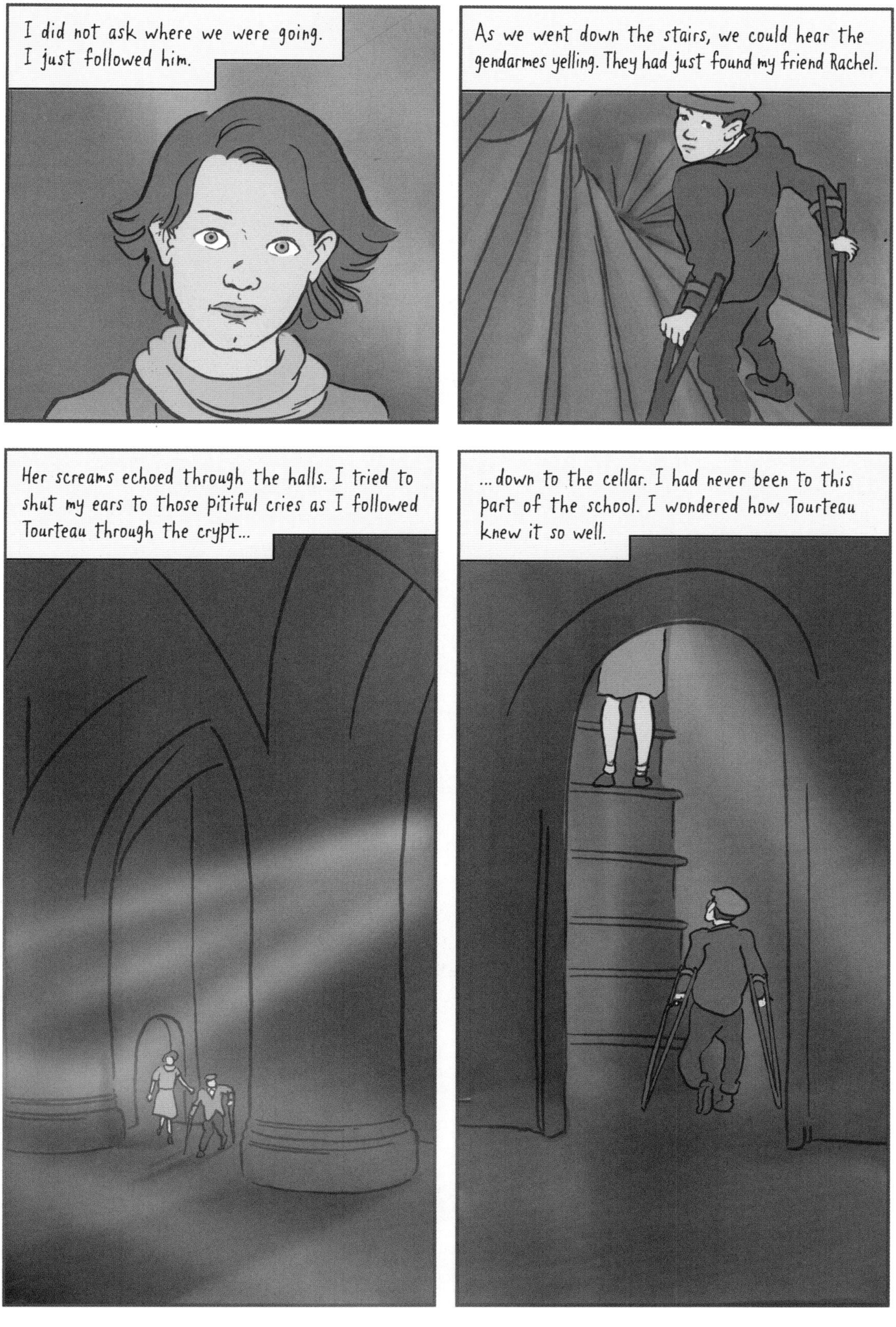
I did not ask where we were going. I just followed him.
As we went down the stairs, we could hear the gendarmes yelling. They had just found my friend Rachel.
Her screams echoed through the halls. I tried to shut my ears to those pitiful cries as I followed Tourteau through the crypt...
...down to the cellar. I had never been to this part of the school. I wondered how Tourteau knew it so well.

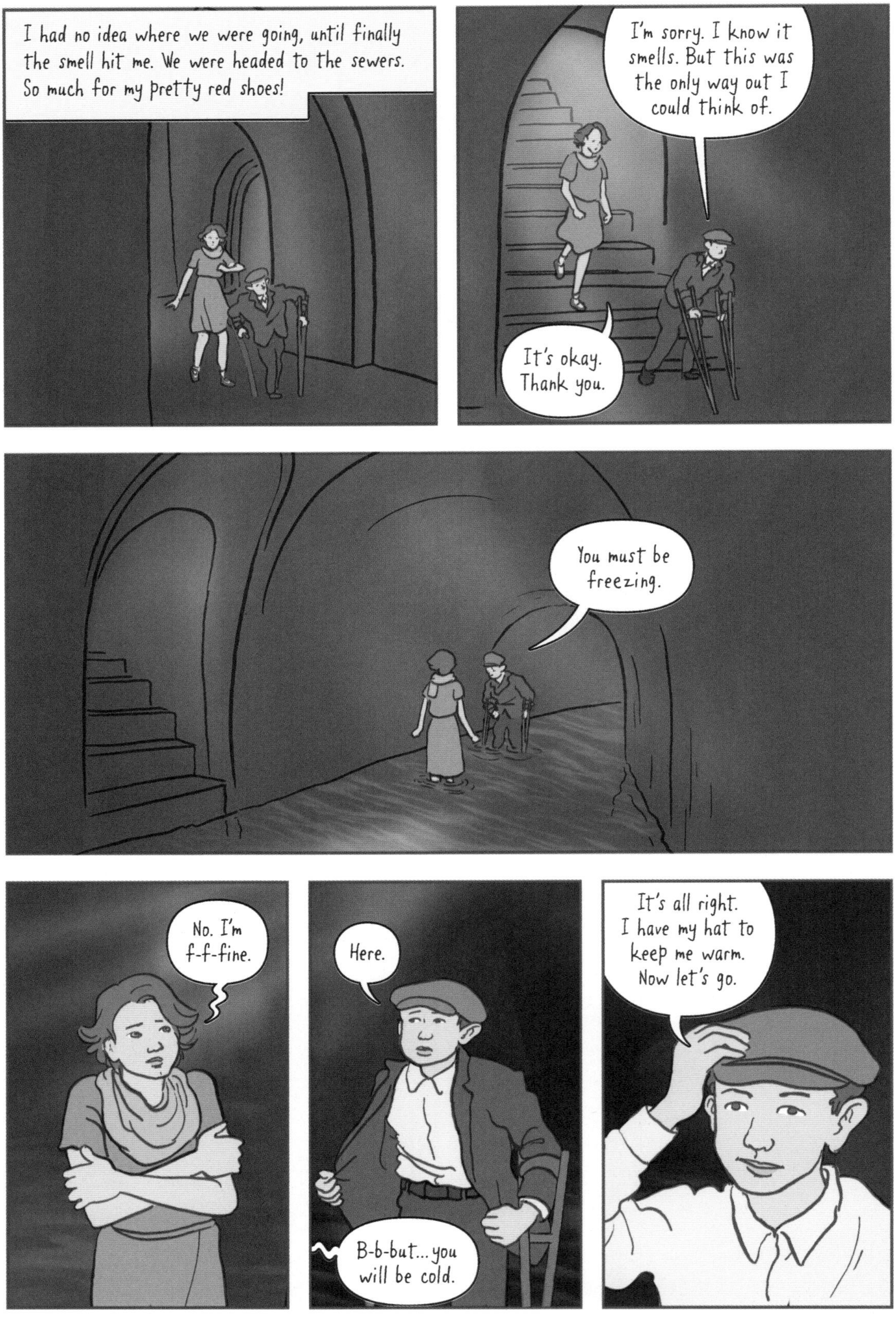
I had no idea where we were going, until finally the smell hit me. We were headed to the sewers. So much for my pretty red shoes!
I'm sorry. I know it smells. But this was the only way out I could think of.
It's okay. Thank you.
You must be freezing.
No. I'm f-f-fine.
Here.
B-b-but... you will be cold.
It's all right. I have my hat to keep me warm. Now let's go.

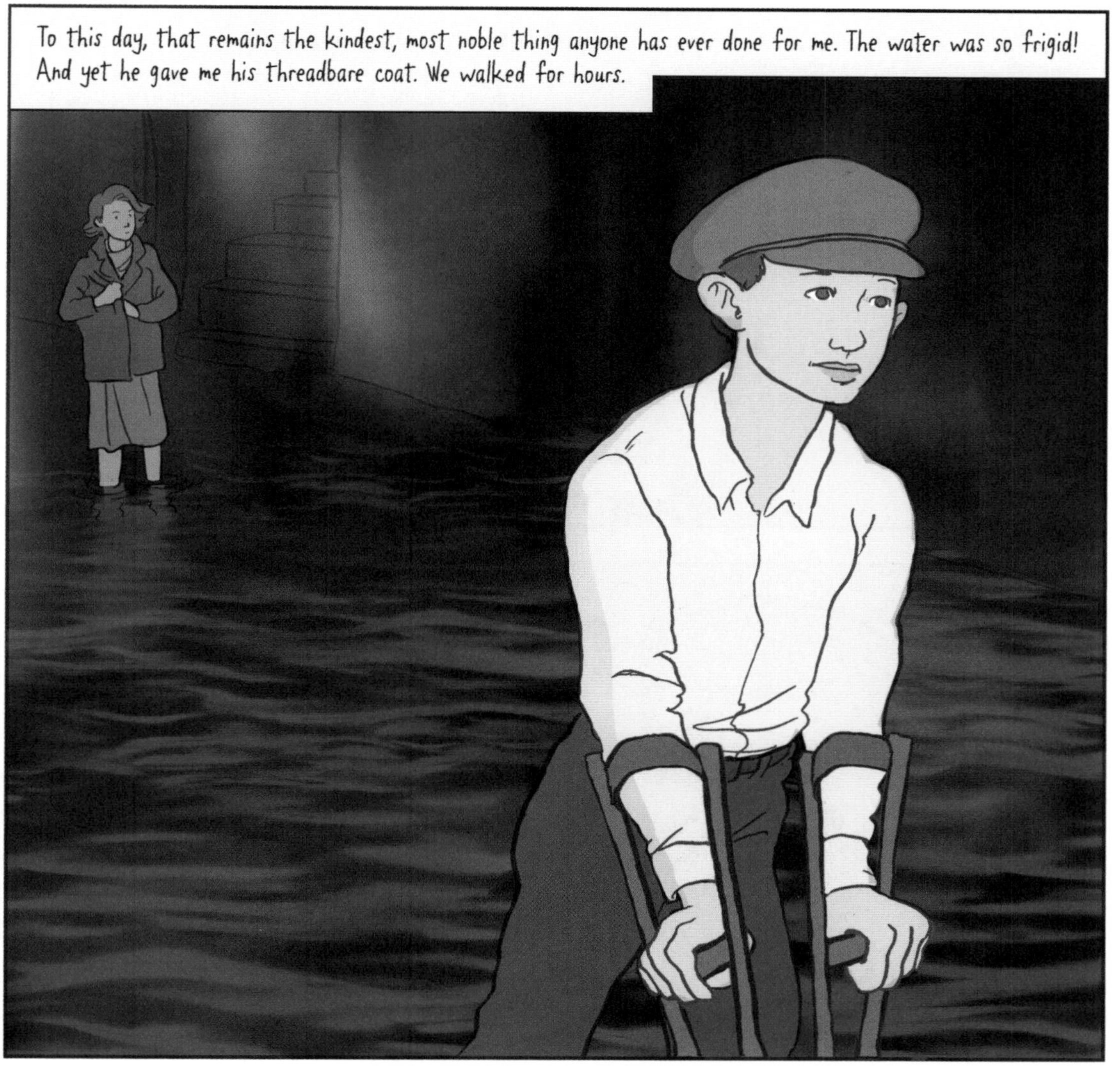
To this day, that remains the kindest, most noble thing anyone has ever done for me. The water was so frigid! And yet he gave me his threadbare coat. We walked for hours.

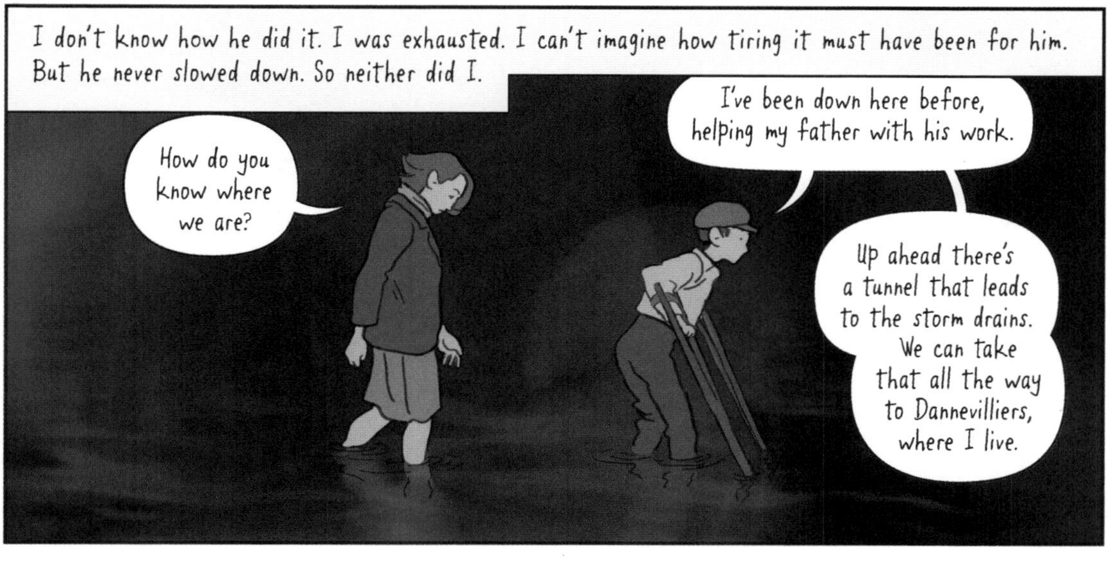
I don't know how he did it. I was exhausted. I can't imagine how tiring it must have been for him. But he never slowed down. So neither did I.
How do you know where we are?
I've been down here before, helping my father with his work.
Up ahead there's a tunnel that leads to the storm drains. We can take that all the way to Dannevilliers, where I live.

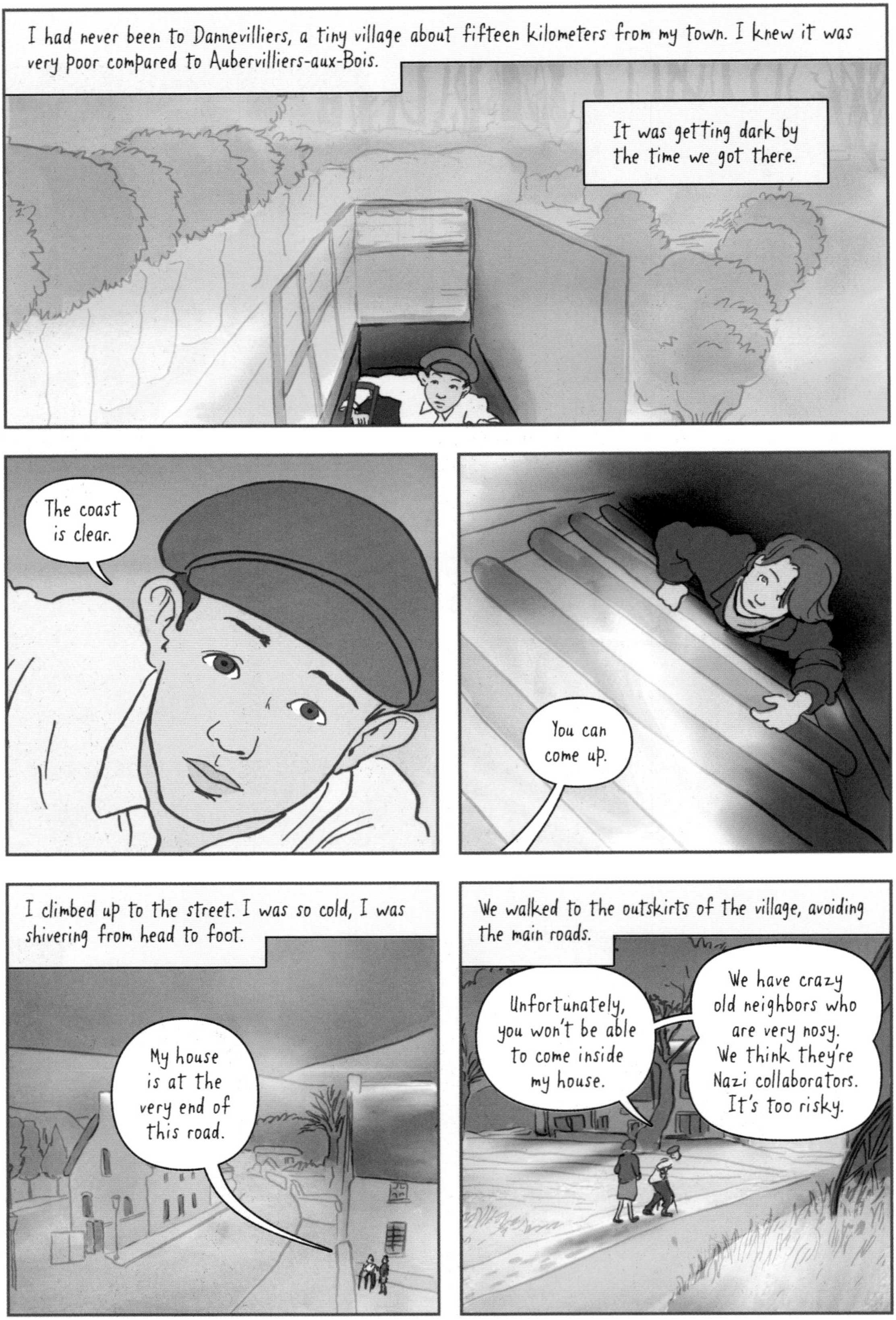
I had never been to Dannevilliers, a tiny village about fifteen kilometers from my town. I knew it was very poor compared to Aubervilliers-aux-Bois.
It was getting dark by the time we got there.
The coast is clear.
You can come up.
I climbed up to the street. I was so cold, I was shivering from head to foot.
My house is at the very end of this road.
We walked to the outskirts of the village, avoiding the main roads.
Unfortunately, you won't be able to come inside my house.
We have crazy old neighbors who are very nosy. We think they're Nazi collaborators. It's too risky.

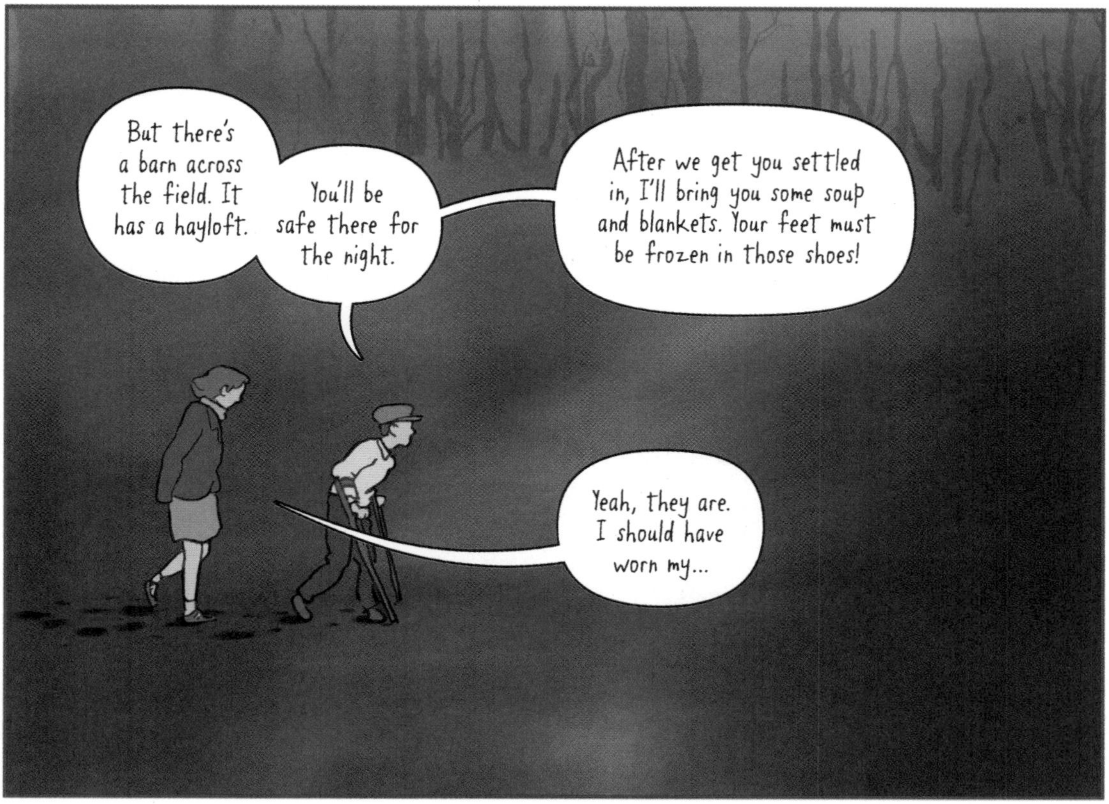
But there's a barn across the field. It has a hayloft.
You'll be safe there for the night.
After we get you settled in, I'll bring you some soup and blankets. Your feet must be frozen in those shoes!
Yeah, they are. I should have worn my...

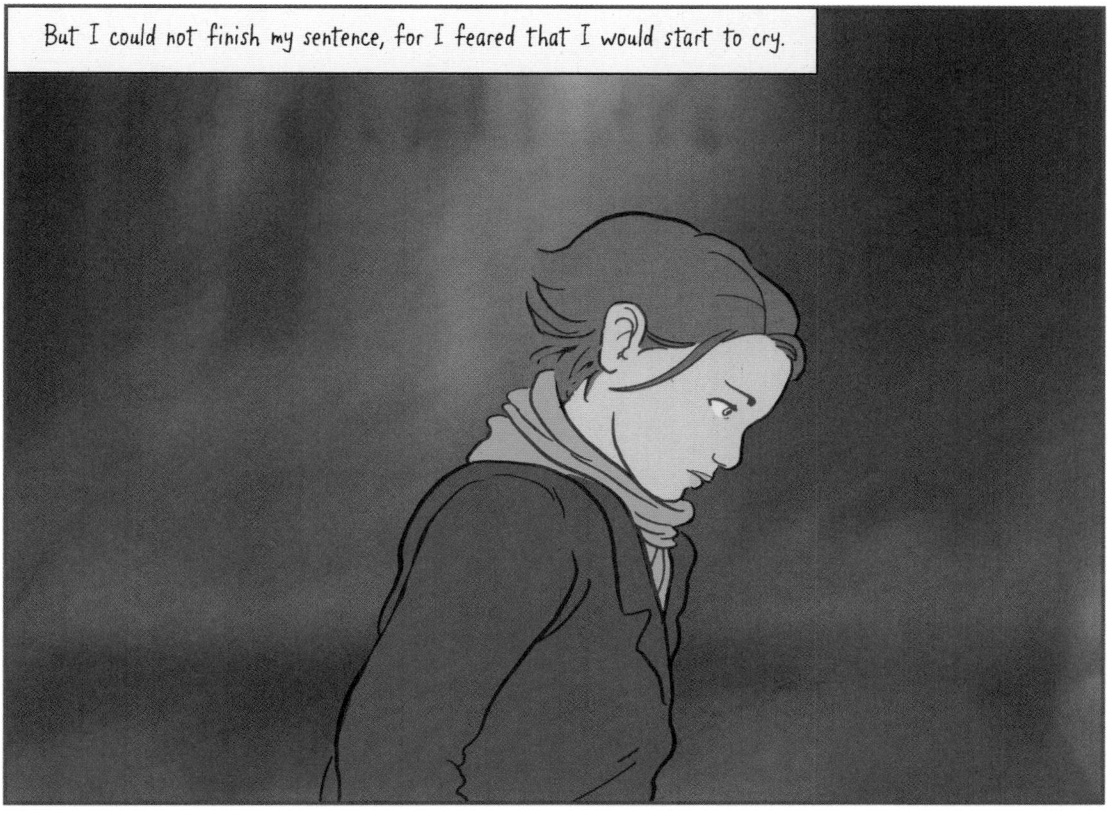
But I could not finish my sentence, for I feared that I would start to cry.

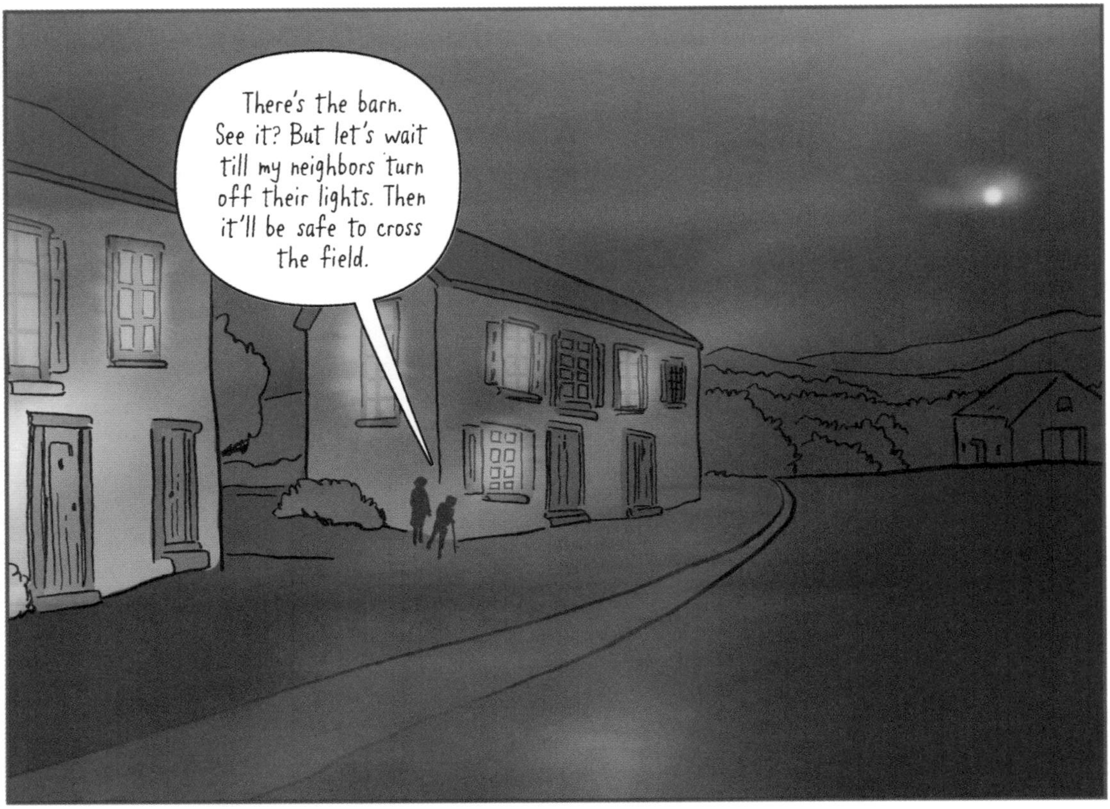
There's the barn. See it? But let's wait till my neighbors turn off their lights. Then it'll be safe to cross the field.

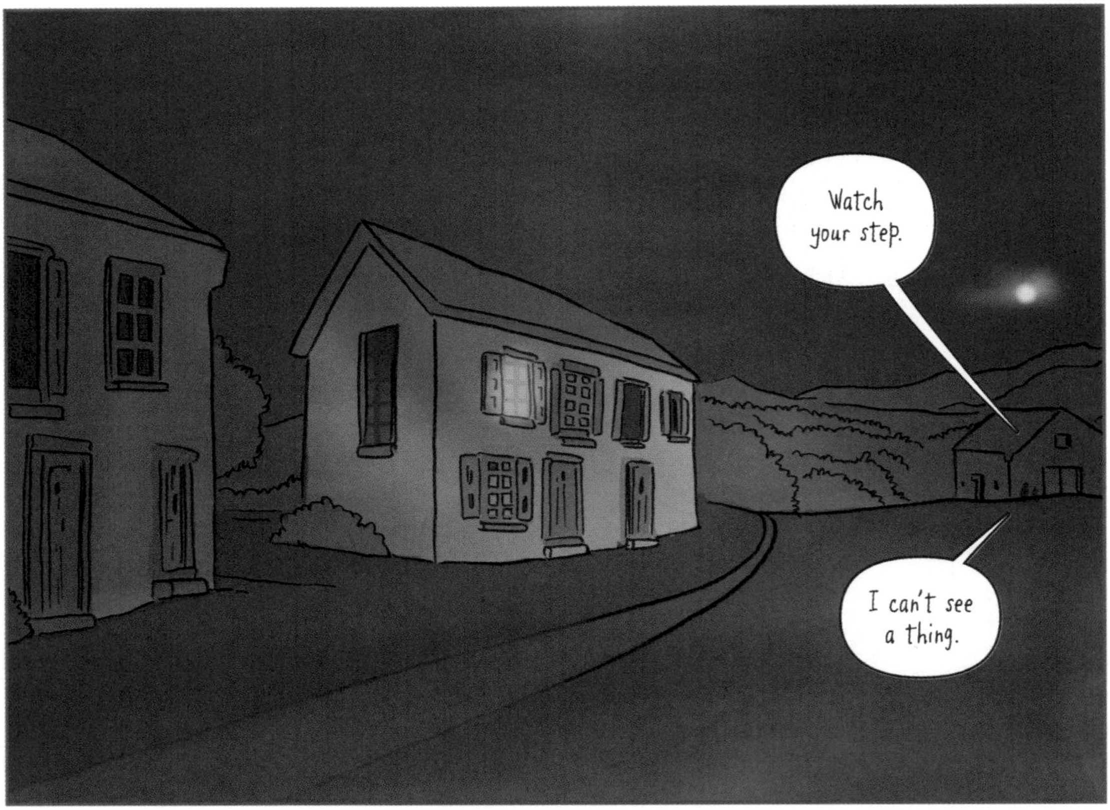
Watch your step.
I can't see a thing.

CHAPTER 9

IT WAS FOR THE BEST THAT I DID NOT GET A GOOD LOOK AT THE OUTSIDE OF THE BARN. I MIGHT HAVE BEEN TOO SCARED TO ENTER IF I HAD!

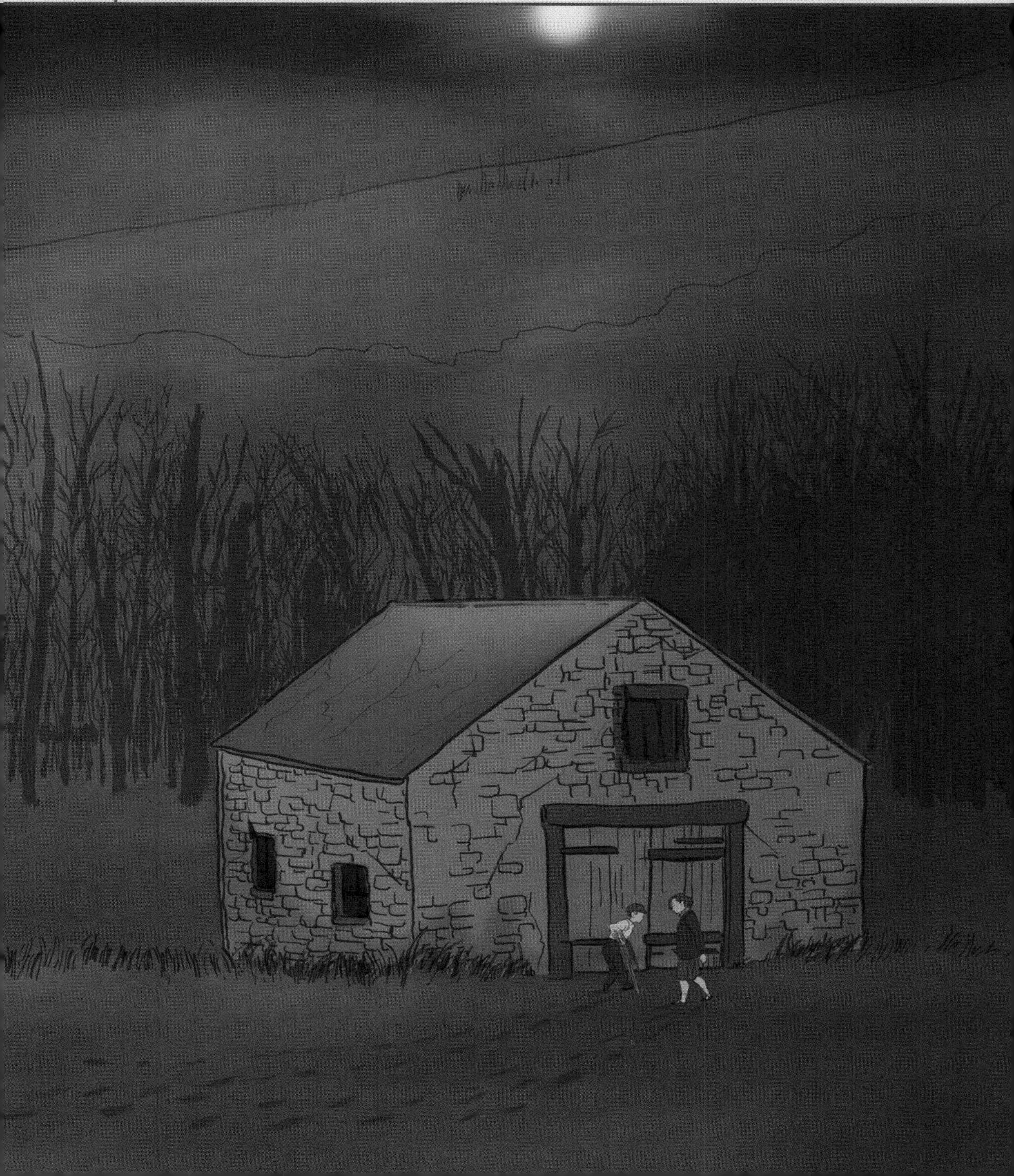

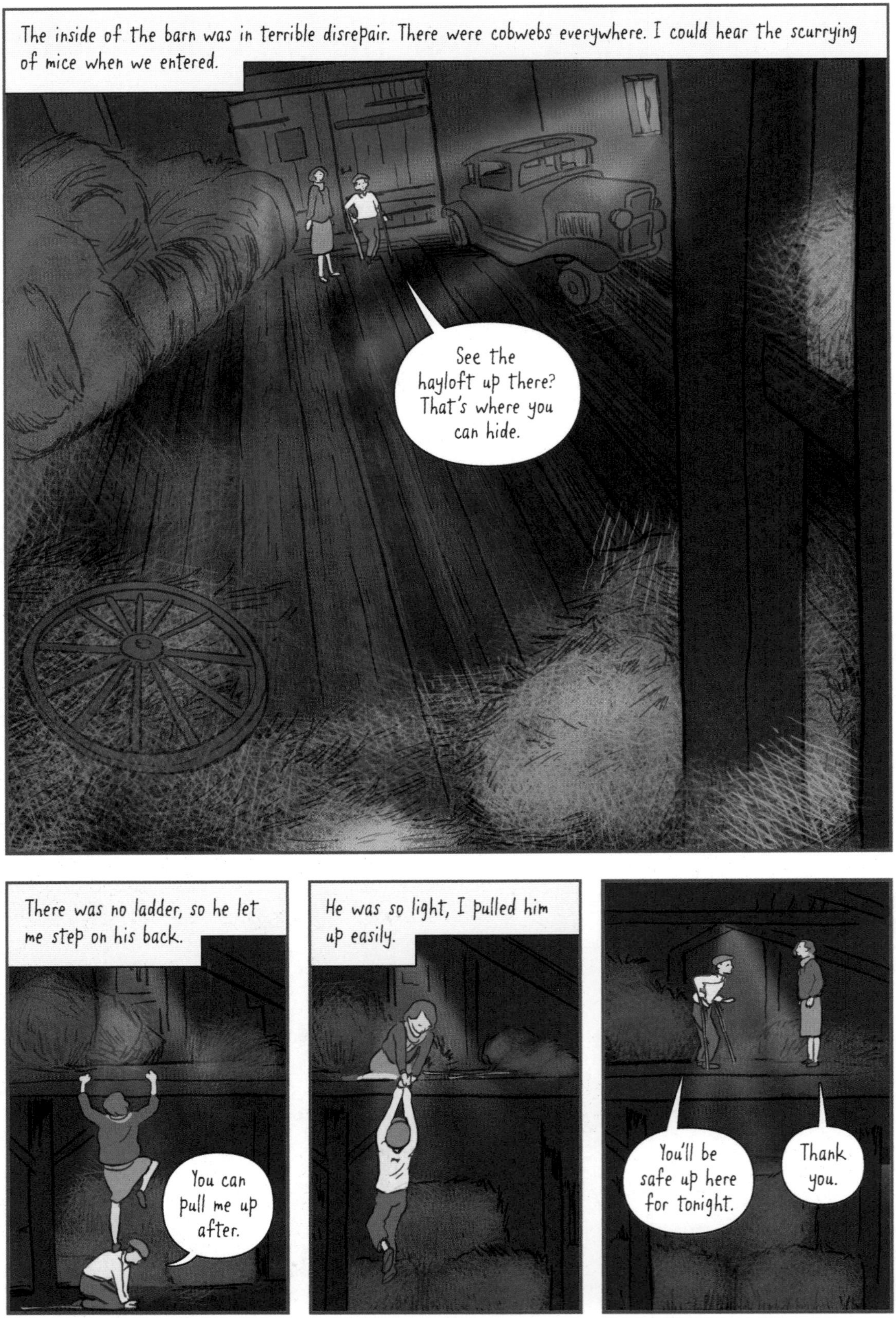
The inside of the barn was in terrible disrepair. There were cobwebs everywhere. I could hear the scurrying of mice when we entered.
See the hayloft up there? That's where you can hide.
There was no ladder, so he let me step on his back.
You can pull me up after.
He was so light, I pulled him up easily.
You'll be safe up here for tonight.
Thank you.

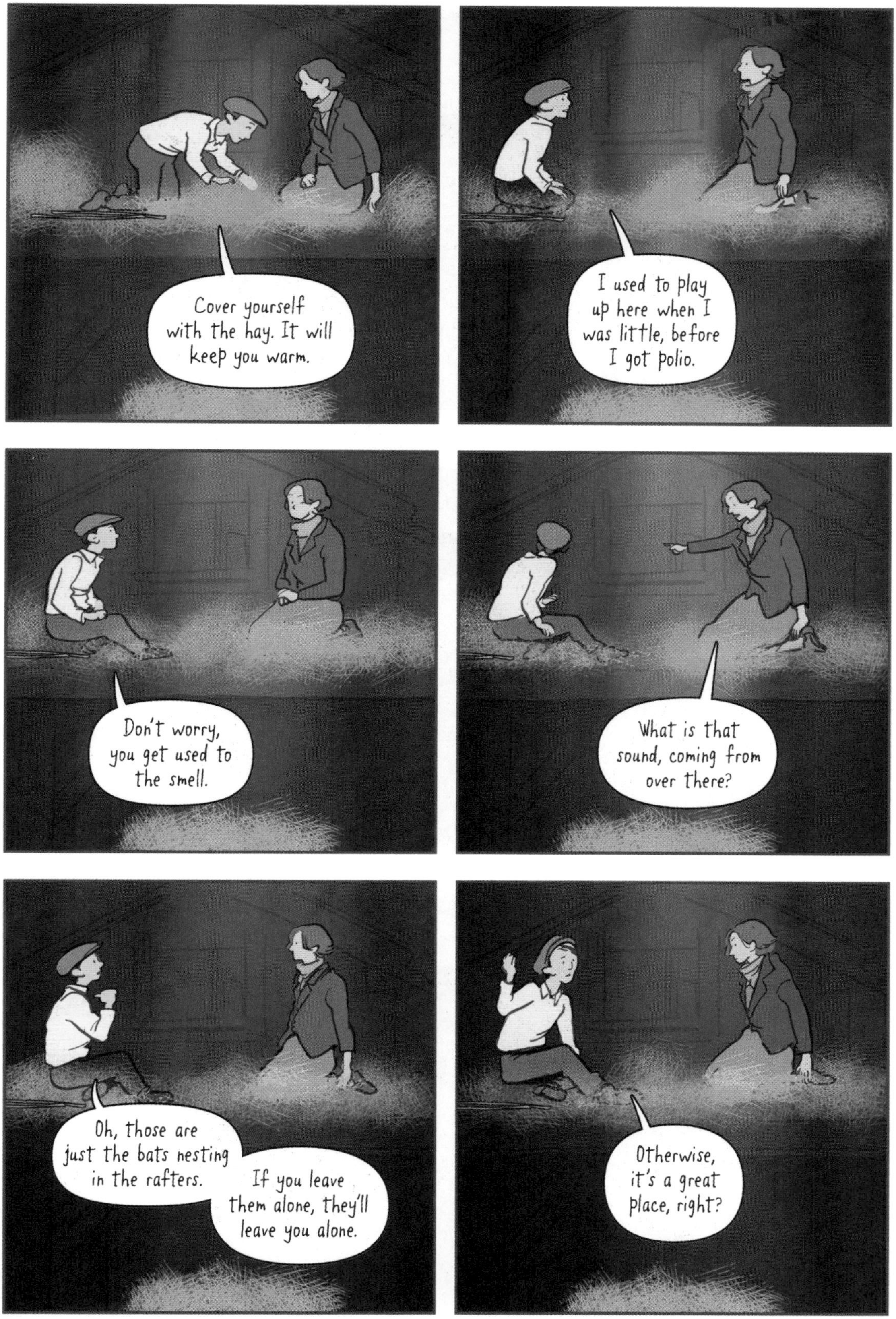
Cover yourself with the hay. It will keep you warm.
I used to play up here when I was little, before I got polio.
Don't worry, you get used to the smell.
What is that sound, coming from over there?
Oh, those are just the bats nesting in the rafters.
If you leave them alone, they'll leave you alone.
Otherwise, it's a great place, right?

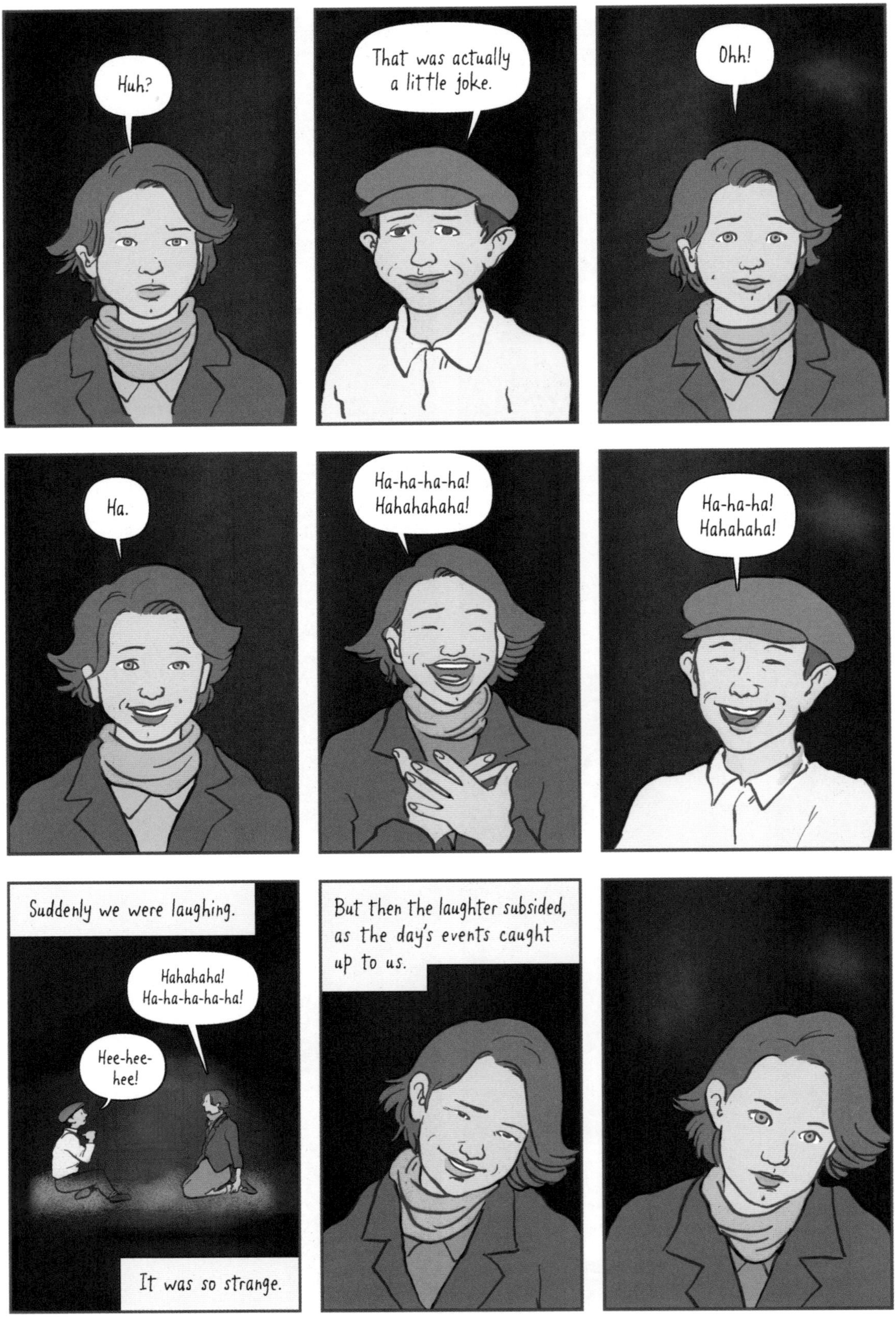
Huh?
That was actually a little joke.
Ohh!
Ha.
Ha-ha-ha-ha! Hahahahaha!
Ha-ha-ha! Hahahaha!
Suddenly we were laughing.
Hahahaha! Ha-ha-ha-ha-ha!
Hee-hee-hee!
It was so strange.
But then the laughter subsided, as the day's events caught up to us.

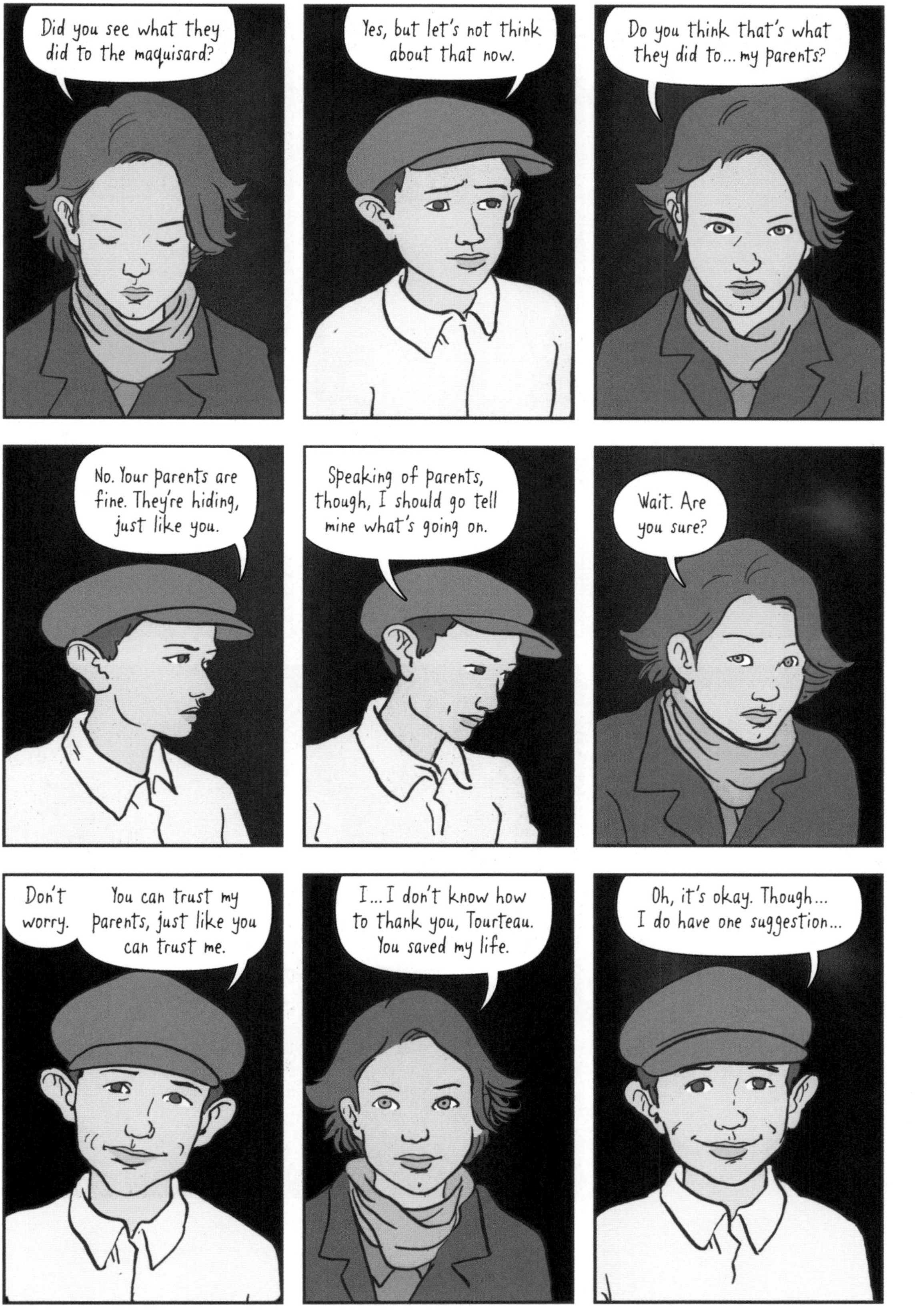
Did you see what they did to the maquisard?
Yes, but let's not think about that now.
Do you think that's what they did to... my parents?
No. Your parents are fine. They're hiding, just like you.
Speaking of parents, though, I should go tell mine what's going on.
Wait. Are you sure?
Don't worry.
You can trust my parents, just like you can trust me.
I... I don't know how to thank you, Tourteau. You saved my life.
Oh, it's okay. Though... I do have one suggestion...

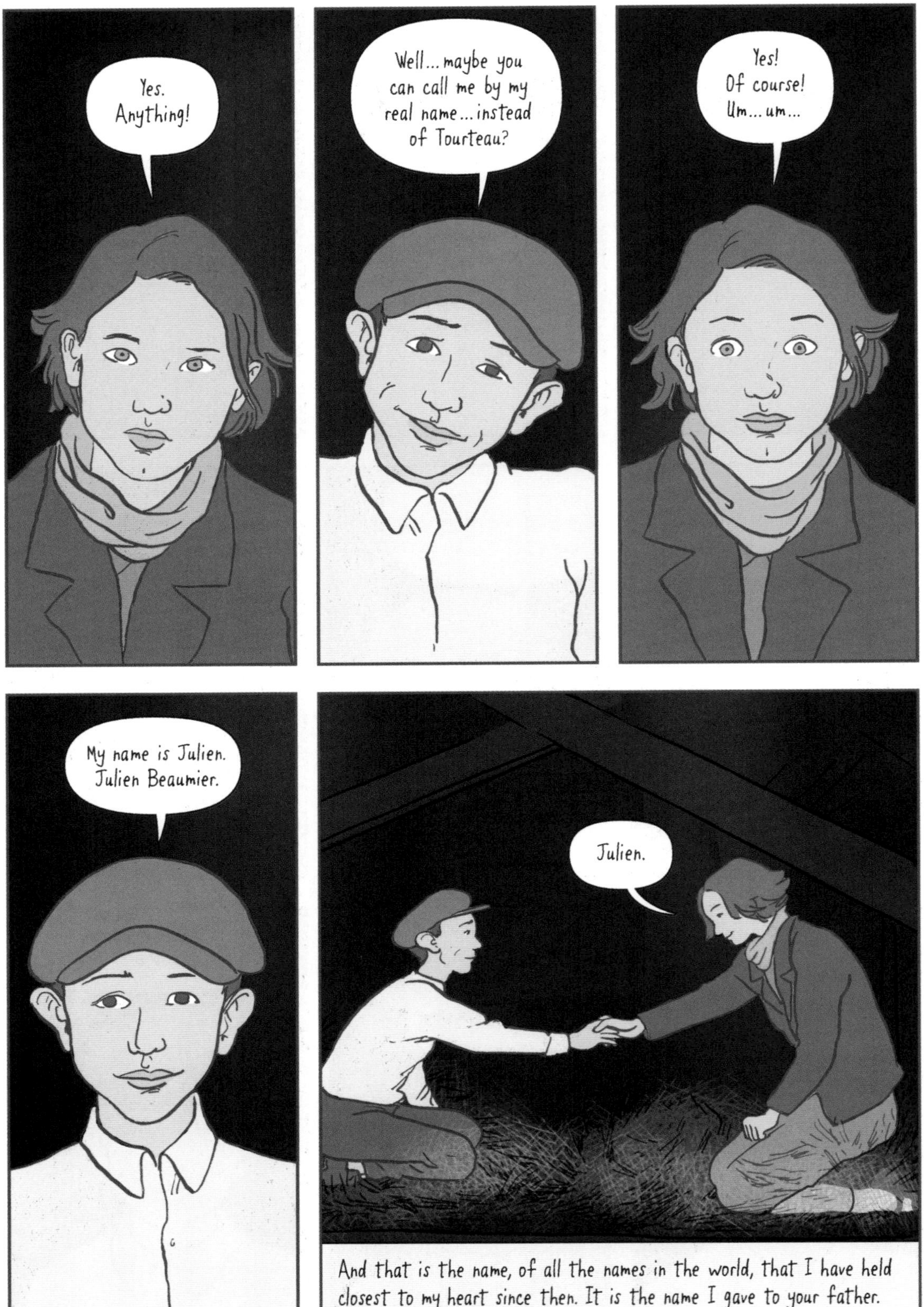
Yes. Anything!
Well... maybe you can call me by my real name... instead of Tourteau?
Yes! Of course! Um... um...
My name is Julien. Julien Beaumier.
Julien.
And that is the name, of all the names in the world, that I have held closest to my heart since then. It is the name I gave to your father. It is the name he gave to you. Julian.

CHAPTER 10

JULIEN RETURNED TO THE BARN WITH HIS PARENTS A SHORT WHILE LATER. THEY BROUGHT ME SOUP AND DRY CLOTHES. AND WARM WORDS.

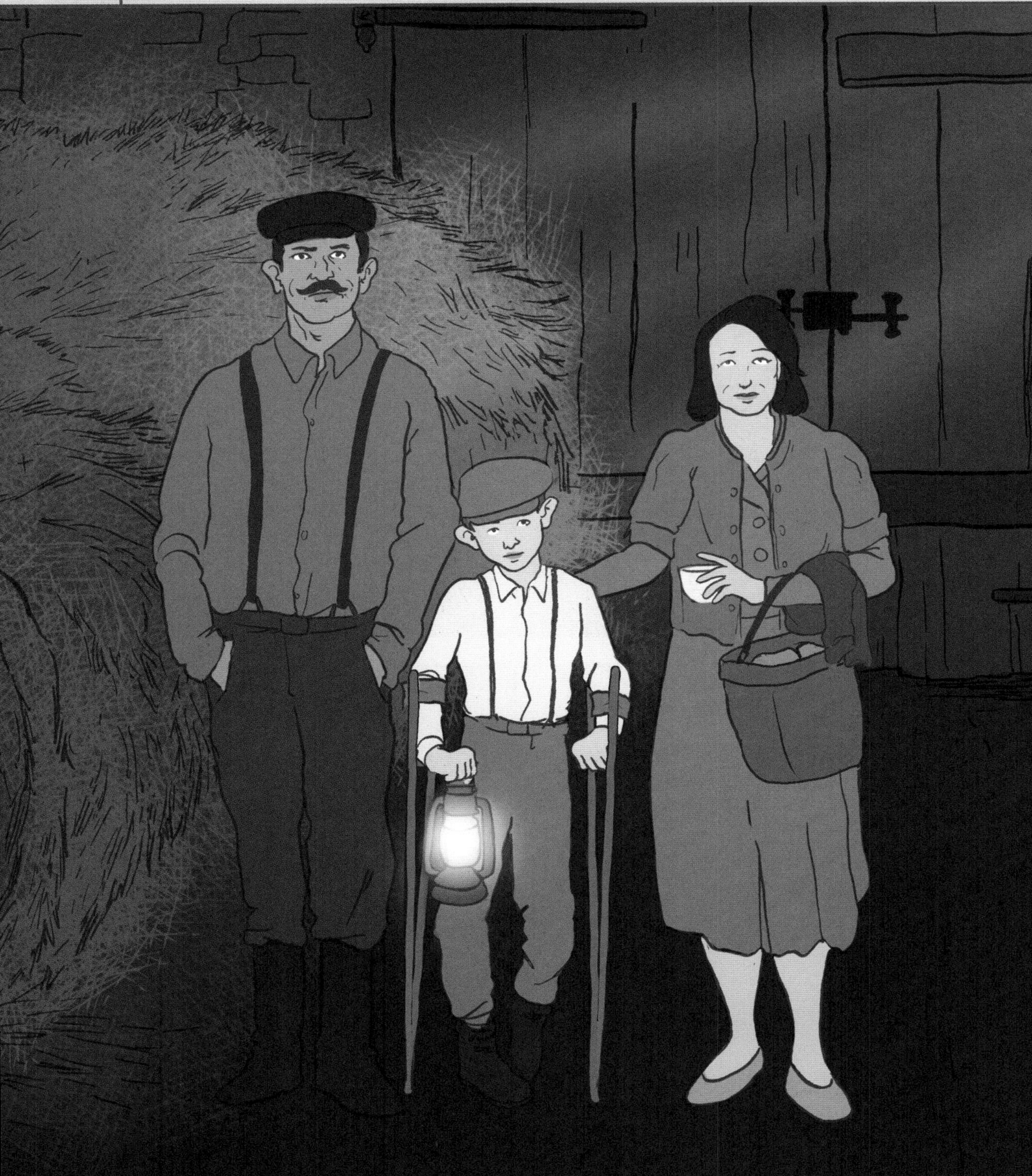

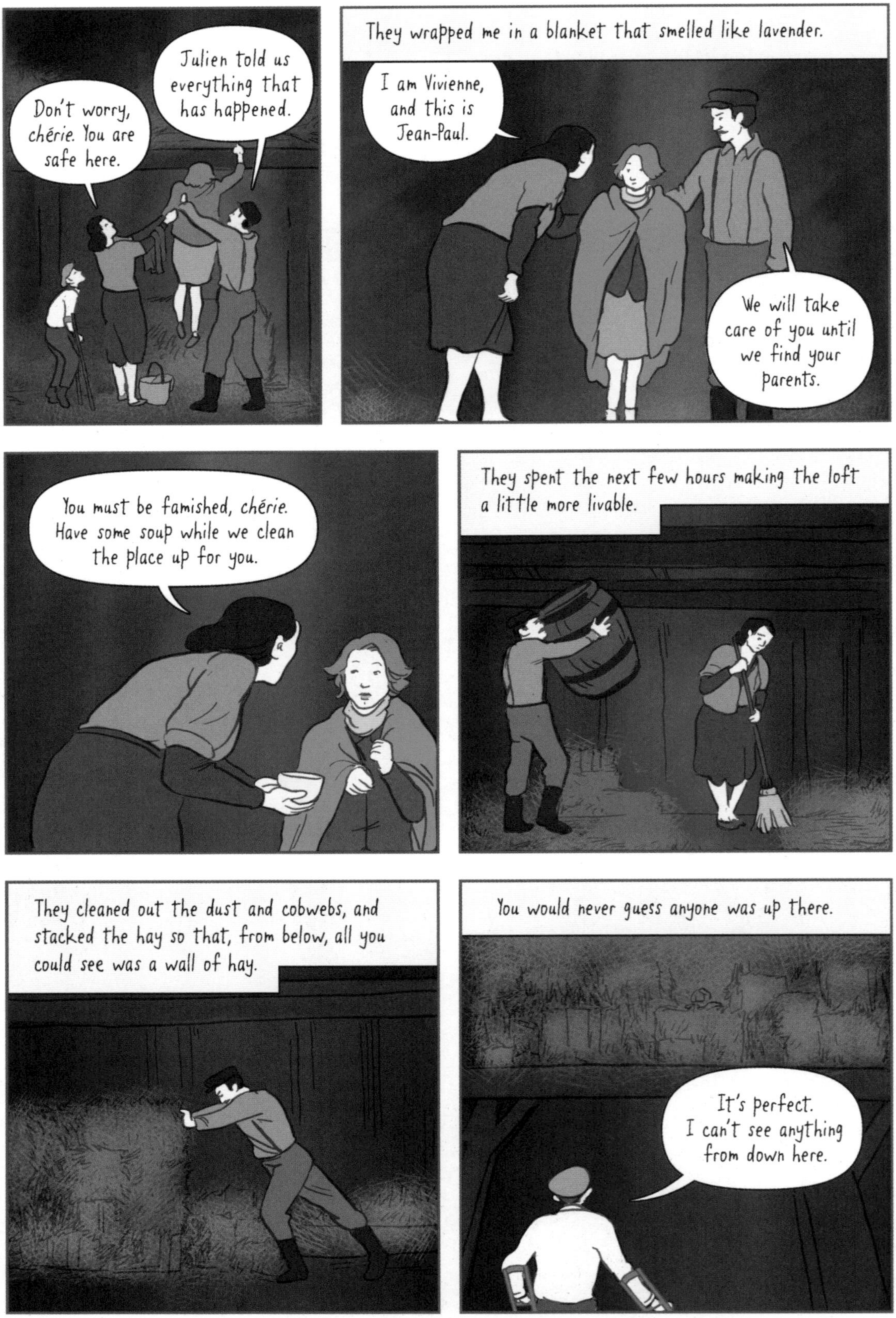
Julien told us everything that has happened.
Don't worry, chérie. You are safe here.
They wrapped me in a blanket that smelled like lavender.
I am Vivienne, and this is Jean-Paul.
We will take care of you until we find your parents.
You must be famished, chérie. Have some soup while we clean the place up for you.
They spent the next few hours making the loft a little more livable.
They cleaned out the dust and cobwebs, and stacked the hay so that, from below, all you could see was a wall of hay.
You would never guess anyone was up there.
It's perfect. I can't see anything from down here.

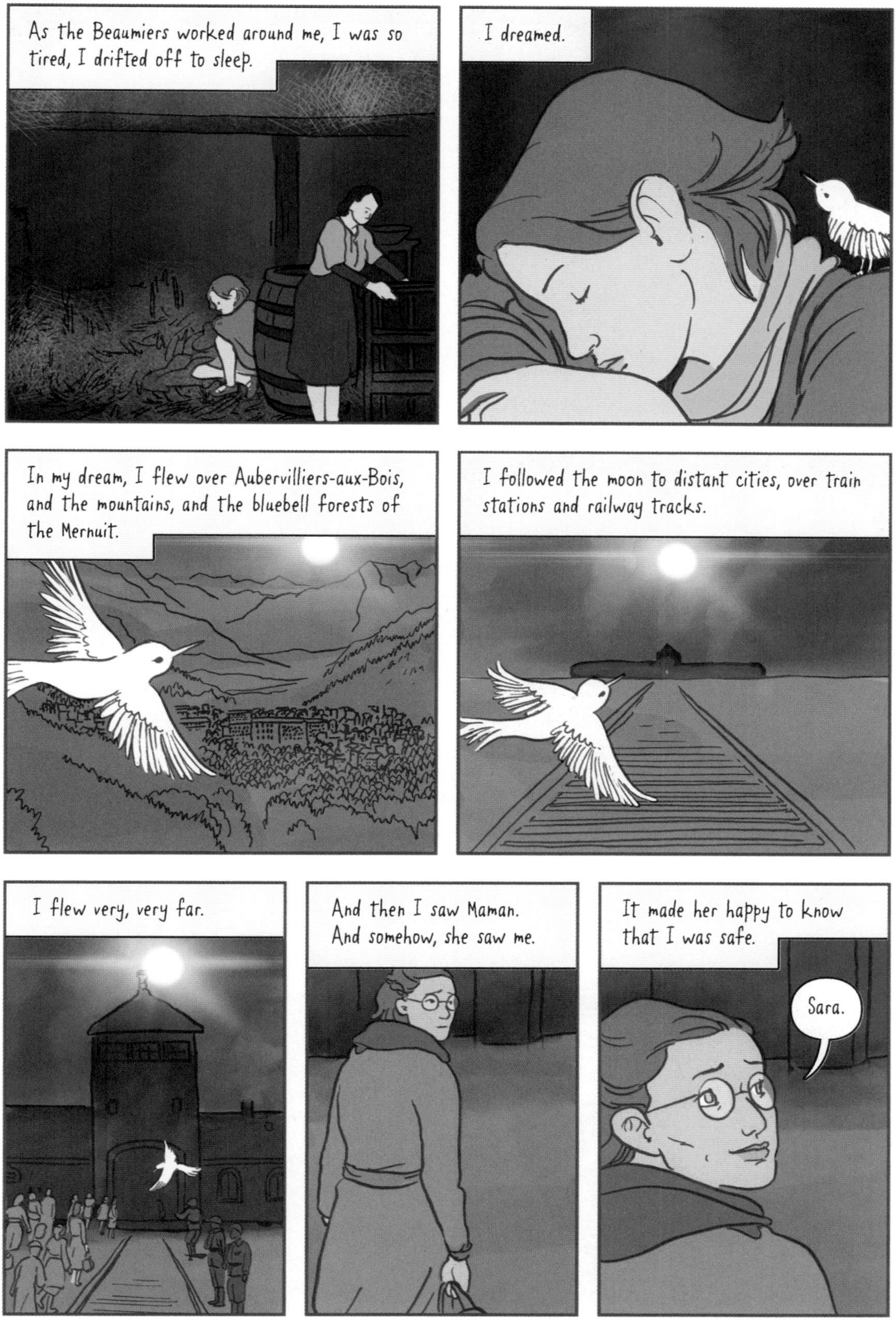
As the Beaumiers worked around me, I was so tired, I drifted off to sleep.
I dreamed.
In my dream, I flew over Aubervilliers-aux-Bois, and the mountains, and the bluebell forests of the Mernuit.
I followed the moon to distant cities, over train stations and railway tracks.
I flew very, very far.
And then I saw Maman. And somehow, she saw me.
It made her happy to know that I was safe.
Sara.

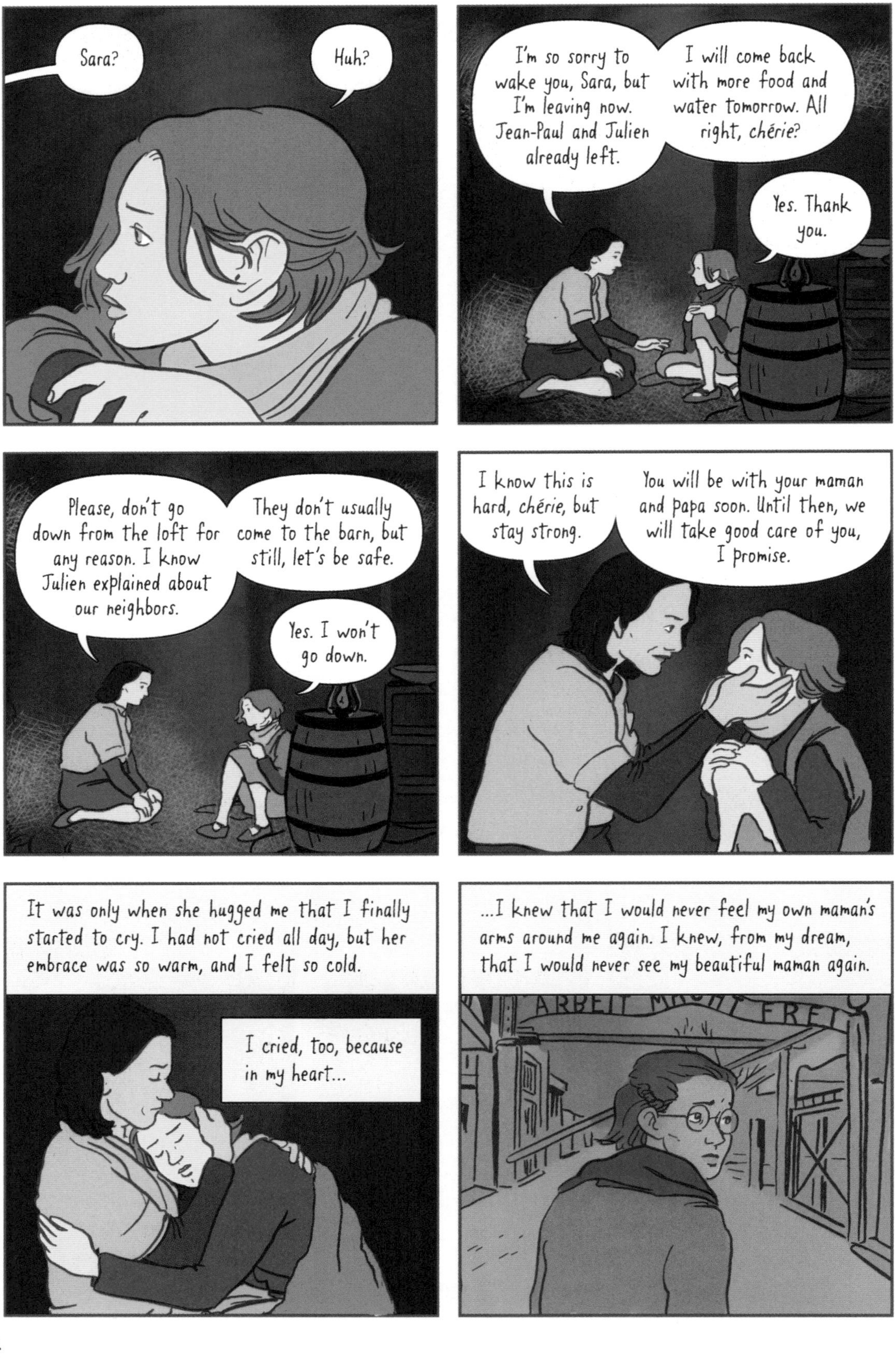
Sara?
Huh?
I'm so sorry to wake you, Sara, but I'm leaving now. Jean-Paul and Julien already left.
I will come back with more food and water tomorrow. All right, *chérie*?
Yes. Thank you.
Please, don't go down from the loft for any reason. I know Julien explained about our neighbors.
They don't usually come to the barn, but still, let's be safe.
Yes. I won't go down.
I know this is hard, *chérie*, but stay strong.
You will be with your maman and papa soon. Until then, we will take good care of you, I promise.
It was only when she hugged me that I finally started to cry. I had not cried all day, but her embrace was so warm, and I felt so cold.
I cried, too, because in my heart...
...I knew that I would never feel my own maman's arms around me again. I knew, from my dream, that I would never see my beautiful maman again.

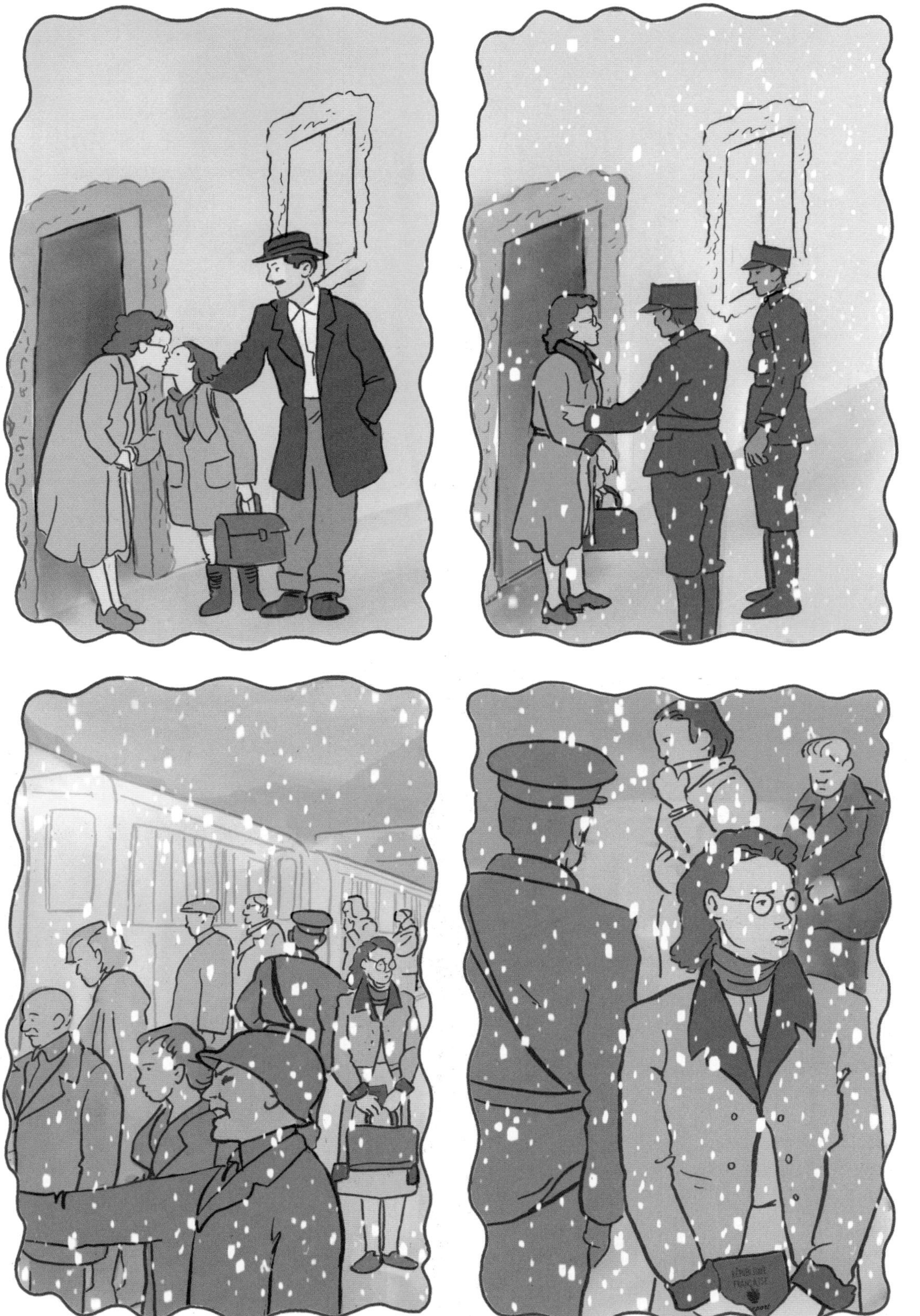

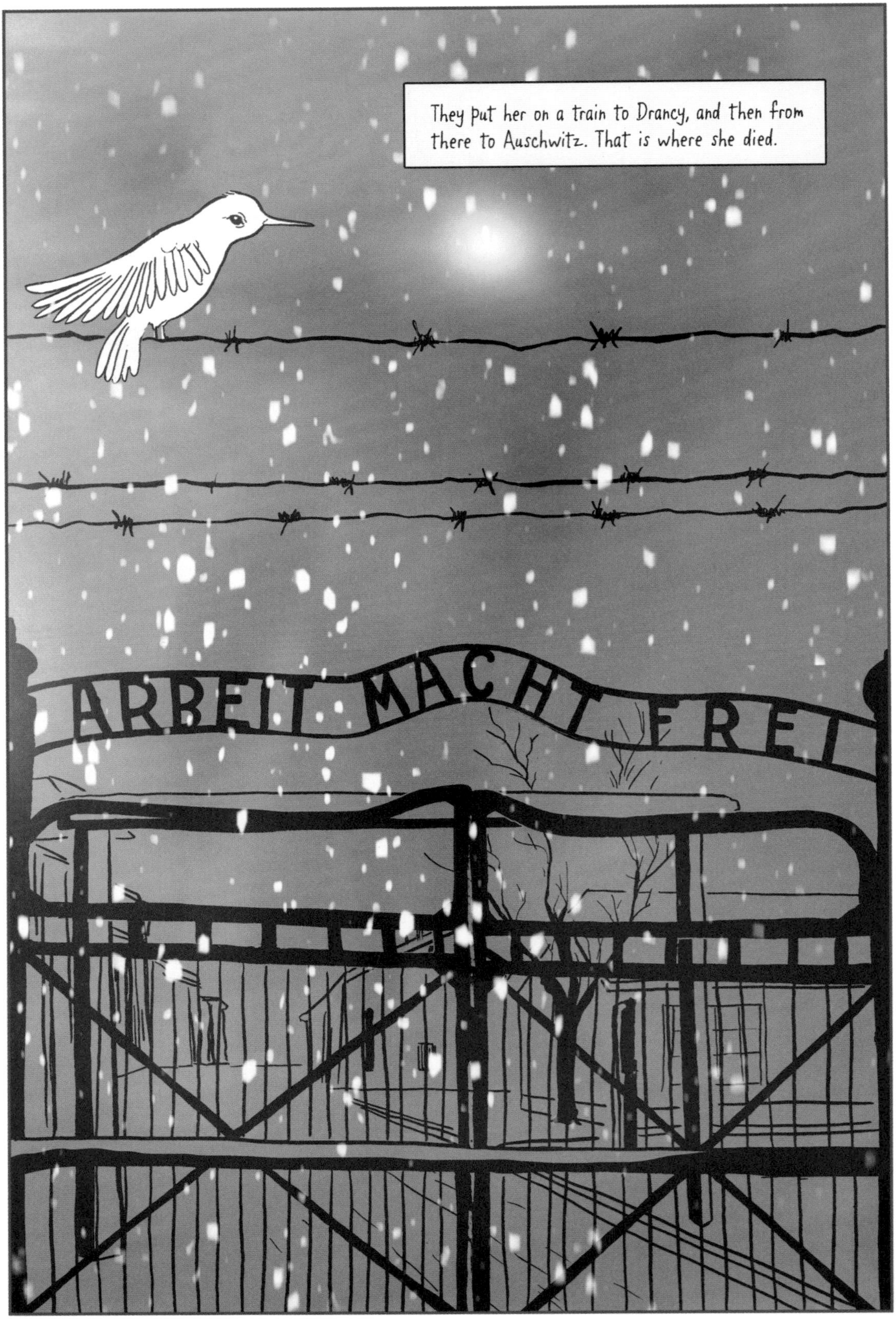
They put her on a train to Drancy, and then from there to Auschwitz. That is where she died.
ARBEIT MACHT FREI

PART TWO

I hear your cries, you little voices of children...
-Muriel Rukeyser, "Seventh Elegy: The Dream-Singing Elegy"

THOSE NEXT FEW DAYS AND NIGHTS WERE THE HARDEST OF MY LIFE. I WAS SO SCARED. I MISSED MY PARENTS DESPERATELY. WHEN WOULD I BE ABLE TO LEAVE? WHERE WOULD I GO?

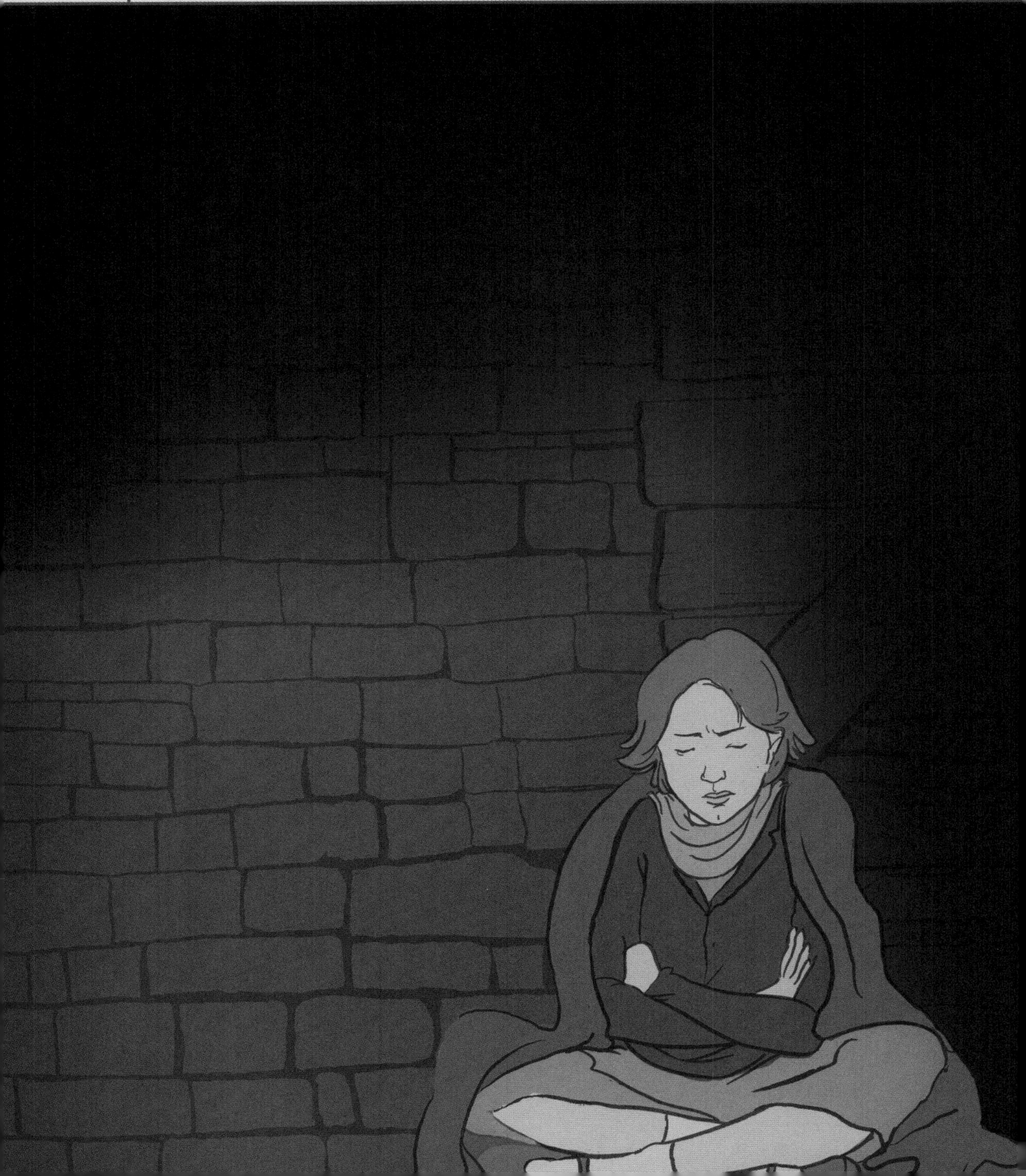

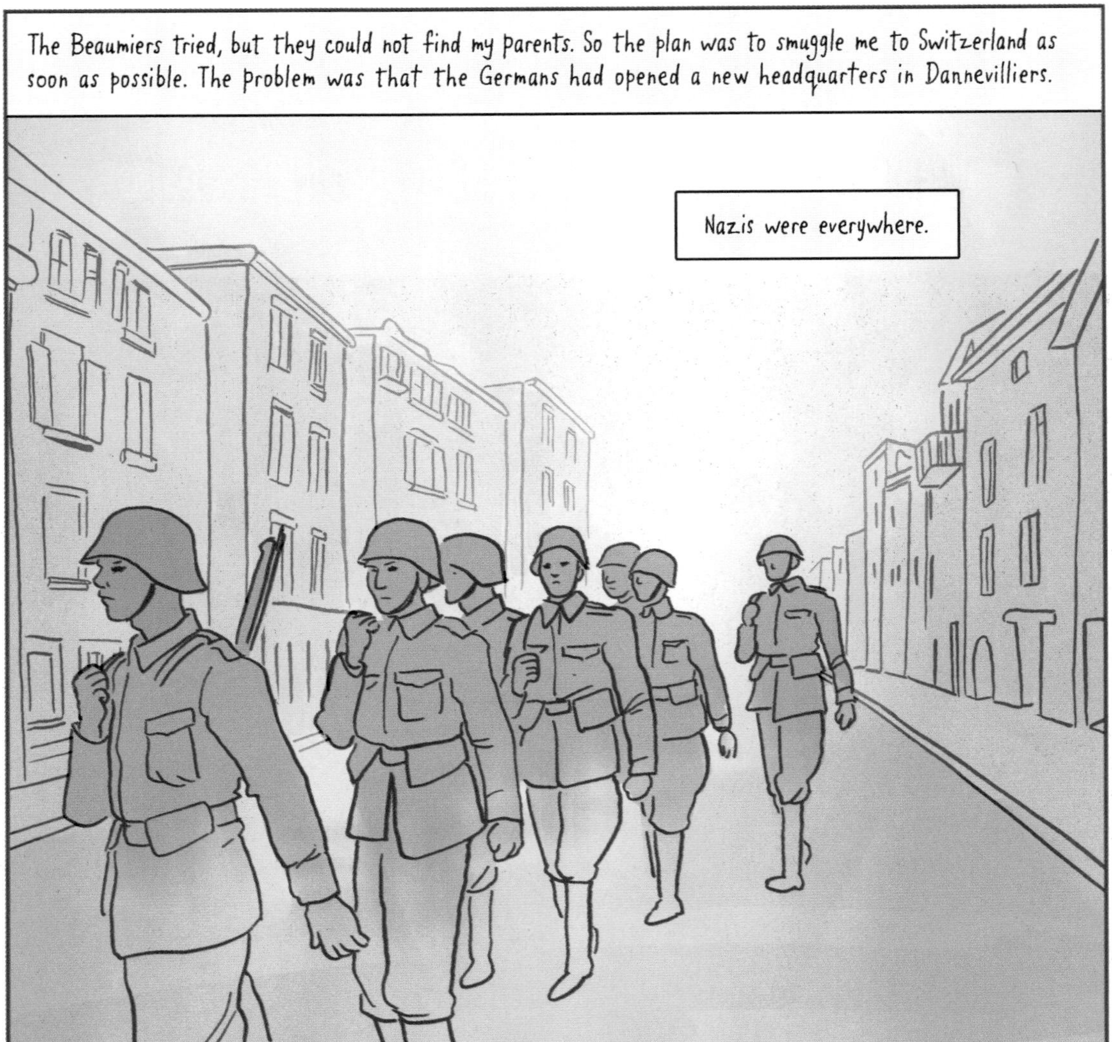
The Beaumiers tried, but they could not find my parents. So the plan was to smuggle me to Switzerland as soon as possible. The problem was that the Germans had opened a new headquarters in Dannevilliers.
Nazis were everywhere.

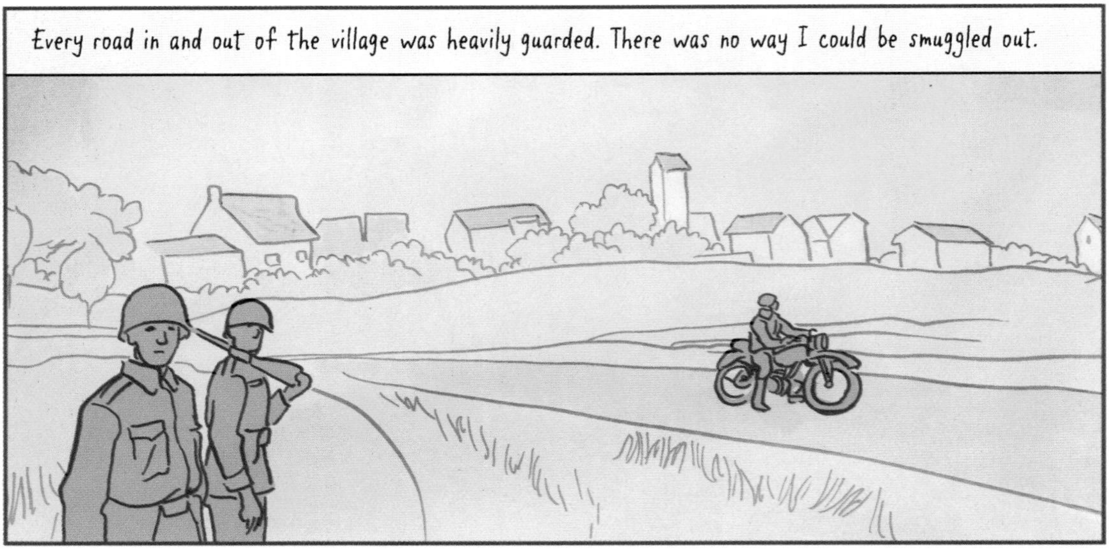
Every road in and out of the village was heavily guarded. There was no way I could be smuggled out.

Nor could I hide inside Julien's house. Their next-door neighbors, the Lafleurs, sat by their front window all day long, watching everything.

Vivienne believed they were spying for the Nazis. Before the war, she had been on friendly terms with Madame Lafleur.

Bonjour, Madame Lafleur! I brought you milk from the market.

Merci, Madame Beaumier!

But after the Occupation began, the Lafleurs changed. They became reclusive. Secretive. They stopped speaking to the Beaumiers.

Bonjour, Madame Lafleur!

...

Vivienne still brought them milk from the market every day, though.

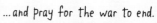

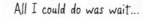

But it was because of the Lafleurs that I could not leave the barn.

All I could do was wait...

...and pray for the war to end.

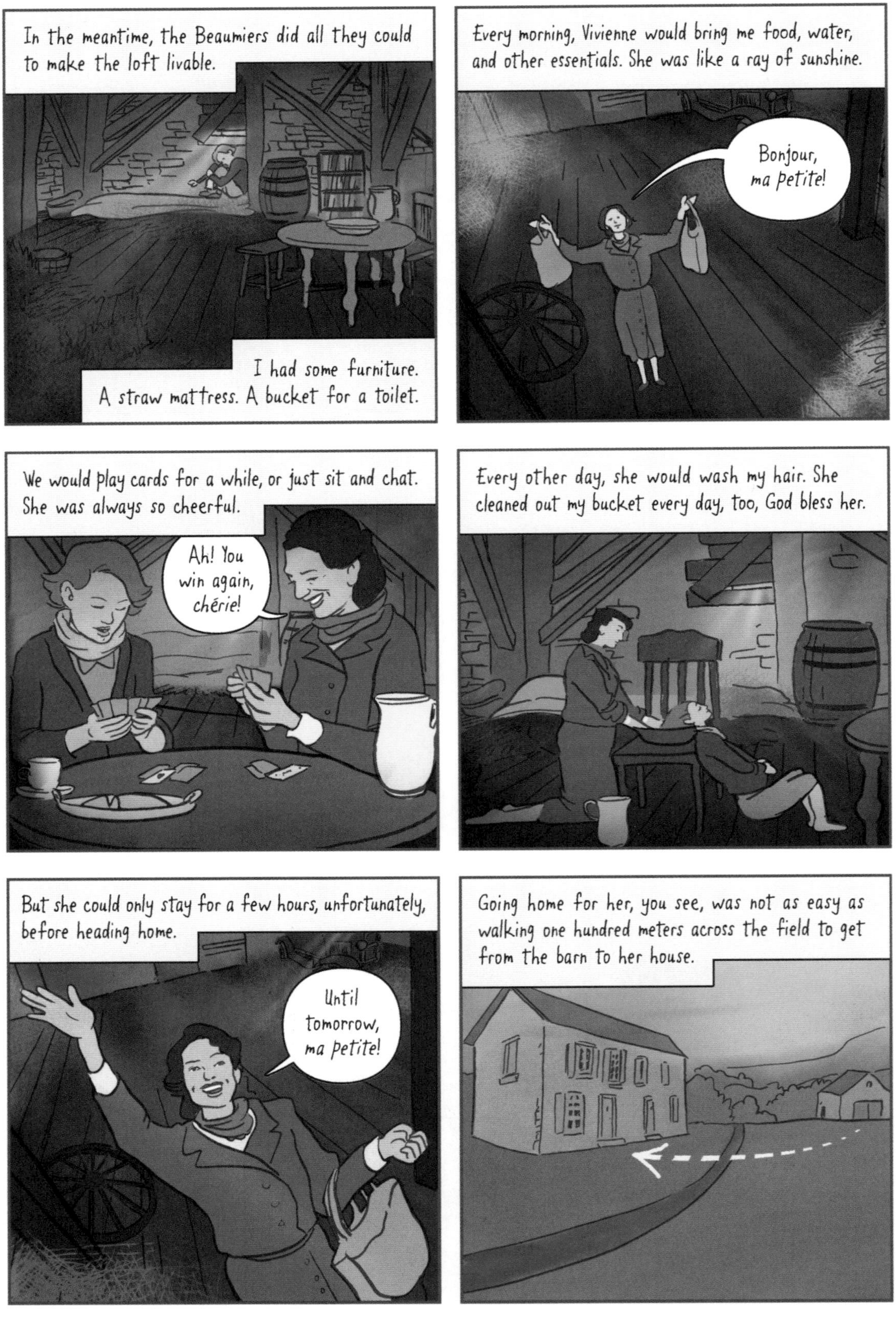
In the meantime, the Beaumiers did all they could to make the loft livable.
I had some furniture. A straw mattress. A bucket for a toilet.
Every morning, Vivienne would bring me food, water, and other essentials. She was like a ray of sunshine.
Bonjour, ma petite!
We would play cards for a while, or just sit and chat. She was always so cheerful.
Ah! You win again, chérie!
Every other day, she would wash my hair. She cleaned out my bucket every day, too, God bless her.
But she could only stay for a few hours, unfortunately, before heading home.
Until tomorrow, ma petite!
Going home for her, you see, was not as easy as walking one hundred meters across the field to get from the barn to her house.

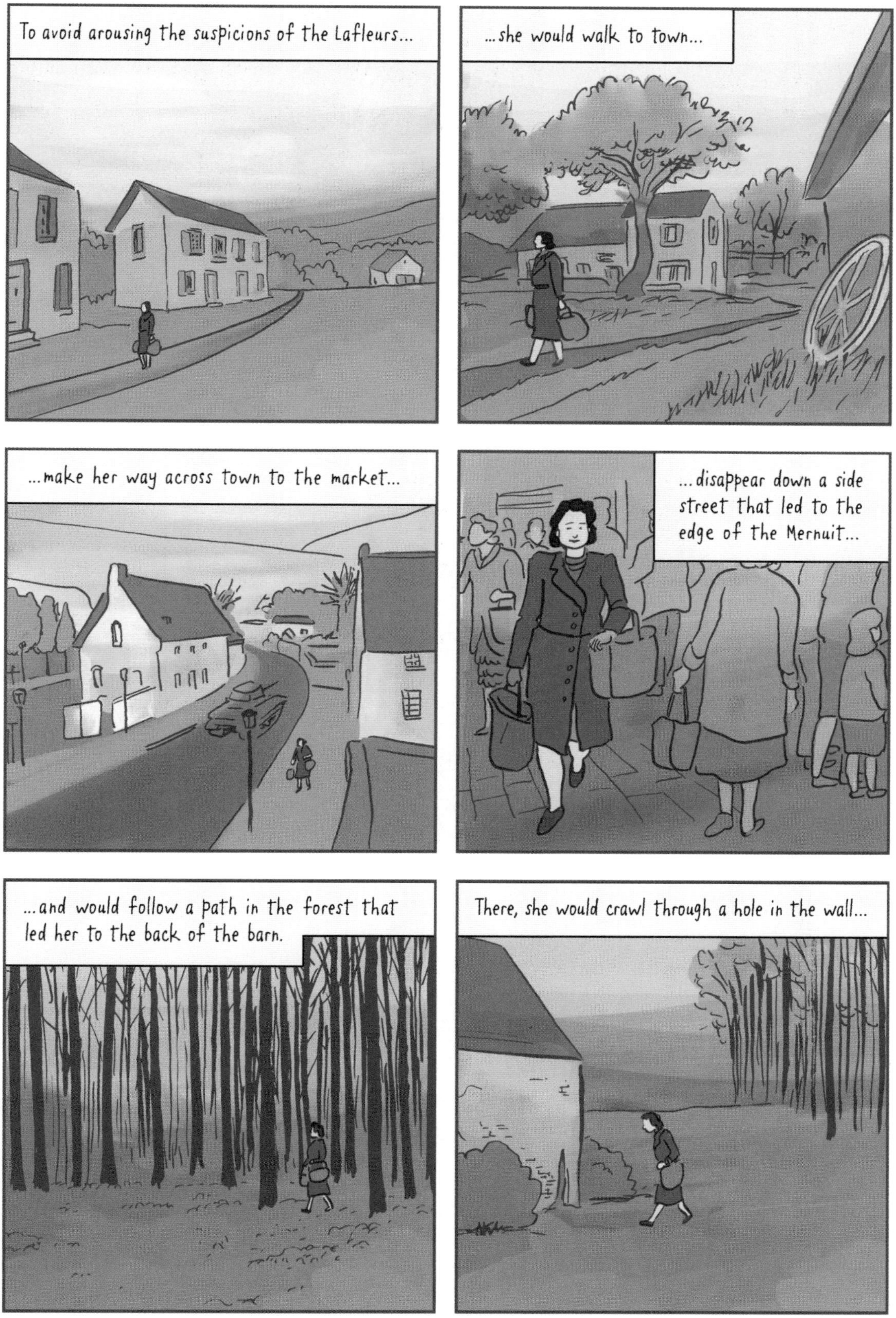
To avoid arousing the suspicions of the Lafleurs...
...she would walk to town...
...make her way across town to the market...
...disappear down a side street that led to the edge of the Mernuit...
...and would follow a path in the forest that led her to the back of the barn.
There, she would crawl through a hole in the wall...

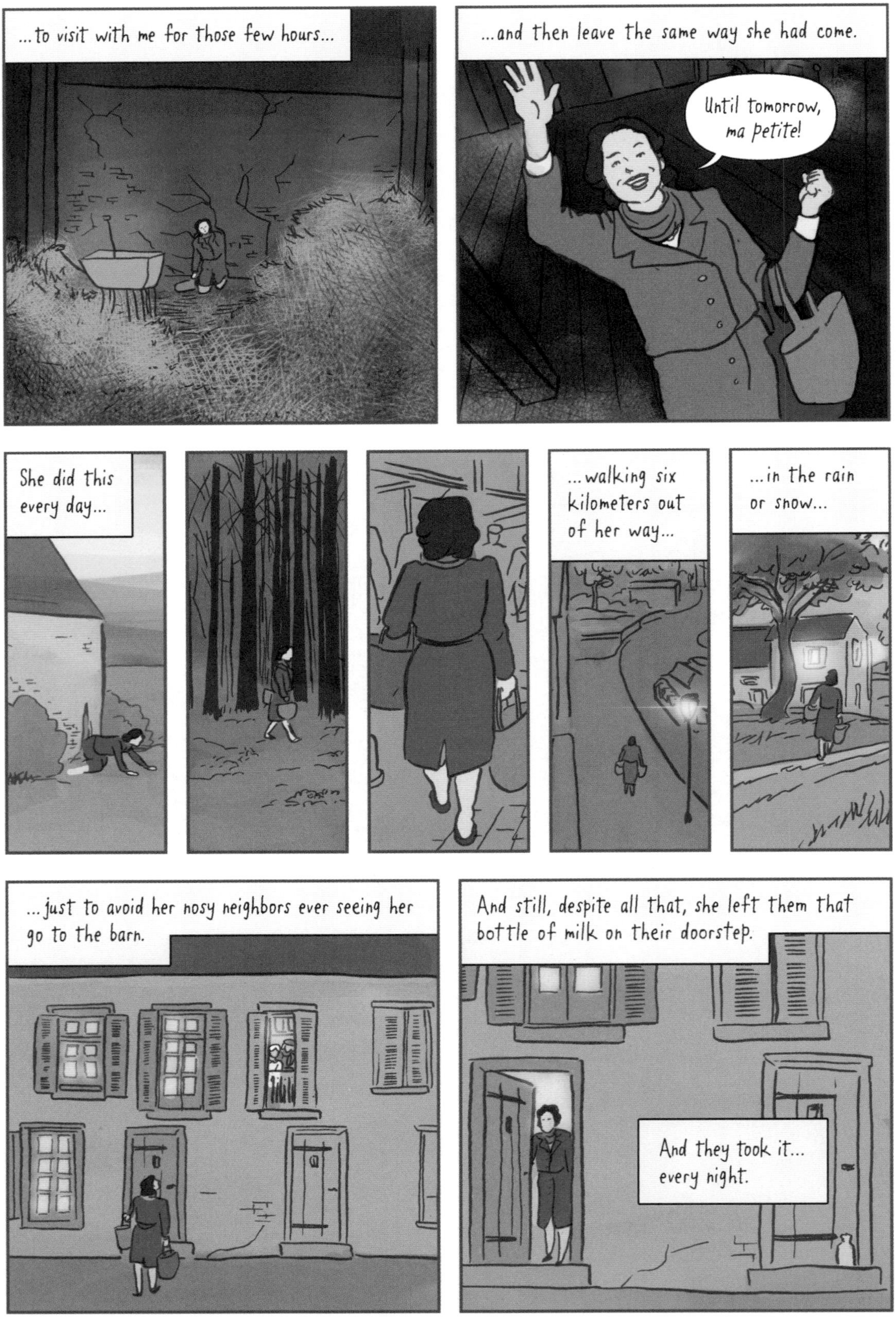
...to visit with me for those few hours...
...and then leave the same way she had come.
Until tomorrow, ma petite!
She did this every day...
...walking six kilometers out of her way...
...in the rain or snow...
...just to avoid her nosy neighbors ever seeing her go to the barn.
And still, despite all that, she left them that bottle of milk on their doorstep.
And they took it... every night.

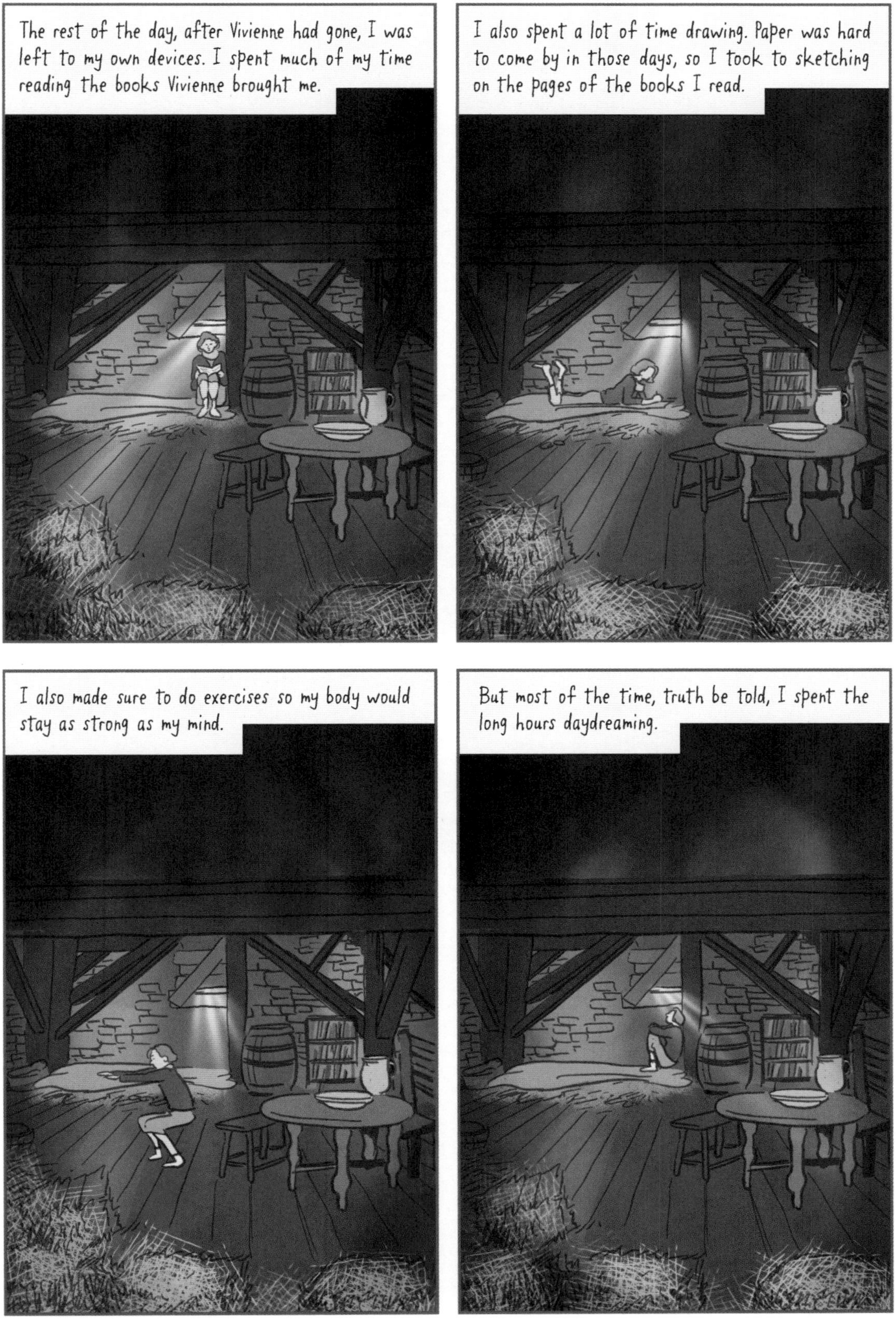
The rest of the day, after Vivienne had gone, I was left to my own devices. I spent much of my time reading the books Vivienne brought me.
I also spent a lot of time drawing. Paper was hard to come by in those days, so I took to sketching on the pages of the books I read.
I also made sure to do exercises so my body would stay as strong as my mind.
But most of the time, truth be told, I spent the long hours daydreaming.

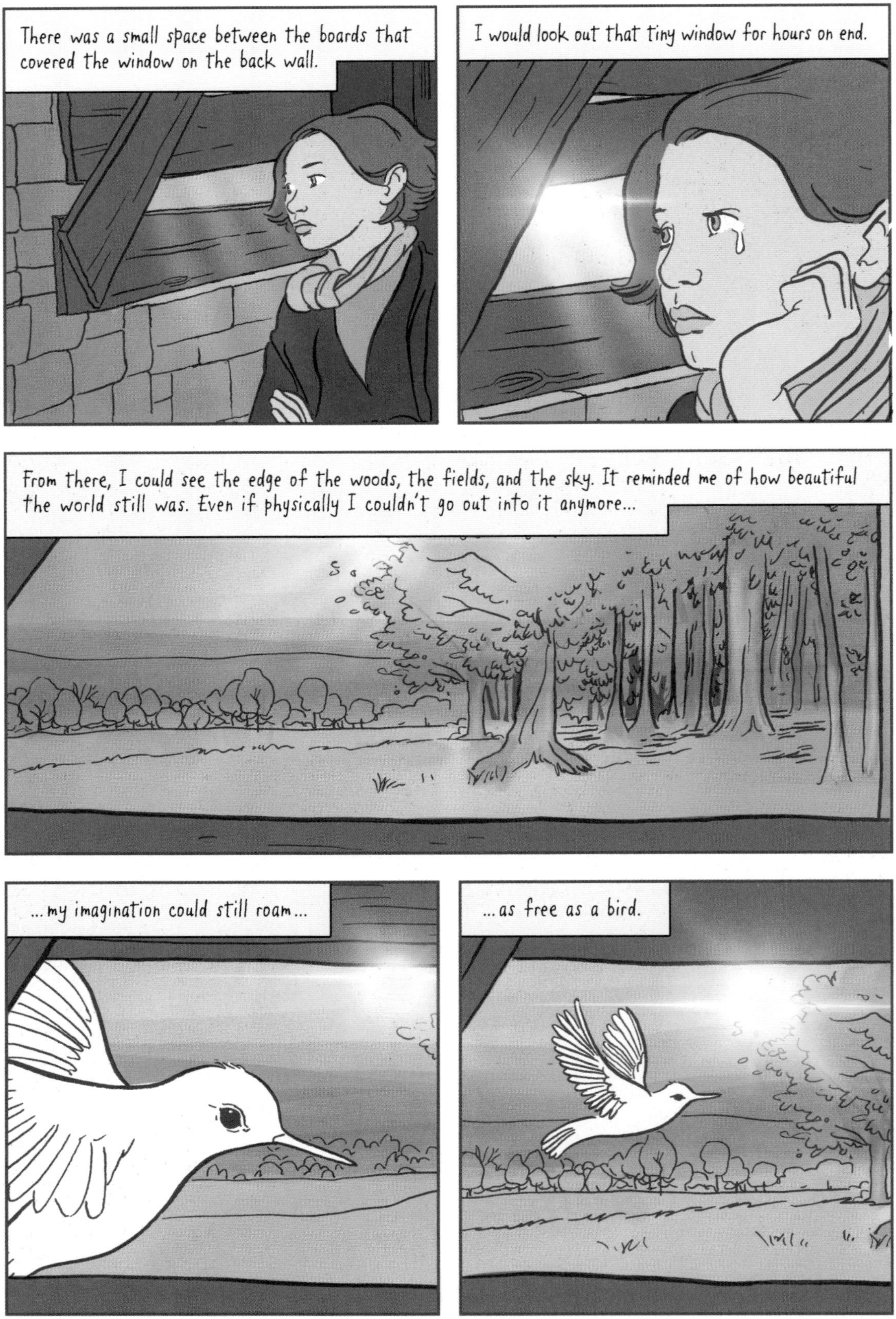

There was a small space between the boards that covered the window on the back wall.
I would look out that tiny window for hours on end.
From there, I could see the edge of the woods, the fields, and the sky. It reminded me of how beautiful the world still was. Even if physically I couldn't go out into it anymore...
...my imagination could still roam...
...as free as a bird.

CHAPTER 2

MY FAVORITE TIME OF EVERY DAY WAS NIGHTFALL. THAT IS WHEN JULIEN, UNDER COVER OF DARKNESS, WOULD COME TO THE BARN. OH, HOW I LOOKED FORWARD TO THOSE VISITS!

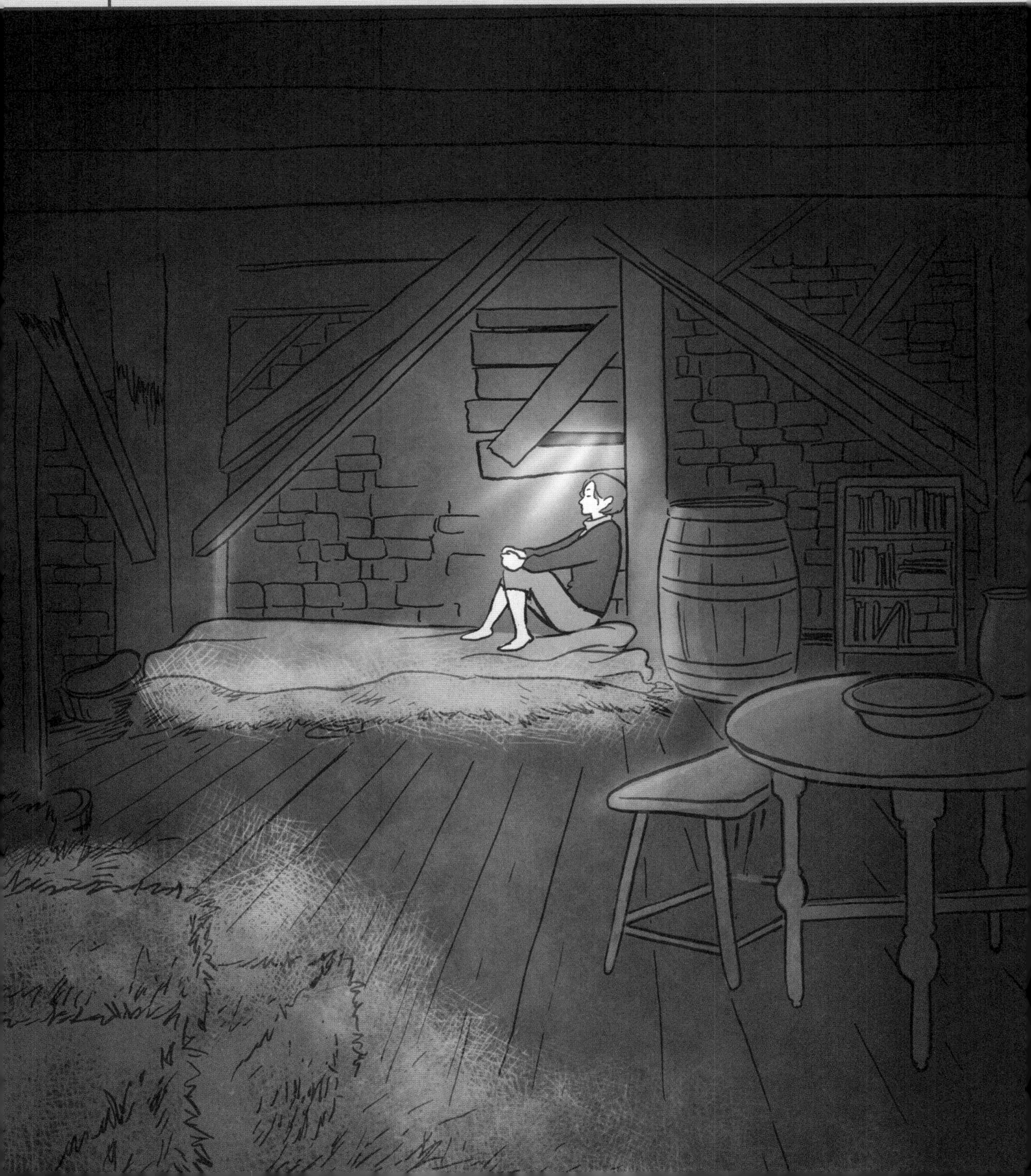

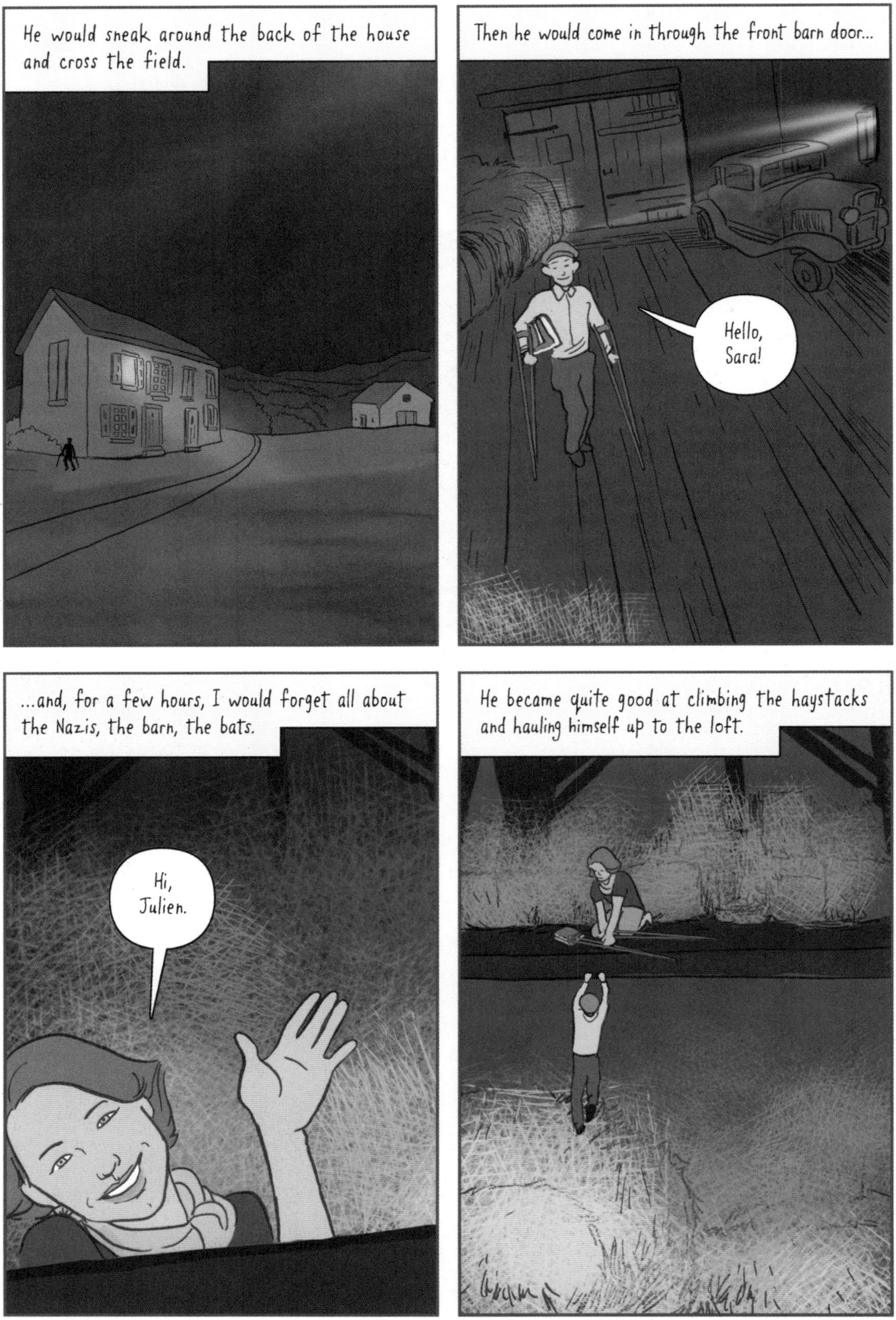
He would sneak around the back of the house and cross the field.
Then he would come in through the front barn door...
Hello, Sara!
...and, for a few hours, I would forget all about the Nazis, the barn, the bats.
Hi, Julien.
He became quite good at climbing the haystacks and hauling himself up to the loft.

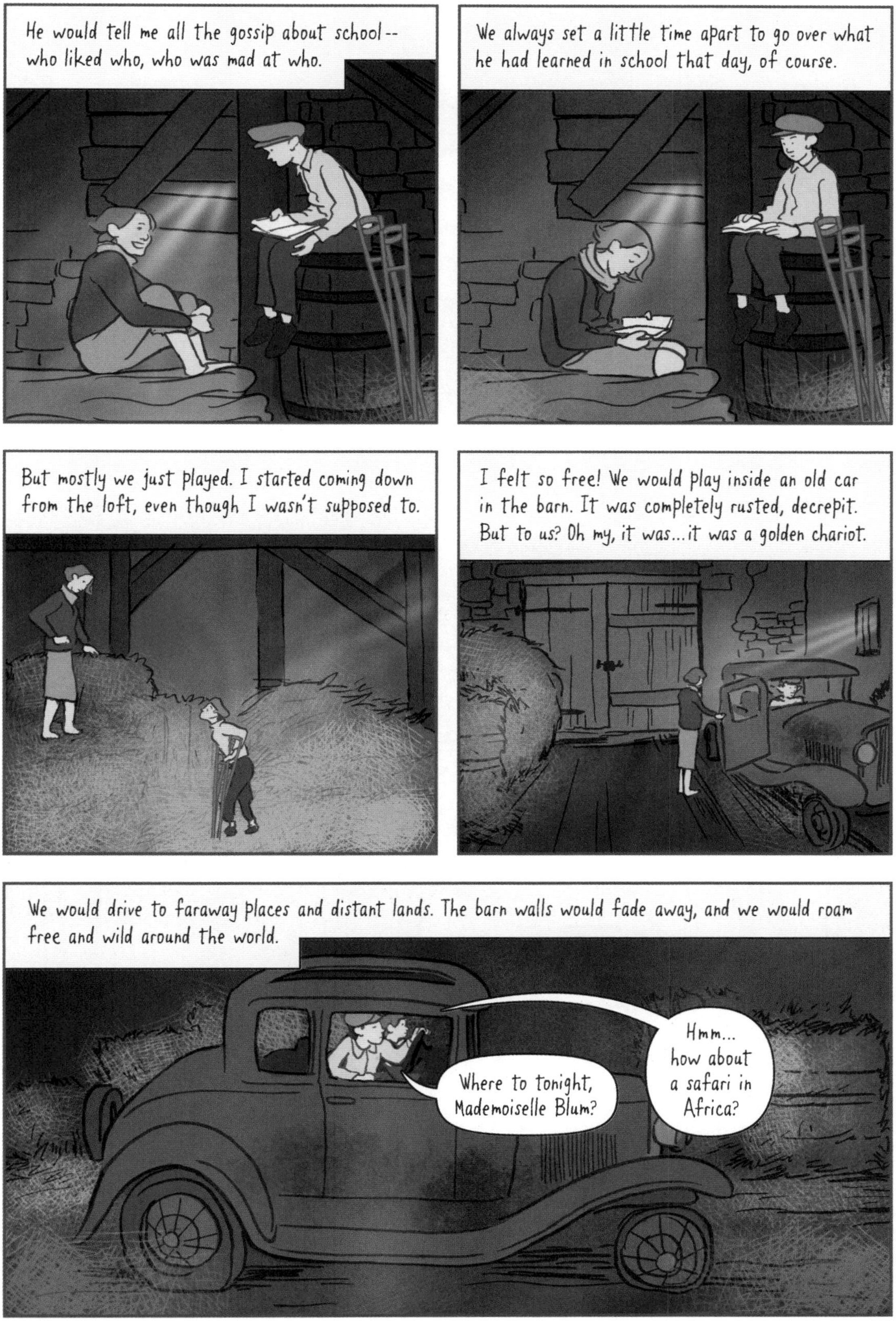
He would tell me all the gossip about school -- who liked who, who was mad at who.
We always set a little time apart to go over what he had learned in school that day, of course.
But mostly we just played. I started coming down from the loft, even though I wasn't supposed to.
I felt so free! We would play inside an old car in the barn. It was completely rusted, decrepit. But to us? Oh my, it was... it was a golden chariot.
We would drive to faraway places and distant lands. The barn walls would fade away, and we would roam free and wild around the world.
Where to tonight, Mademoiselle Blum?
Hmm... how about a safari in Africa?

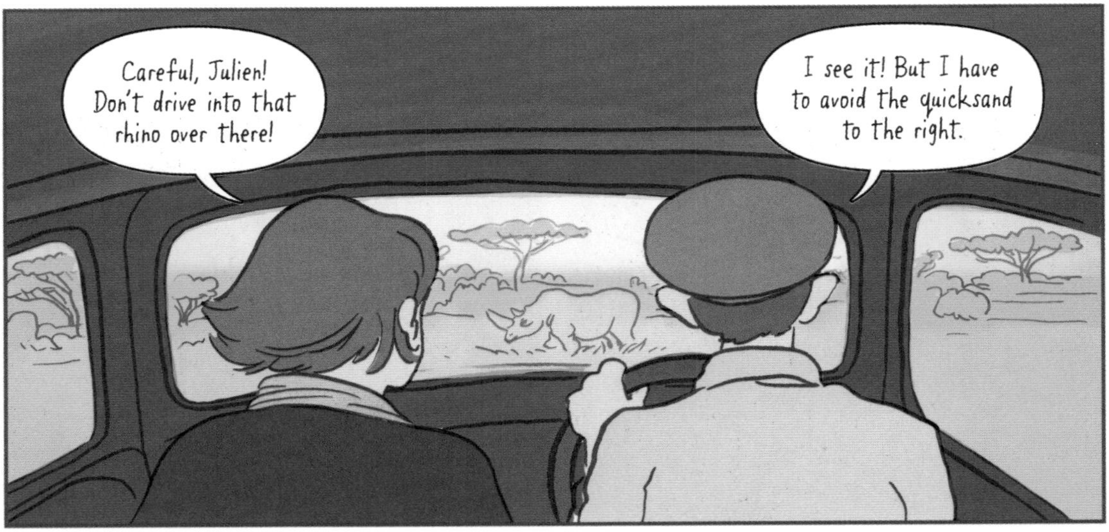
Careful, Julien! Don't drive into that rhino over there!
I see it! But I have to avoid the quicksand to the right.

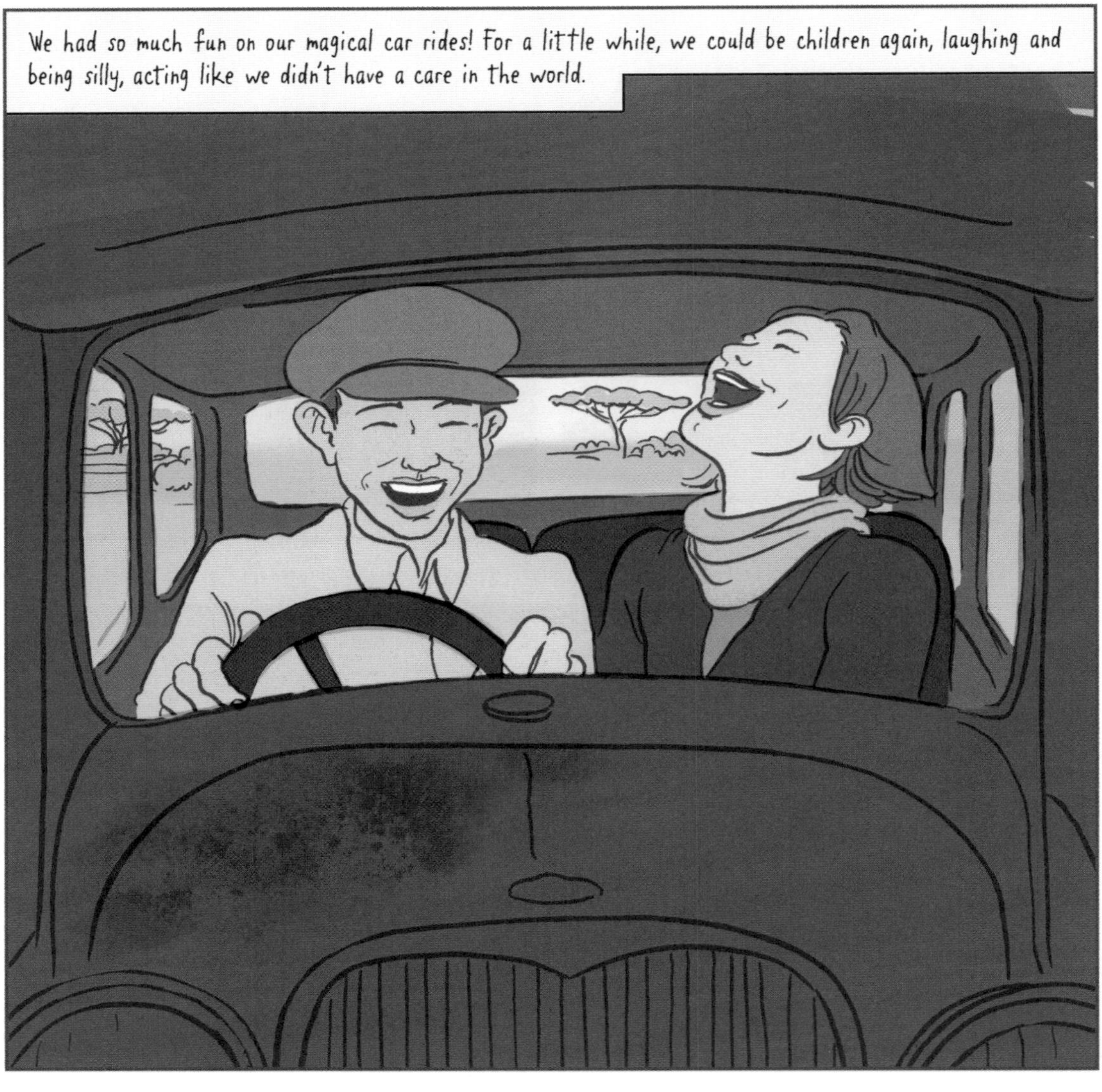
We had so much fun on our magical car rides! For a little while, we could be children again, laughing and being silly, acting like we didn't have a care in the world.

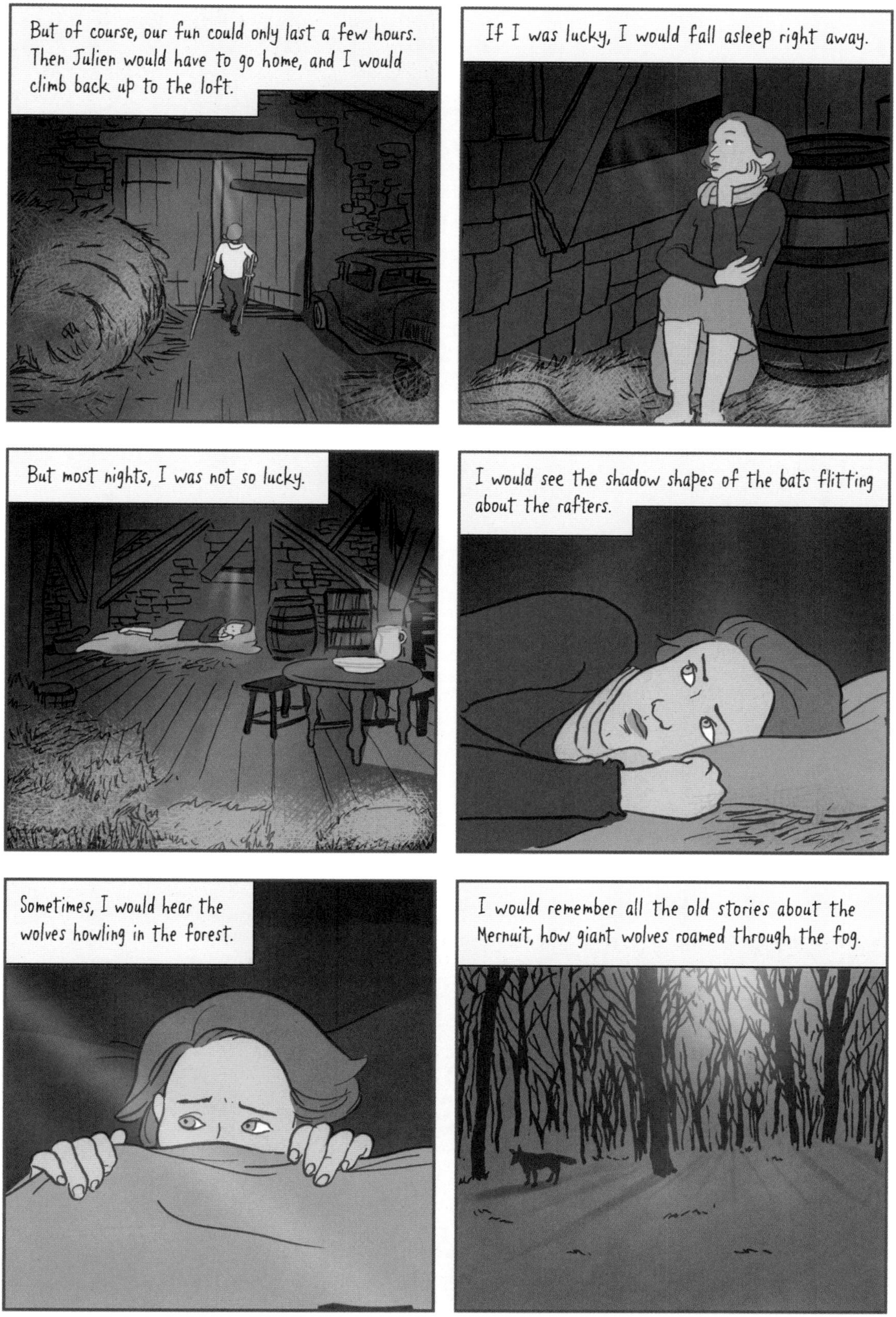
But of course, our fun could only last a few hours. Then Julien would have to go home, and I would climb back up to the loft.
If I was lucky, I would fall asleep right away.
But most nights, I was not so lucky.
I would see the shadow shapes of the bats flitting about the rafters.
Sometimes, I would hear the wolves howling in the forest.
I would remember all the old stories about the Mernuit, how giant wolves roamed through the fog.

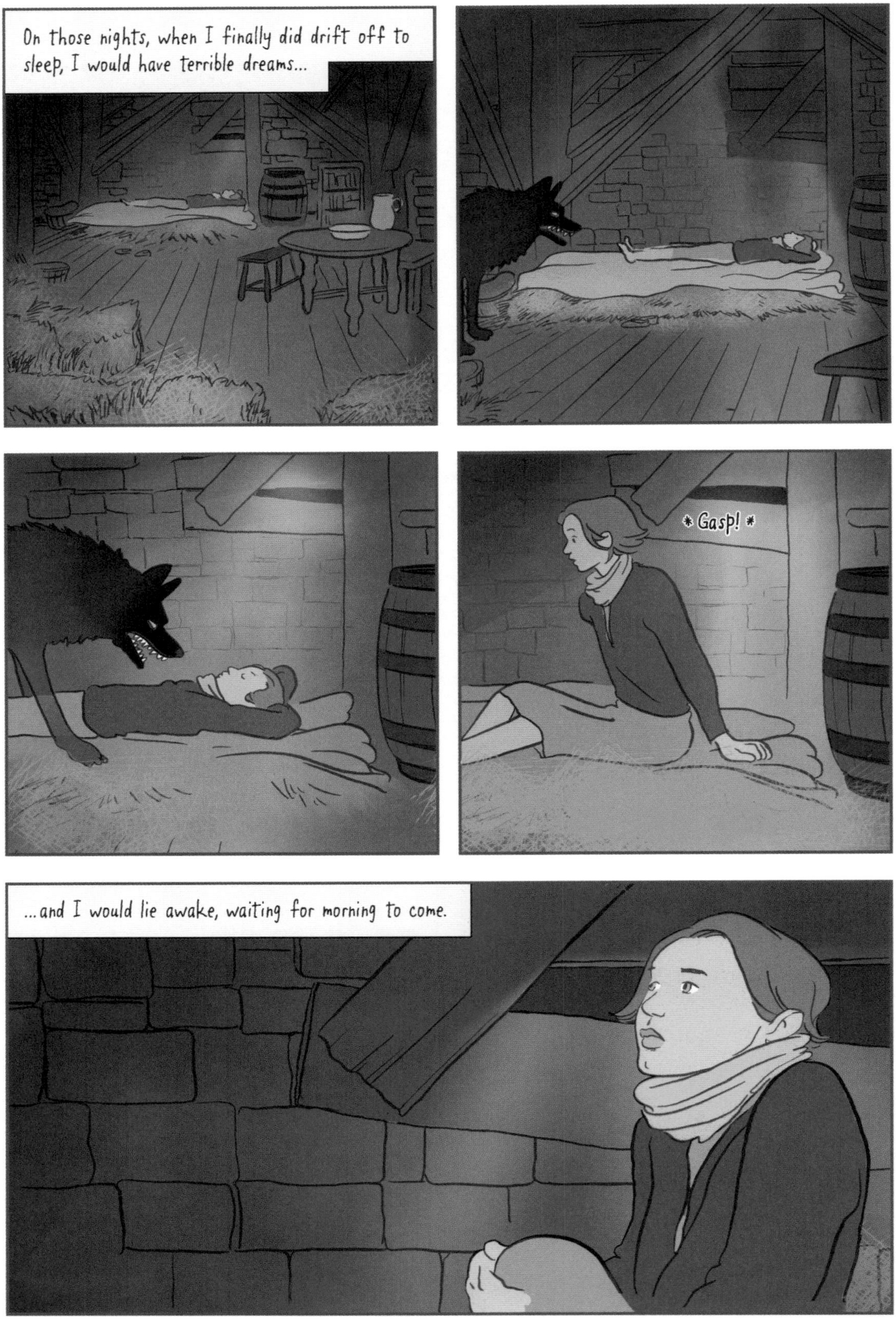
On those nights, when I finally did drift off to sleep, I would have terrible dreams...
* Gasp! *
...and I would lie awake, waiting for morning to come.

CHAPTER 3

IT DID NOT TAKE LONG FOR MY NEW LIFE TO SETTLE INTO A ROUTINE. IN JUST A FEW MONTHS, THE BARN HAD BECOME MY WHOLE WORLD, AND JULIEN THE CENTER OF THAT WORLD.

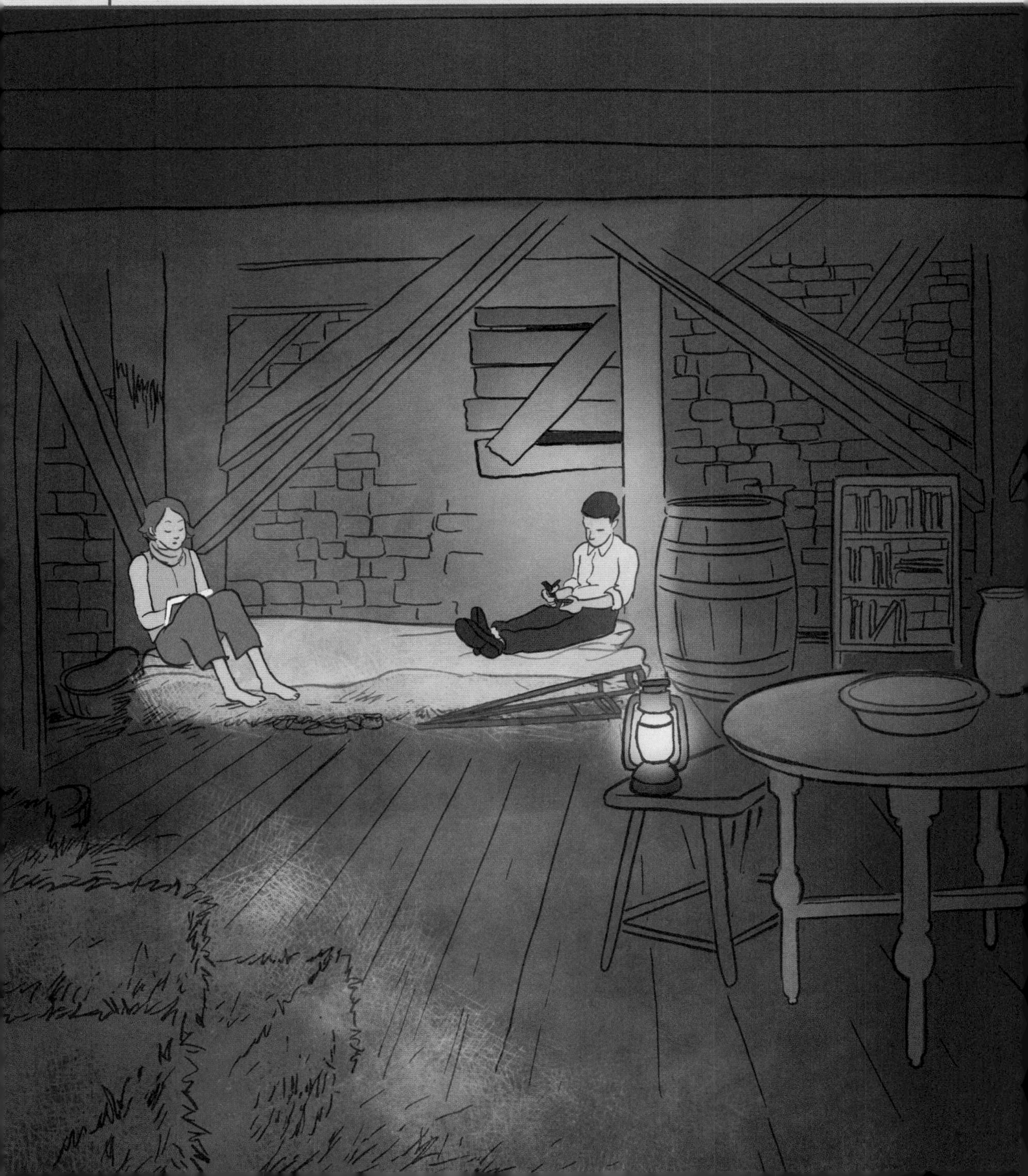

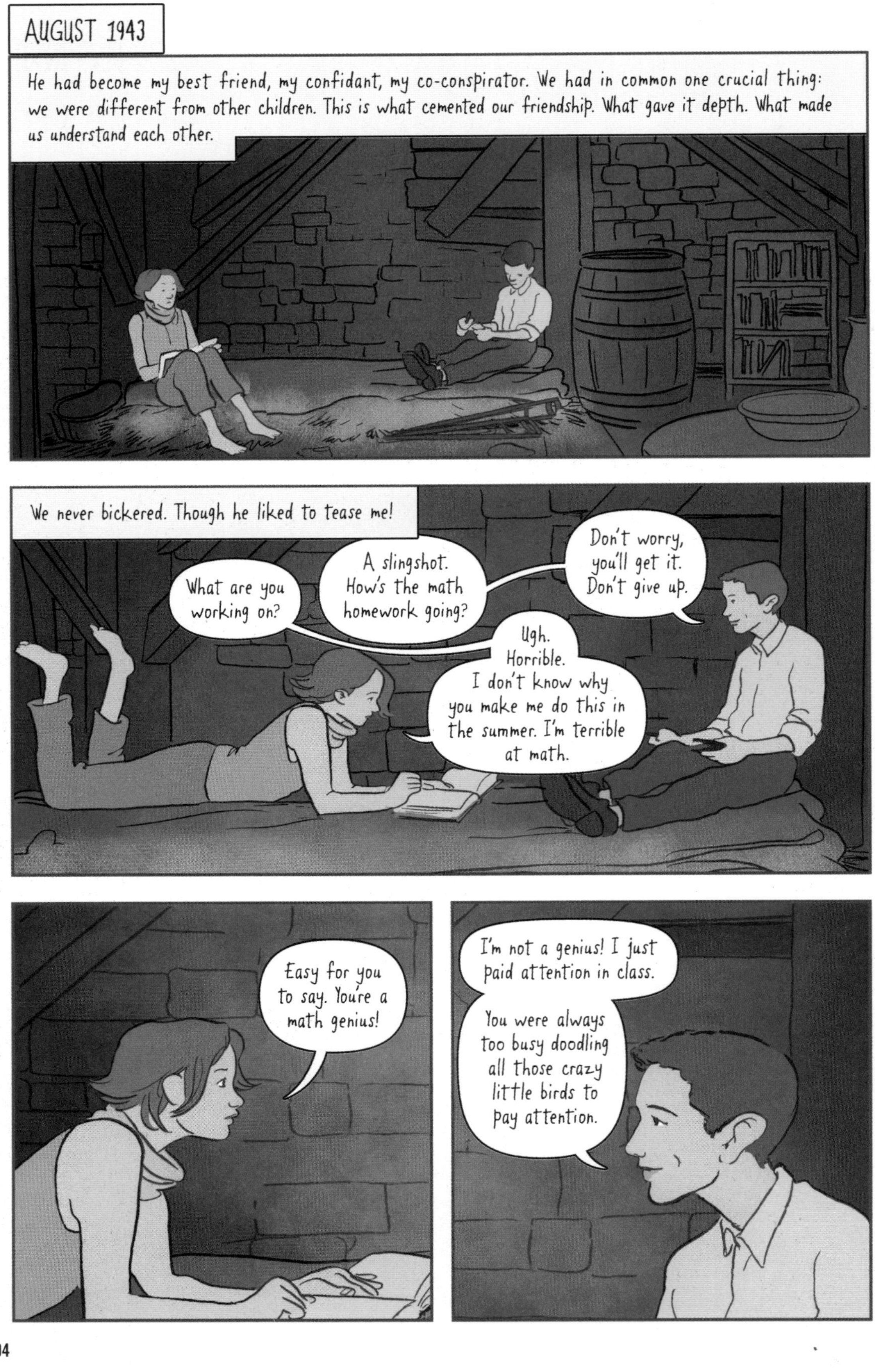
AUGUST 1943
He had become my best friend, my confidant, my co-conspirator. We had in common one crucial thing: we were different from other children. This is what cemented our friendship. What gave it depth. What made us understand each other.
We never bickered. Though he liked to tease me!
What are you working on?
A slingshot. How's the math homework going?
Ugh. Horrible. I don't know why you make me do this in the summer. I'm terrible at math.
Don't worry, you'll get it. Don't give up.
Easy for you to say. You're a math genius!
I'm not a genius! I just paid attention in class.
You were always too busy doodling all those crazy little birds to pay attention.

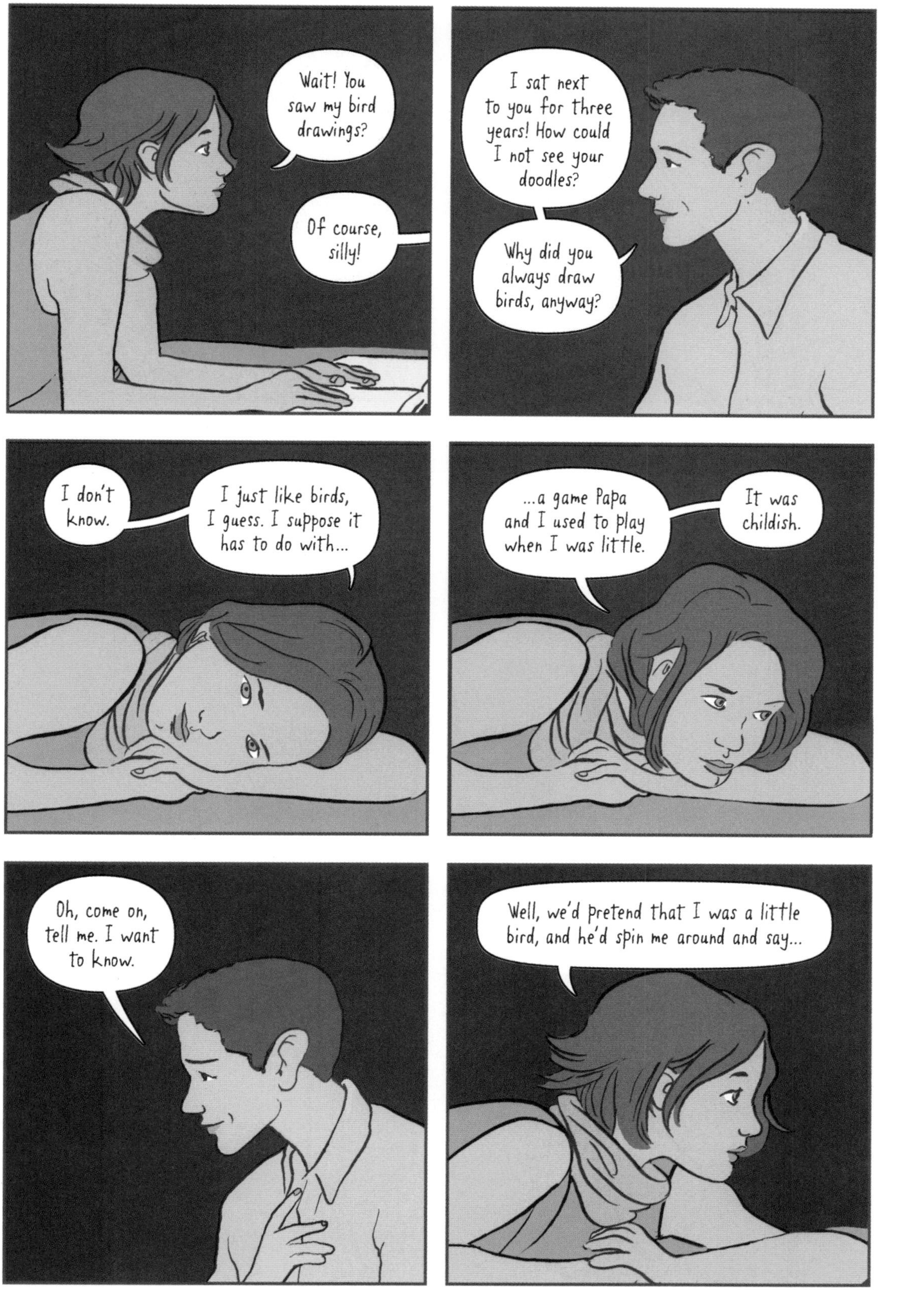
Wait! You saw my bird drawings?
Of course, silly!
I sat next to you for three years! How could I not see your doodles?
Why did you always draw birds, anyway?
I don't know.
I just like birds, I guess. I suppose it has to do with...
...a game Papa and I used to play when I was little.
It was childish.
Oh, come on, tell me. I want to know.
Well, we'd pretend that I was a little bird, and he'd spin me around and say...

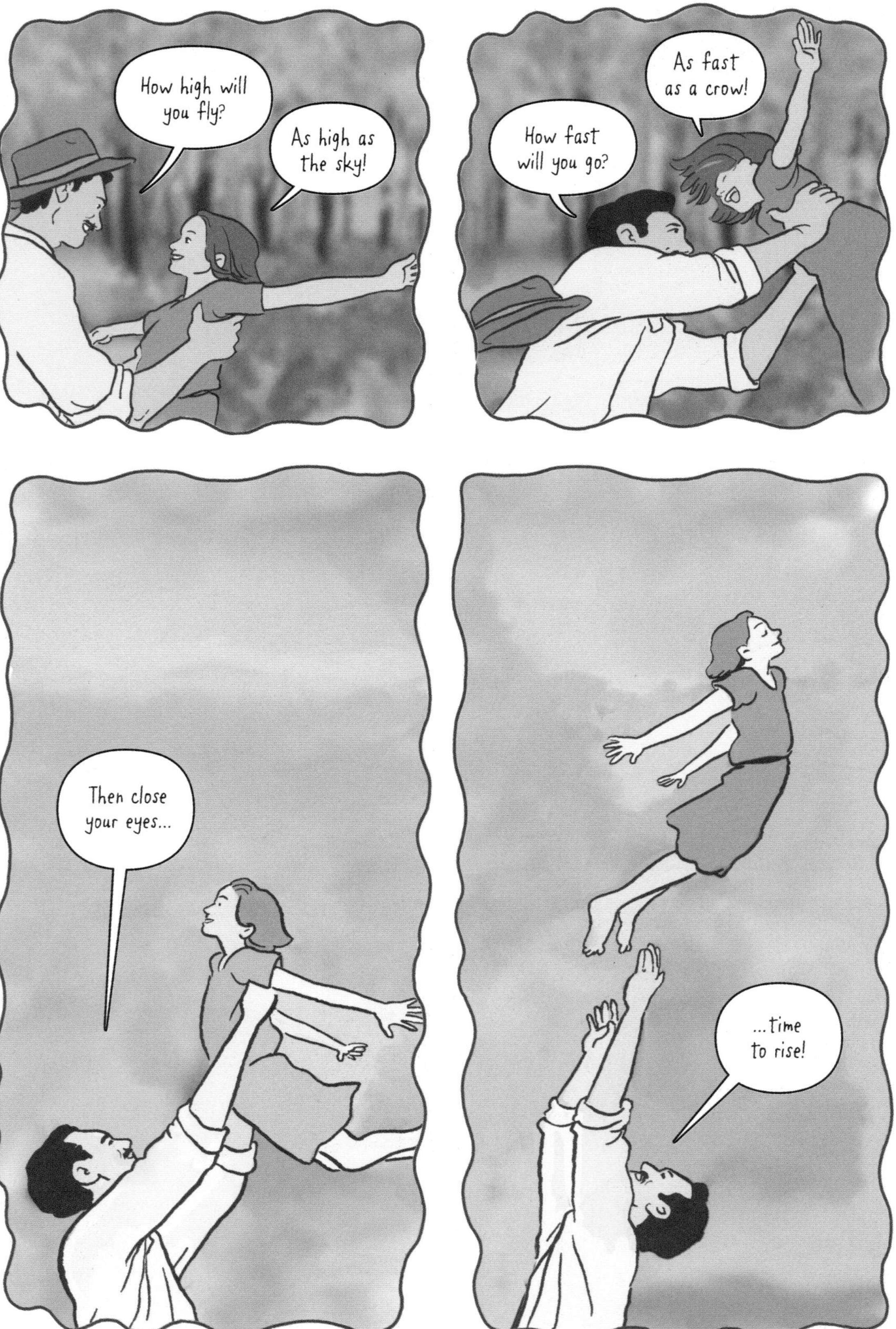
How high will you fly?
As high as the sky!
How fast will you go?
As fast as a crow!
Then close your eyes...
...time to rise!

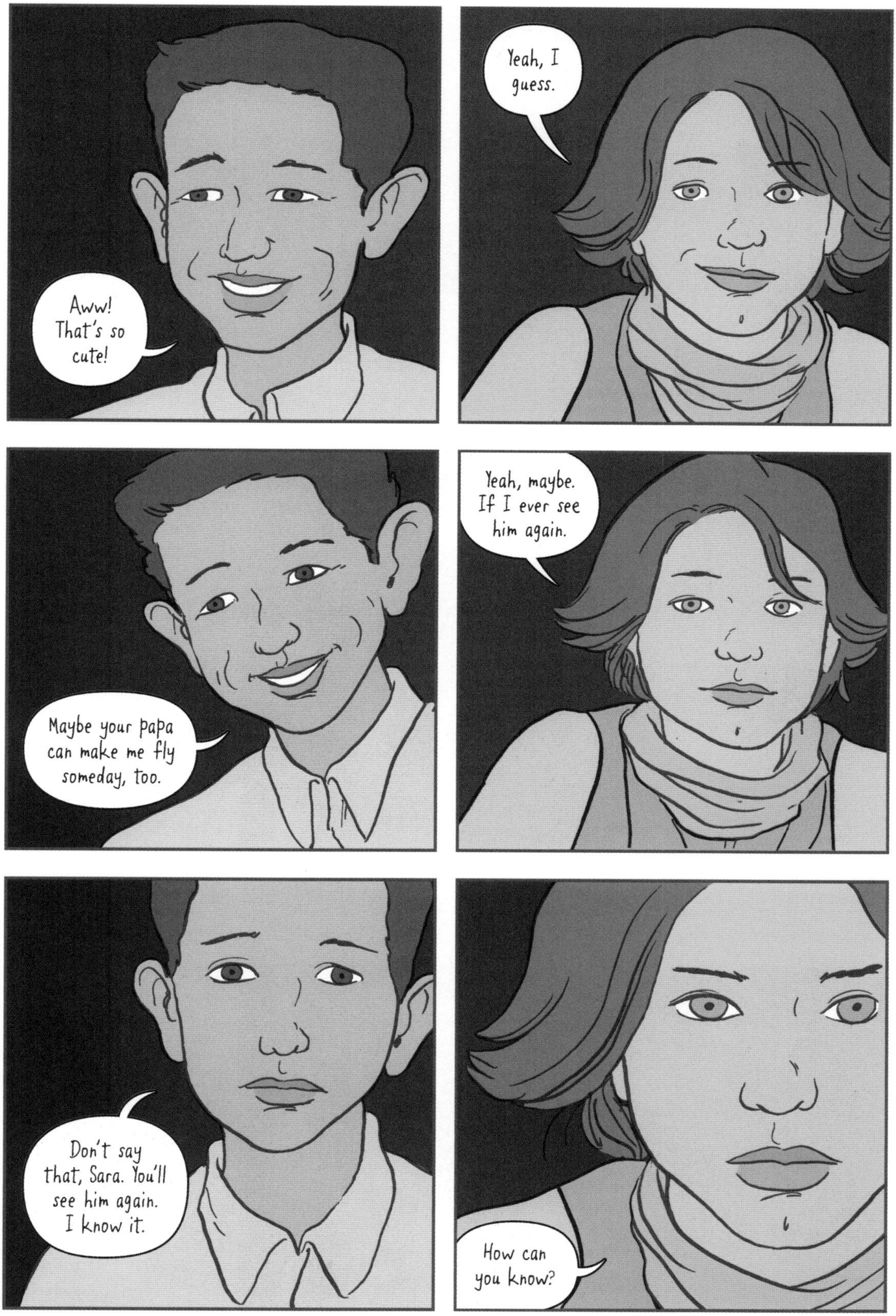
Aww! That's so cute!
Yeah, I guess.
Maybe your papa can make me fly someday, too.
Yeah, maybe. If I ever see him again.
Don't say that, Sara. You'll see him again. I know it.
How can you know?

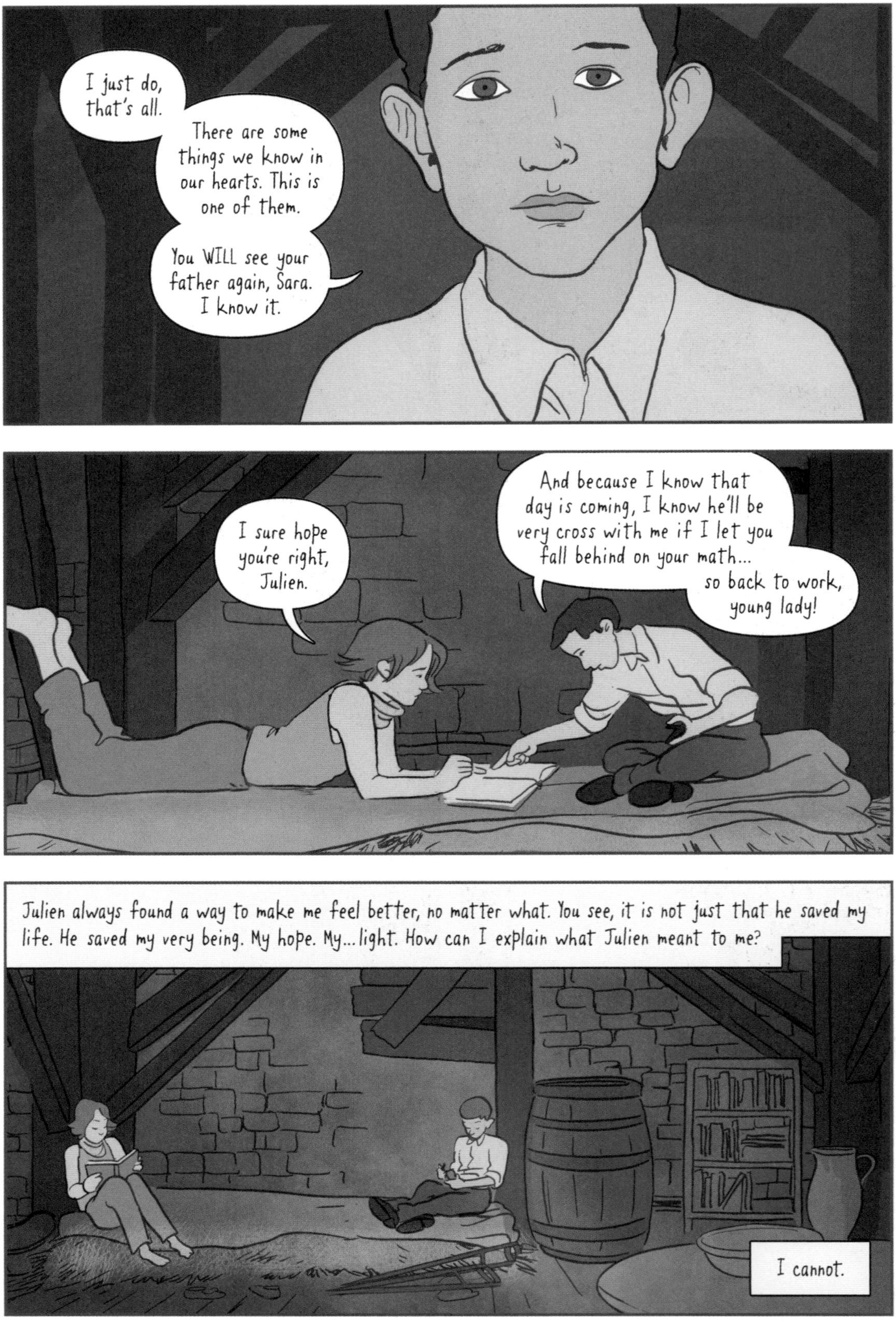
I just do, that's all.
There are some things we know in our hearts. This is one of them.
You WILL see your father again, Sara. I know it.
I sure hope you're right, Julien.
And because I know that day is coming, I know he'll be very cross with me if I let you fall behind on your math... so back to work, young lady!
Julien always found a way to make me feel better, no matter what. You see, it is not just that he saved my life. He saved my very being. My hope. My... light. How can I explain what Julien meant to me?
I cannot.

CHAPTER 4

JULIEN WENT BACK TO SCHOOL IN THE FALL. HE TRULY WAS AN EXCEPTIONAL STUDENT, TOP OF THE CLASS IN EVERY SUBJECT—ESPECIALLY MATHEMATICS.

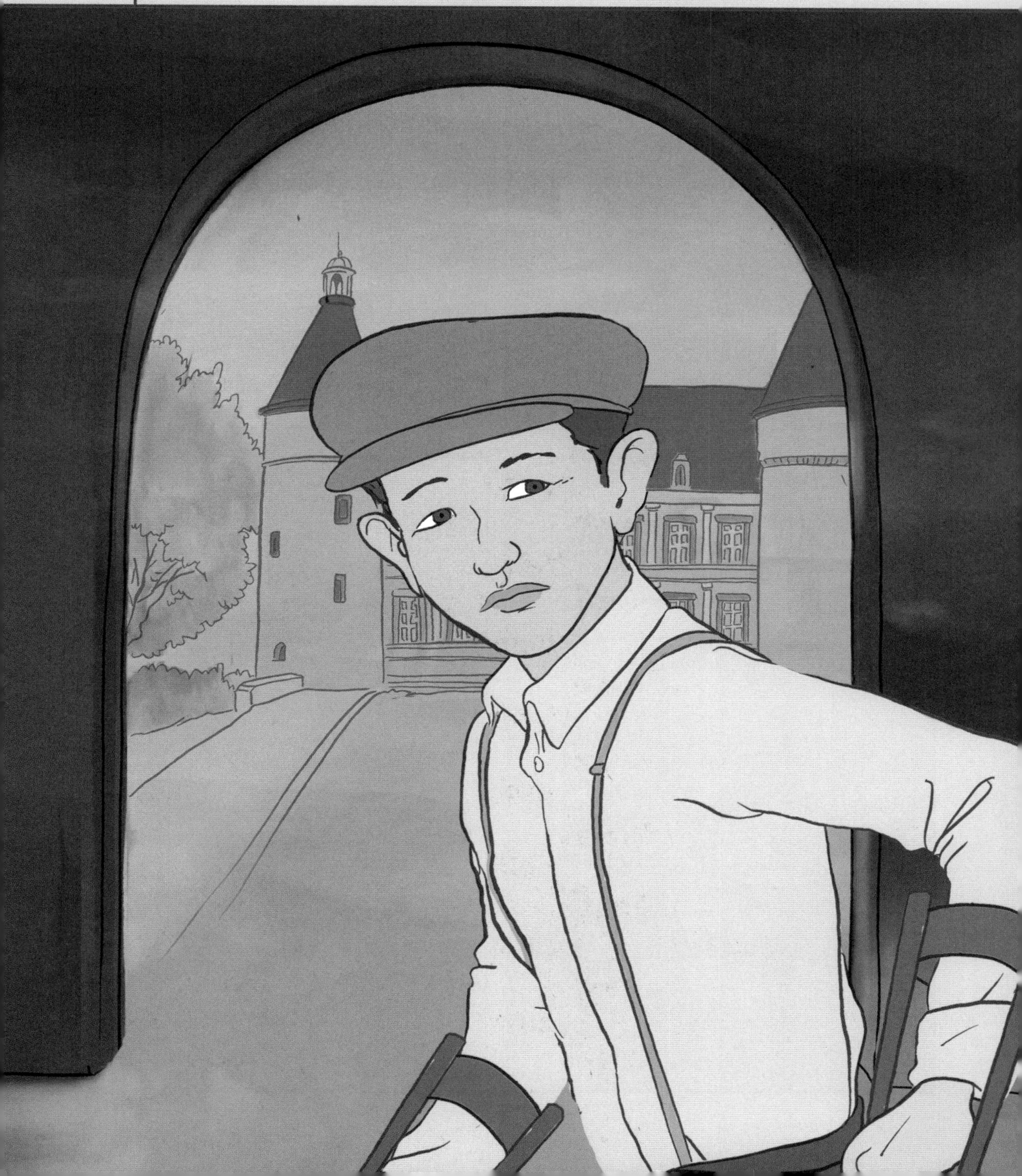

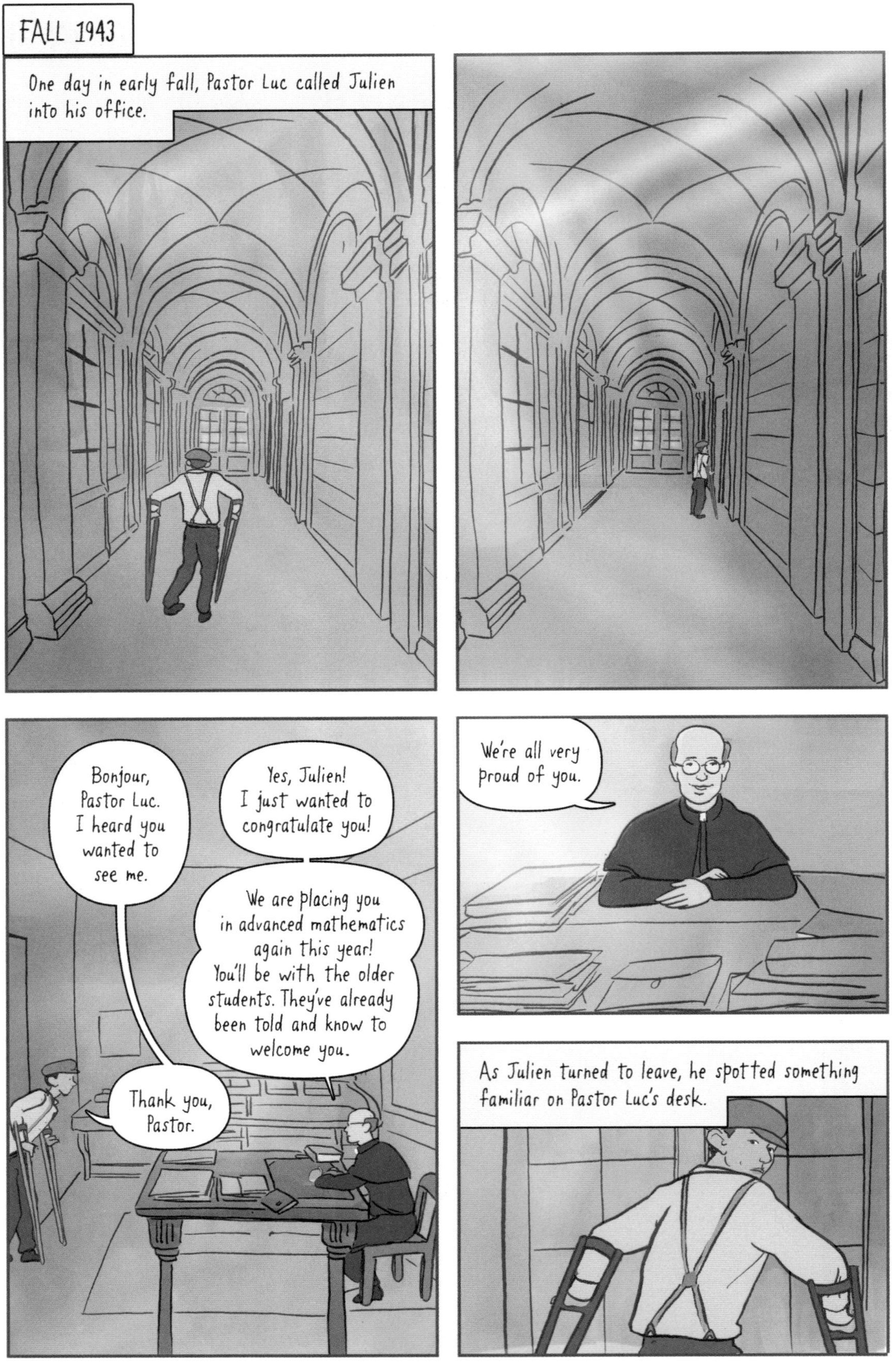
FALL 1943
One day in early fall, Pastor Luc called Julien into his office.
Bonjour, Pastor Luc. I heard you wanted to see me.
Yes, Julien! I just wanted to congratulate you!
We are placing you in advanced mathematics again this year! You'll be with the older students. They've already been told and know to welcome you.
Thank you, Pastor.
We're all very proud of you.
As Julien turned to leave, he spotted something familiar on Pastor Luc's desk.

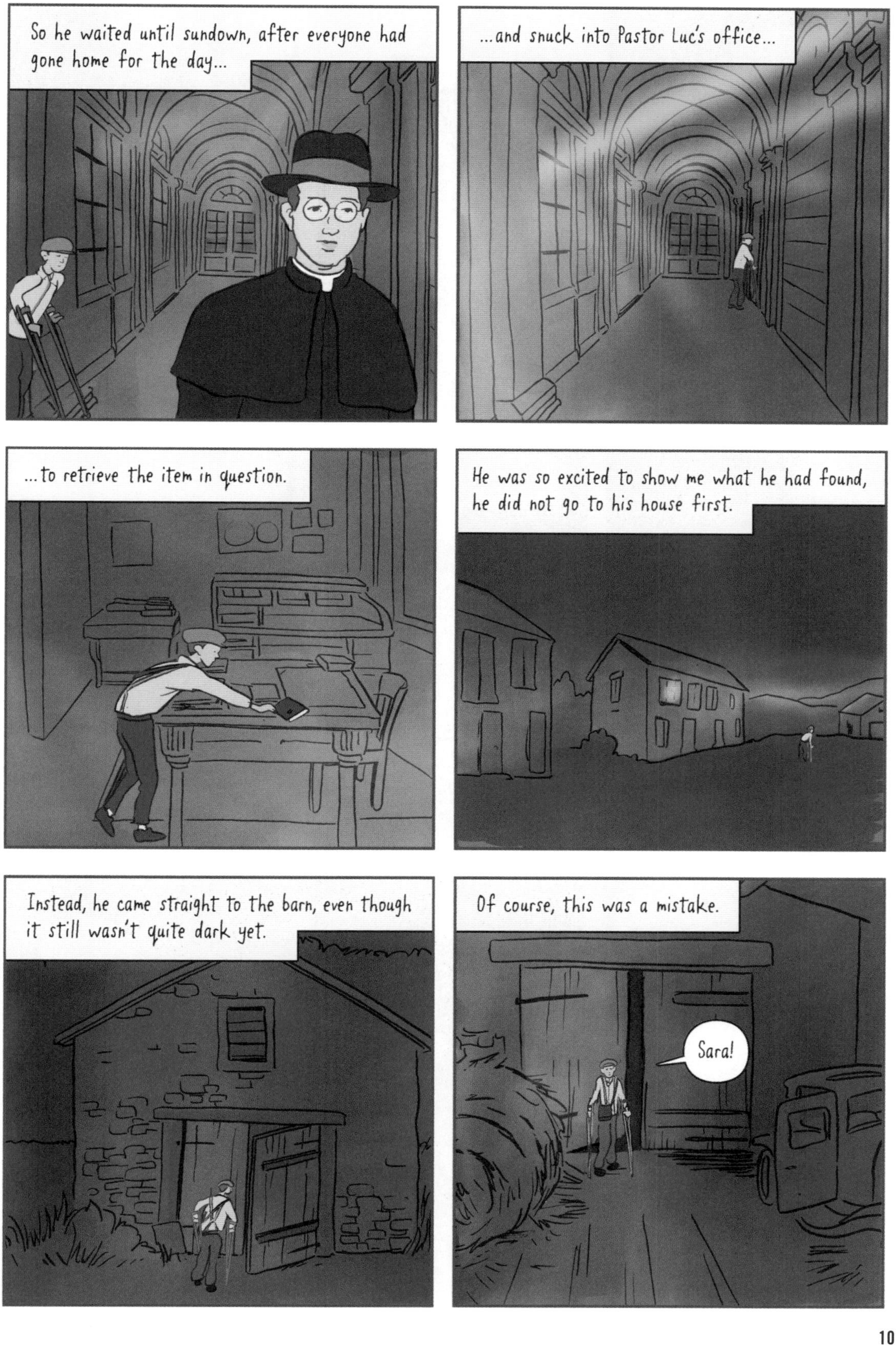
So he waited until sundown, after everyone had gone home for the day...
...and snuck into Pastor Luc's office...
...to retrieve the item in question.
He was so excited to show me what he had found, he did not go to his house first.
Instead, he came straight to the barn, even though it still wasn't quite dark yet.
Of course, this was a mistake.
Sara!

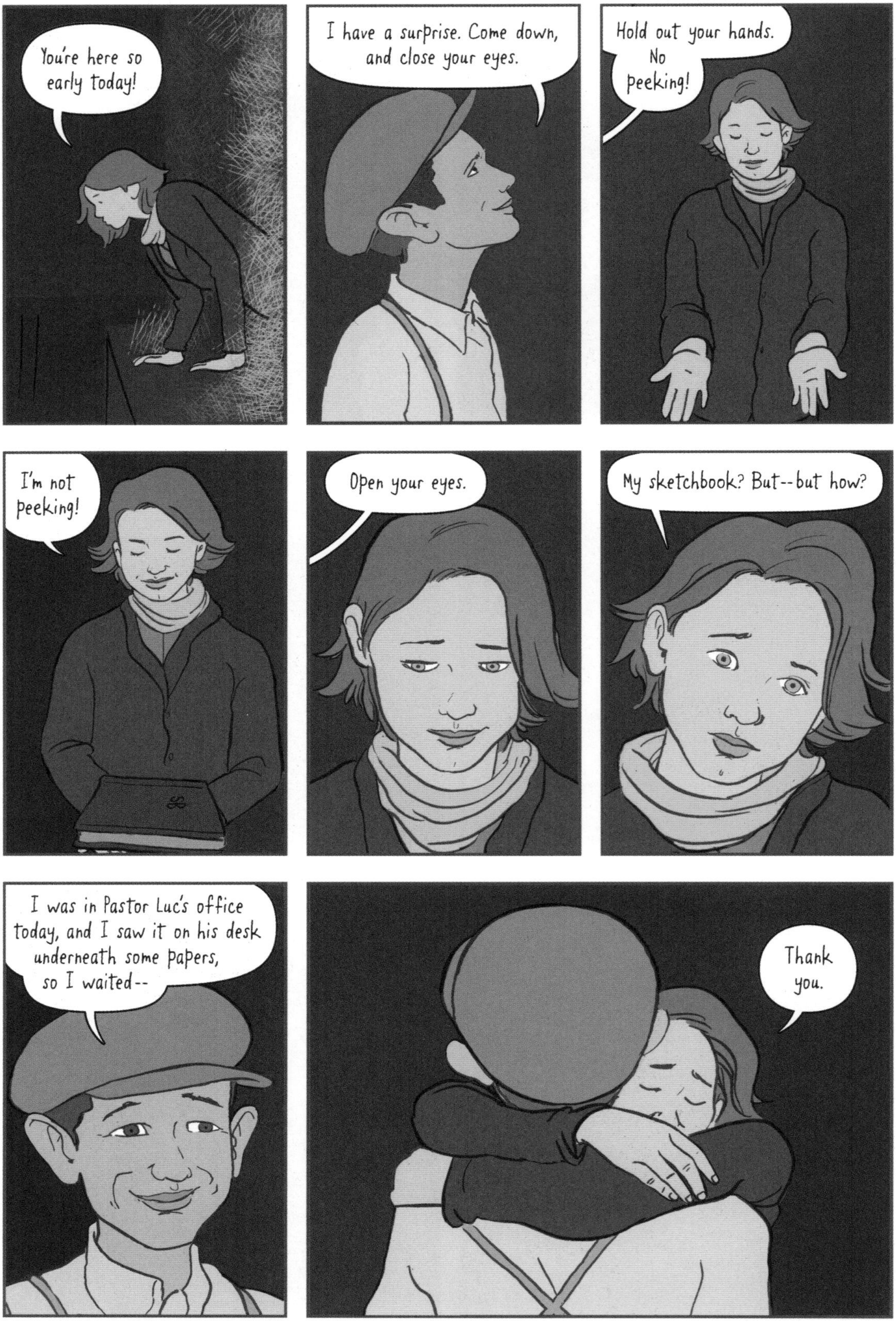
You're here so early today!
I have a surprise. Come down, and close your eyes.
Hold out your hands.
No peeking!
I'm not peeking!
Open your eyes.
My sketchbook? But--but how?
I was in Pastor Luc's office today, and I saw it on his desk underneath some papers, so I waited--
Thank you.

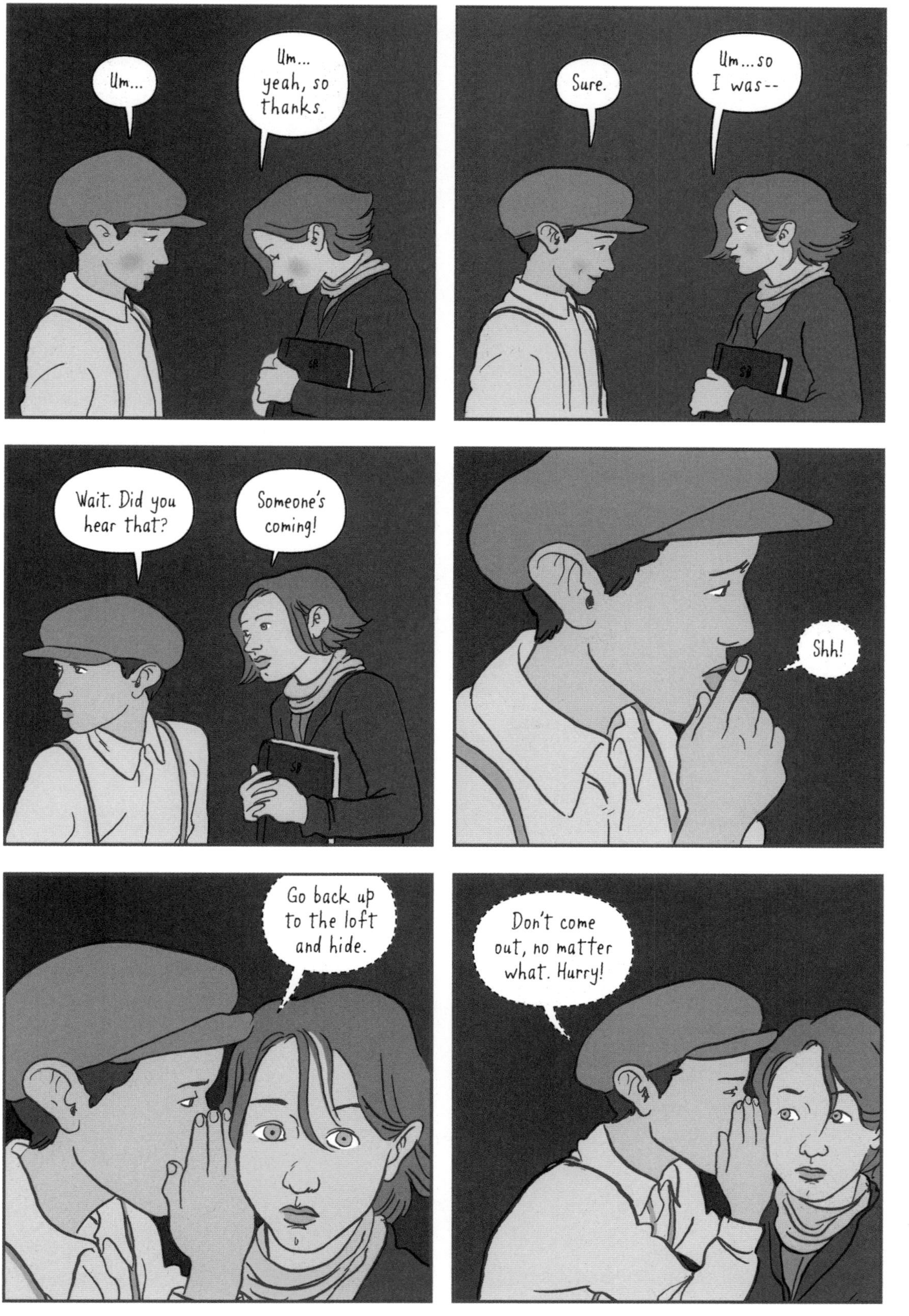
Um...
Um... yeah, so thanks.
Sure.
Um...so I was--
Wait. Did you hear that?
Someone's coming!
Shh!
Go back up to the loft and hide.
Don't come out, no matter what. Hurry!

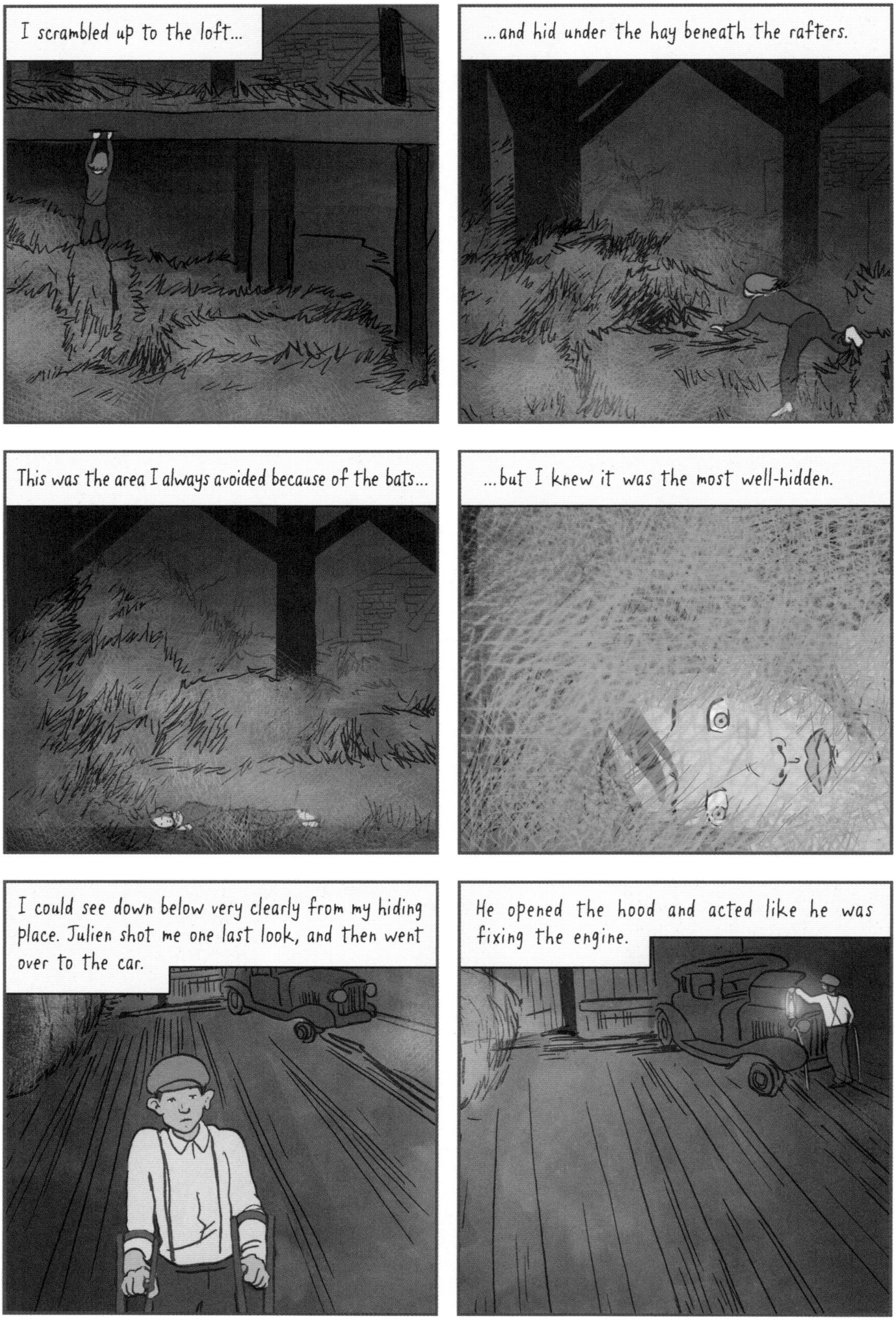
I scrambled up to the loft...
...and hid under the hay beneath the rafters.
This was the area I always avoided because of the bats...
...but I knew it was the most well-hidden.
I could see down below very clearly from my hiding place. Julien shot me one last look, and then went over to the car.
He opened the hood and acted like he was fixing the engine.

CHAPTER 5

I COULD HEAR THE VOICES OUTSIDE COMING CLOSER TO THE BARN. I RECOGNIZED THEM INSTANTLY. IT WAS VINCENT, WITH HIS HENCHMEN, JÉRÔME AND PAUL.

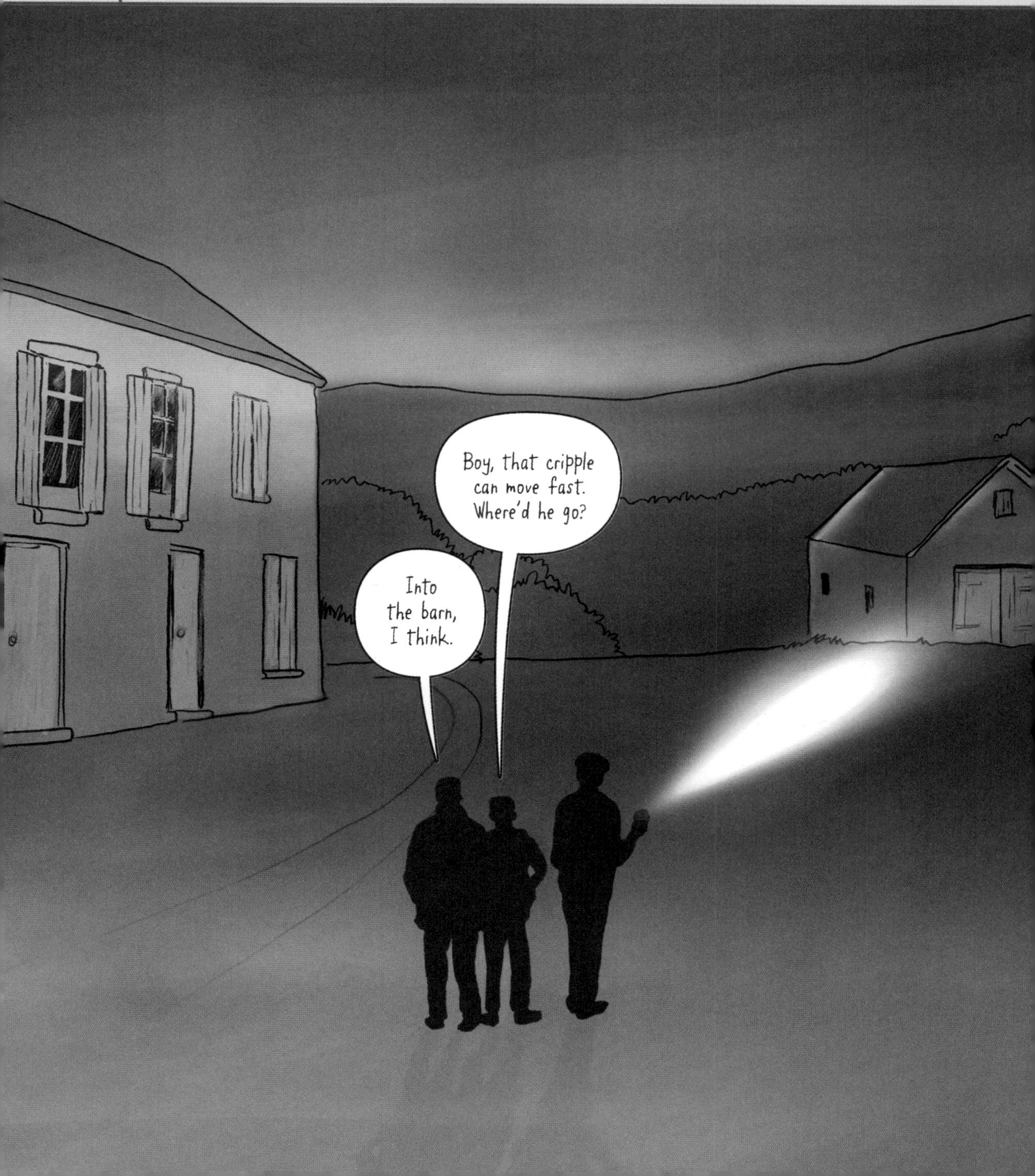
Boy, that cripple can move fast. Where'd he go?
Into the barn, I think.

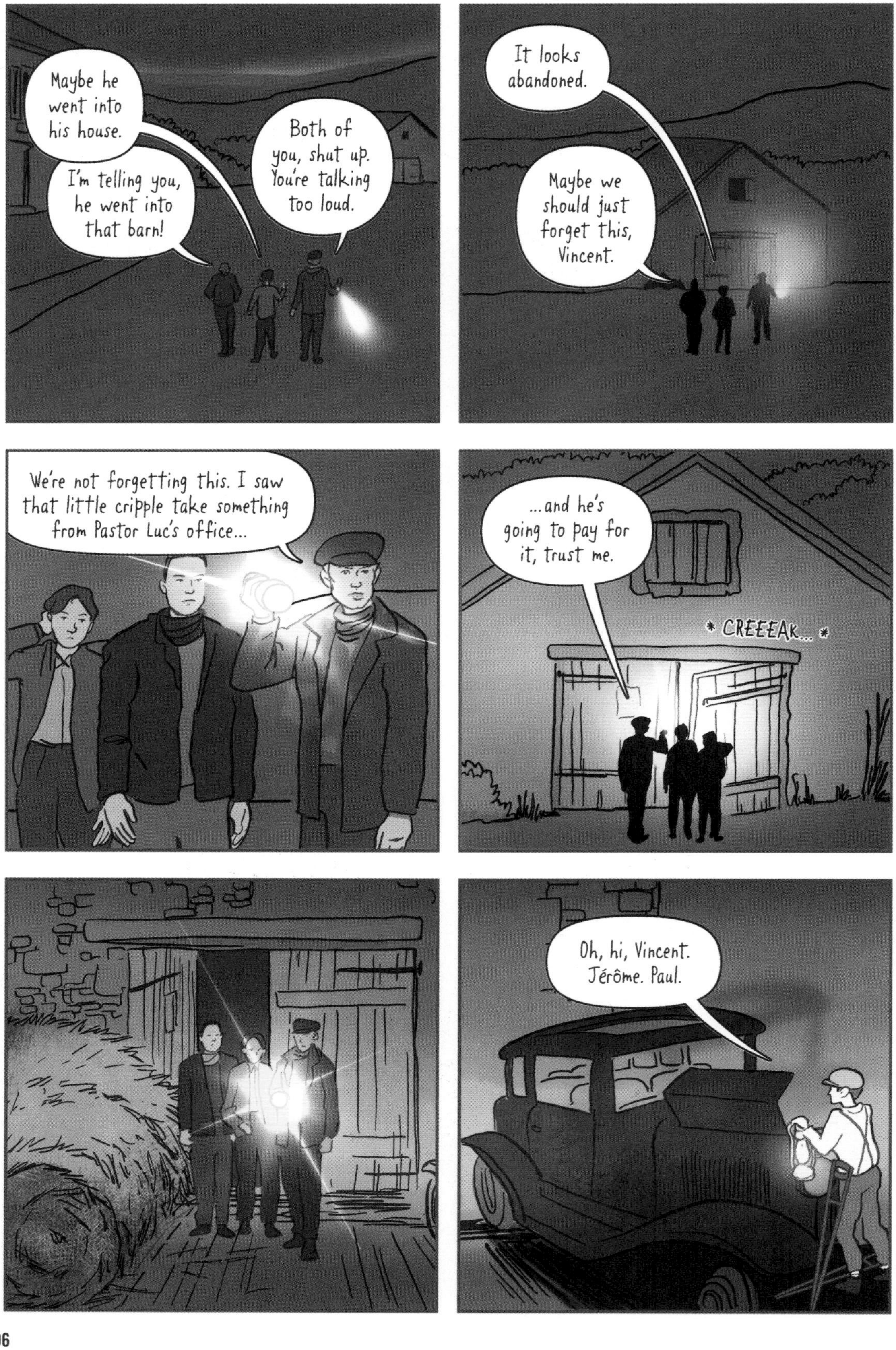
Maybe he went into his house.
I'm telling you, he went into that barn!
Both of you, shut up. You're talking too loud.
It looks abandoned.
Maybe we should just forget this, Vincent.
We're not forgetting this. I saw that little cripple take something from Pastor Luc's office...
...and he's going to pay for it, trust me.
* CREEEAK... *
Oh, hi, Vincent. Jérôme. Paul.

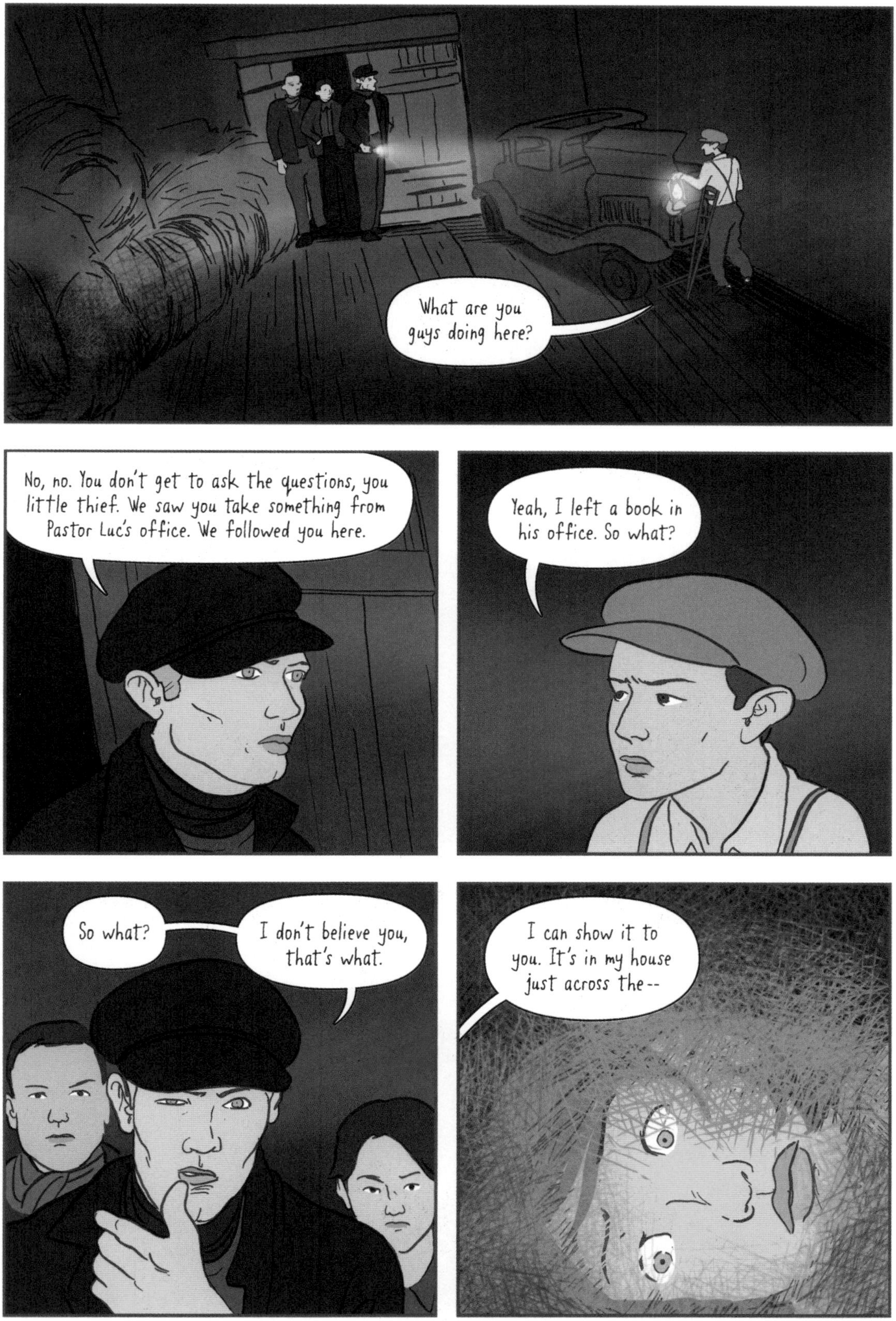
What are you guys doing here?
No, no. You don't get to ask the questions, you little thief. We saw you take something from Pastor Luc's office. We followed you here.
Yeah, I left a book in his office. So what?
So what?
I don't believe you, that's what.
I can show it to you. It's in my house just across the--

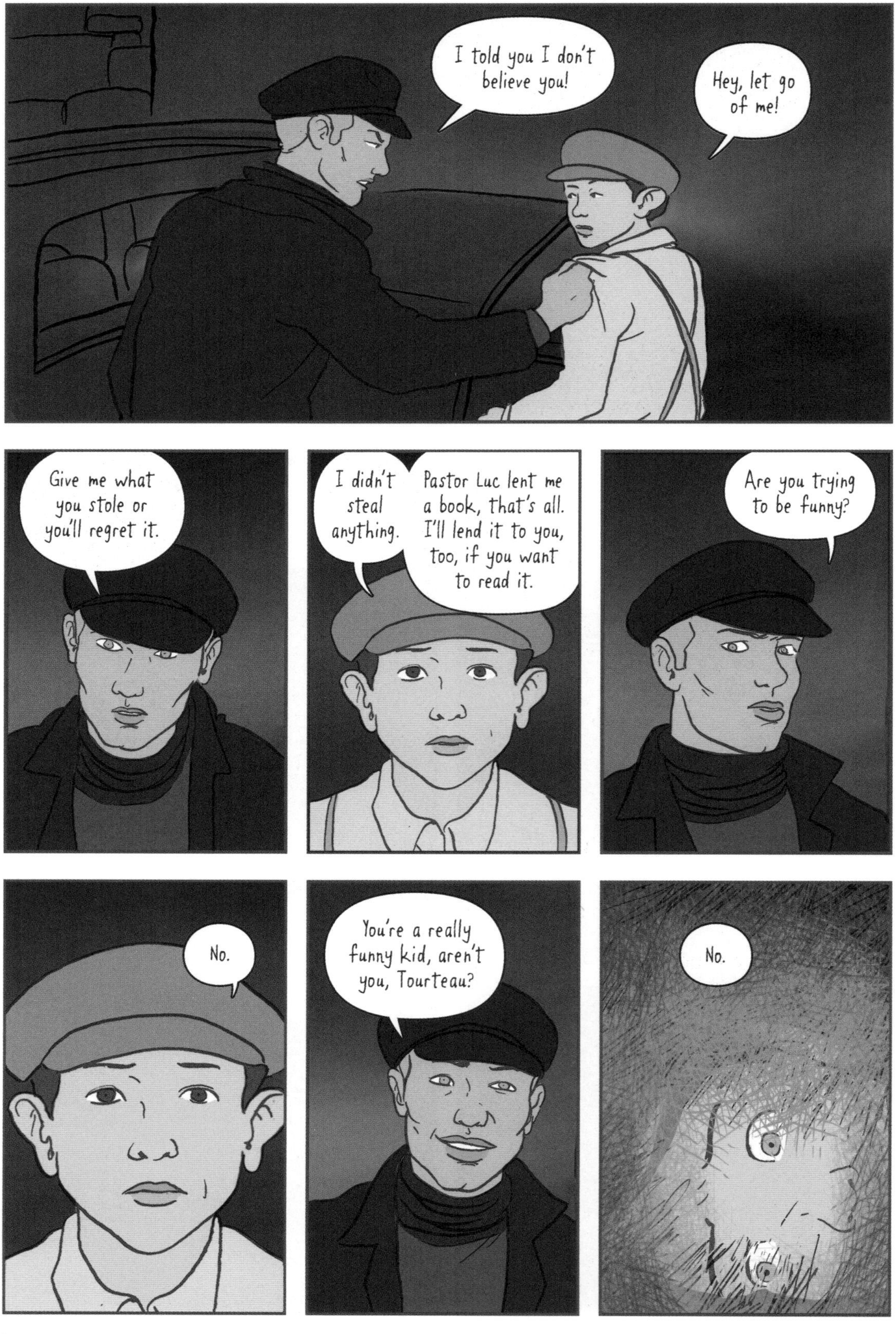
I told you I don't believe you!
Hey, let go of me!
Give me what you stole or you'll regret it.
I didn't steal anything.
Pastor Luc lent me a book, that's all. I'll lend it to you, too, if you want to read it.
Are you trying to be funny?
No.
You're a really funny kid, aren't you, Tourteau?
No.

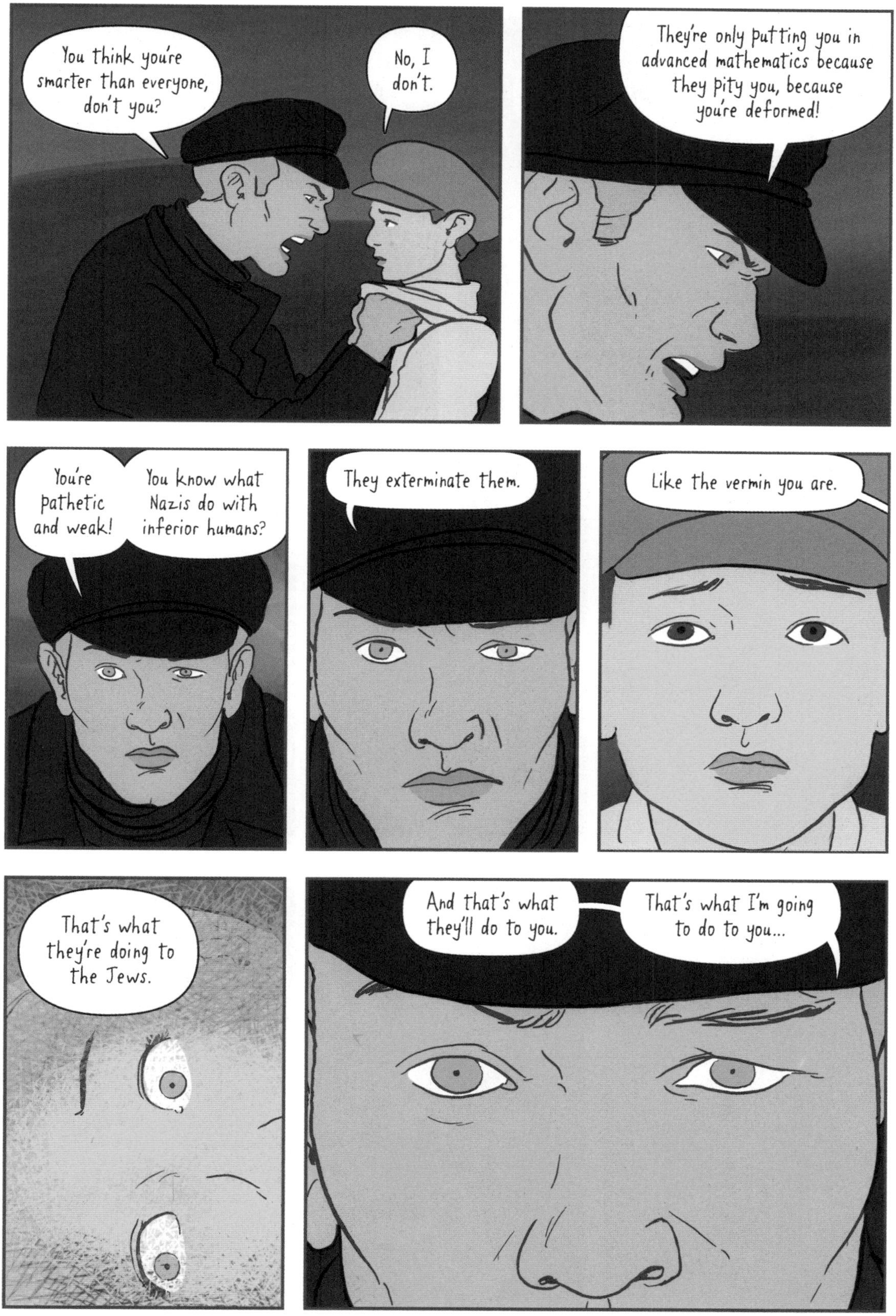
You think you're smarter than everyone, don't you?
No, I don't.
They're only putting you in advanced mathematics because they pity you, because you're deformed!
You're pathetic and weak!
You know what Nazis do with inferior humans?
They exterminate them.
Like the vermin you are.
That's what they're doing to the Jews.
And that's what they'll do to you.
That's what I'm going to do to you...

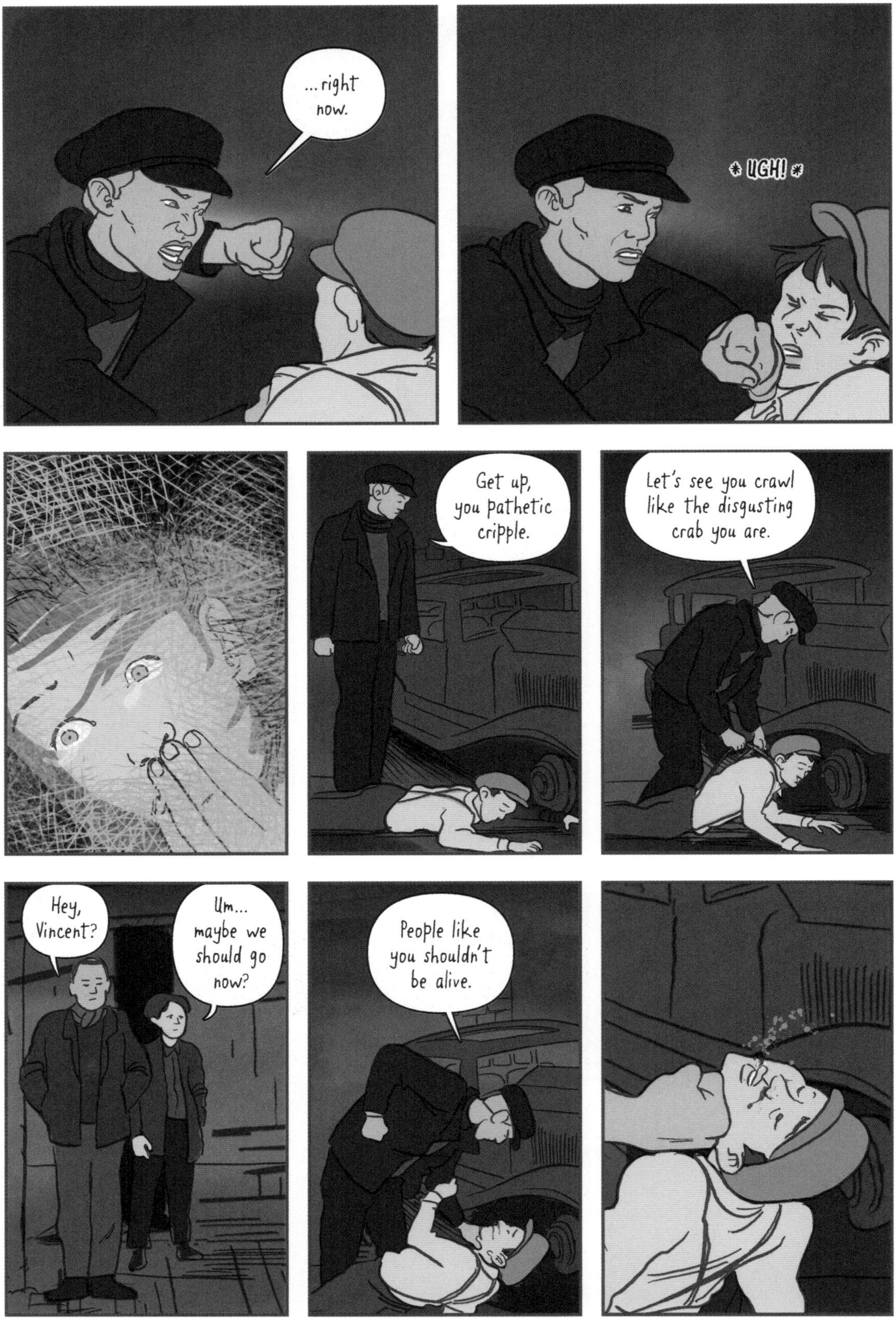

...right now.
* UGH! *
Get up, you pathetic cripple.
Let's see you crawl like the disgusting crab you are.
Hey, Vincent?
Um... maybe we should go now?
People like you shouldn't be alive.

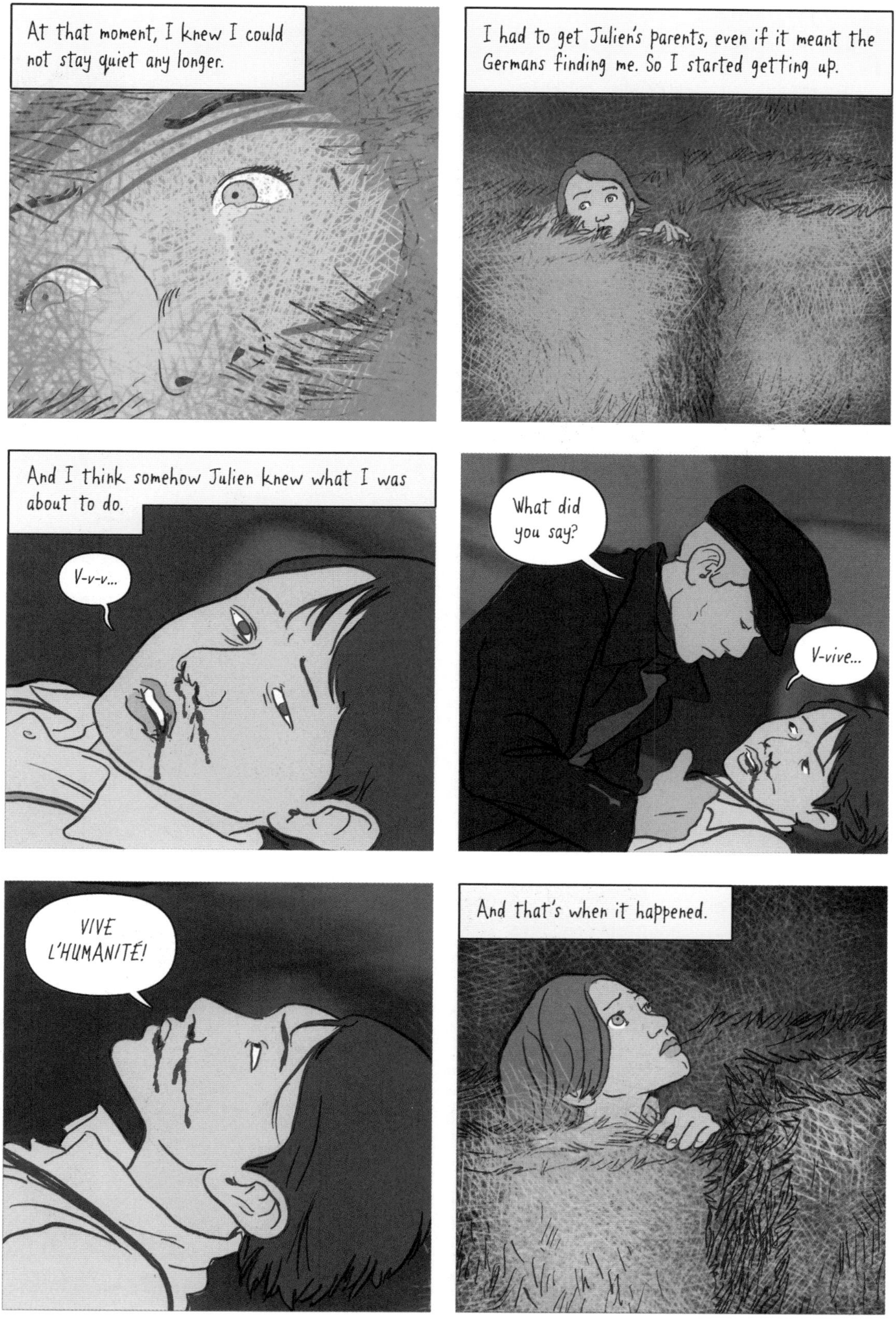
At that moment, I knew I could not stay quiet any longer.
I had to get Julien's parents, even if it meant the Germans finding me. So I started getting up.
And I think somehow Julien knew what I was about to do.
V-v-v...
What did you say?
V-vive...
VIVE L'HUMANITÉ!
And that's when it happened.

Suddenly, without warning, hundreds of bats flew out from the rafters and swarmed the barn below.

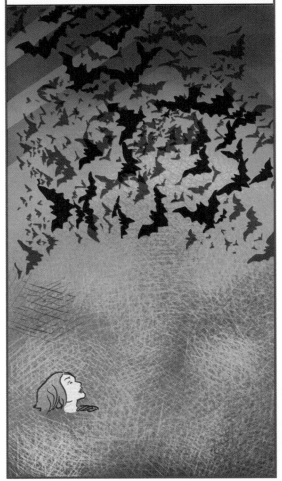

They flew everywhere, shrieking, whooshing through the air like some dark, unholy wind.

What the--?

It was truly terrifying...

...and absolutely glorious!

To this day, I don't know what caused the bats to do that.

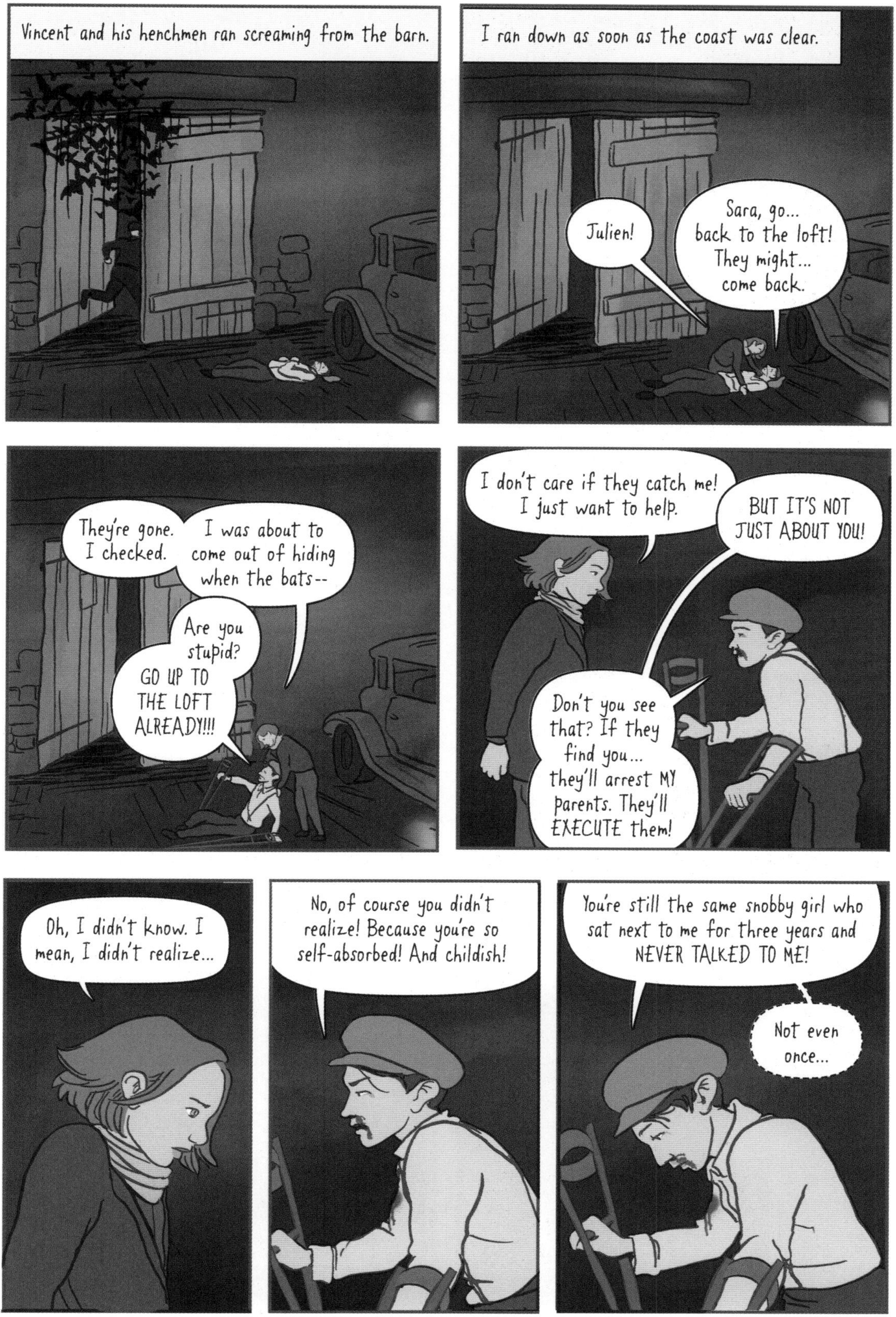
Vincent and his henchmen ran screaming from the barn.
I ran down as soon as the coast was clear.
Julien!
Sara, go... back to the loft! They might... come back.
They're gone. I checked.
I was about to come out of hiding when the bats--
Are you stupid? GO UP TO THE LOFT ALREADY!!!
I don't care if they catch me! I just want to help.
BUT IT'S NOT JUST ABOUT YOU!
Don't you see that? If they find you... they'll arrest MY parents. They'll EXECUTE them!
Oh, I didn't know. I mean, I didn't realize...
No, of course you didn't realize! Because you're so self-absorbed! And childish!
You're still the same snobby girl who sat next to me for three years and NEVER TALKED TO ME!
Not even once...

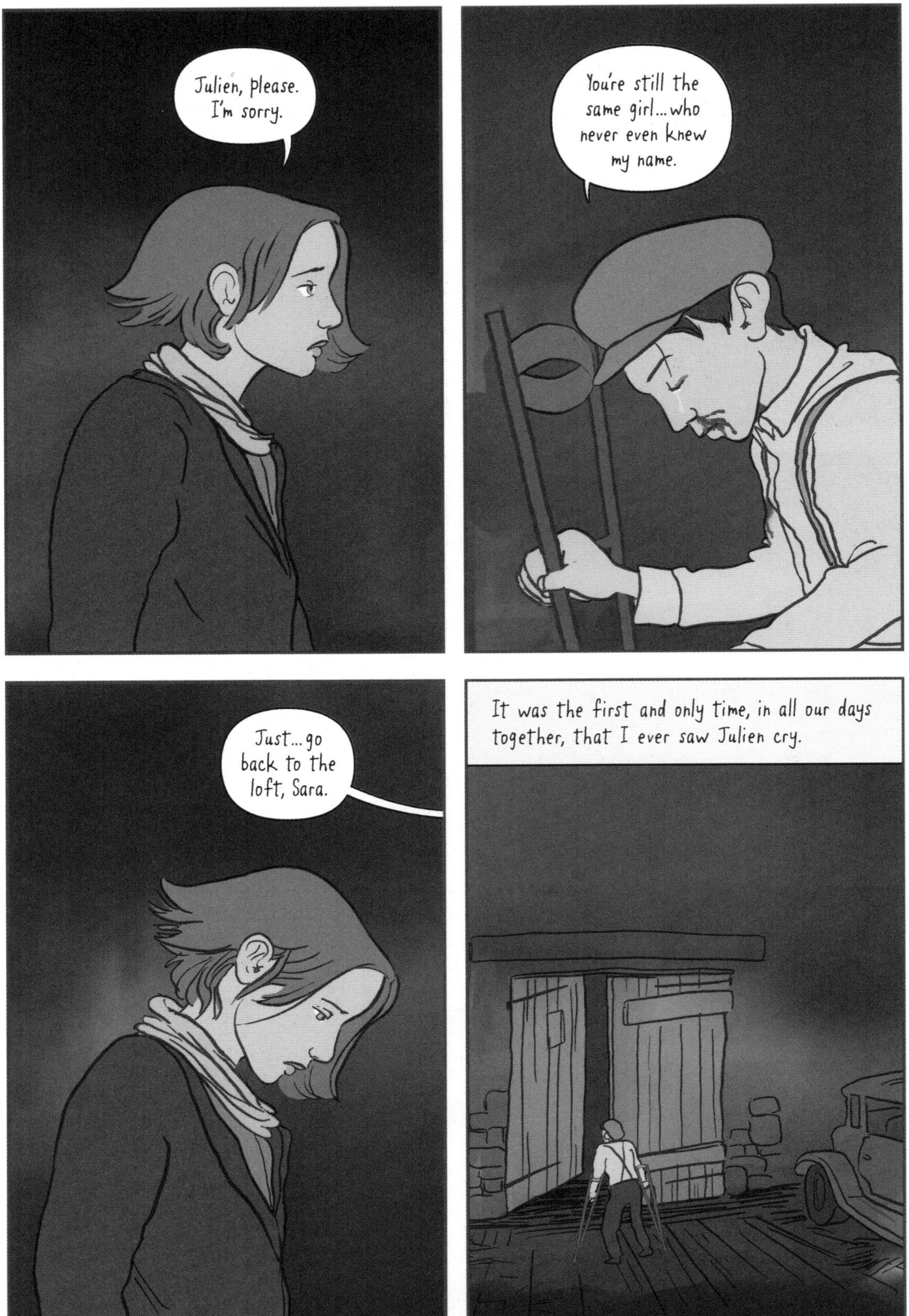
Julien, please. I'm sorry.
You're still the same girl...who never even knew my name.
Just...go back to the loft, Sara.
It was the first and only time, in all our days together, that I ever saw Julien cry.

CHAPTER 6

THE NEXT MORNING, VIVIENNE AND JEAN-PAUL WENT TO THE ÉCOLE LAFAYETTE TO TELL PASTOR LUC ABOUT WHAT VINCENT HAD DONE TO JULIEN.

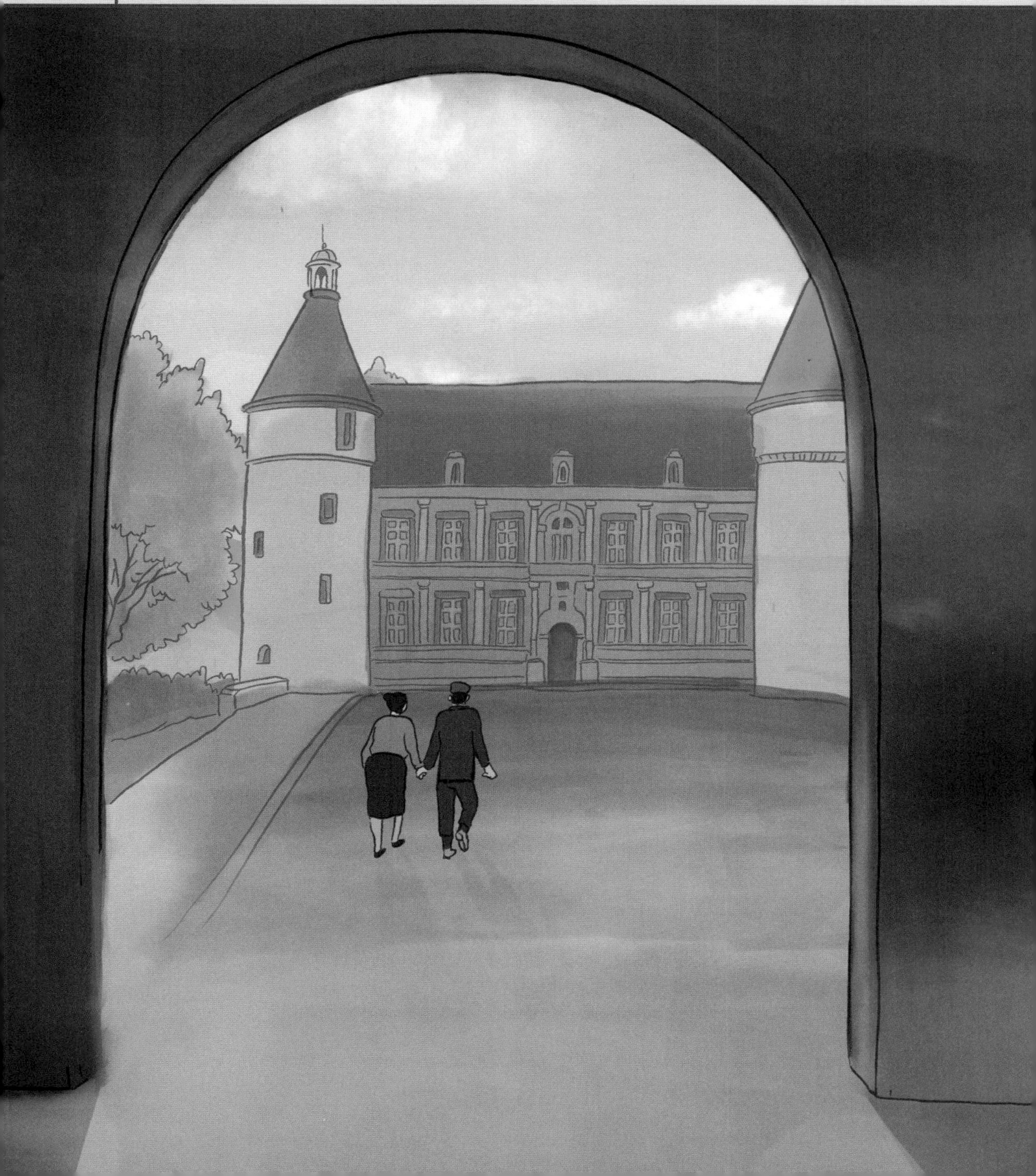

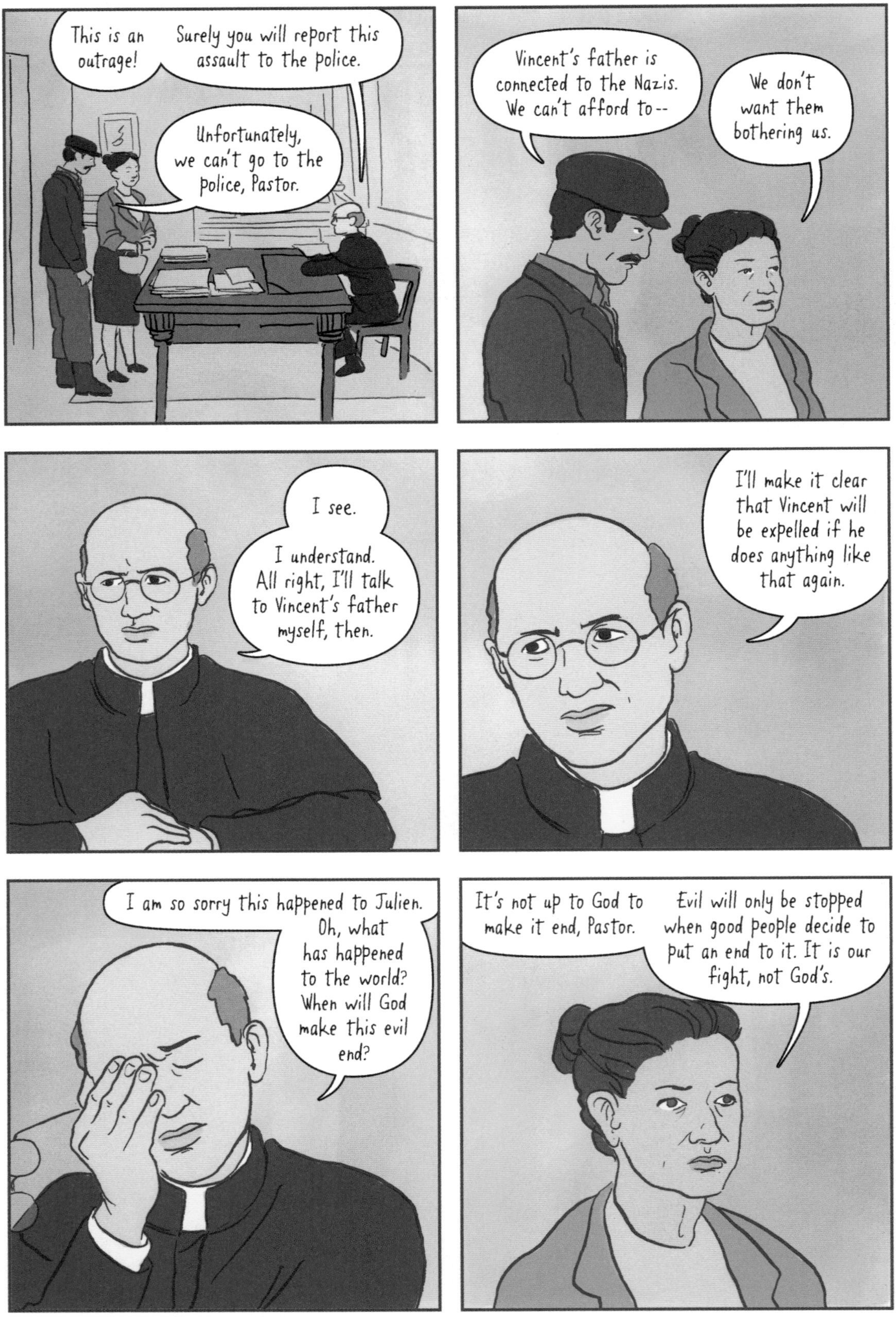

This is an outrage!
Surely you will report this assault to the police.
Unfortunately, we can't go to the police, Pastor.
Vincent's father is connected to the Nazis. We can't afford to--
We don't want them bothering us.
I see.
I understand. All right, I'll talk to Vincent's father myself, then.
I'll make it clear that Vincent will be expelled if he does anything like that again.
I am so sorry this happened to Julien.
Oh, what has happened to the world? When will God make this evil end?
It's not up to God to make it end, Pastor.
Evil will only be stopped when good people decide to put an end to it. It is our fight, not God's.

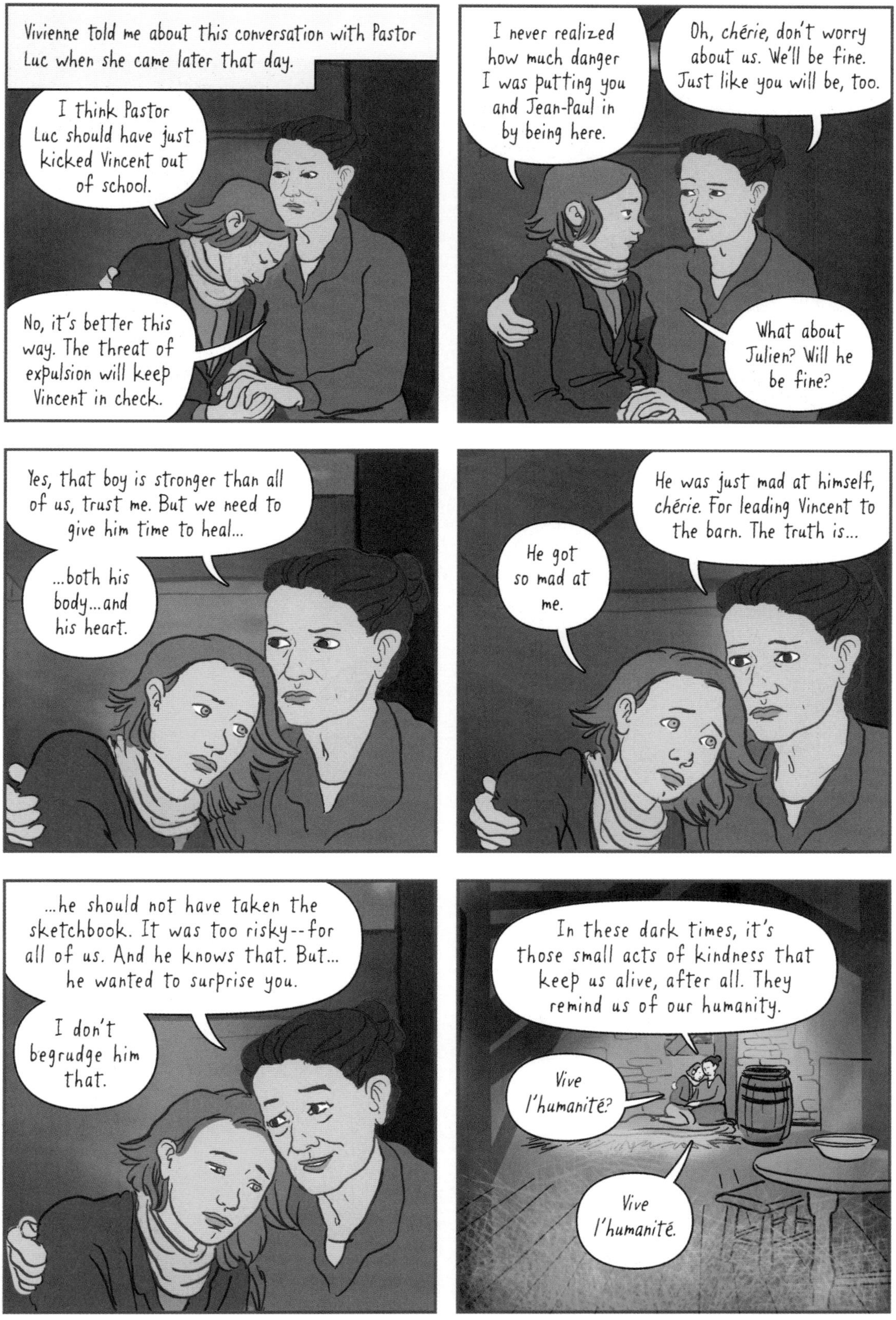

Vivienne told me about this conversation with Pastor Luc when she came later that day.
I think Pastor Luc should have just kicked Vincent out of school.
No, it's better this way. The threat of expulsion will keep Vincent in check.
I never realized how much danger I was putting you and Jean-Paul in by being here.
Oh, chérie, don't worry about us. We'll be fine. Just like you will be, too.
What about Julien? Will he be fine?
Yes, that boy is stronger than all of us, trust me. But we need to give him time to heal...
...both his body...and his heart.
He got so mad at me.
He was just mad at himself, chérie. For leading Vincent to the barn. The truth is...
...he should not have taken the sketchbook. It was too risky--for all of us. And he knows that. But... he wanted to surprise you.
I don't begrudge him that.
In these dark times, it's those small acts of kindness that keep us alive, after all. They remind us of our humanity.
Vive l'humanité?
Vive l'humanité.

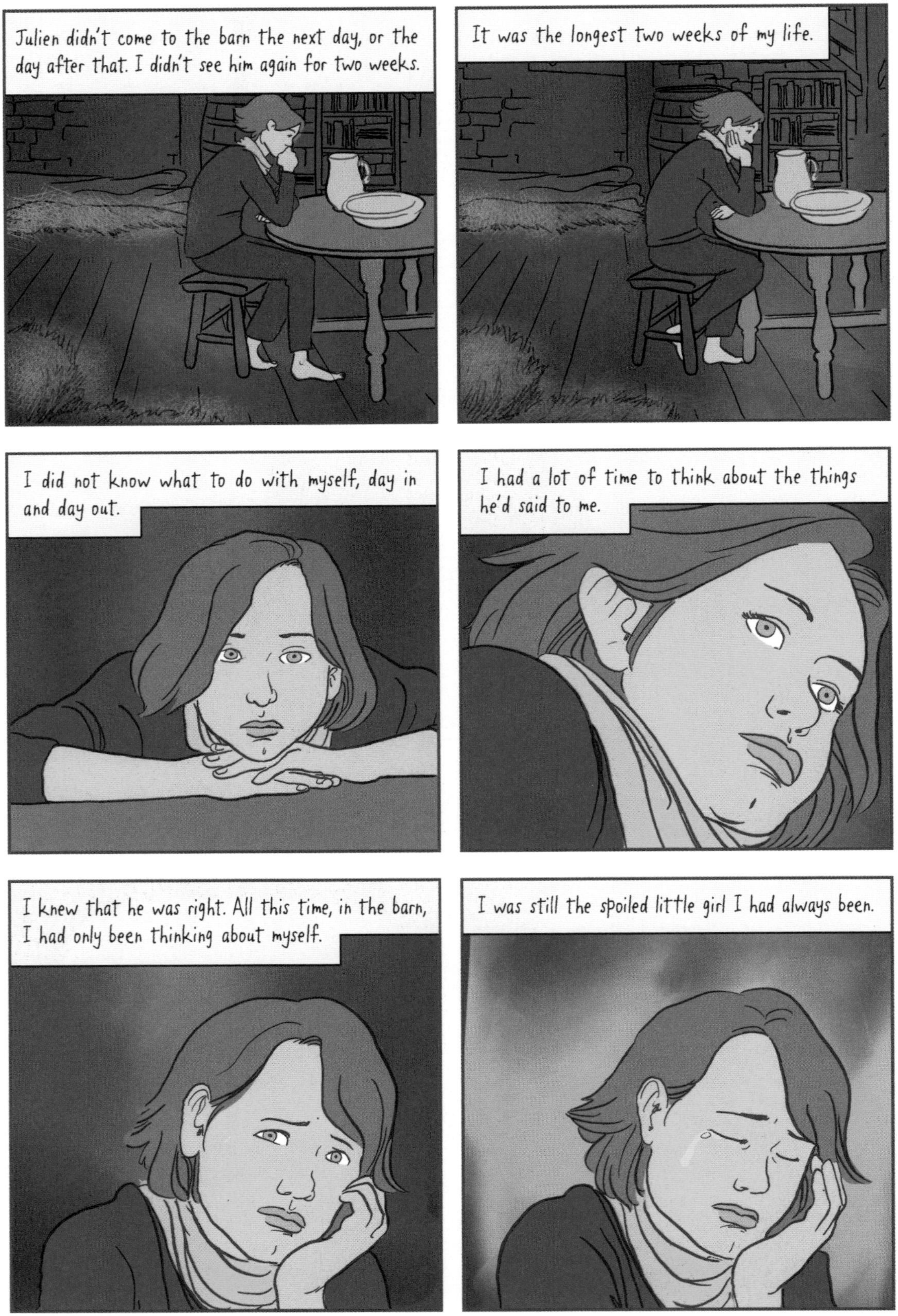
Julien didn't come to the barn the next day, or the day after that. I didn't see him again for two weeks.
It was the longest two weeks of my life.
I did not know what to do with myself, day in and day out.
I had a lot of time to think about the things he'd said to me.
I knew that he was right. All this time, in the barn, I had only been thinking about myself.
I was still the spoiled little girl I had always been.

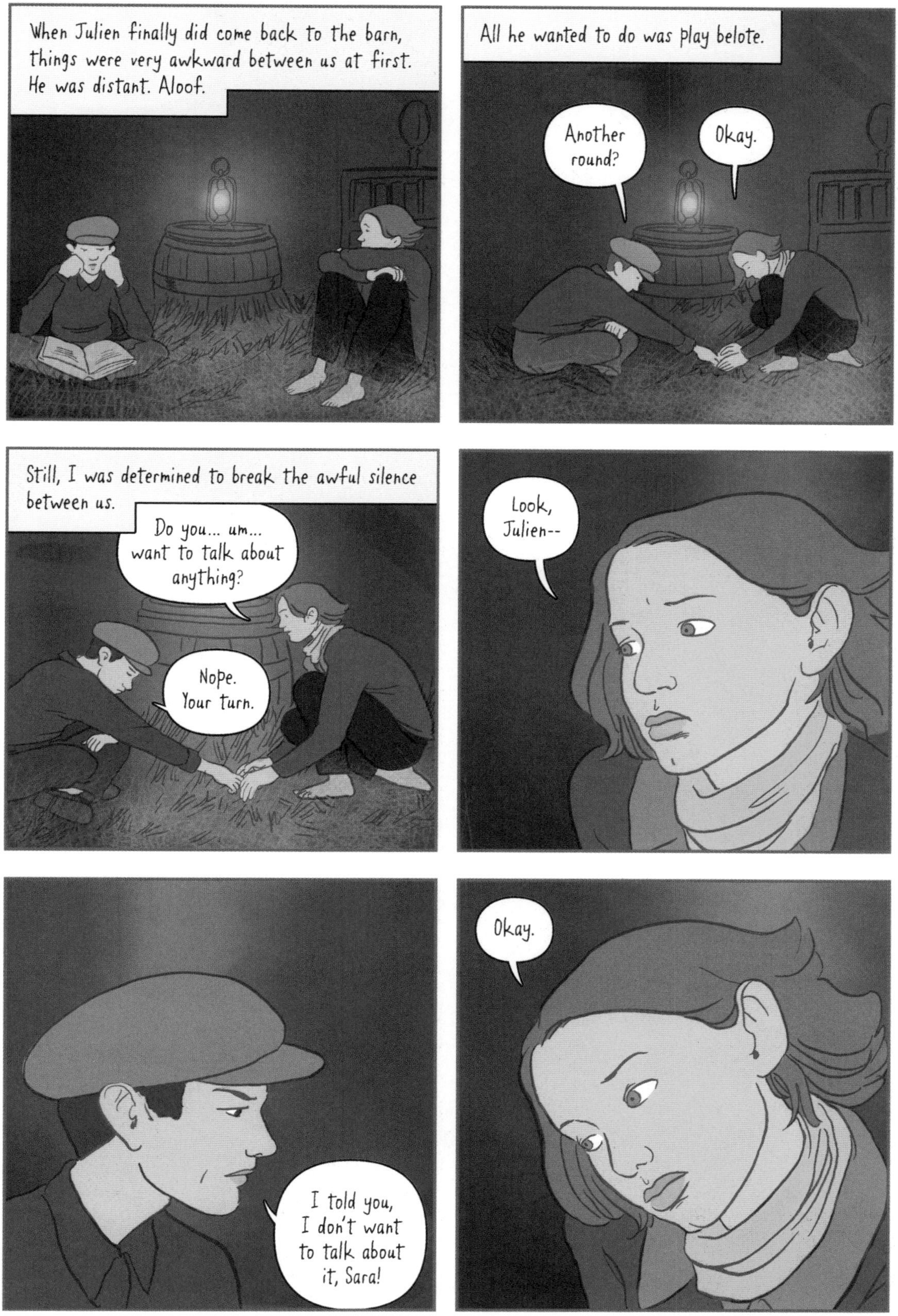
When Julien finally did come back to the barn, things were very awkward between us at first. He was distant. Aloof.
All he wanted to do was play belote.
Another round?
Okay.
Still, I was determined to break the awful silence between us.
Do you... um... want to talk about anything?
Nope. Your turn.
Look, Julien--
I told you, I don't want to talk about it, Sara!
Okay.

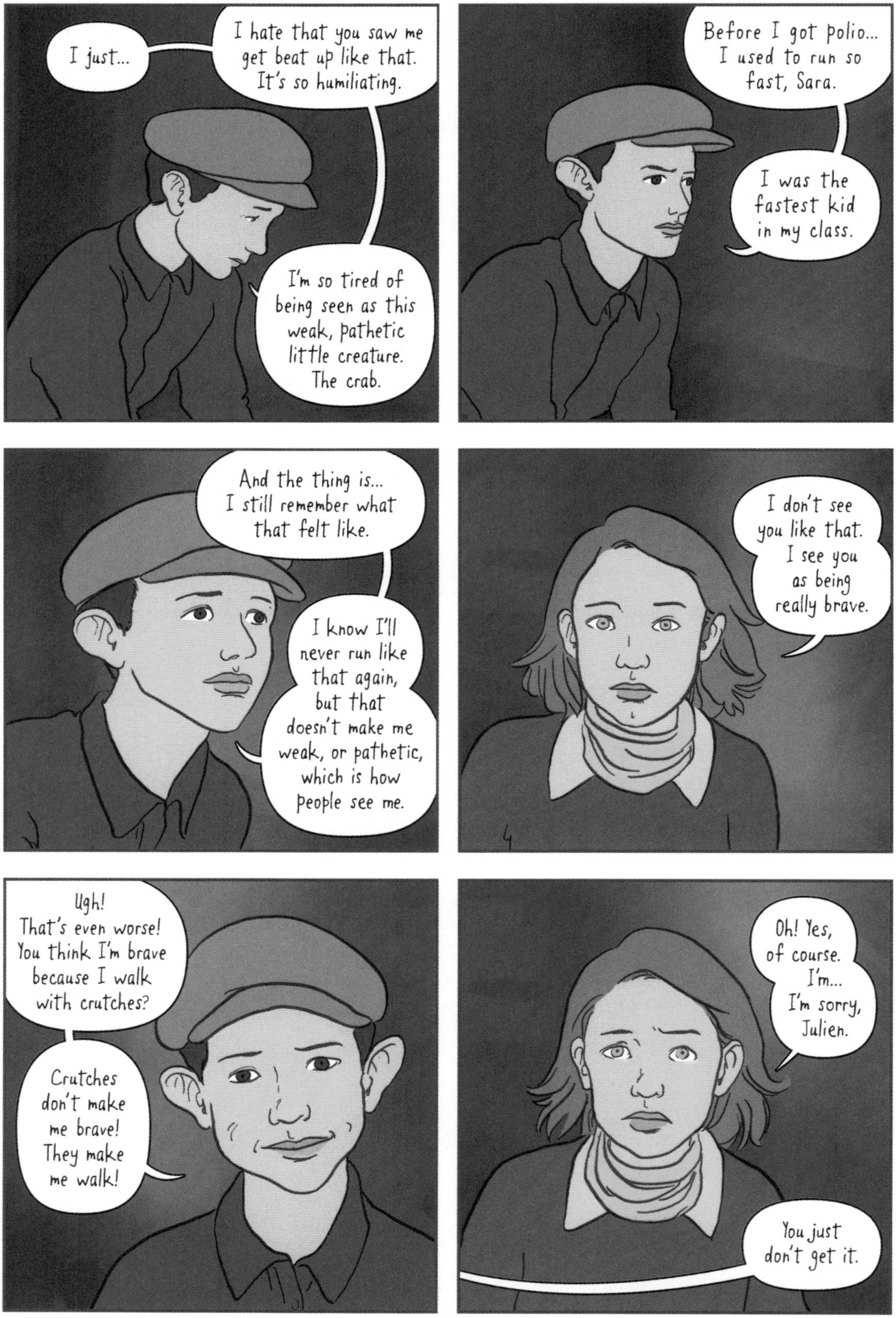
I just...
I hate that you saw me get beat up like that. It's so humiliating.
I'm so tired of being seen as this weak, pathetic little creature. The crab.
Before I got polio... I used to run so fast, Sara.
I was the fastest kid in my class.
And the thing is... I still remember what that felt like.
I know I'll never run like that again, but that doesn't make me weak, or pathetic, which is how people see me.
I don't see you like that. I see you as being really brave.
Ugh! That's even worse! You think I'm brave because I walk with crutches?
Crutches don't make me brave! They make me walk!
Oh! Yes, of course. I'm... I'm sorry, Julien.
You just don't get it.

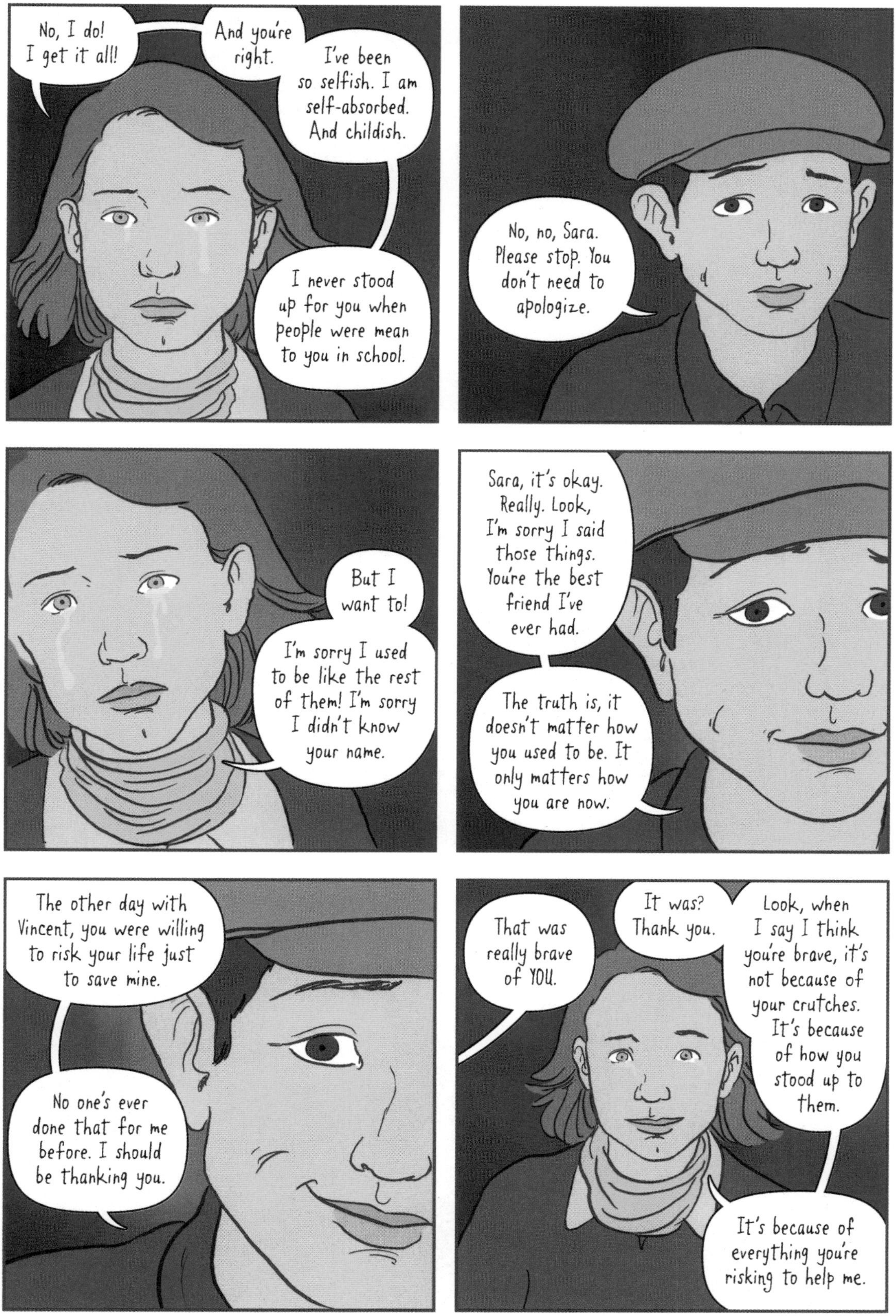
No, I do! I get it all!
And you're right.
I've been so selfish. I am self-absorbed. And childish.
I never stood up for you when people were mean to you in school.
No, no, Sara. Please stop. You don't need to apologize.
But I want to!
I'm sorry I used to be like the rest of them! I'm sorry I didn't know your name.
Sara, it's okay. Really. Look, I'm sorry I said those things. You're the best friend I've ever had.
The truth is, it doesn't matter how you used to be. It only matters how you are now.
The other day with Vincent, you were willing to risk your life just to save mine.
No one's ever done that for me before. I should be thanking you.
That was really brave of YOU.
It was? Thank you.
Look, when I say I think you're brave, it's not because of your crutches. It's because of how you stood up to them.
It's because of everything you're risking to help me.

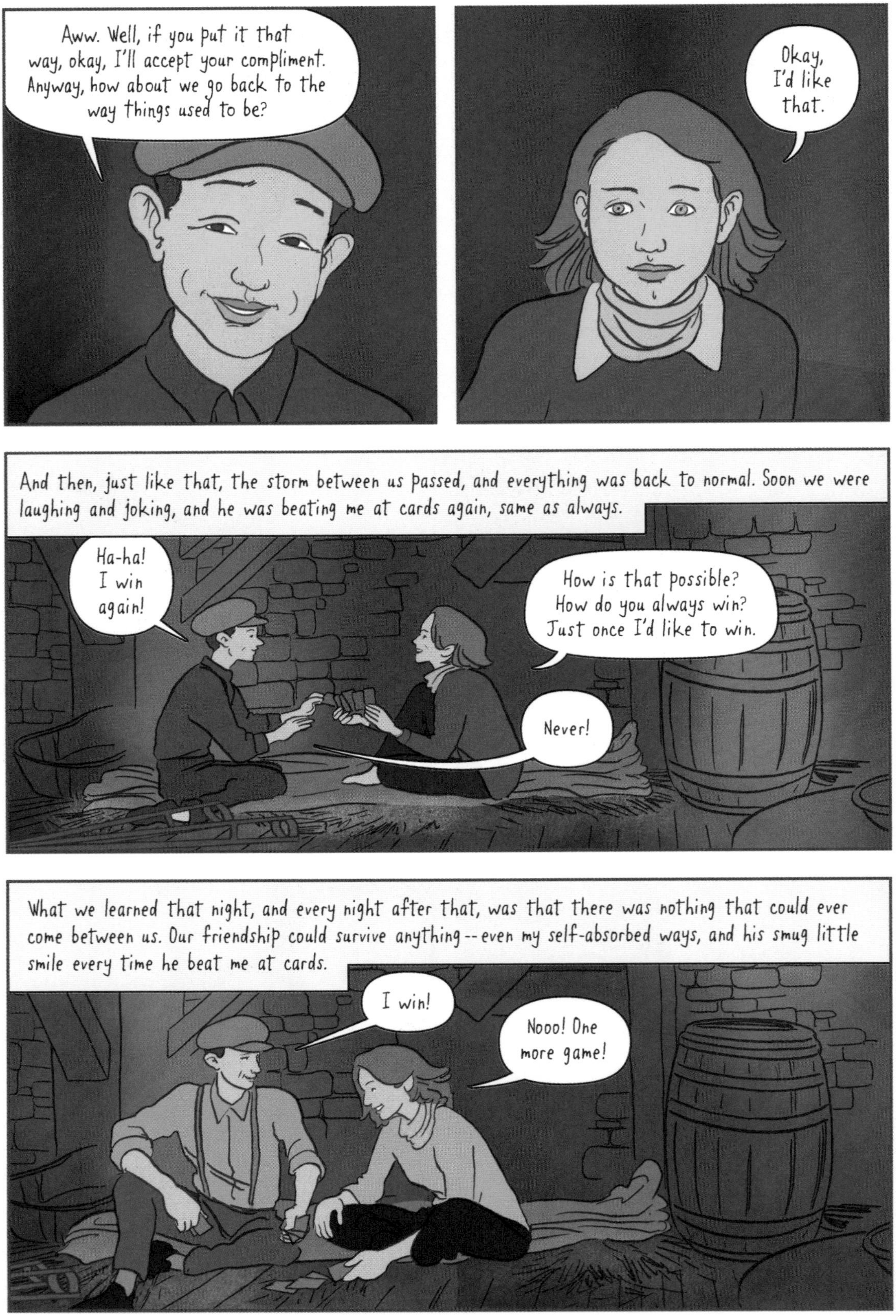
Aww. Well, if you put it that way, okay, I'll accept your compliment. Anyway, how about we go back to the way things used to be?
Okay, I'd like that.
And then, just like that, the storm between us passed, and everything was back to normal. Soon we were laughing and joking, and he was beating me at cards again, same as always.
Ha-ha! I win again!
How is that possible? How do you always win? Just once I'd like to win.
Never!
What we learned that night, and every night after that, was that there was nothing that could ever come between us. Our friendship could survive anything--even my self-absorbed ways, and his smug little smile every time he beat me at cards.
I win!
Nooo! One more game!

PART THREE

But the enemy came like thunder in the wood...

-Muriel Rukeyser, "Seventh Elegy: The Dream-Singing Elegy"

TIME PASSES. THAT IS THE ONLY THING ONE CAN BE SURE OF IN LIFE: TIME DOES NOT STOP. NOT FOR ANYONE. NOT FOR ANYTHING. TIME MARCHES ON, OBLIVIOUS TO ALL.

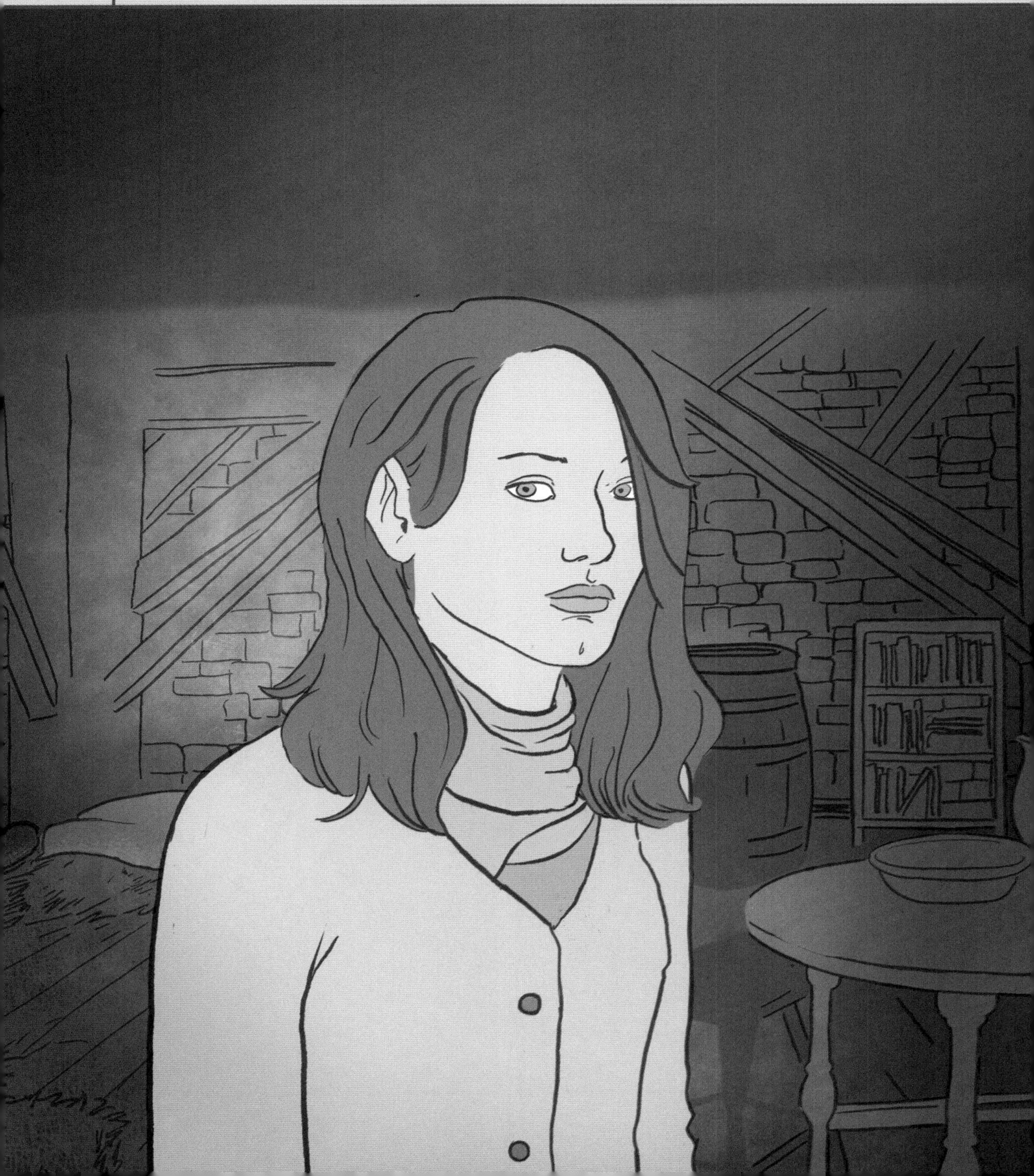

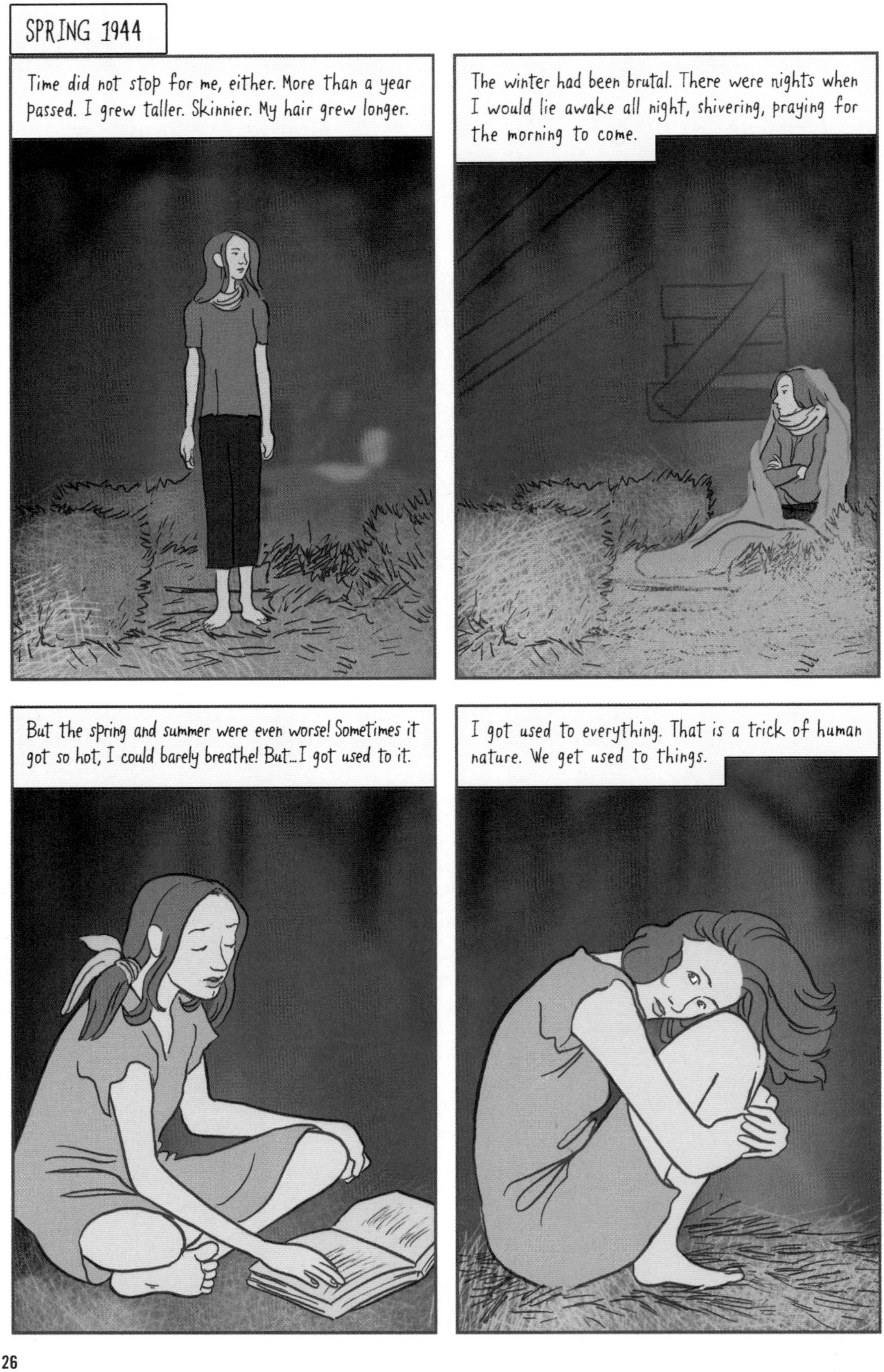
SPRING 1944
Time did not stop for me, either. More than a year passed. I grew taller. Skinnier. My hair grew longer.
The winter had been brutal. There were nights when I would lie awake all night, shivering, praying for the morning to come.
But the spring and summer were even worse! Sometimes it got so hot, I could barely breathe! But...I got used to it.
I got used to everything. That is a trick of human nature. We get used to things.

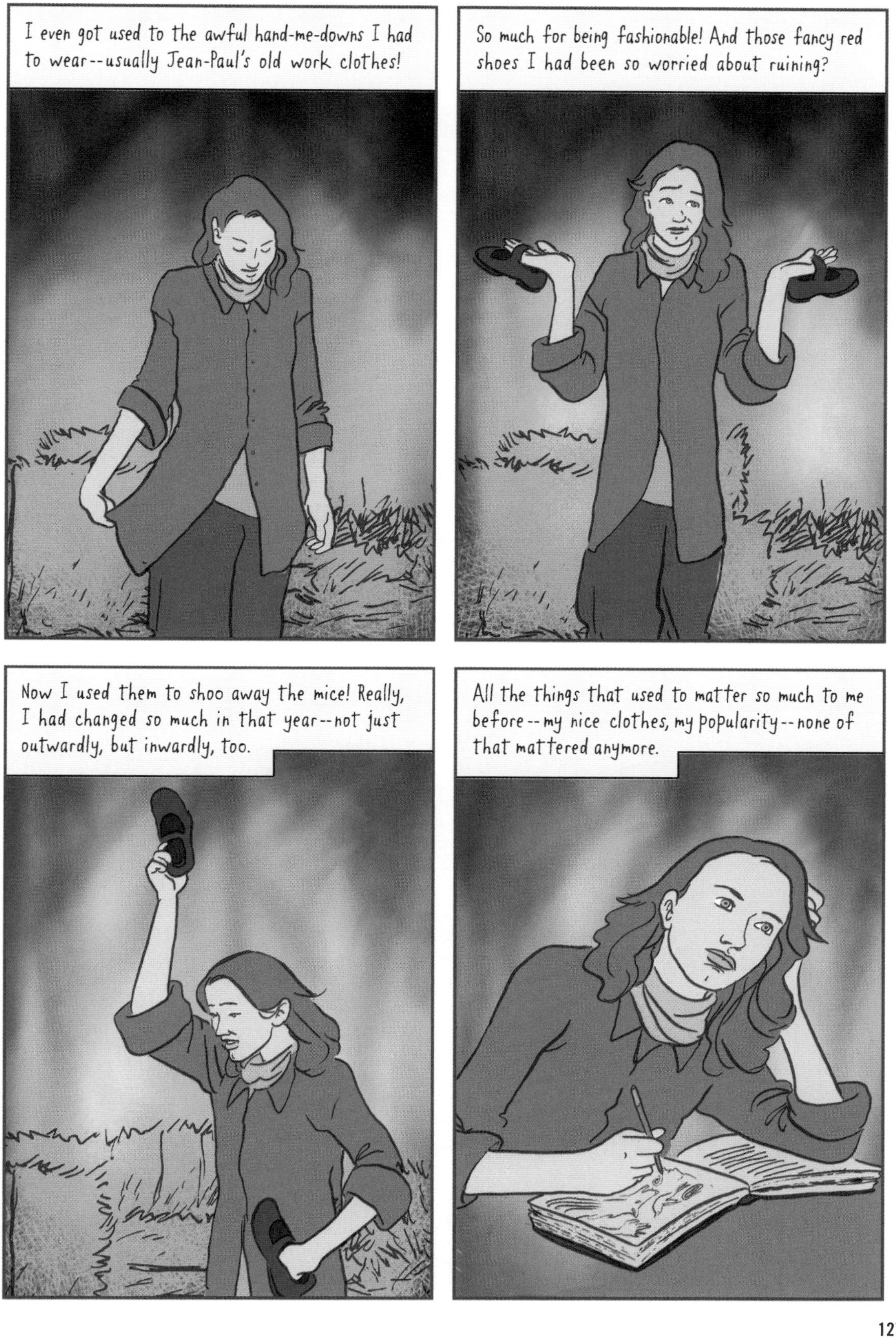
I even got used to the awful hand-me-downs I had to wear--usually Jean-Paul's old work clothes!
So much for being fashionable! And those fancy red shoes I had been so worried about ruining?
Now I used them to shoo away the mice! Really, I had changed so much in that year--not just outwardly, but inwardly, too.
All the things that used to matter so much to me before--my nice clothes, my popularity--none of that mattered anymore.

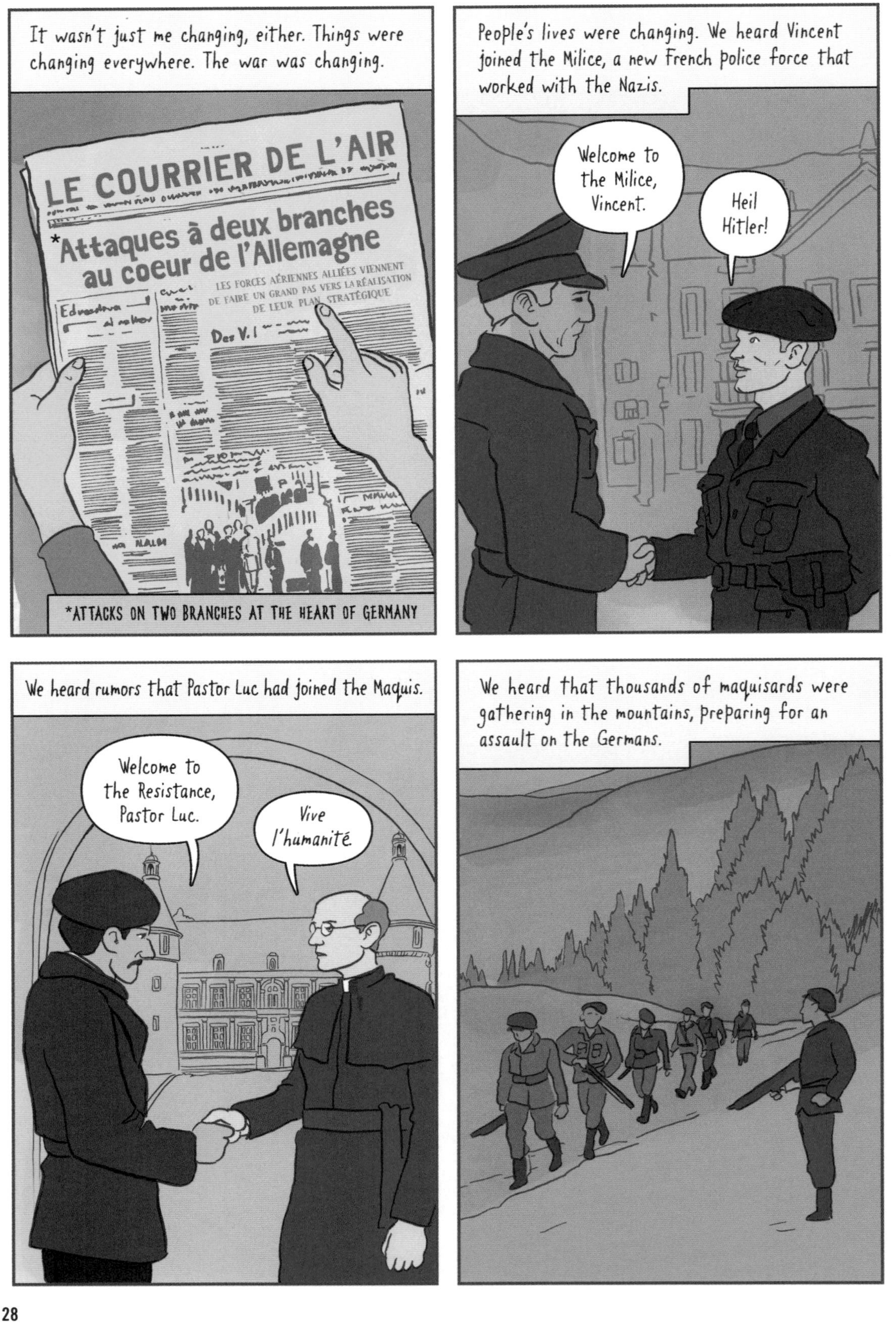
It wasn't just me changing, either. Things were changing everywhere. The war was changing.
LE COURRIER DE L'AIR
*Attaques à deux branches au coeur de l'Allemagne
LES FORCES AÉRIENNES ALLIÉES VIENNENT DE FAIRE UN GRAND PAS VERS LA RÉALISATION DE LEUR PLAN STRATÉGIQUE
Des V. 1
*ATTACKS ON TWO BRANCHES AT THE HEART OF GERMANY
People's lives were changing. We heard Vincent joined the Milice, a new French police force that worked with the Nazis.
Welcome to the Milice, Vincent.
Heil Hitler!
We heard rumors that Pastor Luc had joined the Maquis.
Welcome to the Resistance, Pastor Luc.
Vive l'humanité.
We heard that thousands of maquisards were gathering in the mountains, preparing for an assault on the Germans.

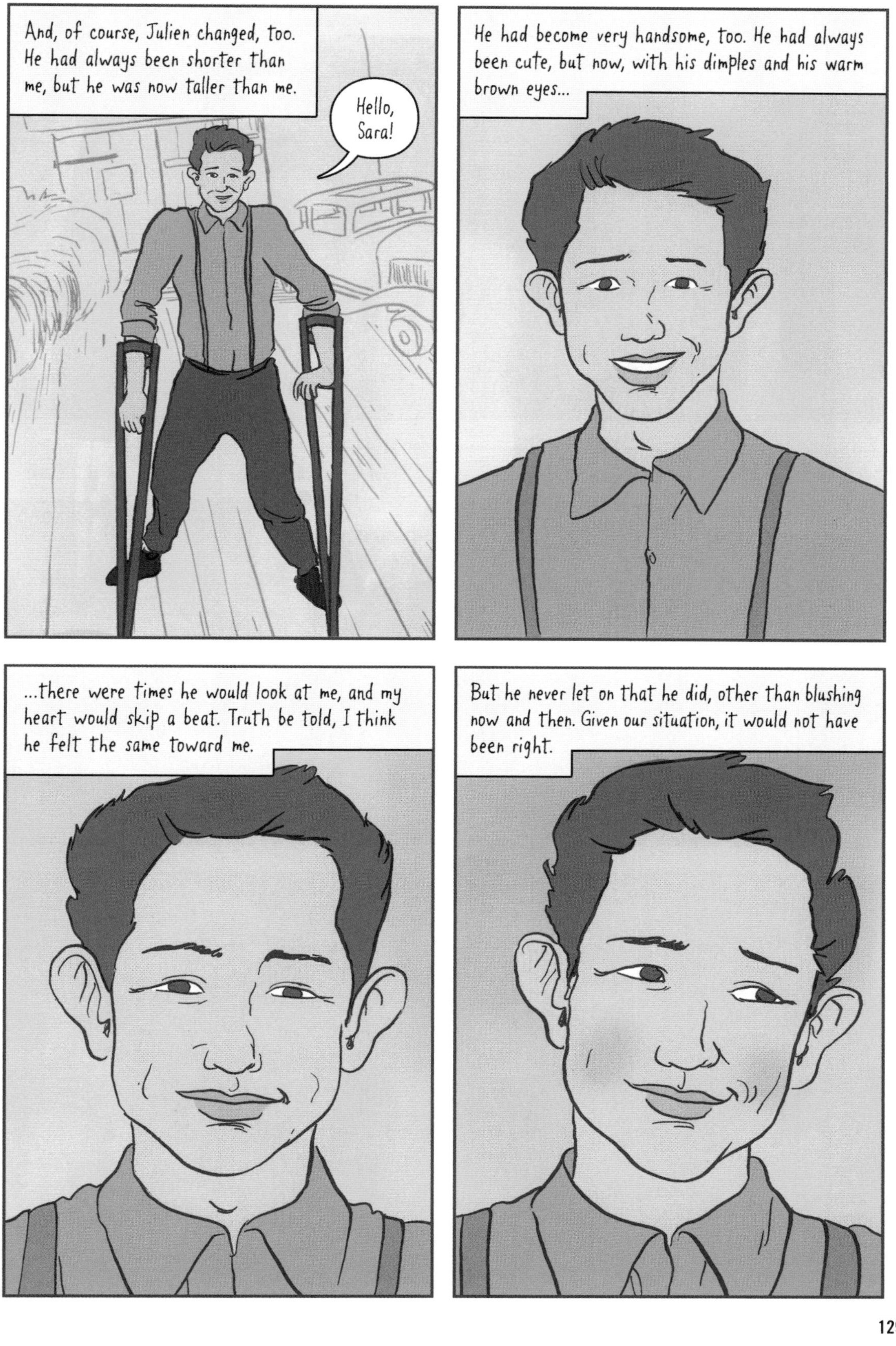
And, of course, Julien changed, too. He had always been shorter than me, but he was now taller than me.
Hello, Sara!
He had become very handsome, too. He had always been cute, but now, with his dimples and his warm brown eyes...
...there were times he would look at me, and my heart would skip a beat. Truth be told, I think he felt the same toward me.
But he never let on that he did, other than blushing now and then. Given our situation, it would not have been right.

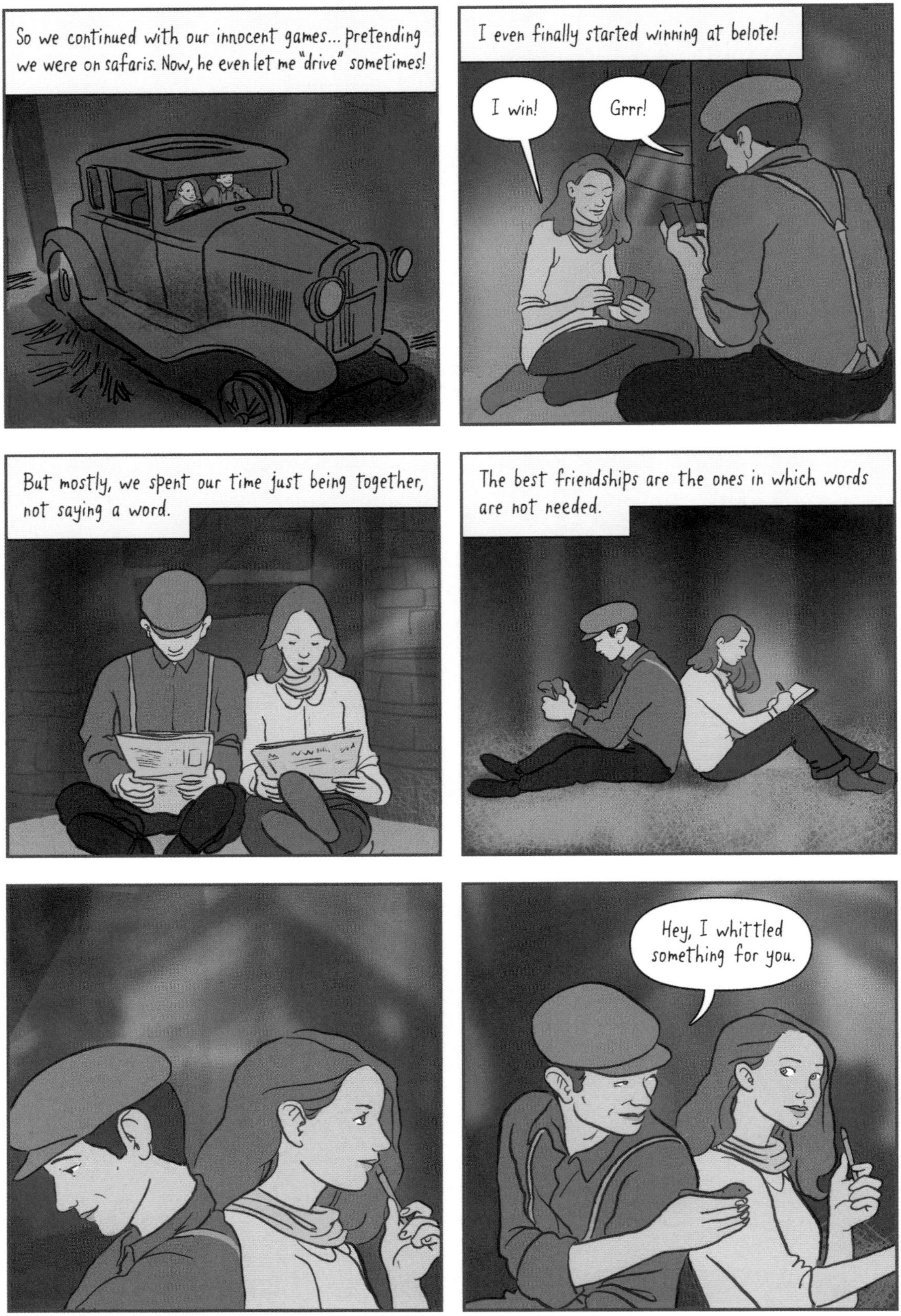
So we continued with our innocent games... pretending we were on safaris. Now, he even let me "drive" sometimes!
I even finally started winning at belote!
I win!
Grrr!
But mostly, we spent our time just being together, not saying a word.
The best friendships are the ones in which words are not needed.
Hey, I whittled something for you.

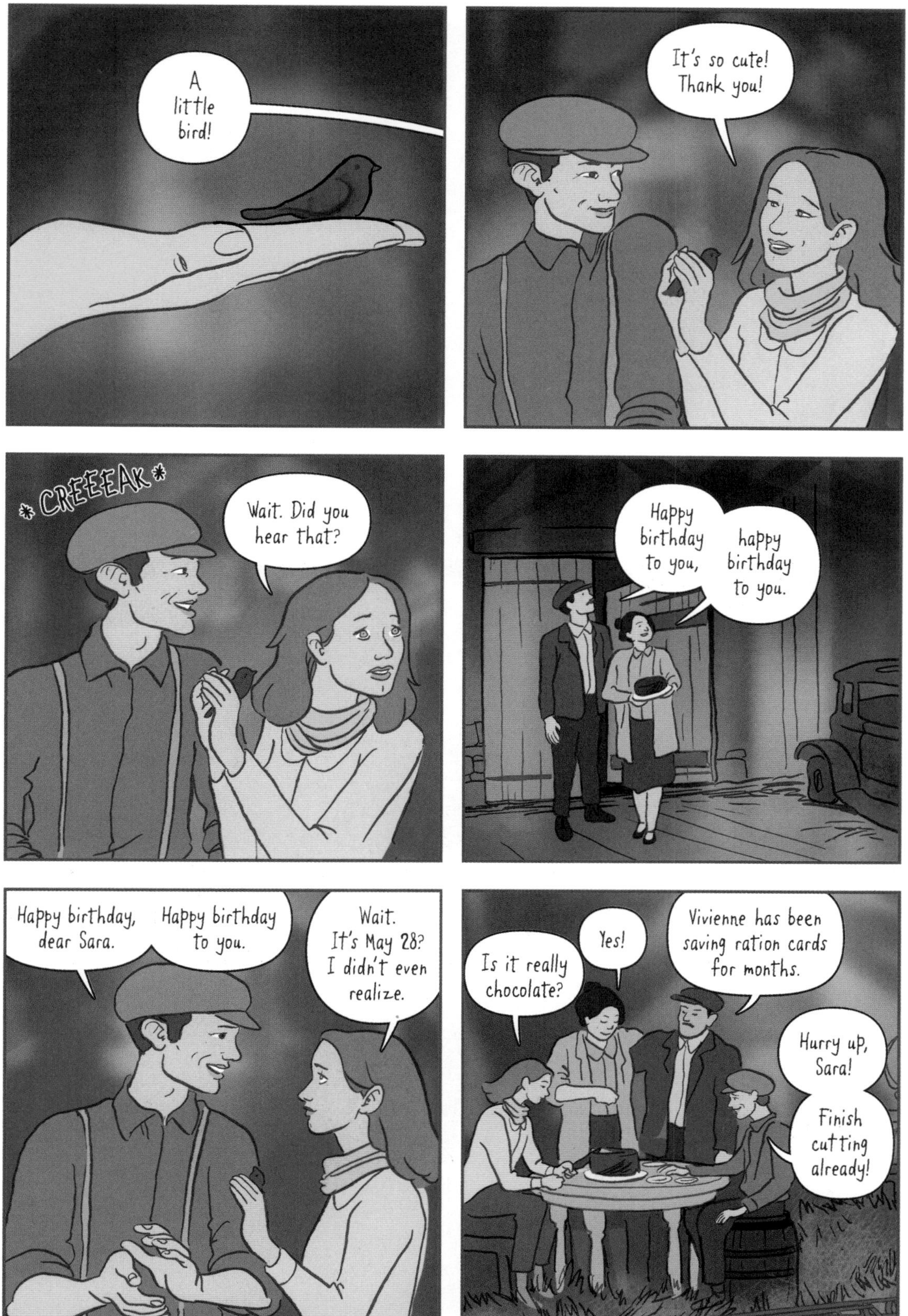
A little bird!
It's so cute! Thank you!
* CREEEAK *
Wait. Did you hear that?
Happy birthday to you,
happy birthday to you.
Happy birthday, dear Sara.
Happy birthday to you.
Wait. It's May 28? I didn't even realize.
Is it really chocolate?
Yes!
Vivienne has been saving ration cards for months.
Hurry up, Sara!
Finish cutting already!

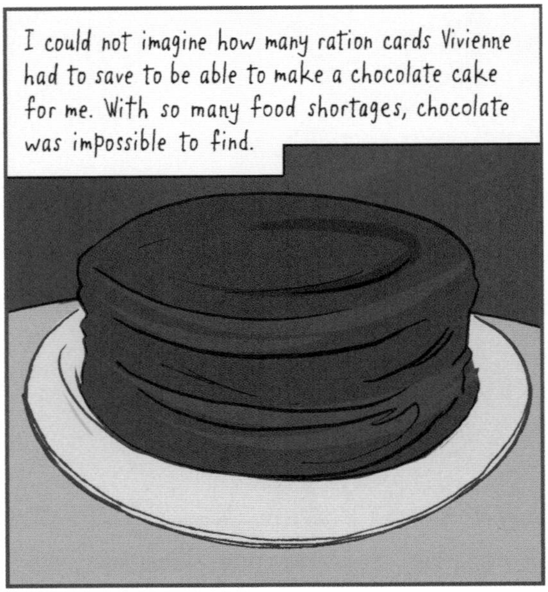
I could not imagine how many ration cards Vivienne had to save to be able to make a chocolate cake for me. With so many food shortages, chocolate was impossible to find.

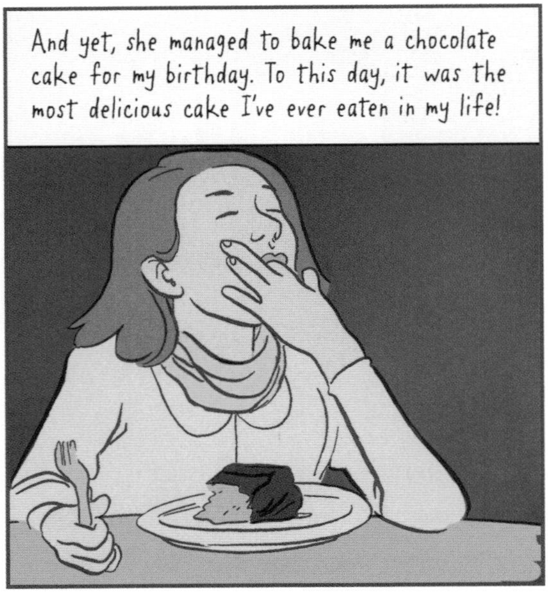
And yet, she managed to bake me a chocolate cake for my birthday. To this day, it was the most delicious cake I've ever eaten in my life!

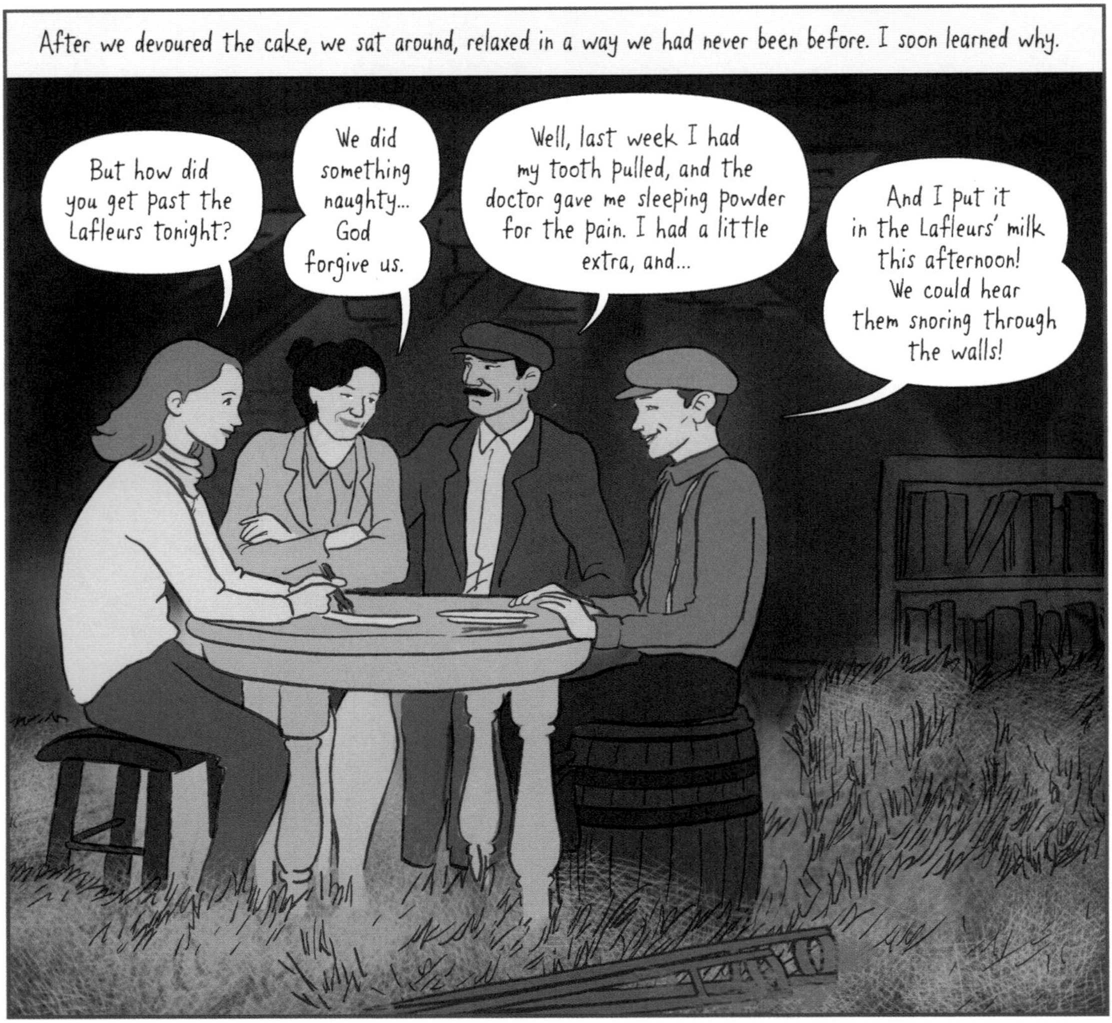
After we devoured the cake, we sat around, relaxed in a way we had never been before. I soon learned why.
But how did you get past the Lafleurs tonight?
We did something naughty... God forgive us.
Well, last week I had my tooth pulled, and the doctor gave me sleeping powder for the pain. I had a little extra, and...
And I put it in the Lafleurs' milk this afternoon! We could hear them snoring through the walls!

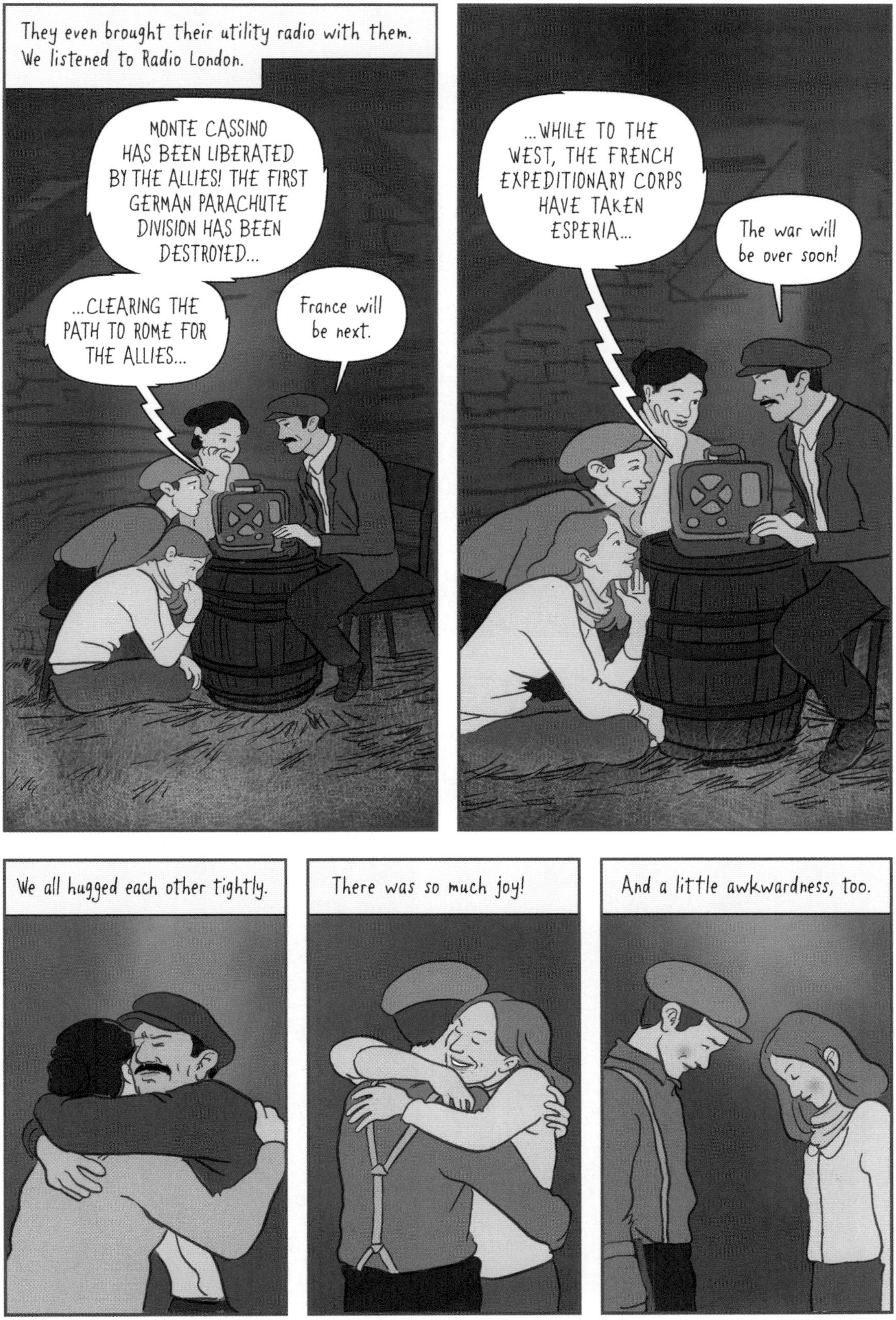
They even brought their utility radio with them. We listened to Radio London.
MONTE CASSINO HAS BEEN LIBERATED BY THE ALLIES! THE FIRST GERMAN PARACHUTE DIVISION HAS BEEN DESTROYED...
...CLEARING THE PATH TO ROME FOR THE ALLIES...
France will be next.
...WHILE TO THE WEST, THE FRENCH EXPEDITIONARY CORPS HAVE TAKEN ESPERIA...
The war will be over soon!
We all hugged each other tightly.
There was so much joy!
And a little awkwardness, too.

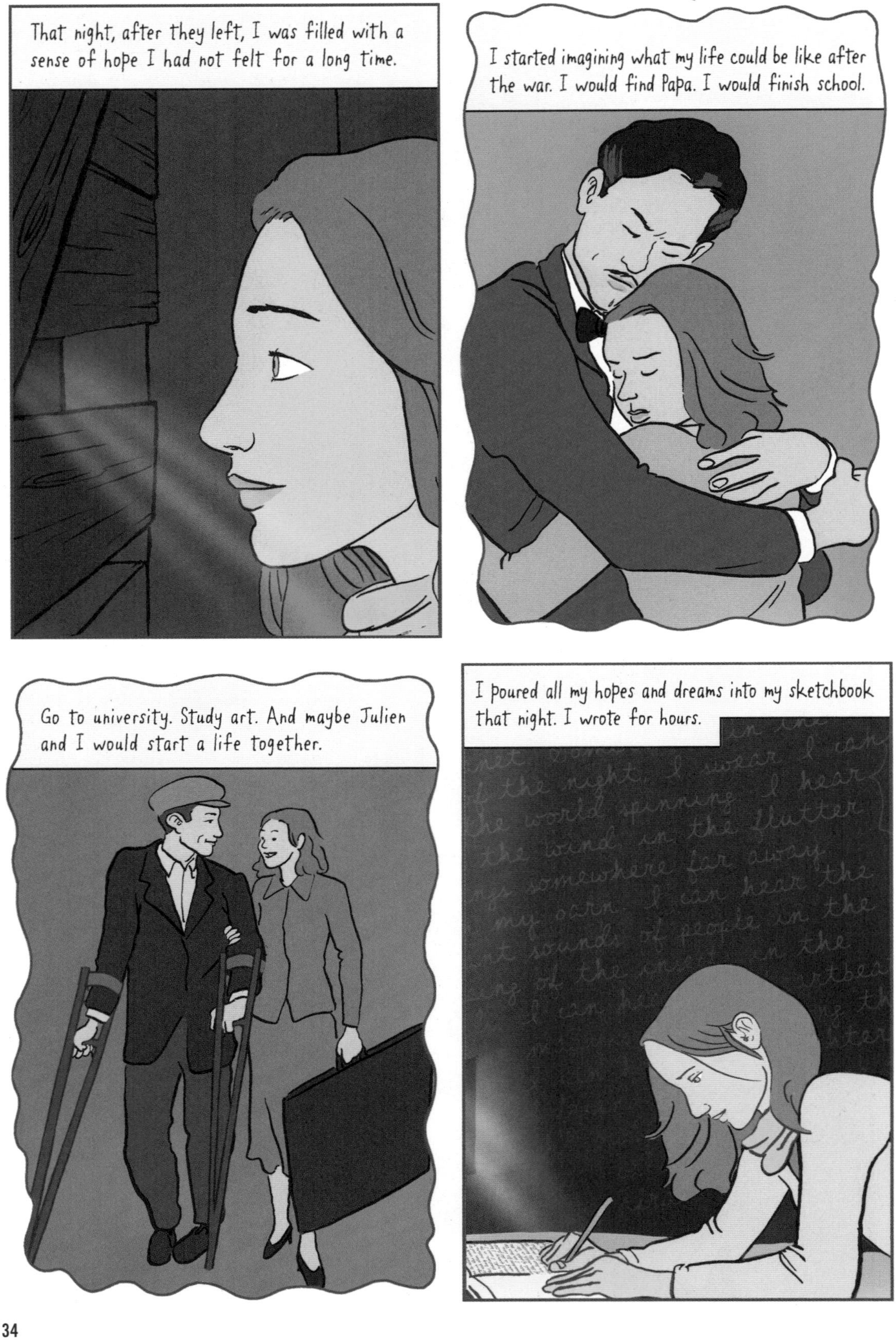
That night, after they left, I was filled with a sense of hope I had not felt for a long time.
I started imagining what my life could be like after the war. I would find Papa. I would finish school.
Go to university. Study art. And maybe Julien and I would start a life together.
I poured all my hopes and dreams into my sketchbook that night. I wrote for hours.

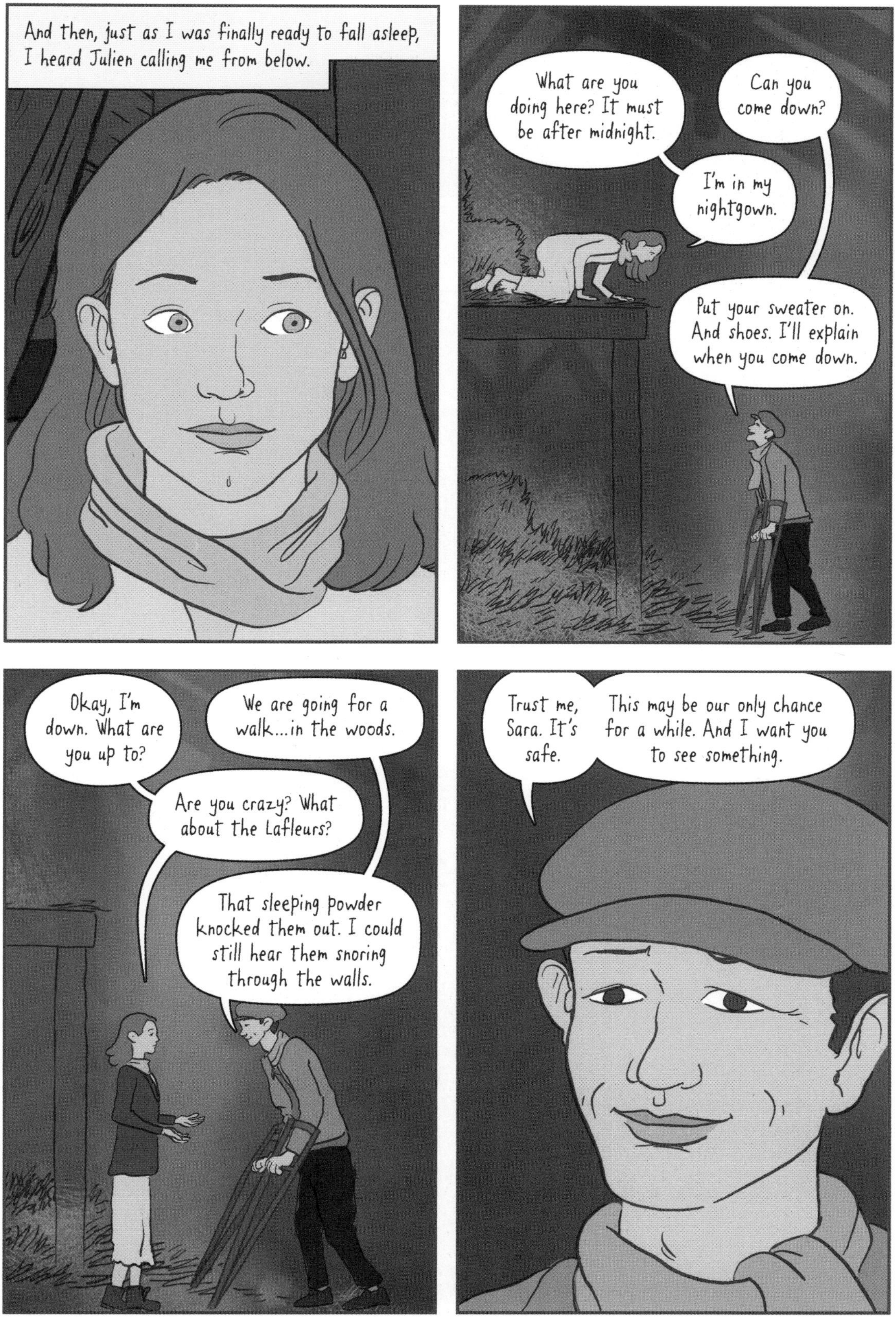
And then, just as I was finally ready to fall asleep, I heard Julien calling me from below.
What are you doing here? It must be after midnight.
Can you come down?
I'm in my nightgown.
Put your sweater on. And shoes. I'll explain when you come down.
Okay, I'm down. What are you up to?
We are going for a walk...in the woods.
Are you crazy? What about the Lafleurs?
That sleeping powder knocked them out. I could still hear them snoring through the walls.
Trust me, Sara. It's safe.
This may be our only chance for a while. And I want you to see something.

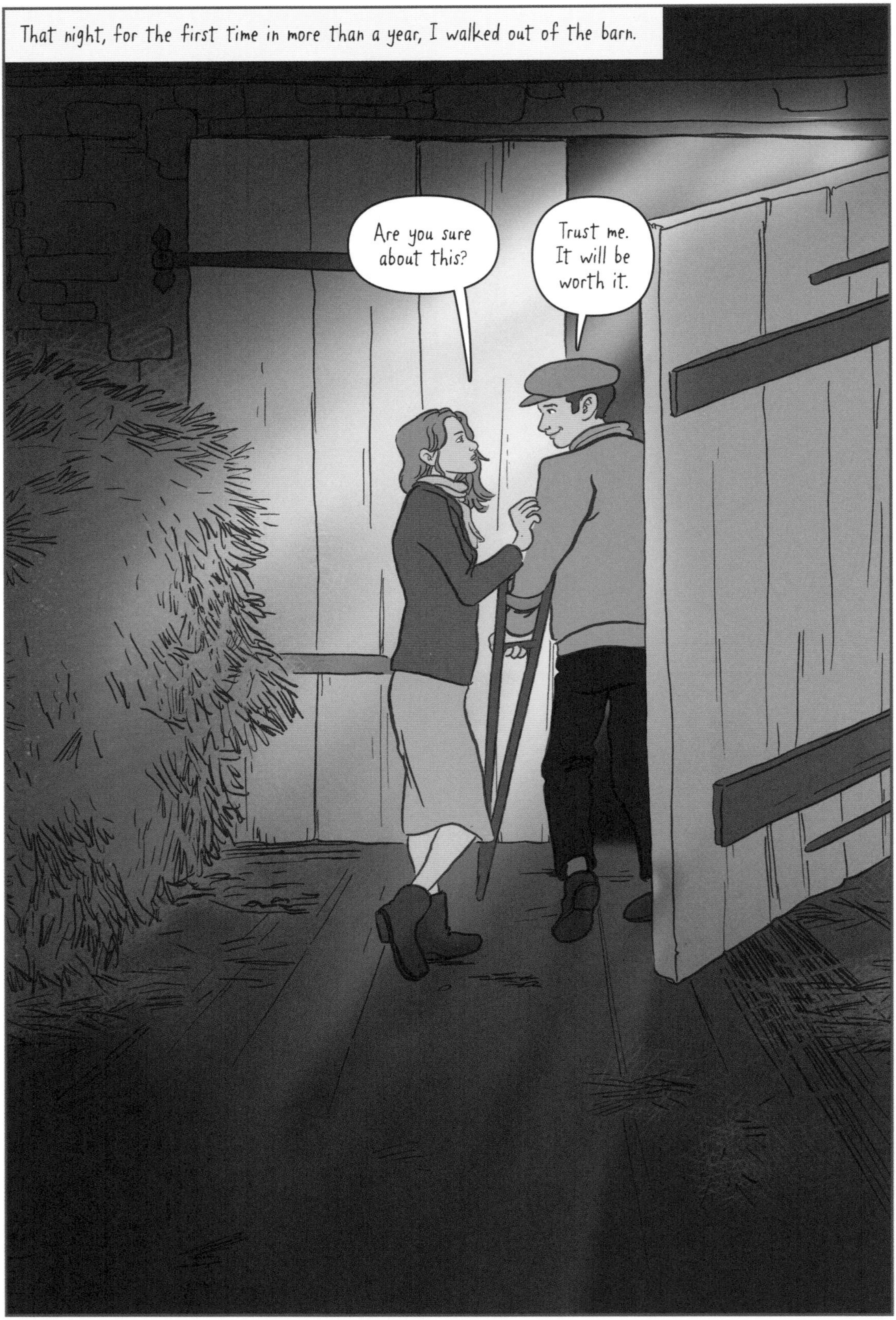
That night, for the first time in more than a year, I walked out of the barn.
Are you sure about this?
Trust me. It will be worth it.

MON DIEU, WAS HE RIGHT! IT WAS WORTH IT! YOU SEE, THE BLUEBELLS HAD JUST COME INTO BLOOM. THE FOREST FLOOR WAS LITERALLY SPARKLING IN THE MOONLIGHT.

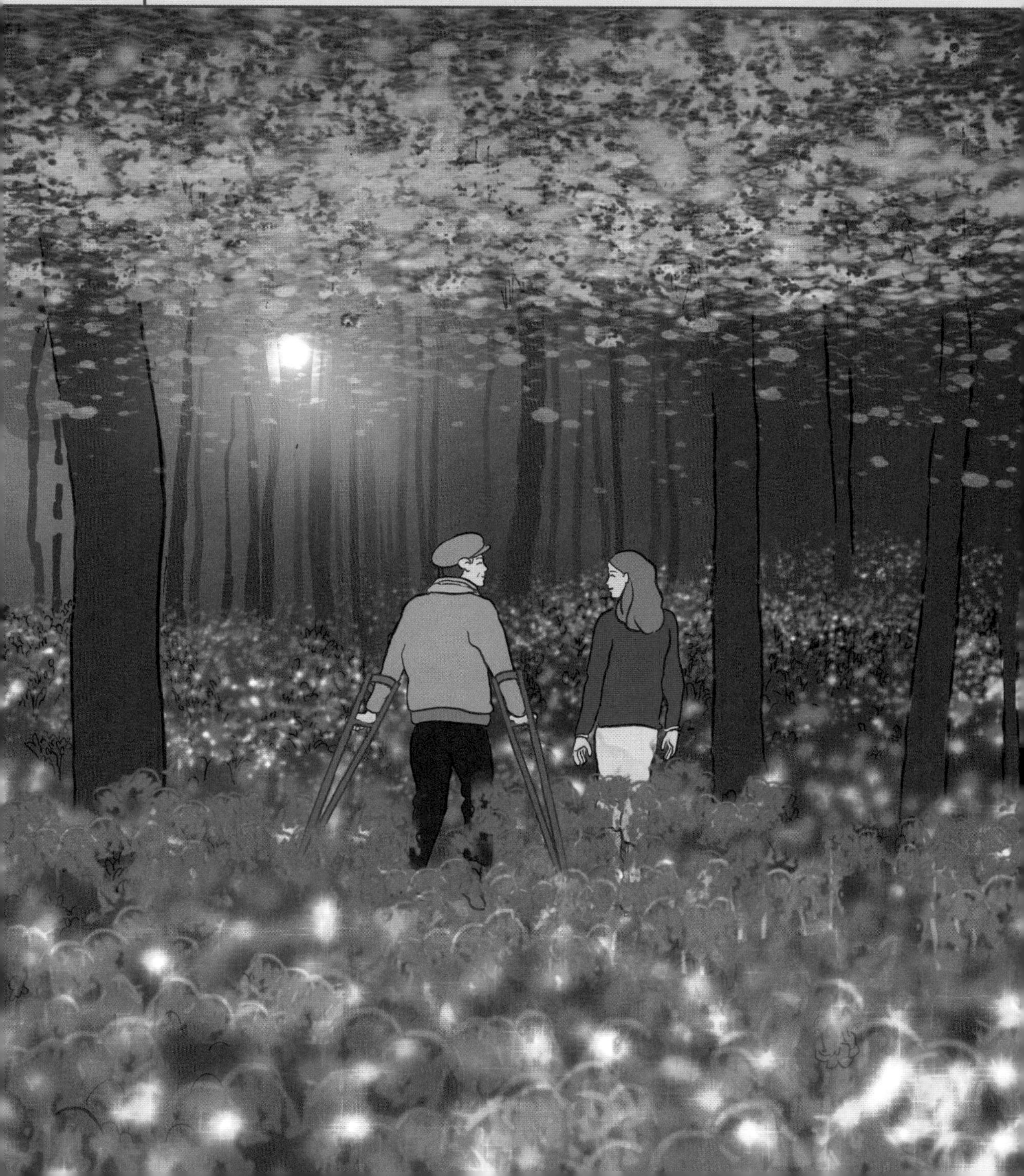

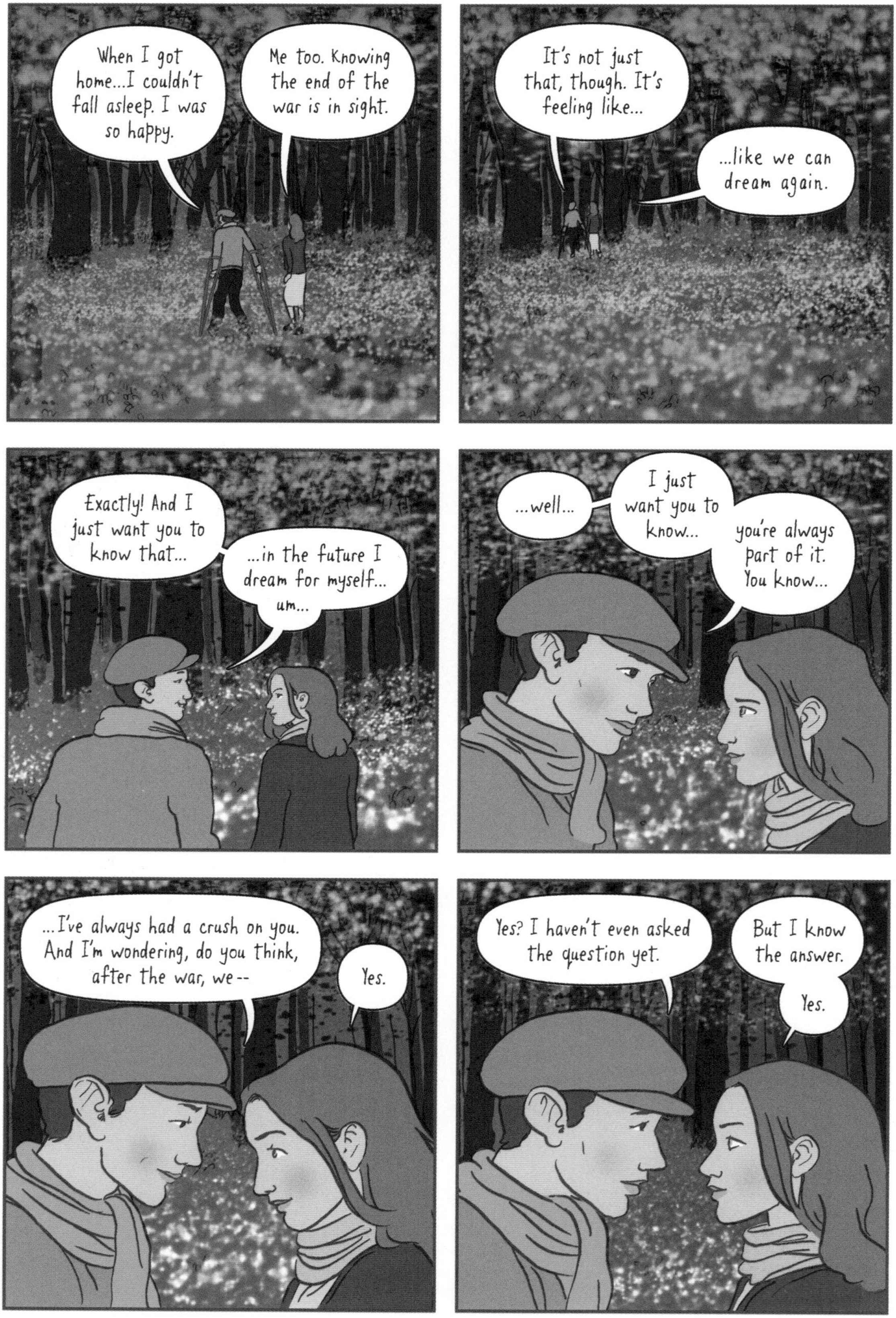
When I got home...I couldn't fall asleep. I was so happy.
Me too. Knowing the end of the war is in sight.
It's not just that, though. It's feeling like...
...like we can dream again.
Exactly! And I just want you to know that...
...in the future I dream for myself... um...
...well...
I just want you to know...
you're always part of it. You know...
...I've always had a crush on you. And I'm wondering, do you think, after the war, we--
Yes.
Yes? I haven't even asked the question yet.
But I know the answer.
Yes.

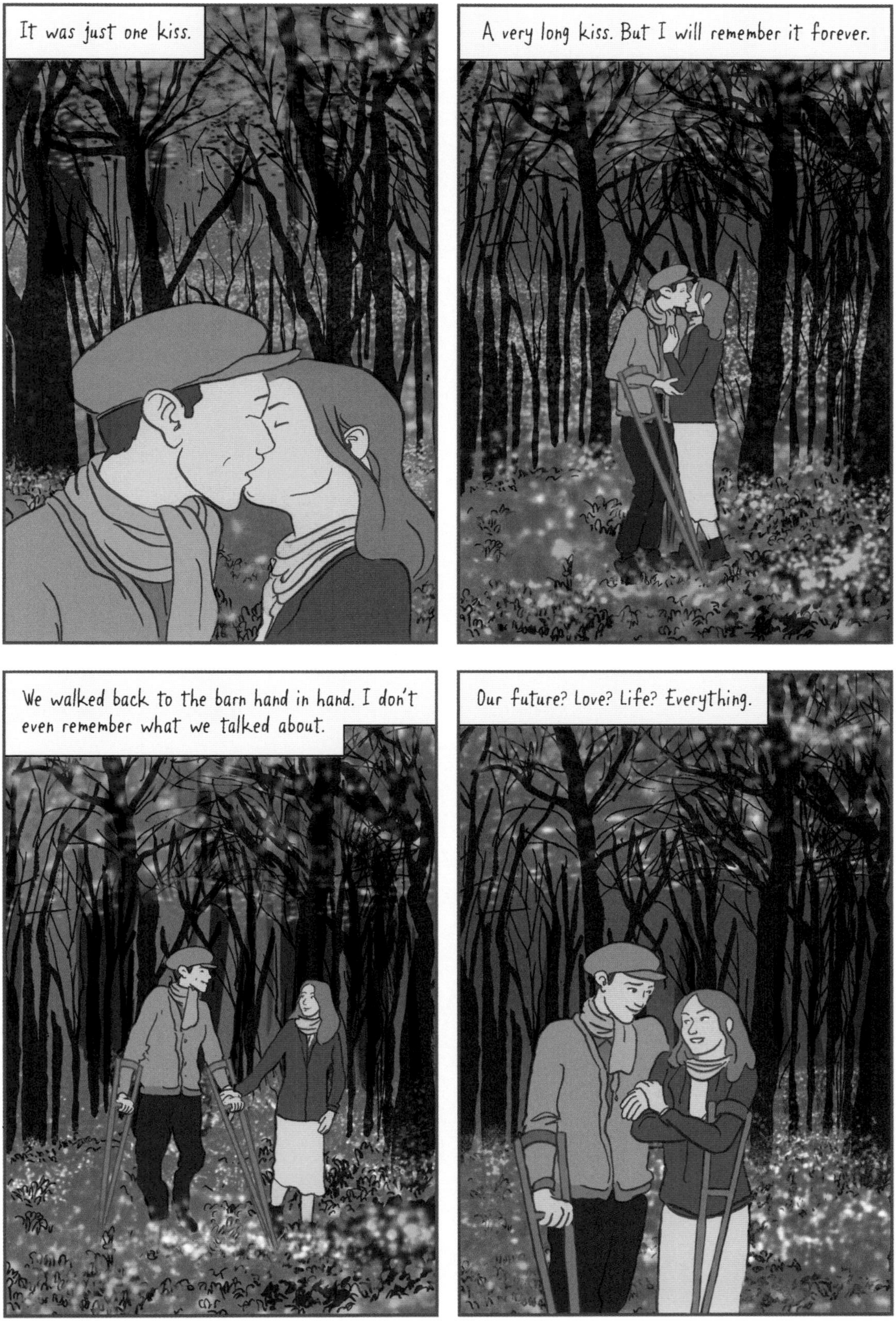
It was just one kiss.
A very long kiss. But I will remember it forever.
We walked back to the barn hand in hand. I don't even remember what we talked about.
Our future? Love? Life? Everything.

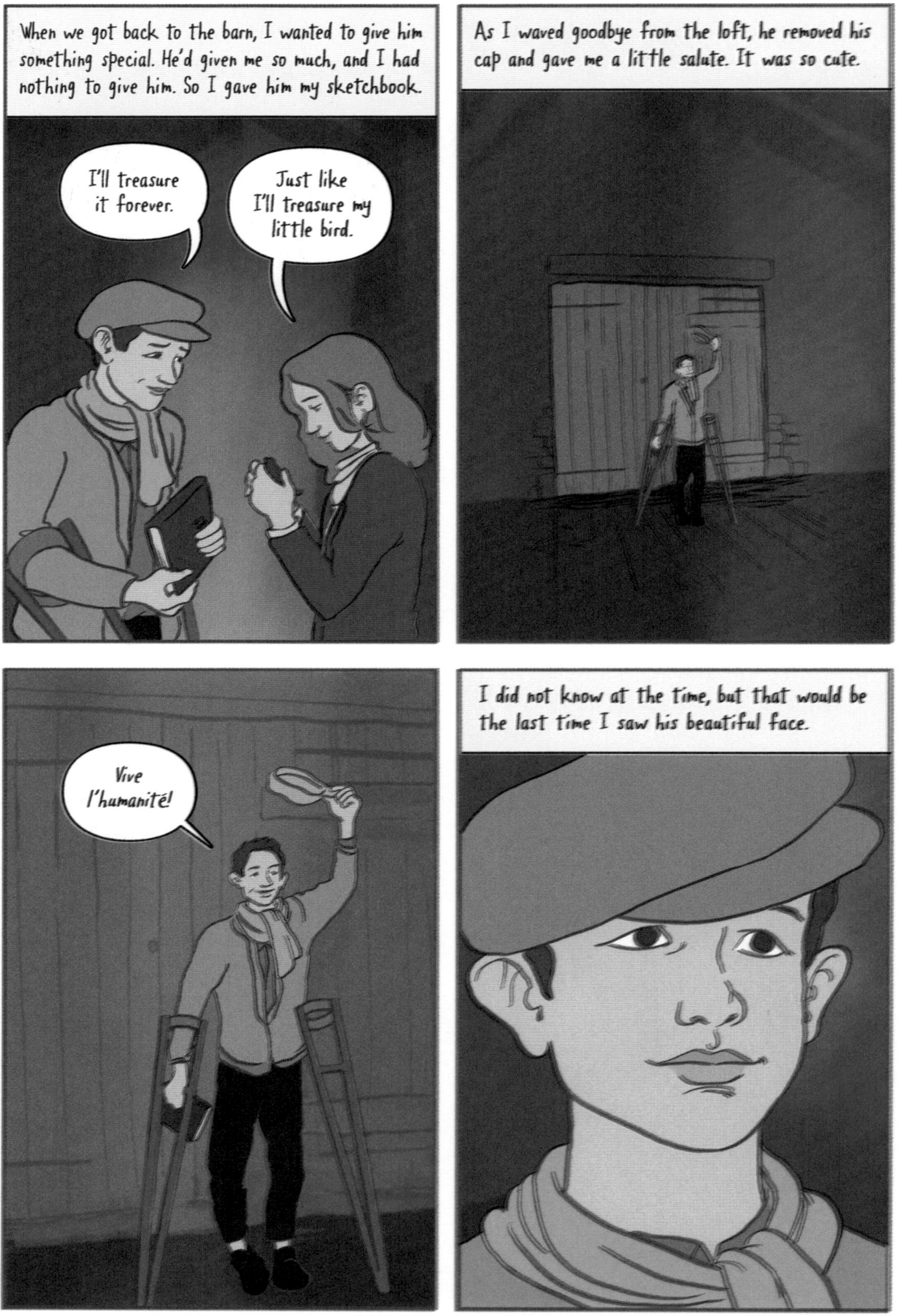
When we got back to the barn, I wanted to give him something special. He'd given me so much, and I had nothing to give him. So I gave him my sketchbook.
I'll treasure it forever.
Just like I'll treasure my little bird.
As I waved goodbye from the loft, he removed his cap and gave me a little salute. It was so cute.
Vive l'humanité!
I did not know at the time, but that would be the last time I saw his beautiful face.

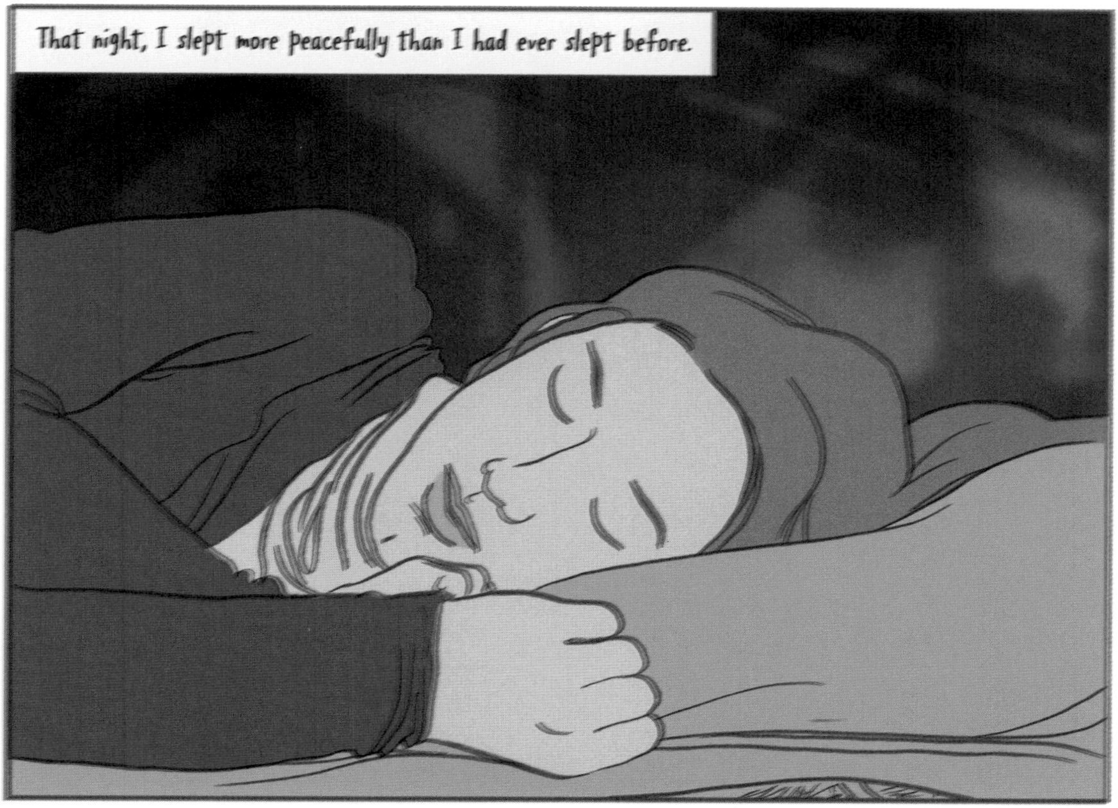
That night, I slept more peacefully than I had ever slept before.

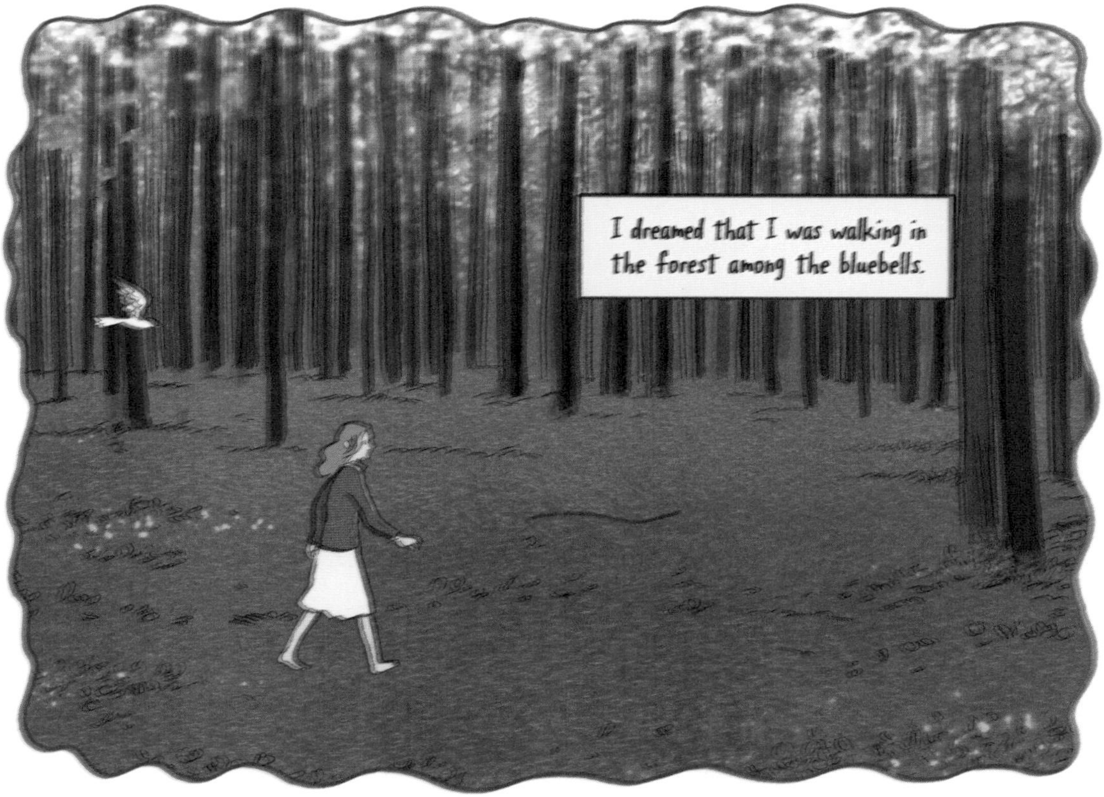
I dreamed that I was walking in the forest among the bluebells.

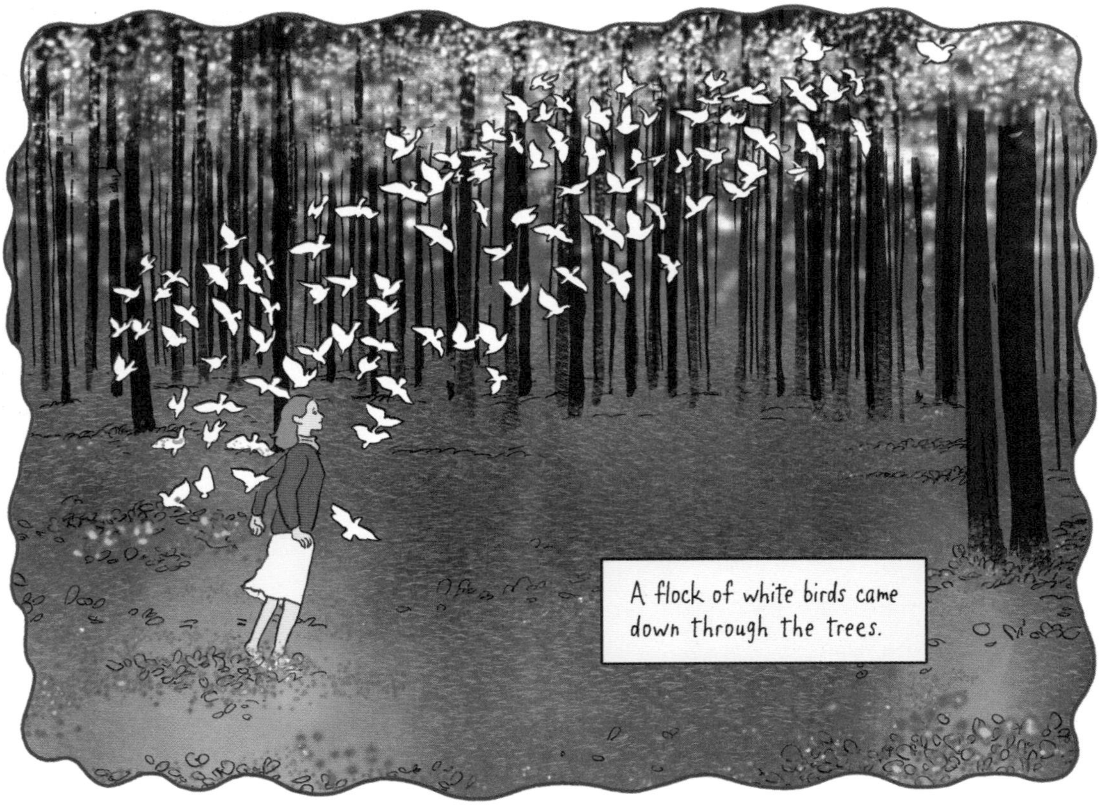
A flock of white birds came down through the trees.

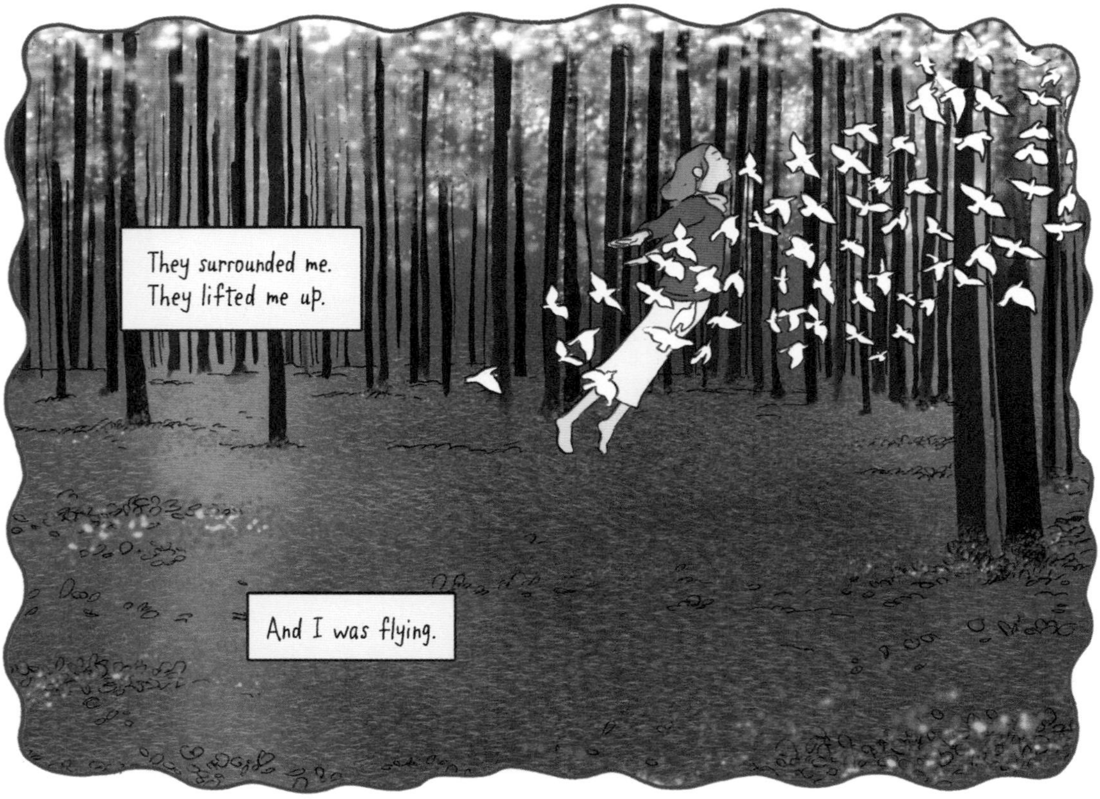
They surrounded me. They lifted me up.
And I was flying.

I HAD POURED MY HEART AND SOUL INTO MY SKETCHBOOK. THE TRUTH IS, I WANTED JULIEN TO READ IT. I WANTED HIM KNOW HOW I FELT ABOUT HIM.

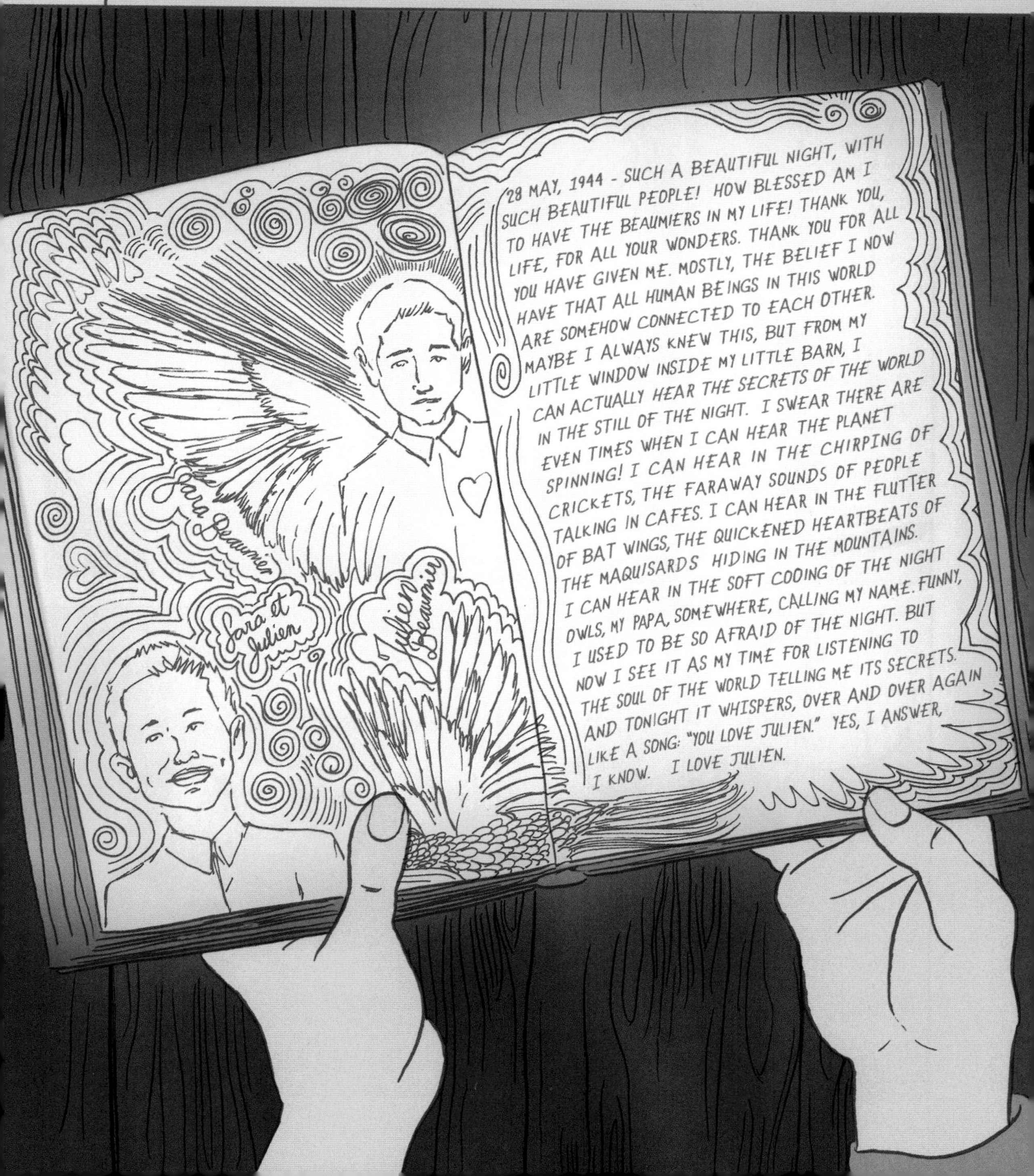
Sara Beaumier
Sara et Julien
Julien Beaumier
28 MAY, 1944 - SUCH A BEAUTIFUL NIGHT, WITH SUCH BEAUTIFUL PEOPLE! HOW BLESSED AM I TO HAVE THE BEAUMIERS IN MY LIFE! THANK YOU, LIFE, FOR ALL YOUR WONDERS. THANK YOU FOR ALL YOU HAVE GIVEN ME. MOSTLY, THE BELIEF I NOW HAVE THAT ALL HUMAN BEINGS IN THIS WORLD ARE SOMEHOW CONNECTED TO EACH OTHER. MAYBE I ALWAYS KNEW THIS, BUT FROM MY LITTLE WINDOW INSIDE MY LITTLE BARN, I CAN ACTUALLY HEAR THE SECRETS OF THE WORLD IN THE STILL OF THE NIGHT. I SWEAR THERE ARE EVEN TIMES WHEN I CAN HEAR THE PLANET SPINNING! I CAN HEAR IN THE CHIRPING OF CRICKETS, THE FARAWAY SOUNDS OF PEOPLE TALKING IN CAFES. I CAN HEAR IN THE FLUTTER OF BAT WINGS, THE QUICKENED HEARTBEATS OF THE MAQUISARDS HIDING IN THE MOUNTAINS. I CAN HEAR IN THE SOFT COOING OF THE NIGHT OWLS, MY PAPA, SOMEWHERE, CALLING MY NAME. FUNNY, I USED TO BE SO AFRAID OF THE NIGHT. BUT NOW I SEE IT AS MY TIME FOR LISTENING TO THE SOUL OF THE WORLD TELLING ME ITS SECRETS. AND TONIGHT IT WHISPERS, OVER AND OVER AGAIN LIKE A SONG: "YOU LOVE JULIEN." YES, I ANSWER, I KNOW. I LOVE JULIEN.

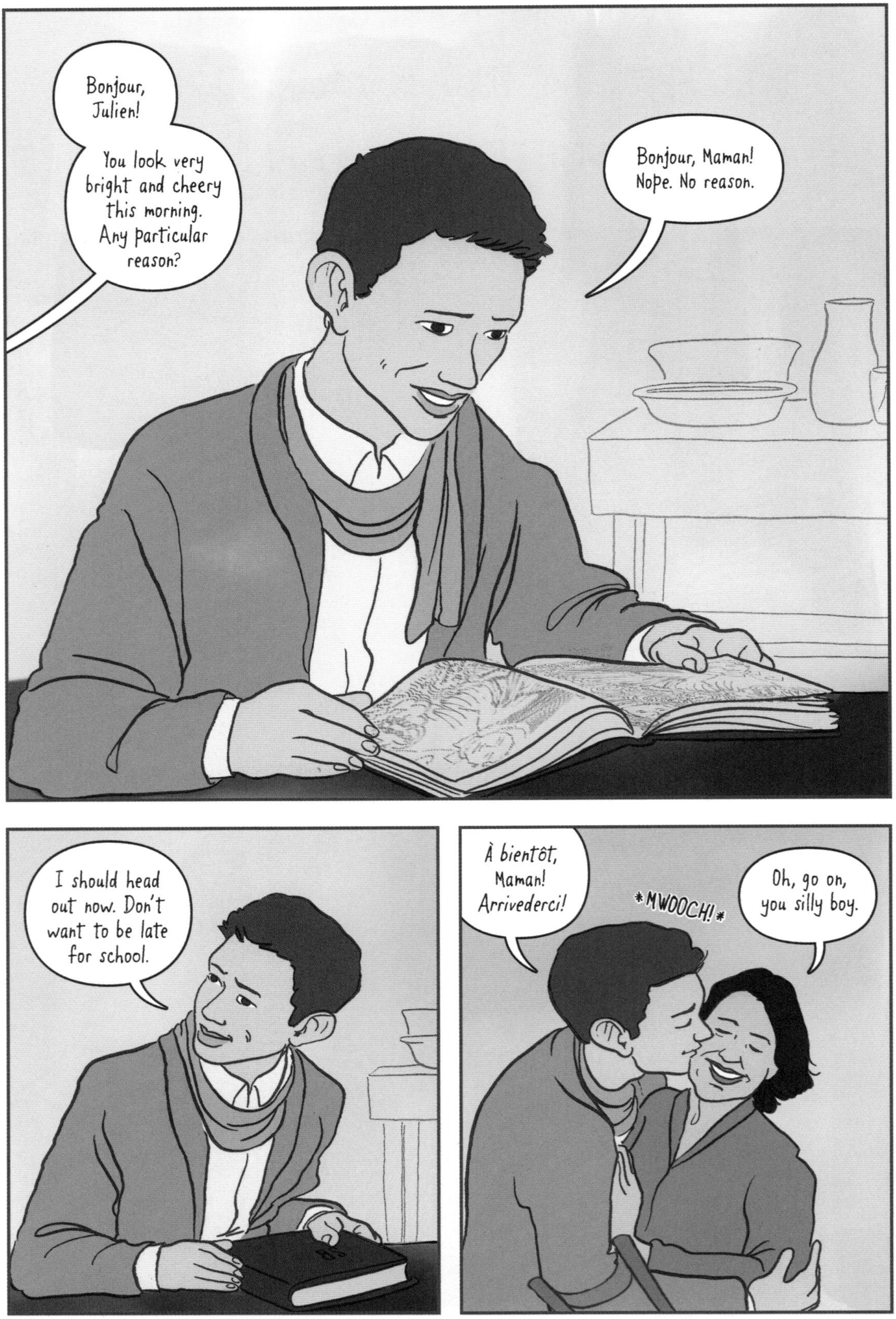
Bonjour, Julien!
You look very bright and cheery this morning. Any particular reason?
Bonjour, Maman! Nope. No reason.
I should head out now. Don't want to be late for school.
À bientôt, Maman! Arrivederci!
MWOOCH!
Oh, go on, you silly boy.

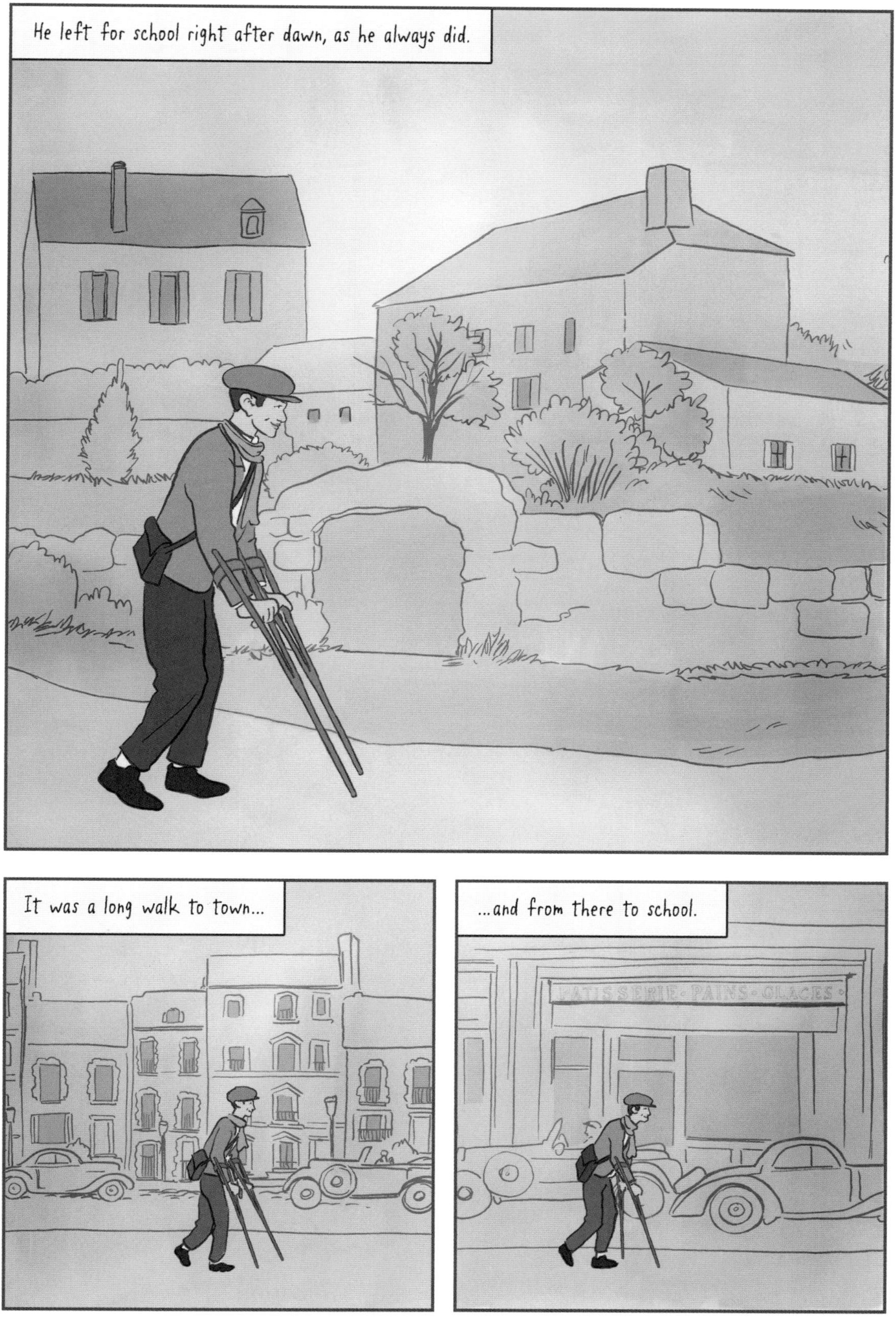
He left for school right after dawn, as he always did.
It was a long walk to town...
...and from there to school.
PATISSERIE·PAINS·GLACES

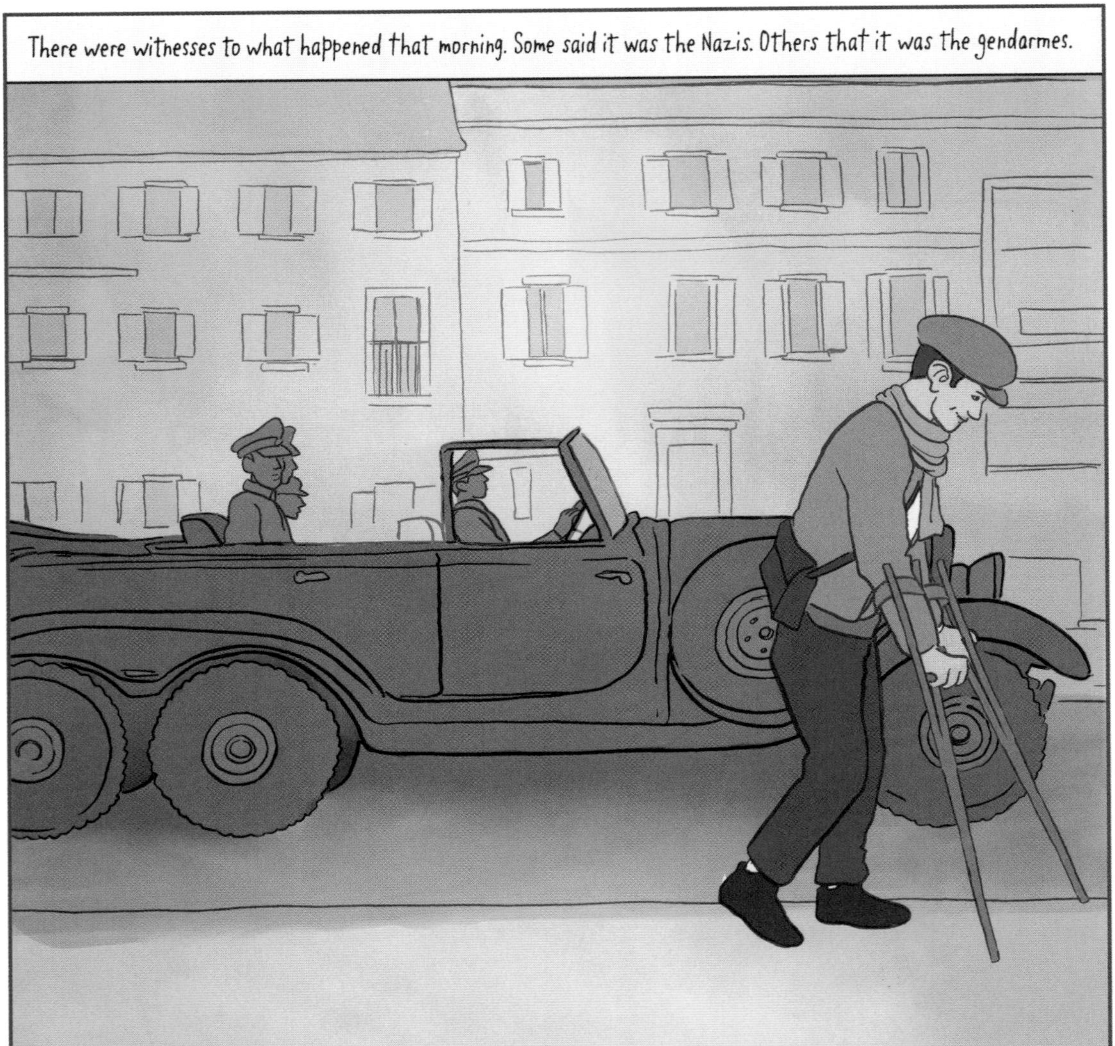
There were witnesses to what happened that morning. Some said it was the Nazis. Others that it was the gendarmes.

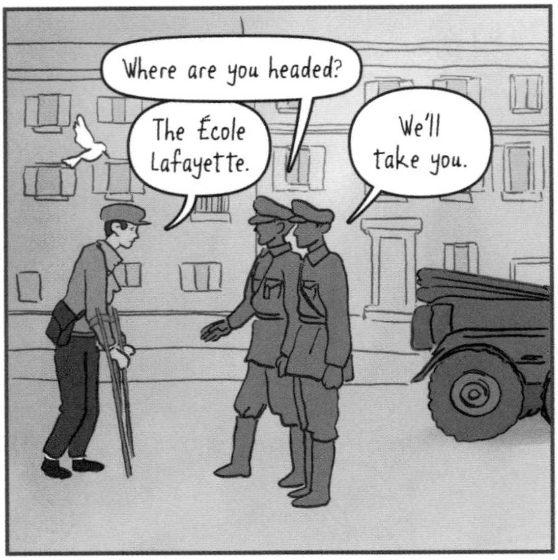
Where are you headed?
The École Lafayette.
We'll take you.

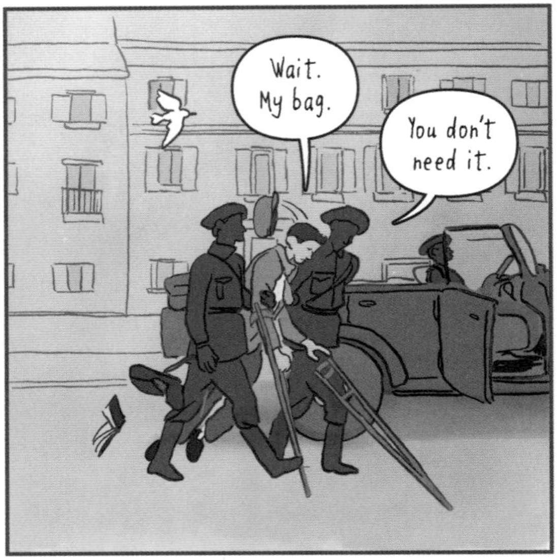
Wait. My bag.
You don't need it.

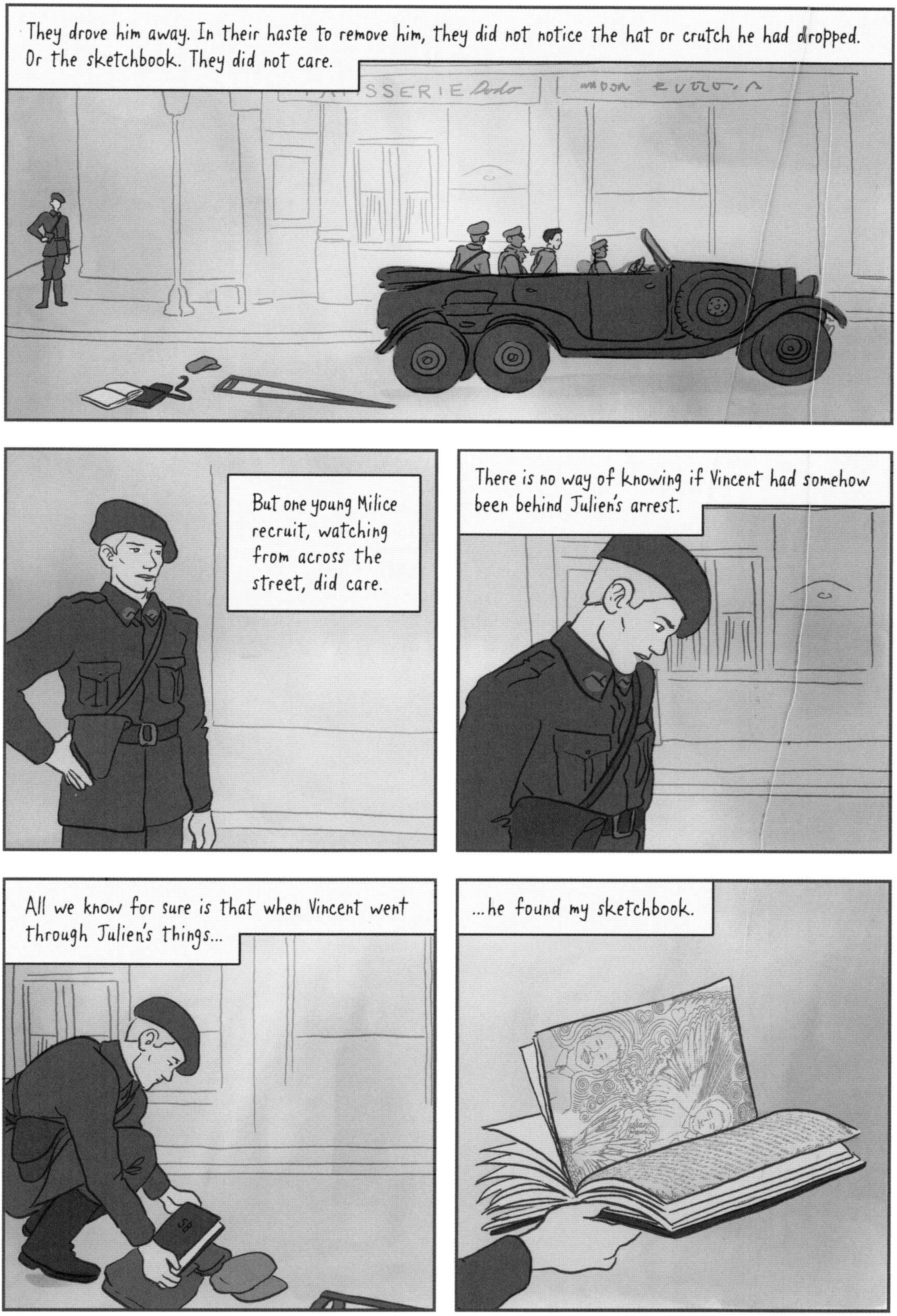
They drove him away. In their haste to remove him, they did not notice the hat or crutch he had dropped. Or the sketchbook. They did not care.
But one young Milice recruit, watching from across the street, did care.
There is no way of knowing if Vincent had somehow been behind Julien's arrest.
All we know for sure is that when Vincent went through Julien's things...
...he found my sketchbook.

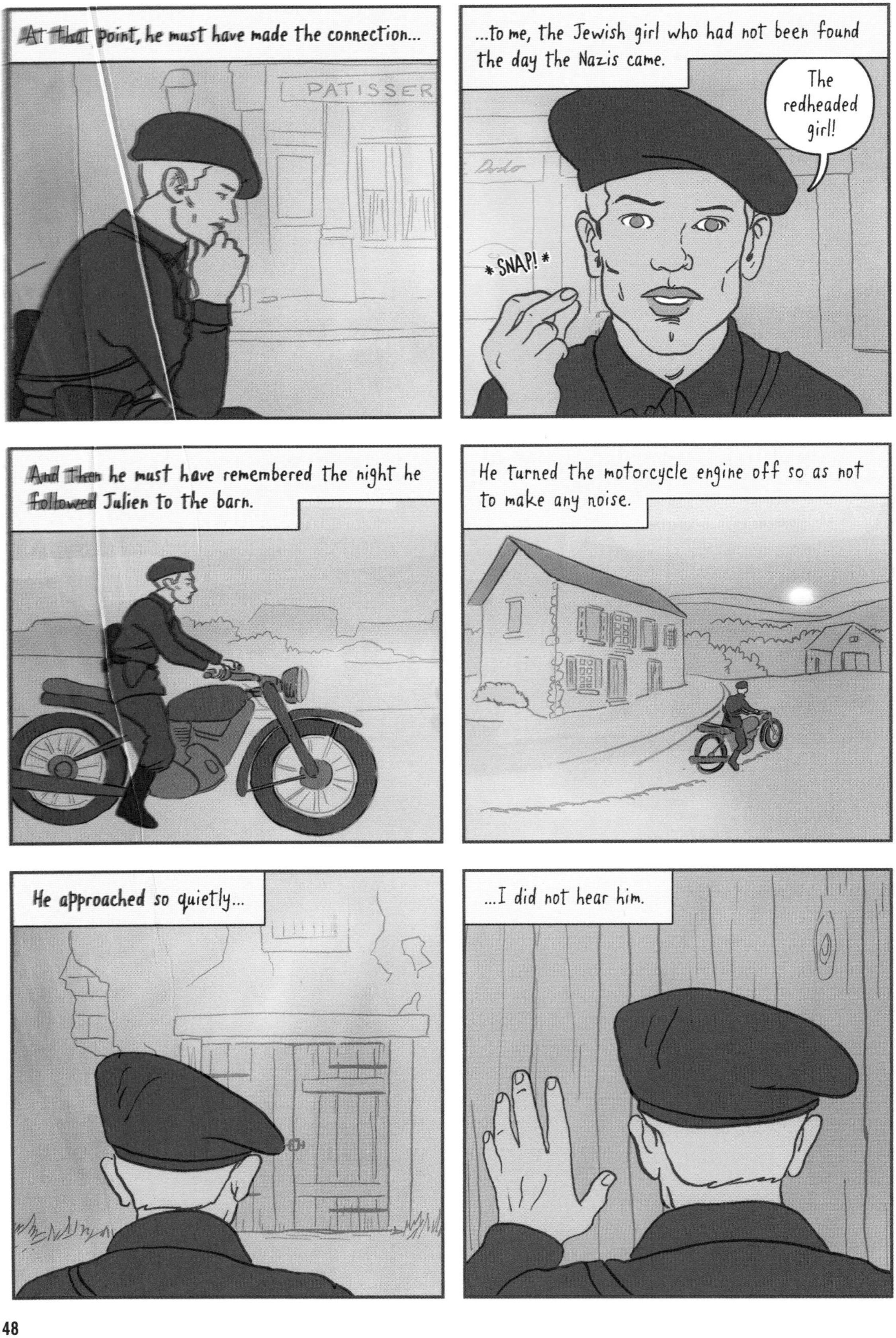
At that point, he must have made the connection...
PATISSER
...to me, the Jewish girl who had not been found the day the Nazis came.
The redheaded girl!
SNAP!
And then he must have remembered the night he followed Julien to the barn.
He turned the motorcycle engine off so as not to make any noise.
He approached so quietly...
...I did not hear him.

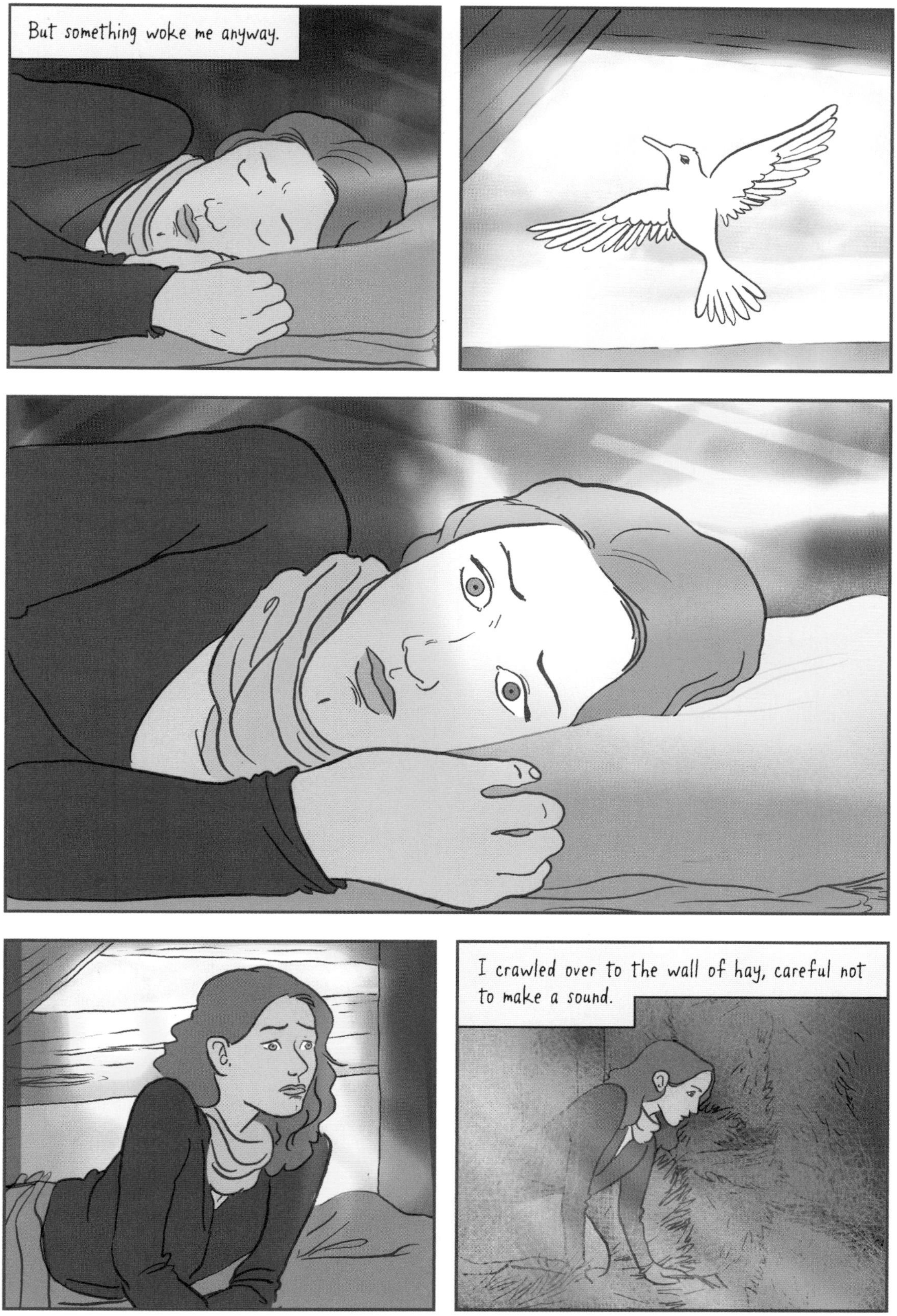
But something woke me anyway.
I crawled over to the wall of hay, careful not to make a sound.

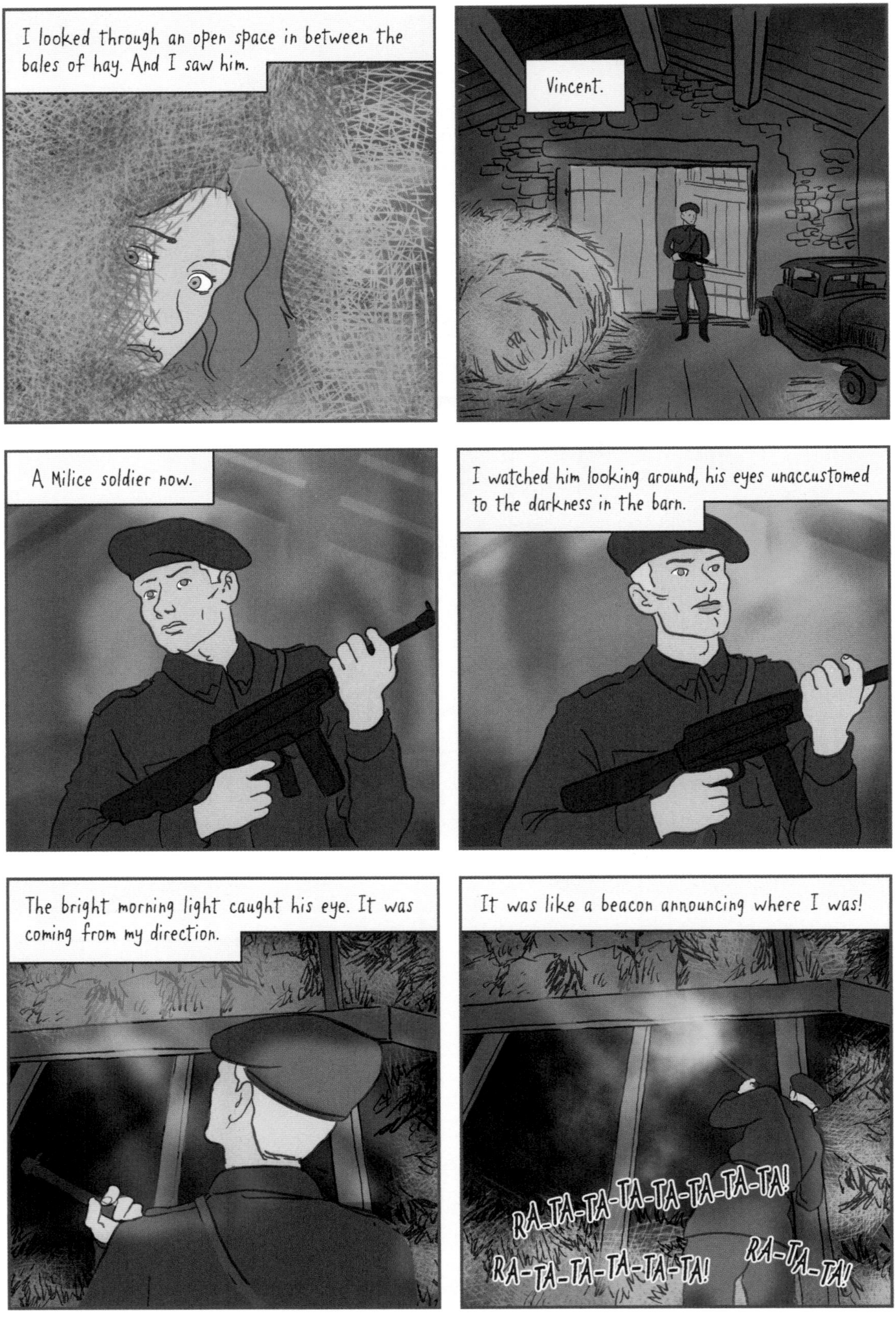
I looked through an open space in between the bales of hay. And I saw him.
Vincent.
A Milice soldier now.
I watched him looking around, his eyes unaccustomed to the darkness in the barn.
The bright morning light caught his eye. It was coming from my direction.
It was like a beacon announcing where I was!
RA-TA-TA-TA-TA-TA-TA-TA!
RA-TA-TA-TA-TA-TA!
RA-TA-TA!

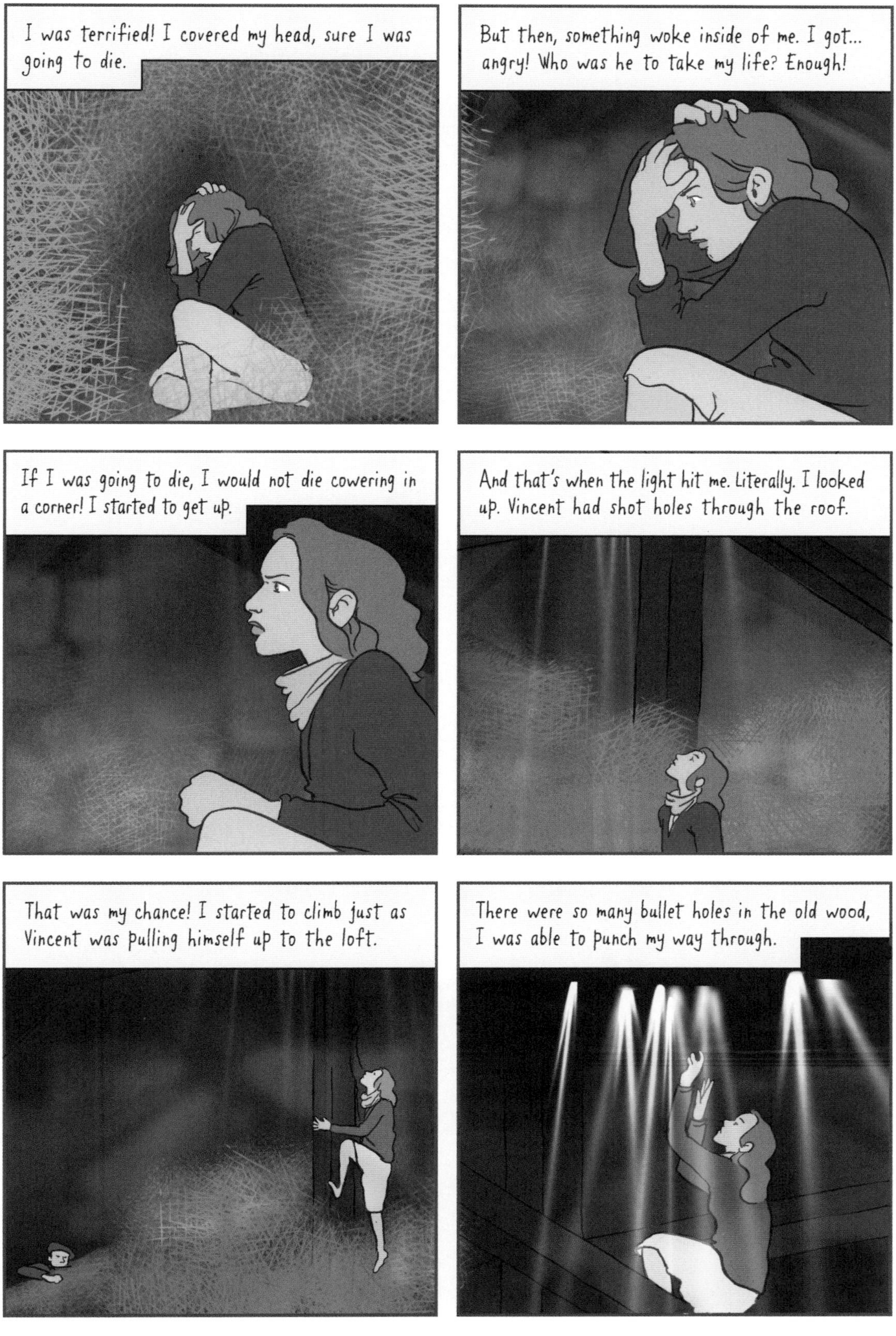
I was terrified! I covered my head, sure I was going to die.
But then, something woke inside of me. I got... angry! Who was he to take my life? Enough!
If I was going to die, I would not die cowering in a corner! I started to get up.
And that's when the light hit me. Literally. I looked up. Vincent had shot holes through the roof.
That was my chance! I started to climb just as Vincent was pulling himself up to the loft.
There were so many bullet holes in the old wood, I was able to punch my way through.

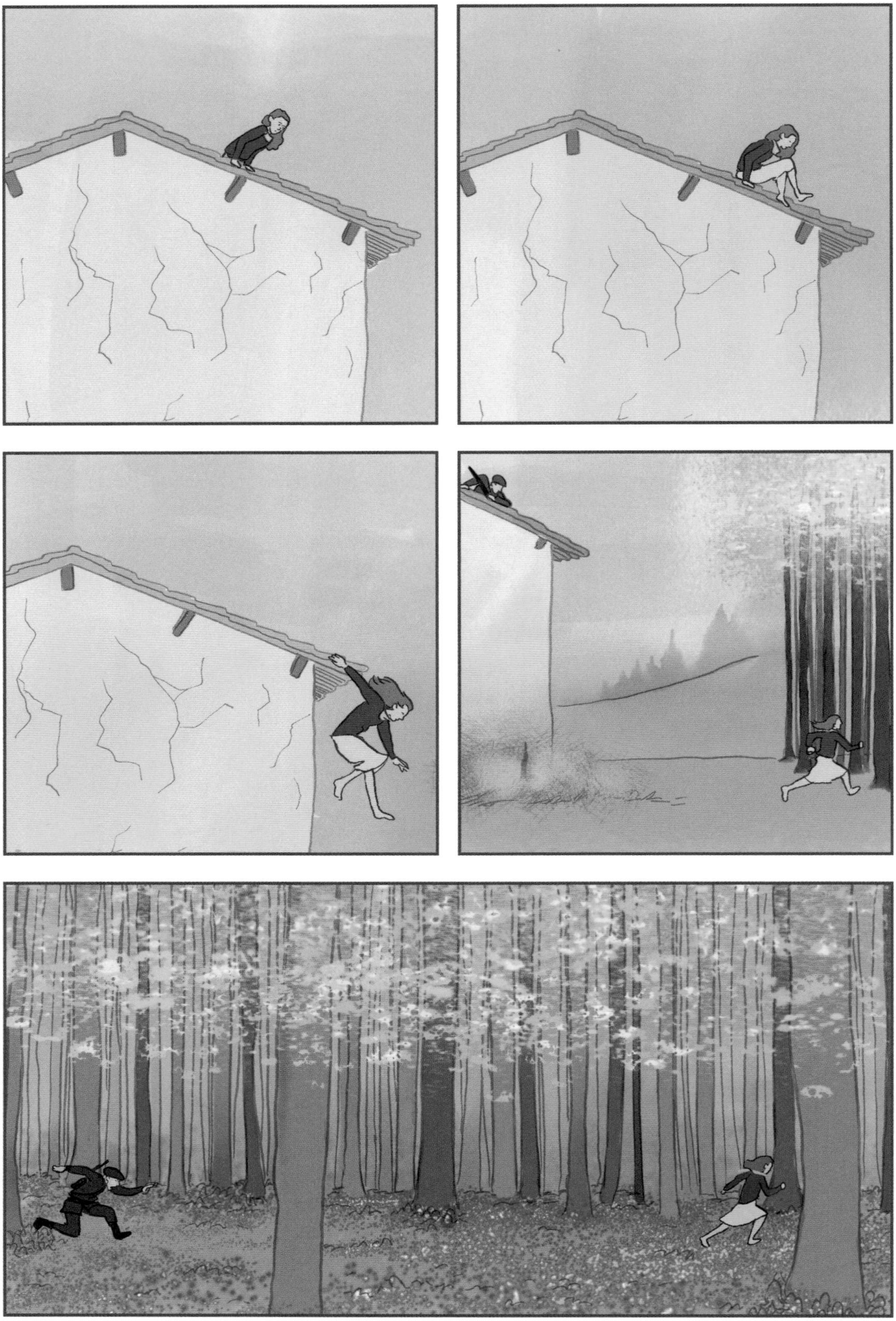

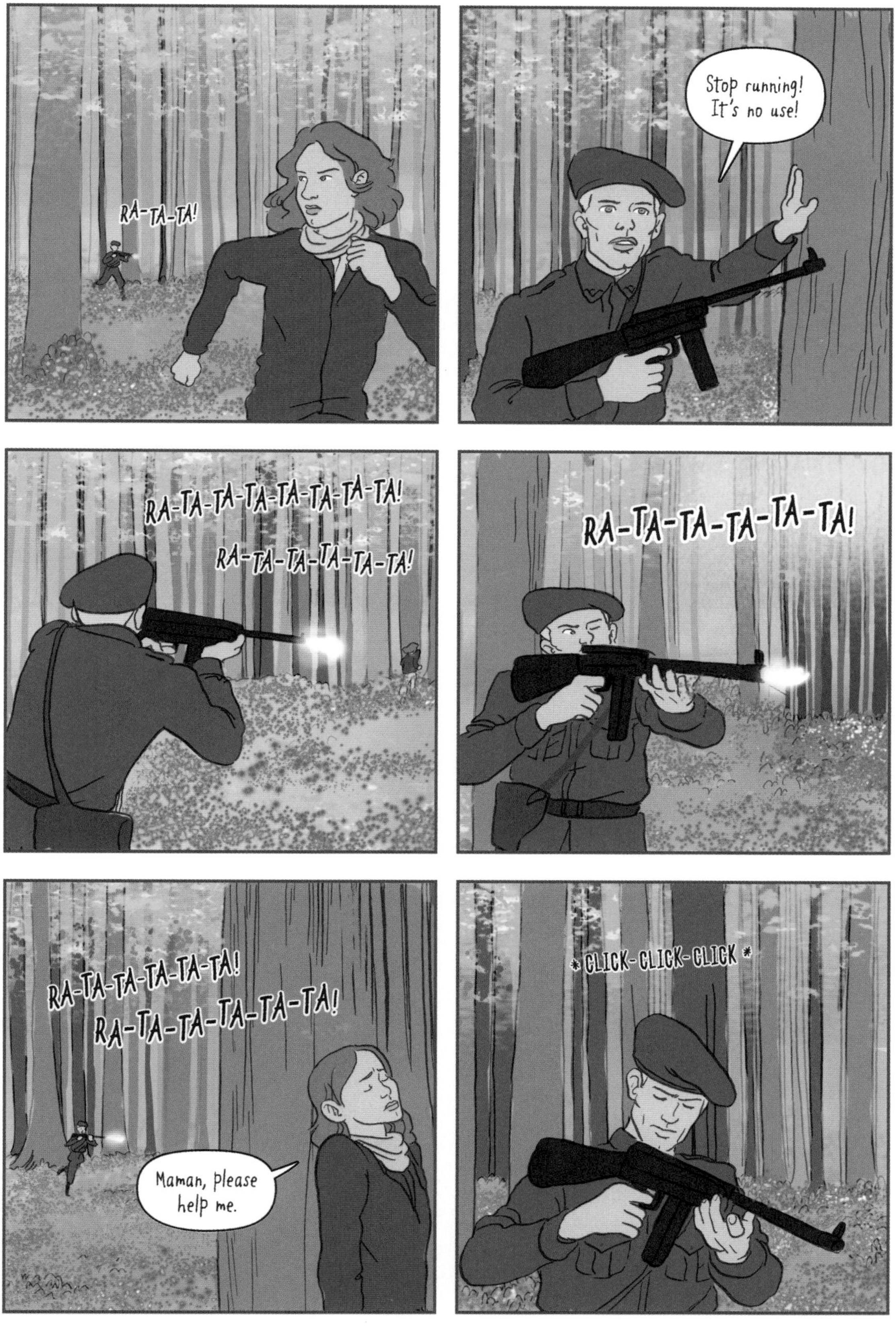
RA-TA-TA!
Stop running! It's no use!
RA-TA-TA-TA-TA-TA-TA-TA!
RA-TA-TA-TA-TA-TA!
RA-TA-TA-TA-TA-TA!
RA-TA-TA-TA-TA-TA!
RA-TA-TA-TA-TA-TA!
Maman, please help me.
* CLICK-CLICK-CLICK *

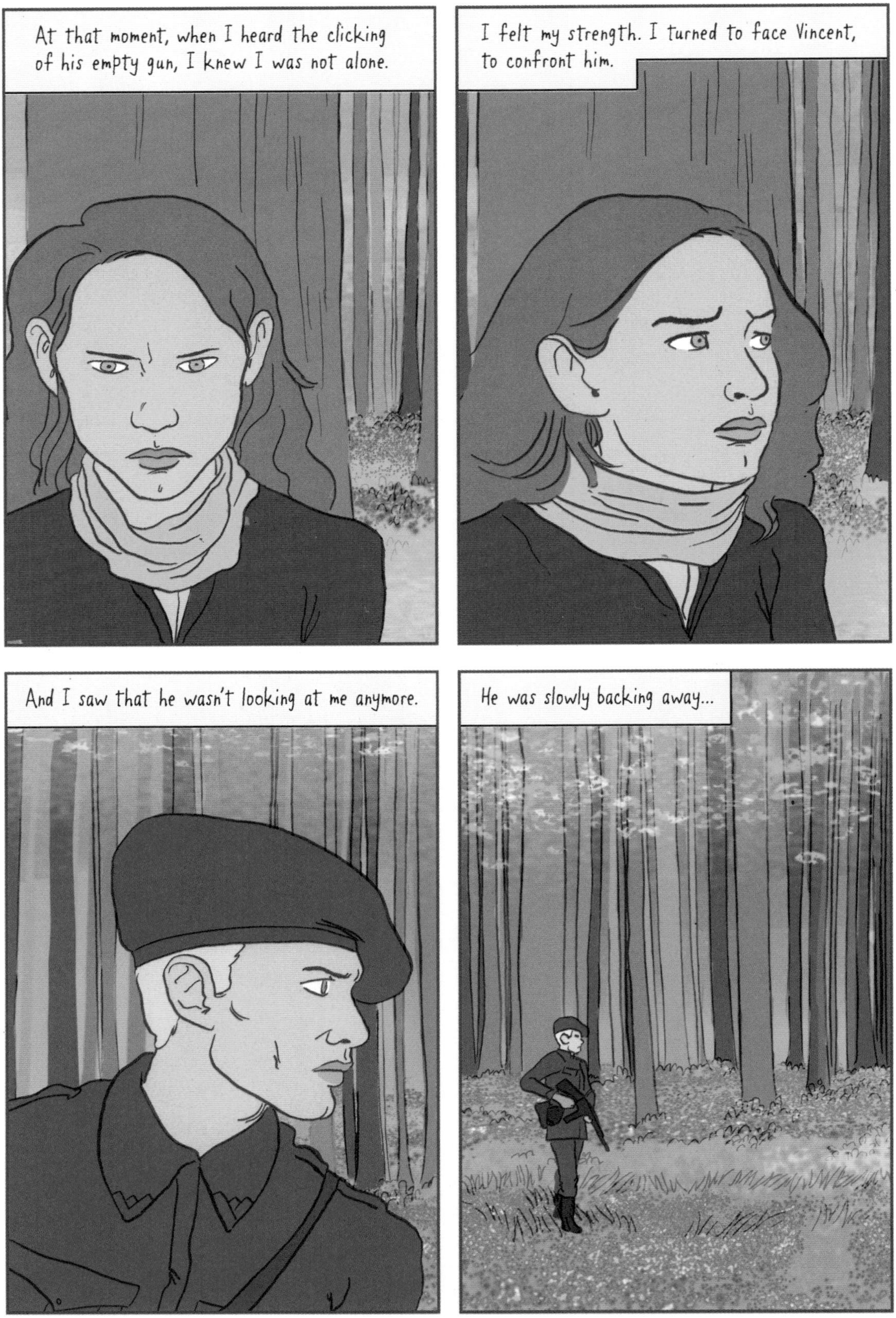
At that moment, when I heard the clicking of his empty gun, I knew I was not alone.
I felt my strength. I turned to face Vincent, to confront him.
And I saw that he wasn't looking at me anymore.
He was slowly backing away...

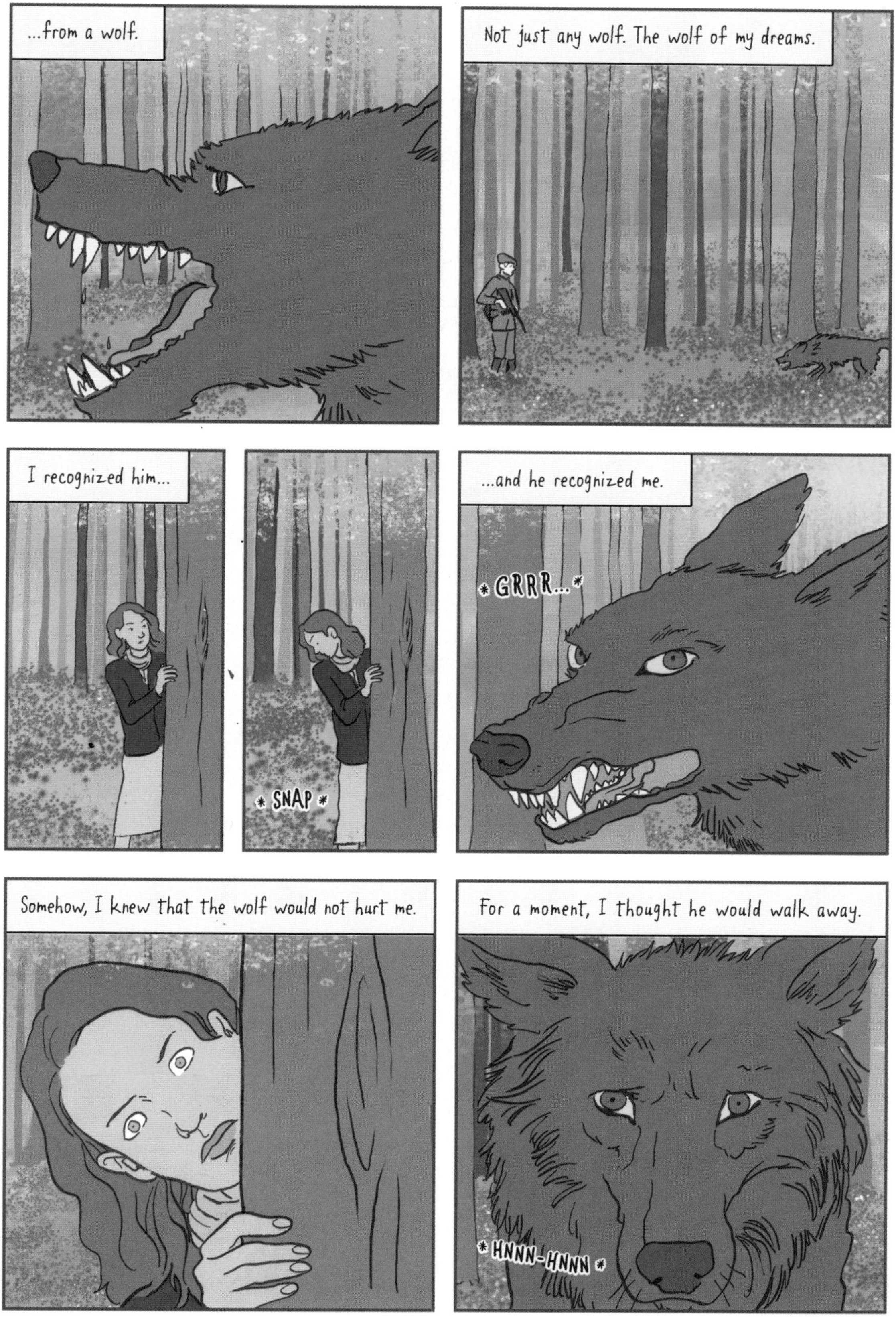
...from a wolf.
Not just any wolf. The wolf of my dreams.
I recognized him...
* SNAP *
...and he recognized me.
* GRRR... *
Somehow, I knew that the wolf would not hurt me.
For a moment, I thought he would walk away.
* HNNN-HNNN *

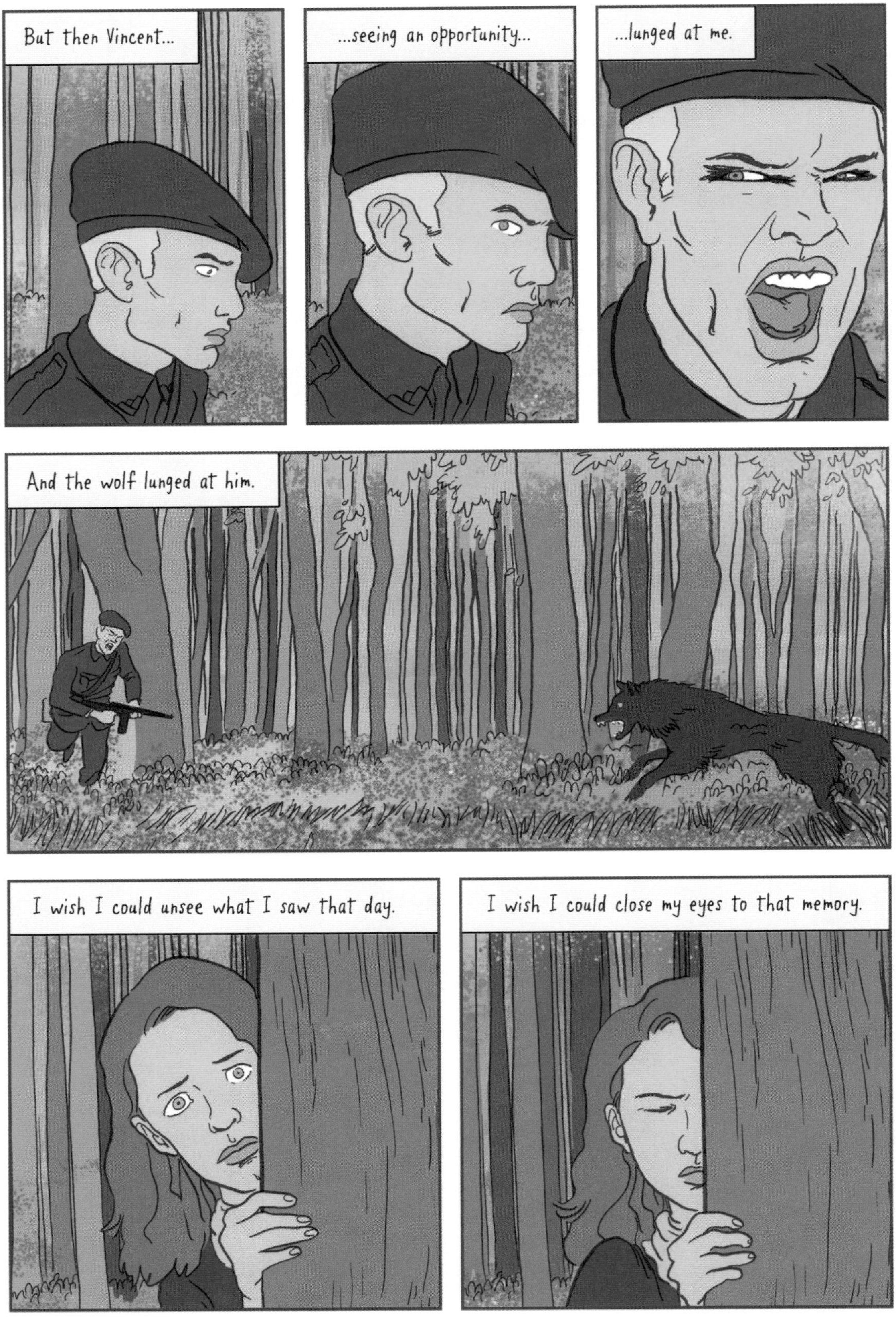
But then Vincent...
...seeing an opportunity...
...lunged at me.
And the wolf lunged at him.
I wish I could unsee what I saw that day.
I wish I could close my eyes to that memory.

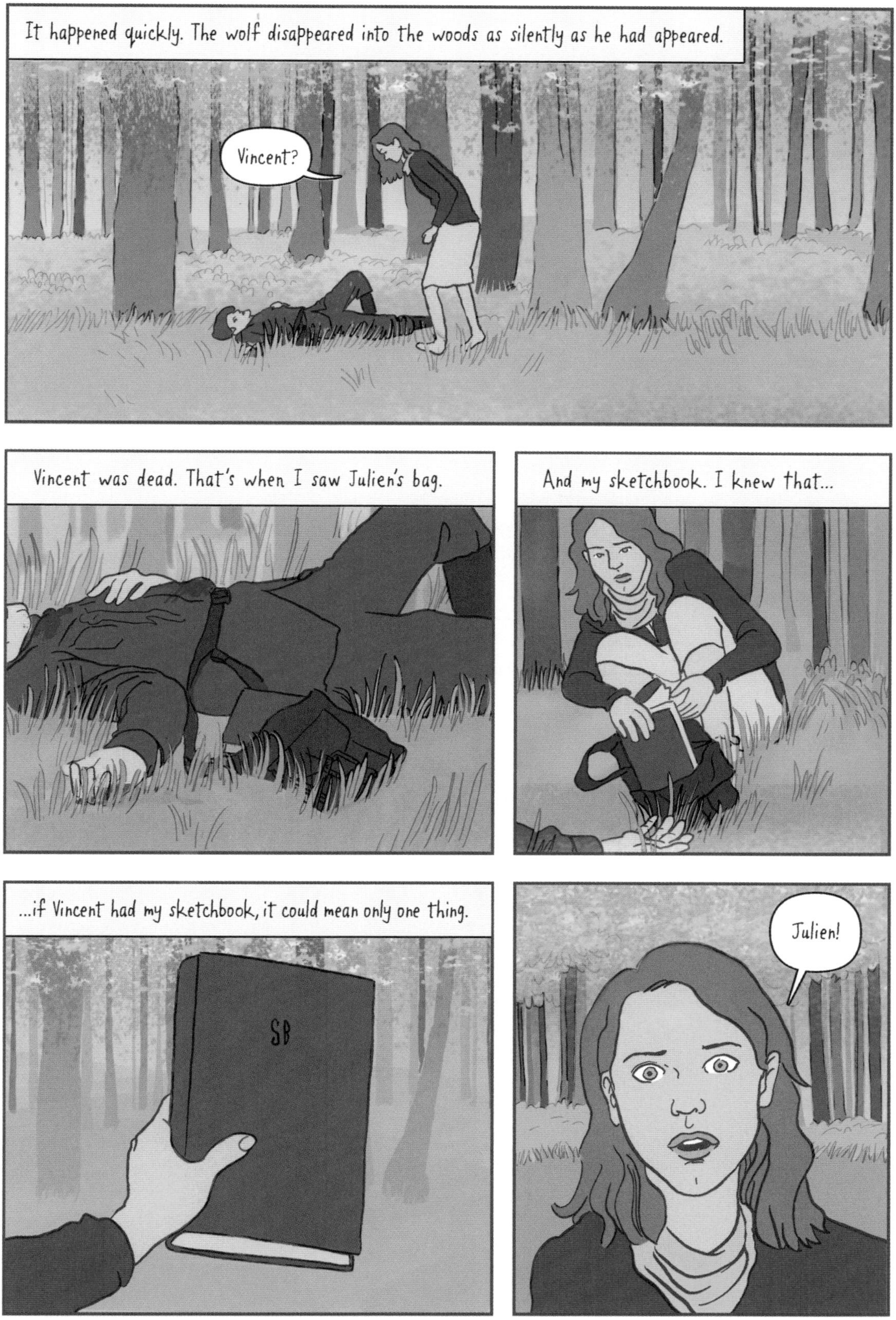
It happened quickly. The wolf disappeared into the woods as silently as he had appeared.
Vincent?
Vincent was dead. That's when I saw Julien's bag.
And my sketchbook. I knew that...
...if Vincent had my sketchbook, it could mean only one thing.
SB
Julien!

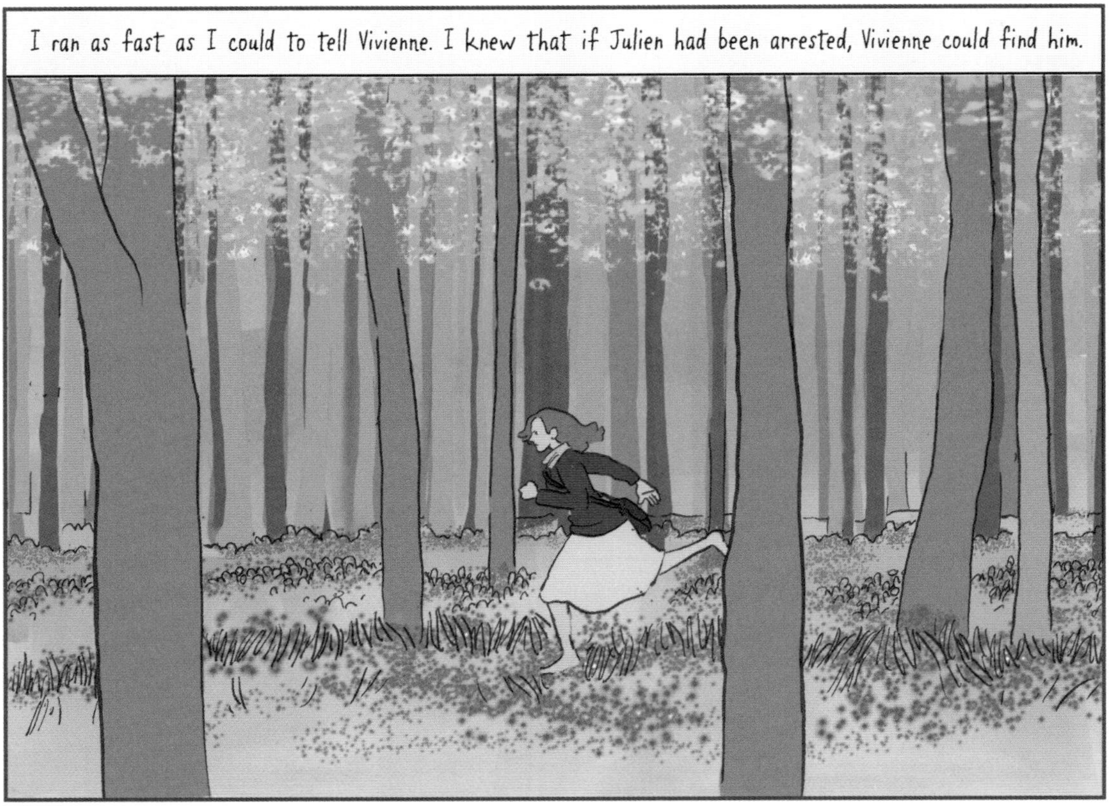
I ran as fast as I could to tell Vivienne. I knew that if Julien had been arrested, Vivienne could find him.

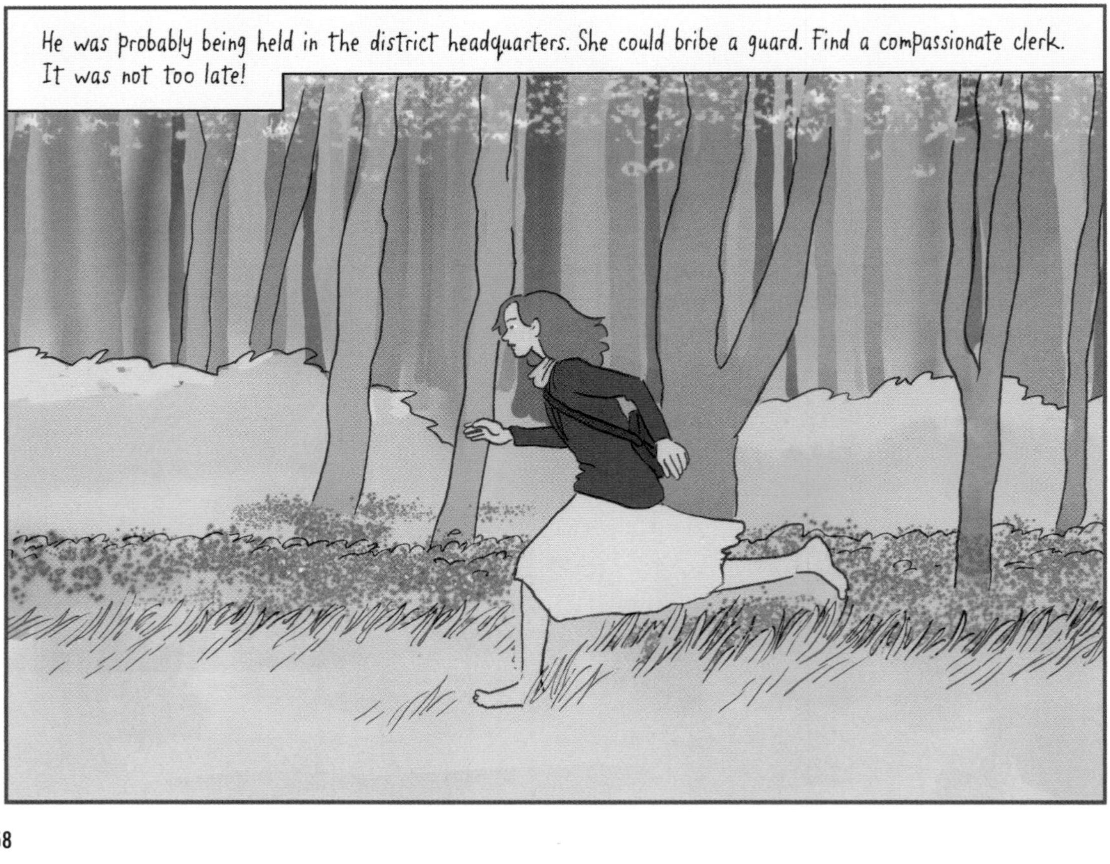
He was probably being held in the district headquarters. She could bribe a guard. Find a compassionate clerk. It was not too late!

CHAPTER 4

I RAN AS FAST AS I HAD EVER RUN IN MY ENTIRE LIFE. I DID NOT EVEN REALIZE THAT MY FEET WERE ALL CUT UP FROM RUNNING THROUGH THE WOODS.

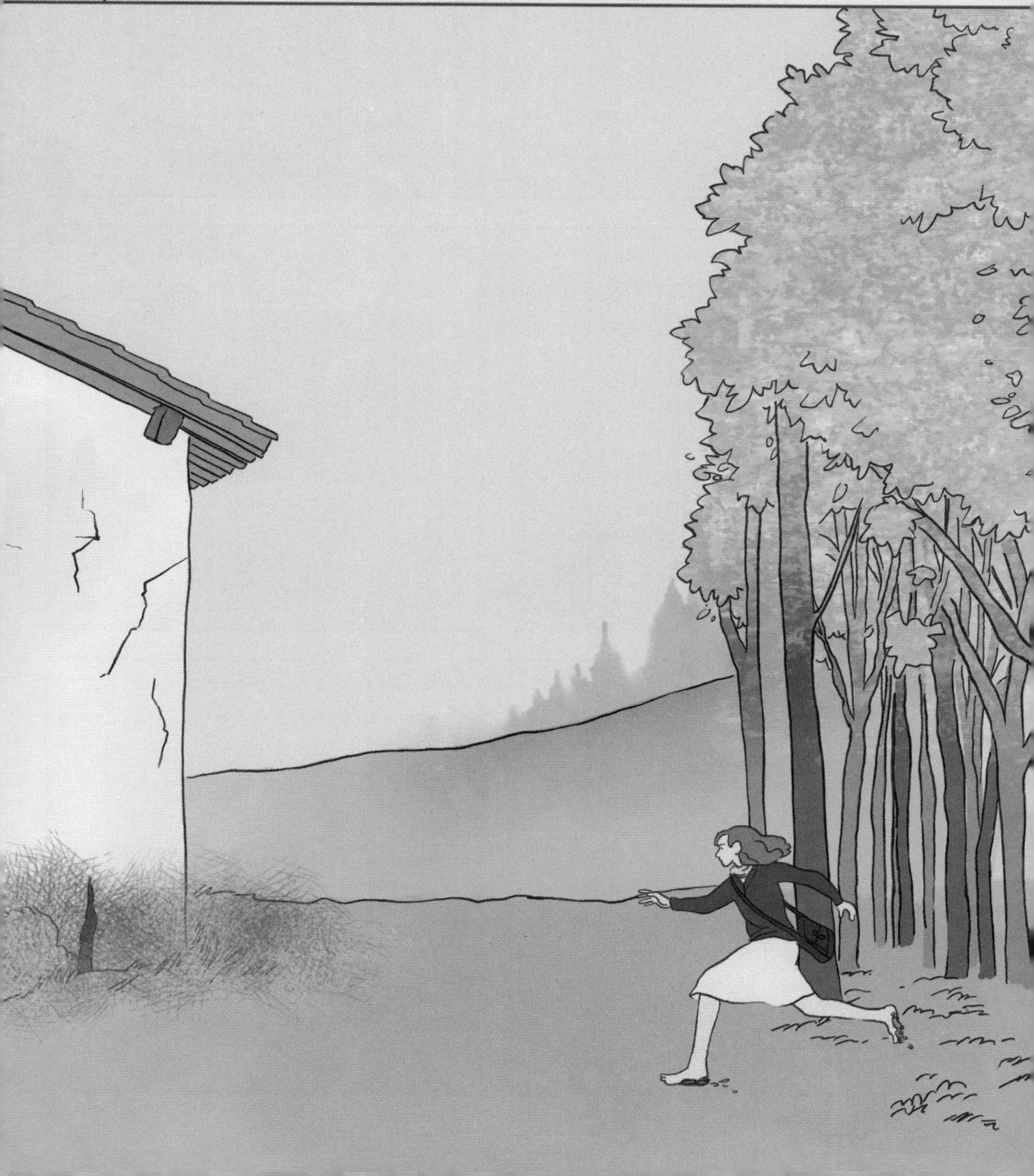

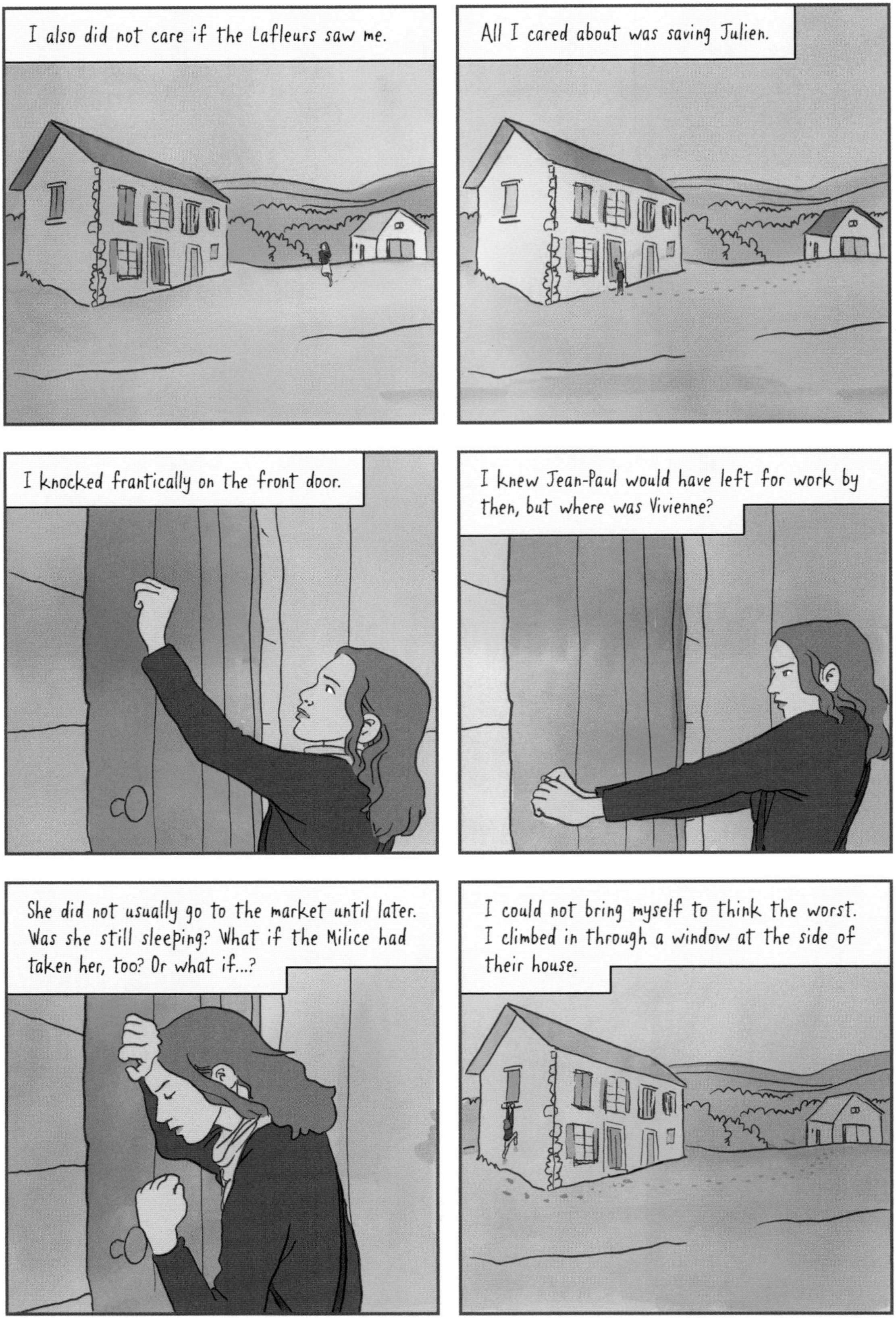
I also did not care if the Lafleurs saw me.
All I cared about was saving Julien.
I knocked frantically on the front door.
I knew Jean-Paul would have left for work by then, but where was Vivienne?
She did not usually go to the market until later. Was she still sleeping? What if the Milice had taken her, too? Or what if...?
I could not bring myself to think the worst. I climbed in through a window at the side of their house.

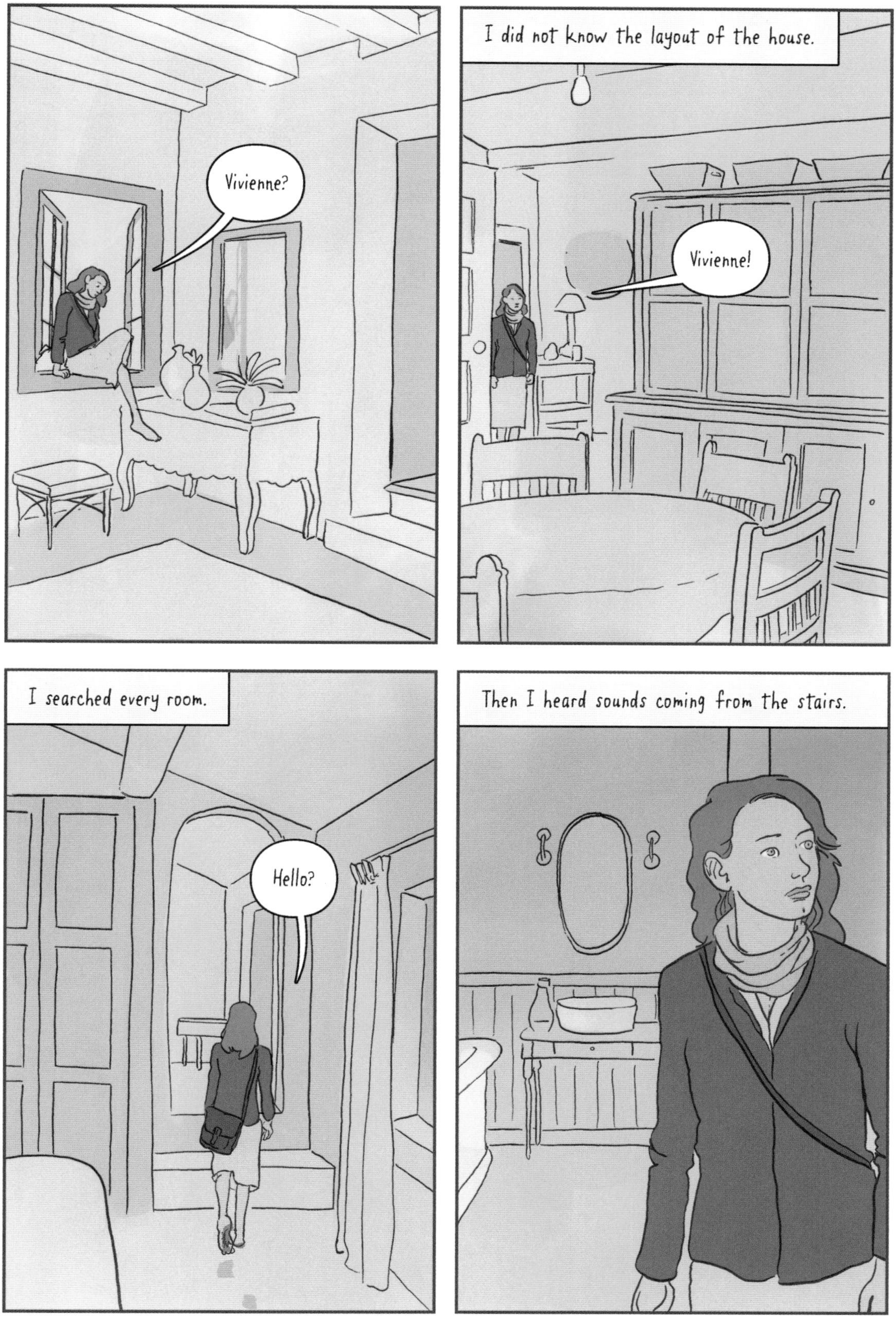
Vivienne?
I did not know the layout of the house.
Vivienne!
I searched every room.
Hello?
Then I heard sounds coming from the stairs.

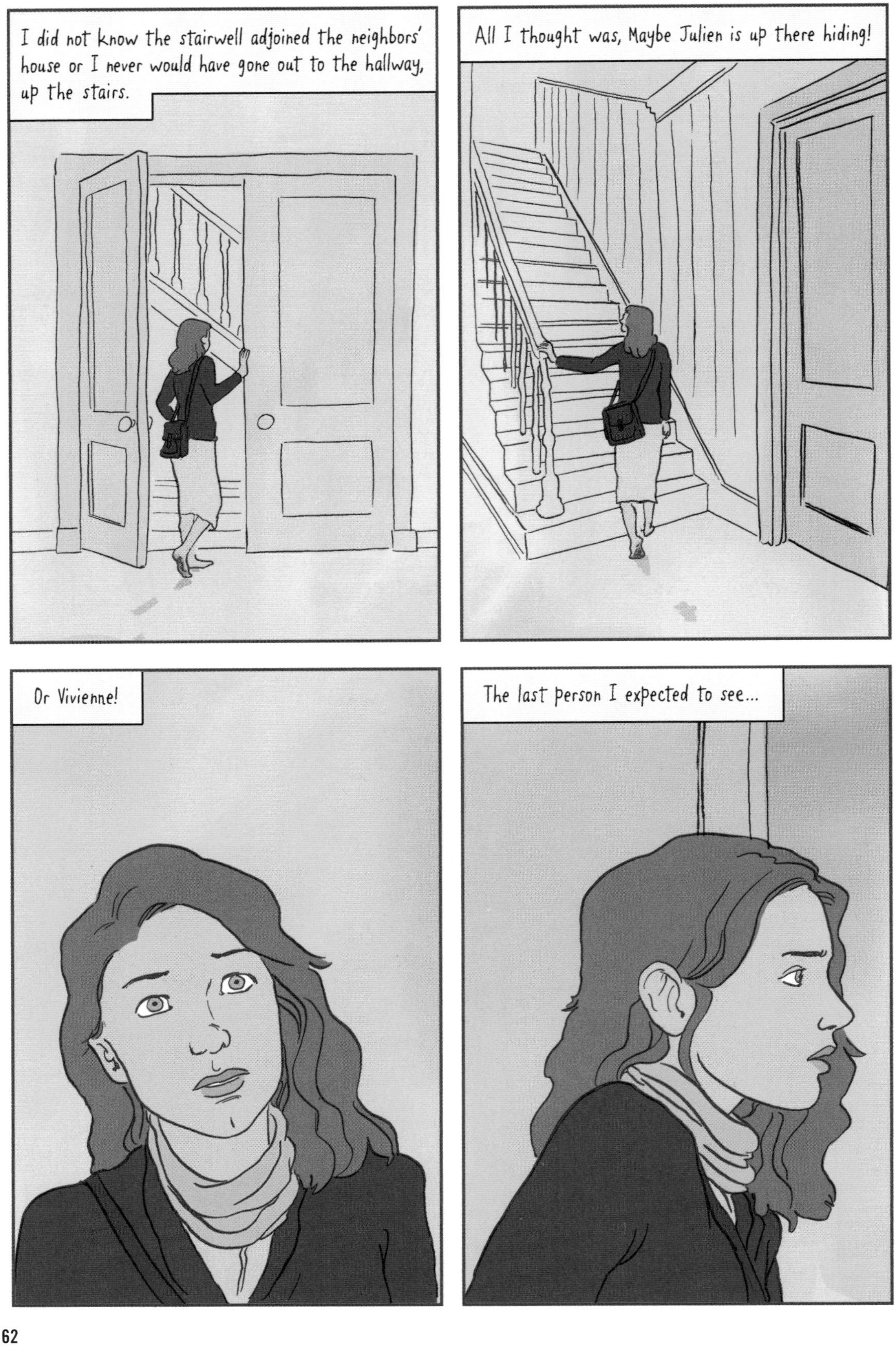
I did not know the stairwell adjoined the neighbors' house or I never would have gone out to the hallway, up the stairs.
All I thought was, Maybe Julien is up there hiding!
Or Vivienne!
The last person I expected to see...

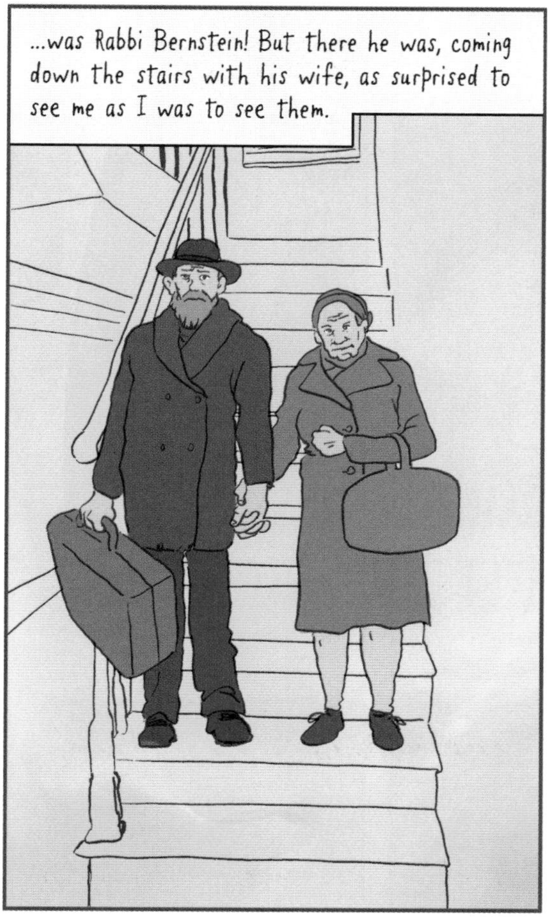
...was Rabbi Bernstein! But there he was, coming down the stairs with his wife, as surprised to see me as I was to see them.

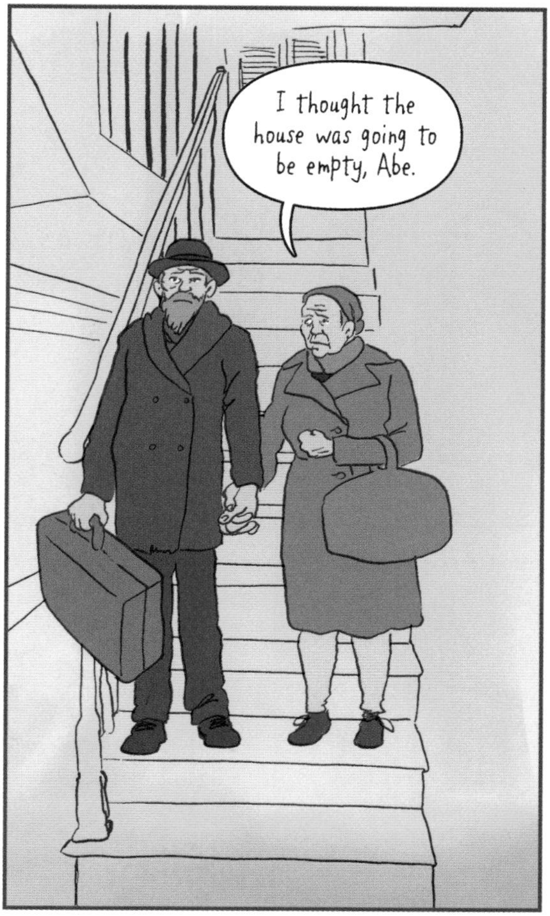
I thought the house was going to be empty, Abe.

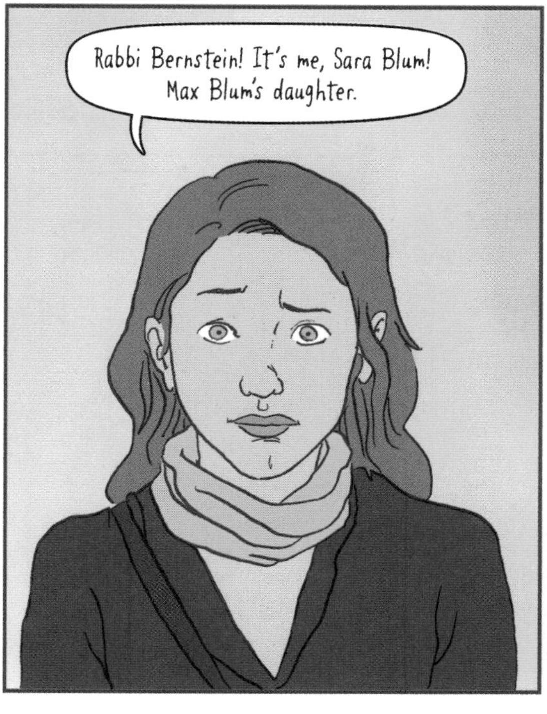
Rabbi Bernstein! It's me, Sara Blum! Max Blum's daughter.

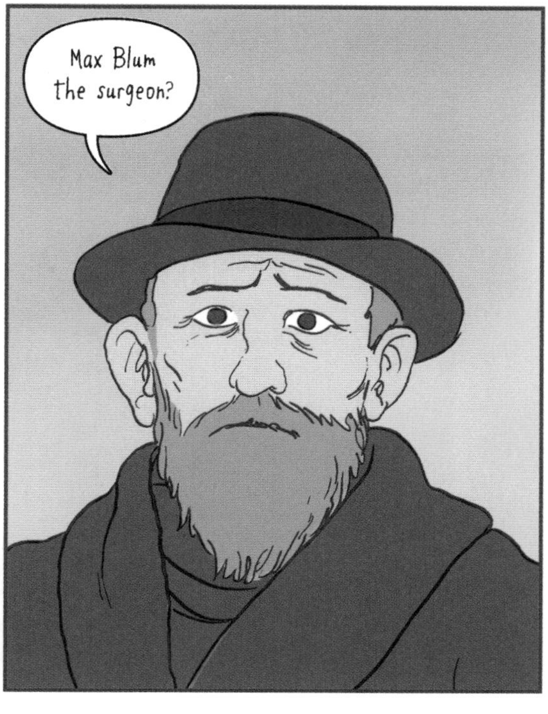
Max Blum the surgeon?

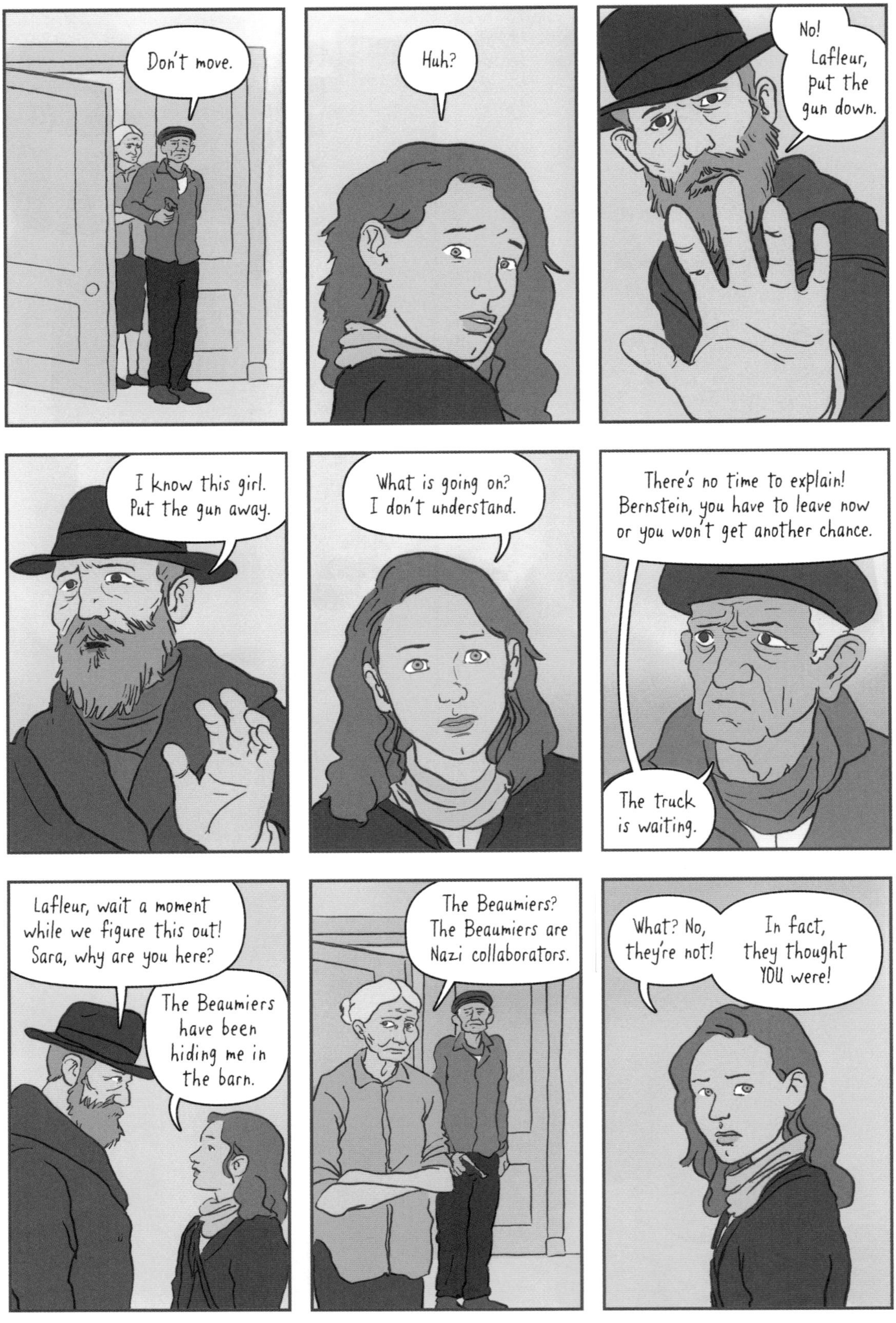
Don't move.
Huh?
No! Lafleur, put the gun down.
I know this girl. Put the gun away.
What is going on? I don't understand.
There's no time to explain! Bernstein, you have to leave now or you won't get another chance.
The truck is waiting.
Lafleur, wait a moment while we figure this out! Sara, why are you here?
The Beaumiers have been hiding me in the barn.
The Beaumiers? The Beaumiers are Nazi collaborators.
What? No, they're not!
In fact, they thought YOU were!

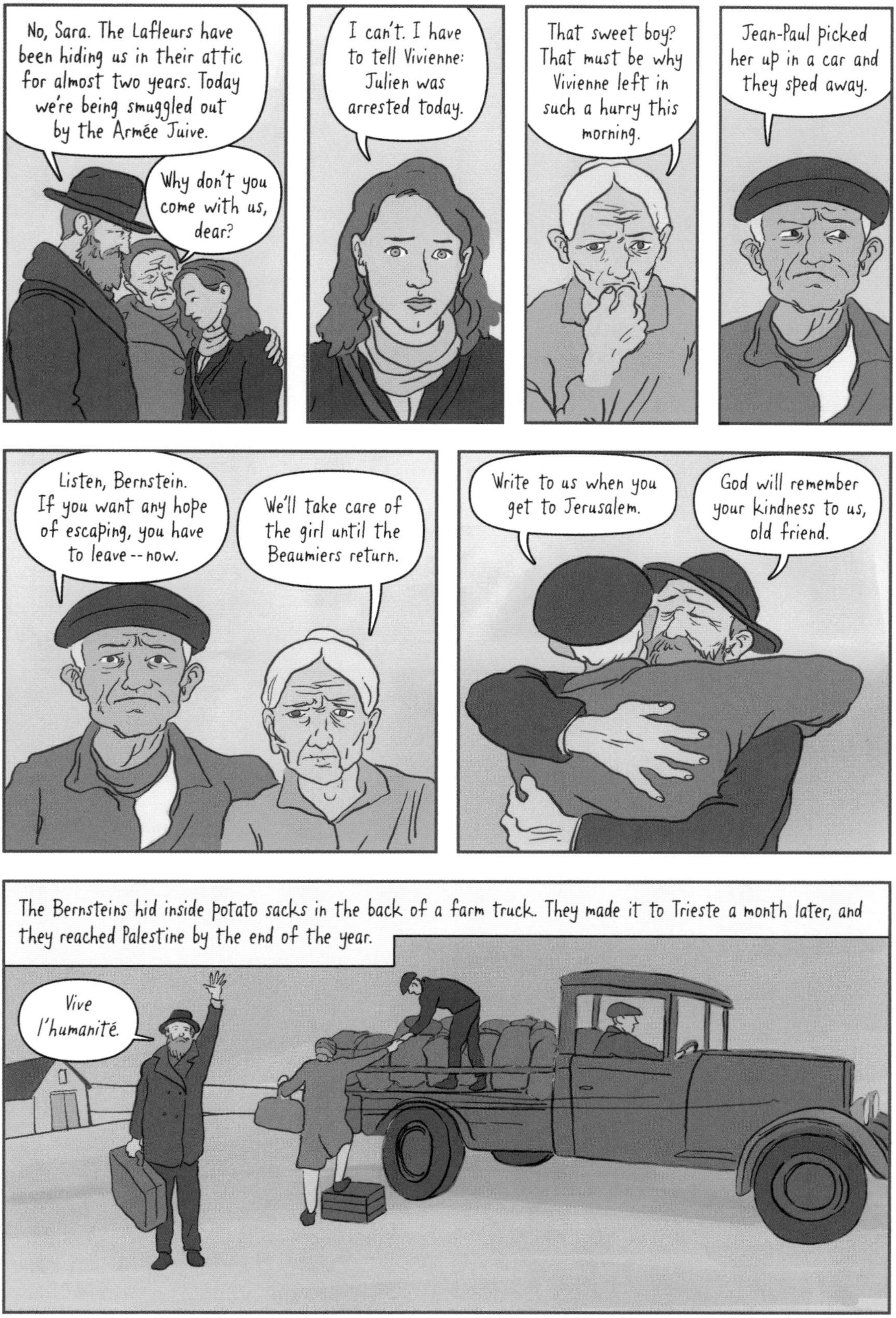
No, Sara. The Lafleurs have been hiding us in their attic for almost two years. Today we're being smuggled out by the Armée Juive.
Why don't you come with us, dear?
I can't. I have to tell Vivienne: Julien was arrested today.
That sweet boy? That must be why Vivienne left in such a hurry this morning.
Jean-Paul picked her up in a car and they sped away.
Listen, Bernstein. If you want any hope of escaping, you have to leave--now.
We'll take care of the girl until the Beaumiers return.
Write to us when you get to Jerusalem.
God will remember your kindness to us, old friend.
The Bernsteins hid inside potato sacks in the back of a farm truck. They made it to Trieste a month later, and they reached Palestine by the end of the year.
Vive l'humanité.

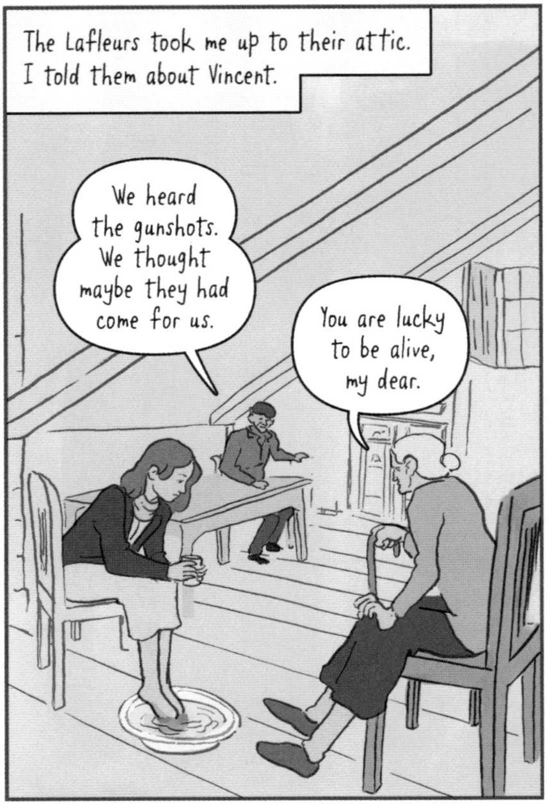
The Lafleurs took me up to their attic. I told them about Vincent.
We heard the gunshots. We thought maybe they had come for us.
You are lucky to be alive, my dear.

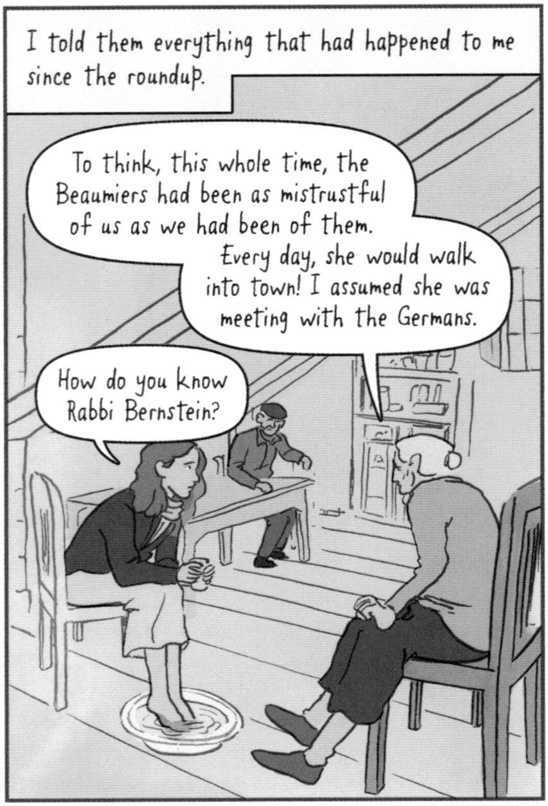
I told them everything that had happened to me since the roundup.
To think, this whole time, the Beaumiers had been as mistrustful of us as we had been of them.
Every day, she would walk into town! I assumed she was meeting with the Germans.
How do you know Rabbi Bernstein?

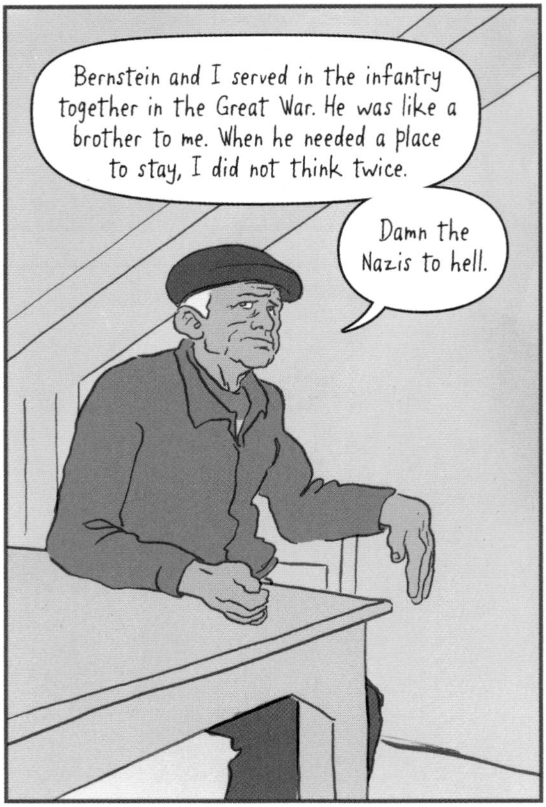
Bernstein and I served in the infantry together in the Great War. He was like a brother to me. When he needed a place to stay, I did not think twice.
Damn the Nazis to hell.

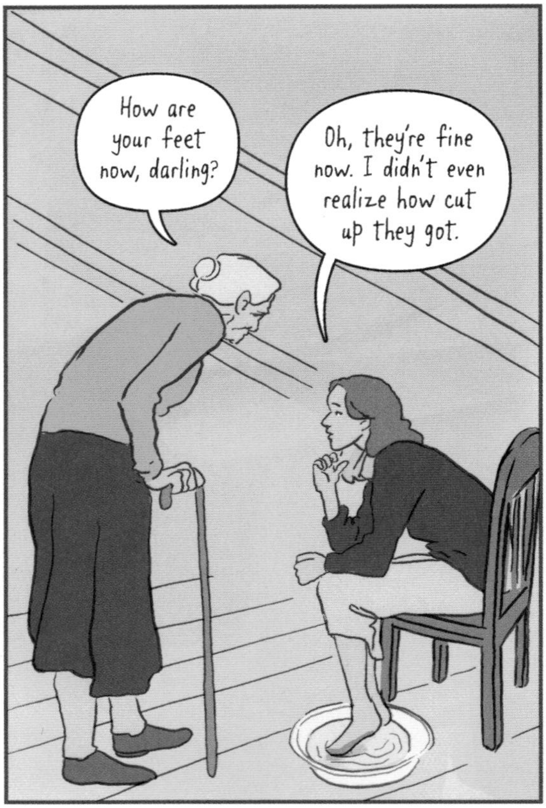
How are your feet now, darling?
Oh, they're fine now. I didn't even realize how cut up they got.

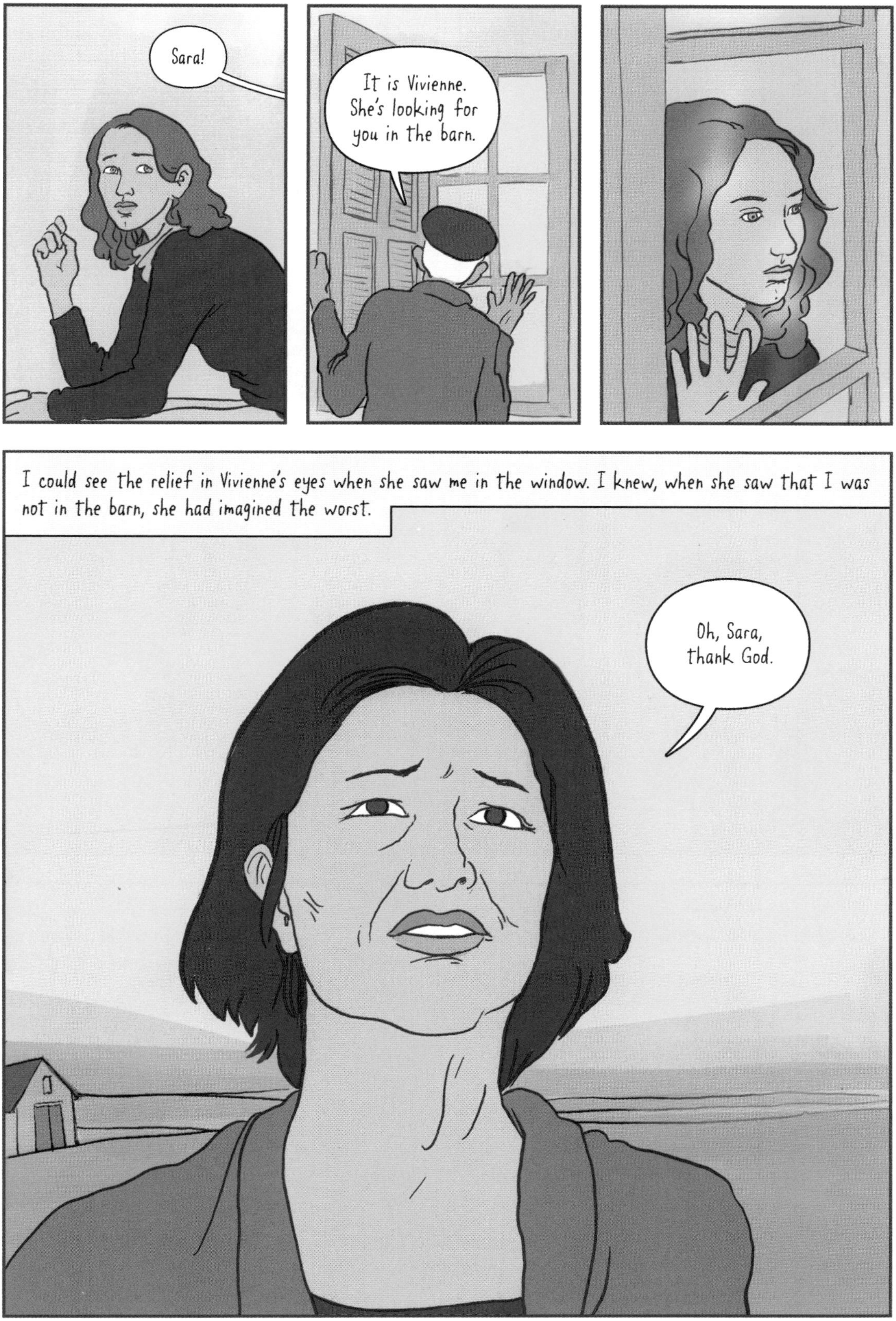
Sara!
It is Vivienne. She's looking for you in the barn.
I could see the relief in Vivienne's eyes when she saw me in the window. I knew, when she saw that I was not in the barn, she had imagined the worst.
Oh, Sara, thank God.

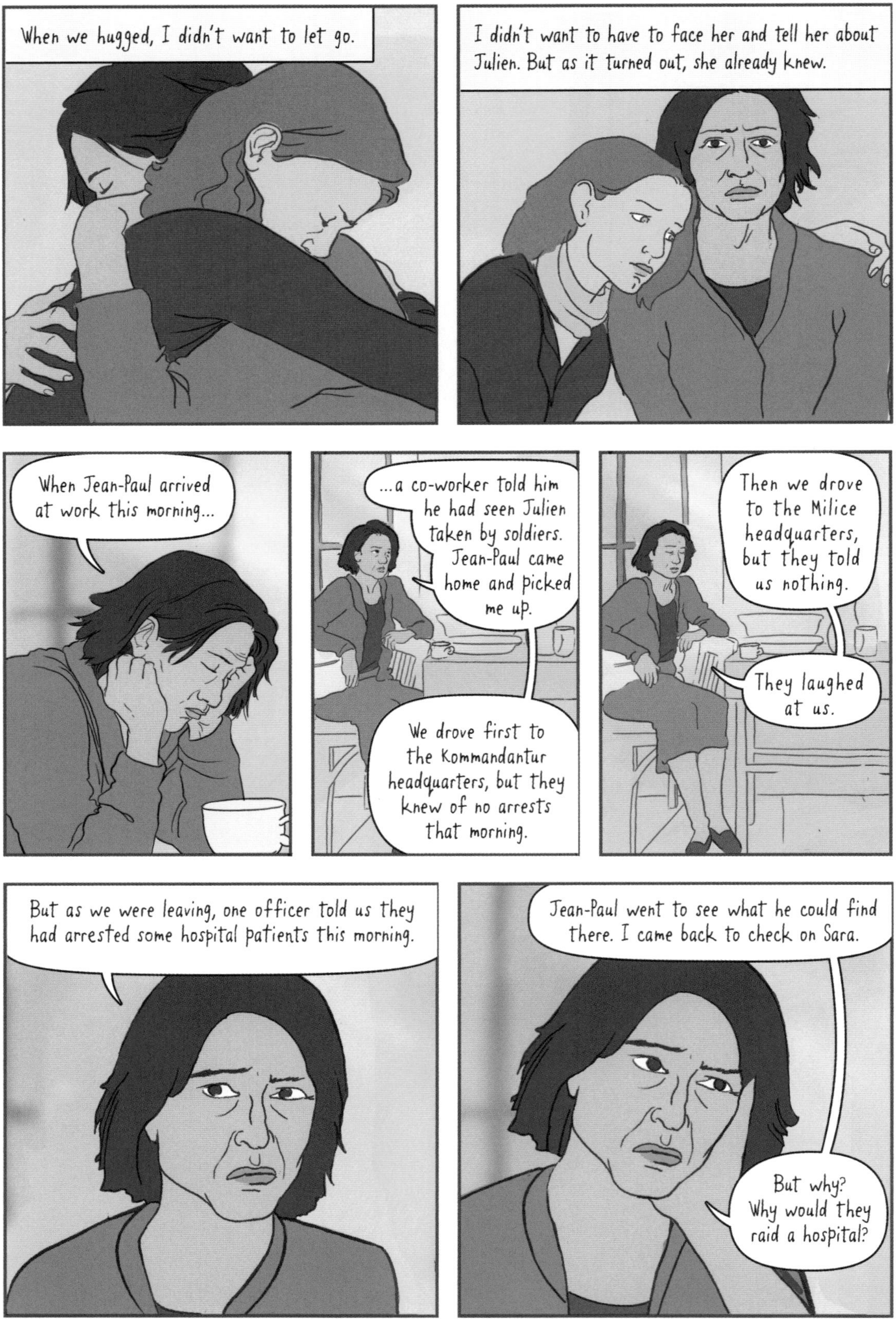

When we hugged, I didn't want to let go.
I didn't want to have to face her and tell her about Julien. But as it turned out, she already knew.
When Jean-Paul arrived at work this morning...
...a co-worker told him he had seen Julien taken by soldiers. Jean-Paul came home and picked me up.
We drove first to the Kommandantur headquarters, but they knew of no arrests that morning.
Then we drove to the Milice headquarters, but they told us nothing.
They laughed at us.
But as we were leaving, one officer told us they had arrested some hospital patients this morning.
Jean-Paul went to see what he could find there. I came back to check on Sara.
But why? Why would they raid a hospital?

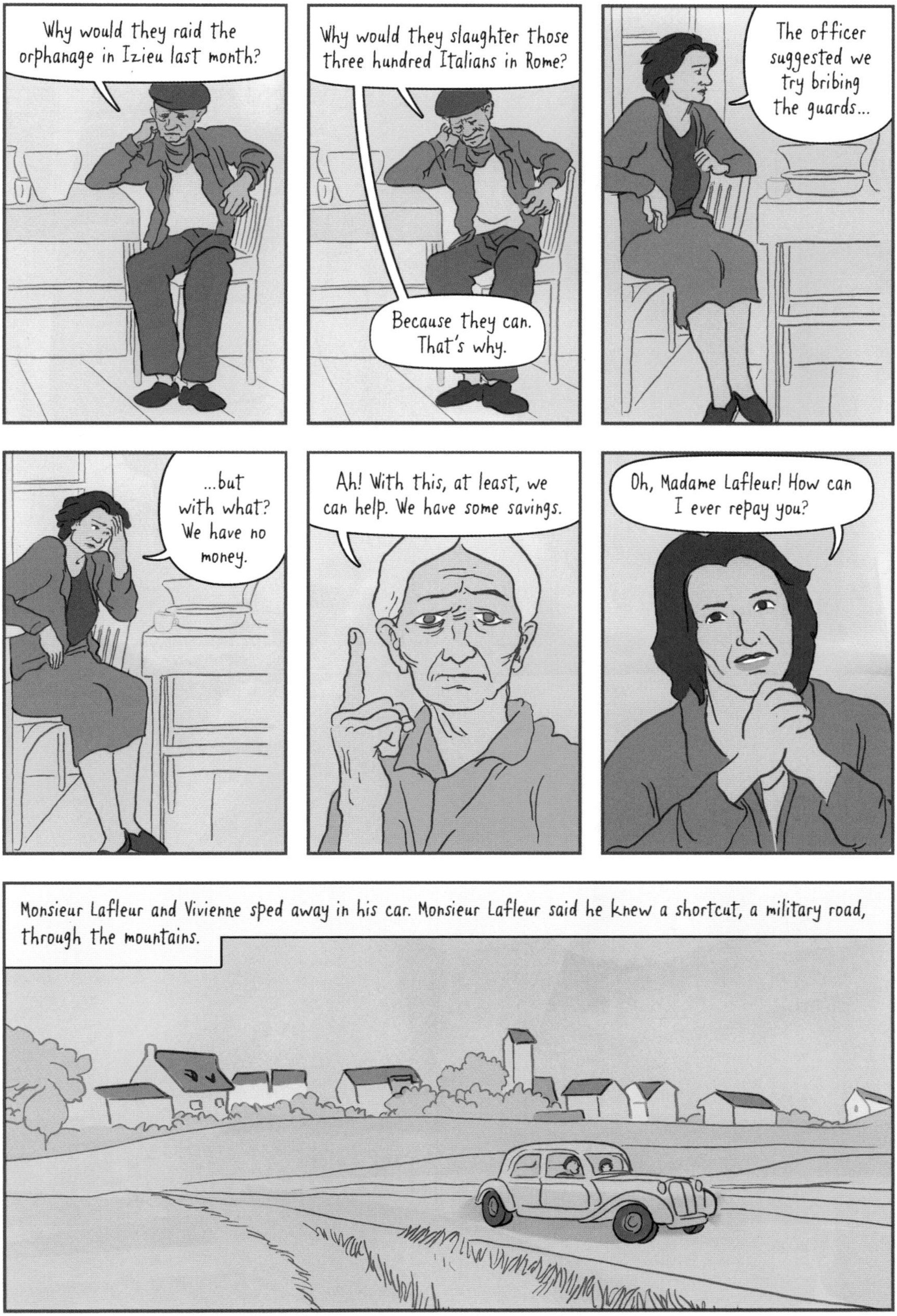
Why would they raid the orphanage in Izieu last month?
Why would they slaughter those three hundred Italians in Rome?
Because they can. That's why.
The officer suggested we try bribing the guards...
...but with what? We have no money.
Ah! With this, at least, we can help. We have some savings.
Oh, Madame Lafleur! How can I ever repay you?
Monsieur Lafleur and Vivienne sped away in his car. Monsieur Lafleur said he knew a shortcut, a military road, through the mountains.

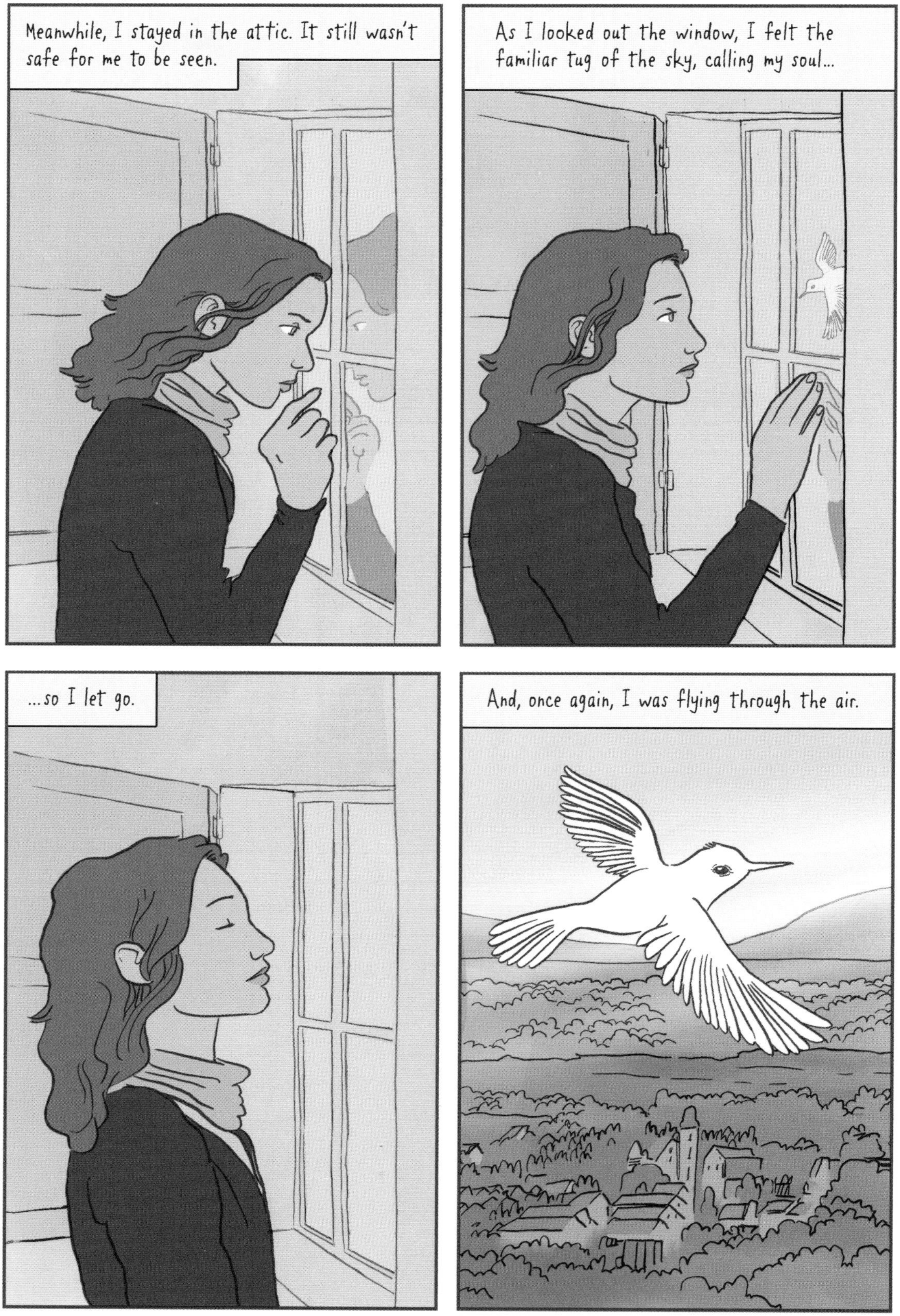
Meanwhile, I stayed in the attic. It still wasn't safe for me to be seen.
As I looked out the window, I felt the familiar tug of the sky, calling my soul...
...so I let go.
And, once again, I was flying through the air.

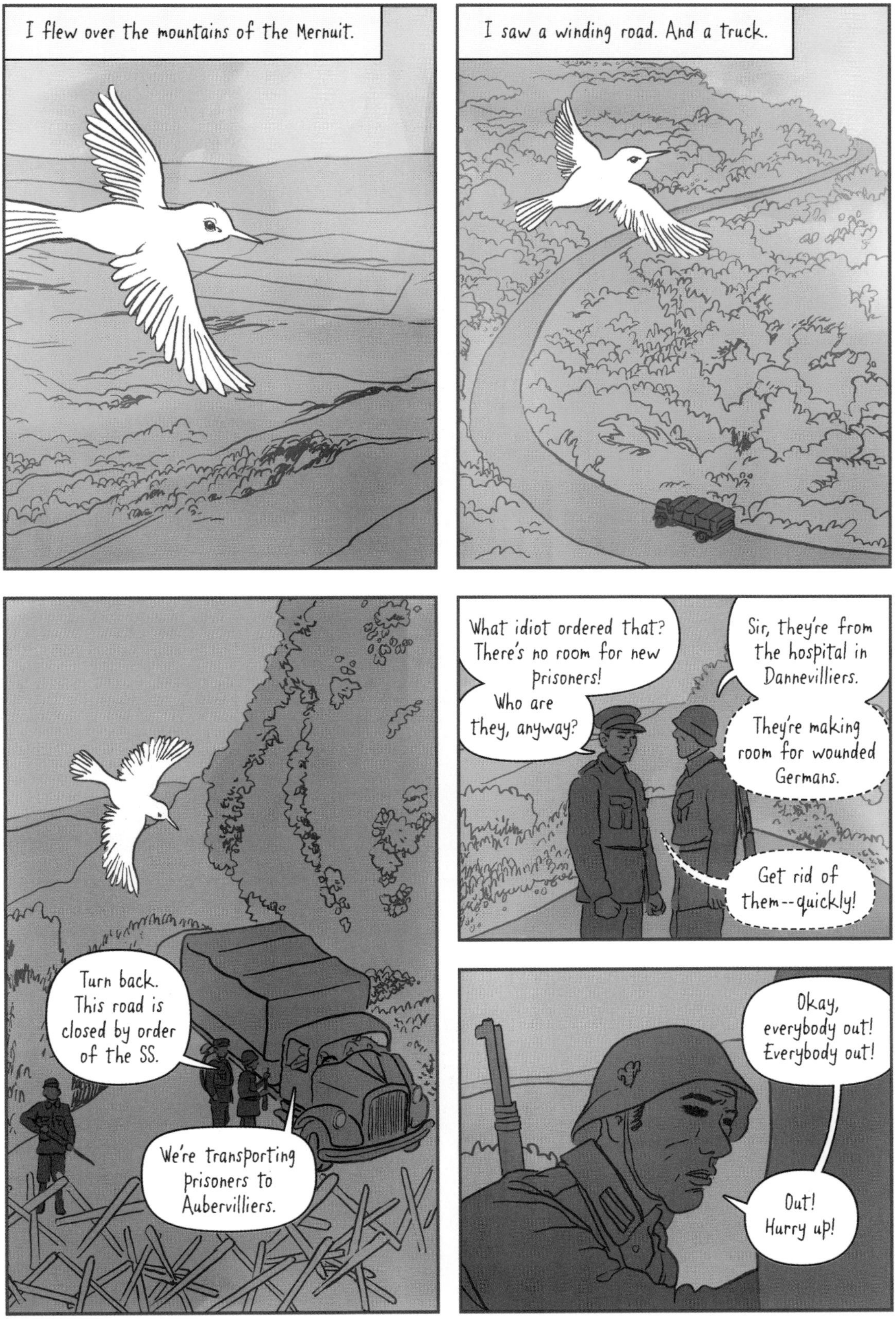
I flew over the mountains of the Mernuit.
I saw a winding road. And a truck.
Turn back. This road is closed by order of the SS.
We're transporting prisoners to Aubervilliers.
What idiot ordered that? There's no room for new prisoners!
Who are they, anyway?
Sir, they're from the hospital in Dannevilliers.
They're making room for wounded Germans.
Get rid of them--quickly!
Okay, everybody out! Everybody out!
Out! Hurry up!

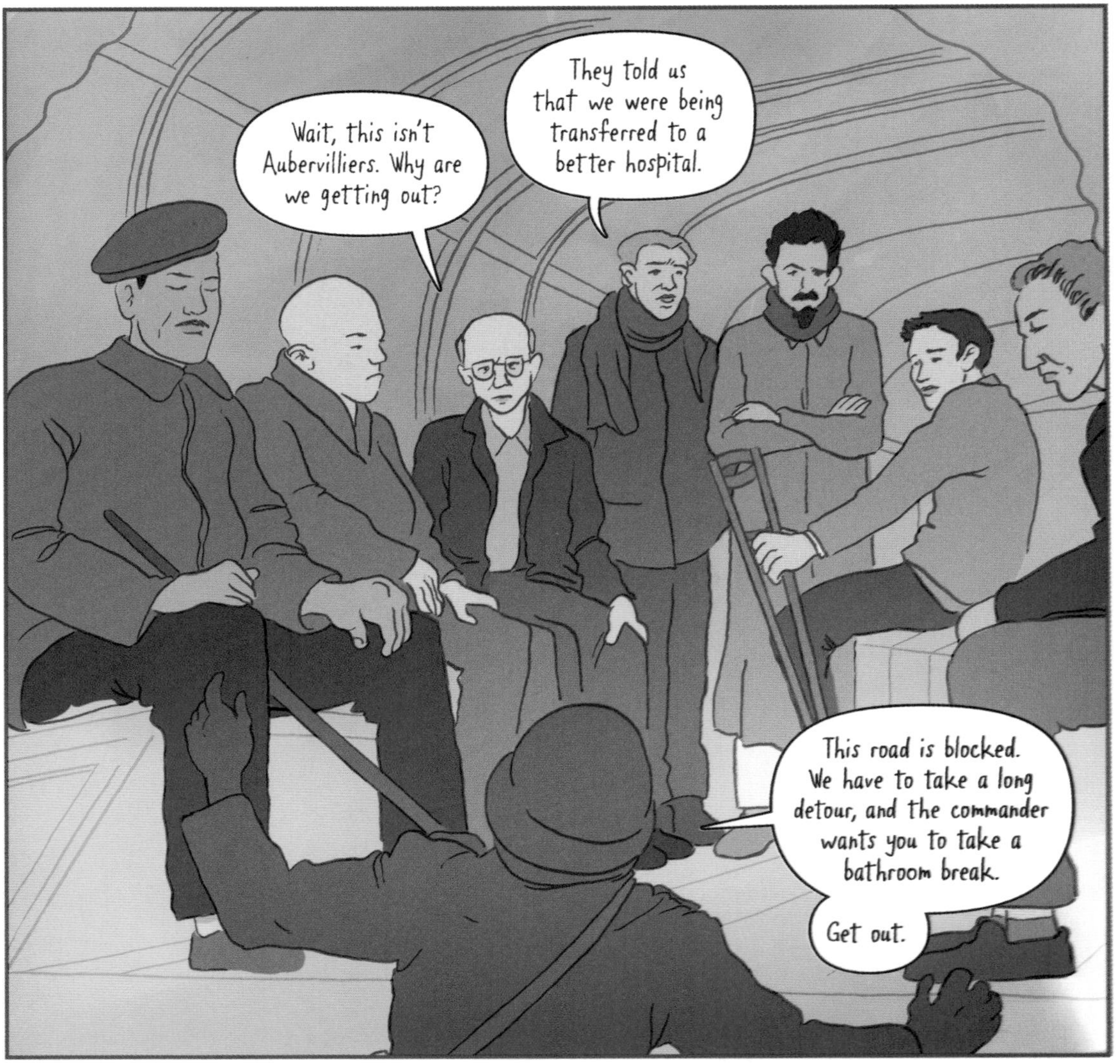
Wait, this isn't Aubervilliers. Why are we getting out?
They told us that we were being transferred to a better hospital.
This road is blocked. We have to take a long detour, and the commander wants you to take a bathroom break.
Get out.

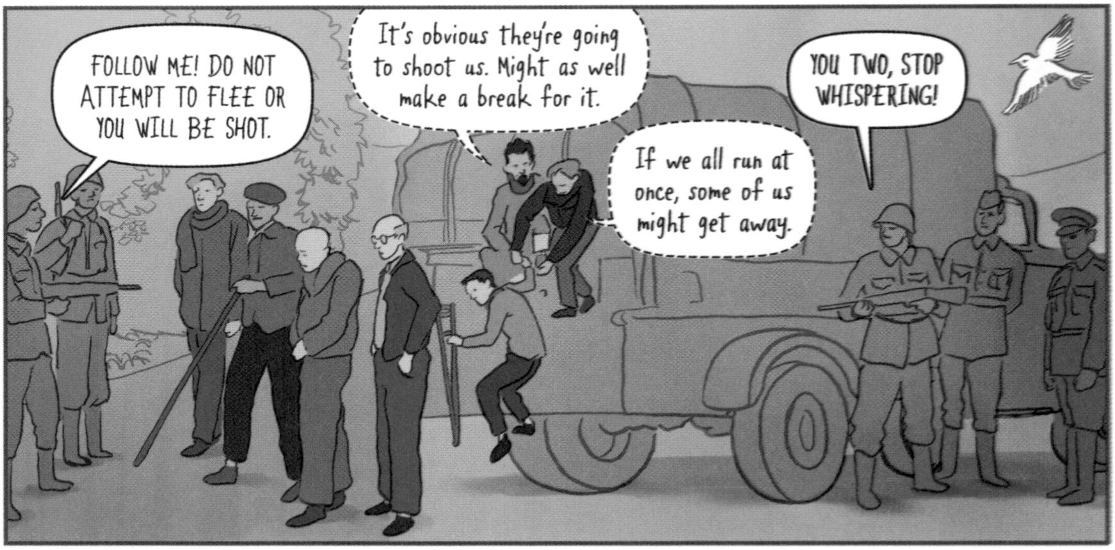
FOLLOW ME! DO NOT ATTEMPT TO FLEE OR YOU WILL BE SHOT.
It's obvious they're going to shoot us. Might as well make a break for it.
If we all run at once, some of us might get away.
YOU TWO, STOP WHISPERING!

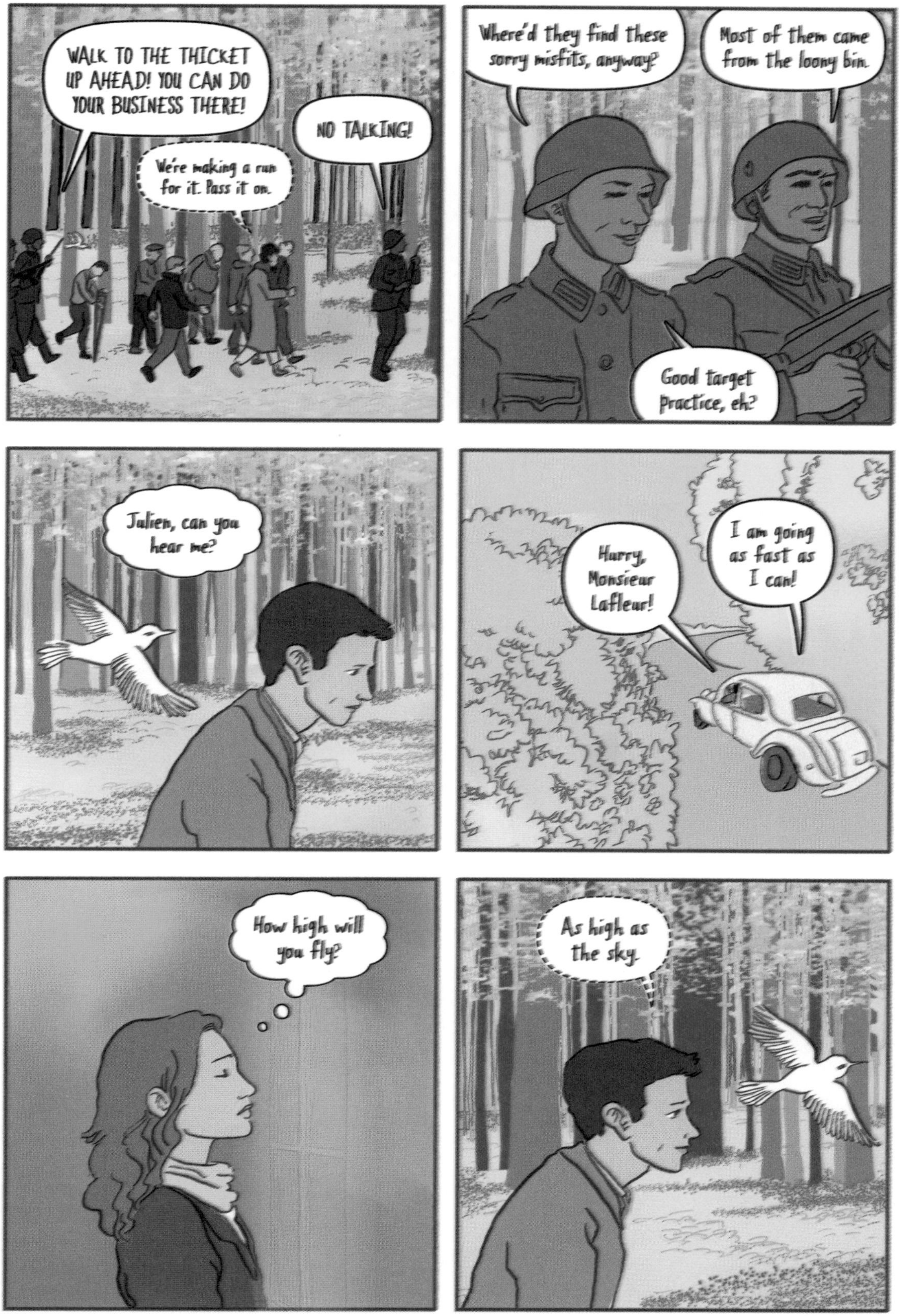

WALK TO THE THICKET UP AHEAD! YOU CAN DO YOUR BUSINESS THERE!
We're making a run for it. Pass it on.
NO TALKING!
Where'd they find these sorry misfits, anyway?
Most of them came from the loony bin.
Good target practice, eh?
Julien, can you hear me?
Hurry, Monsieur Lafleur!
I am going as fast as I can!
How high will you fly?
As high as the sky.

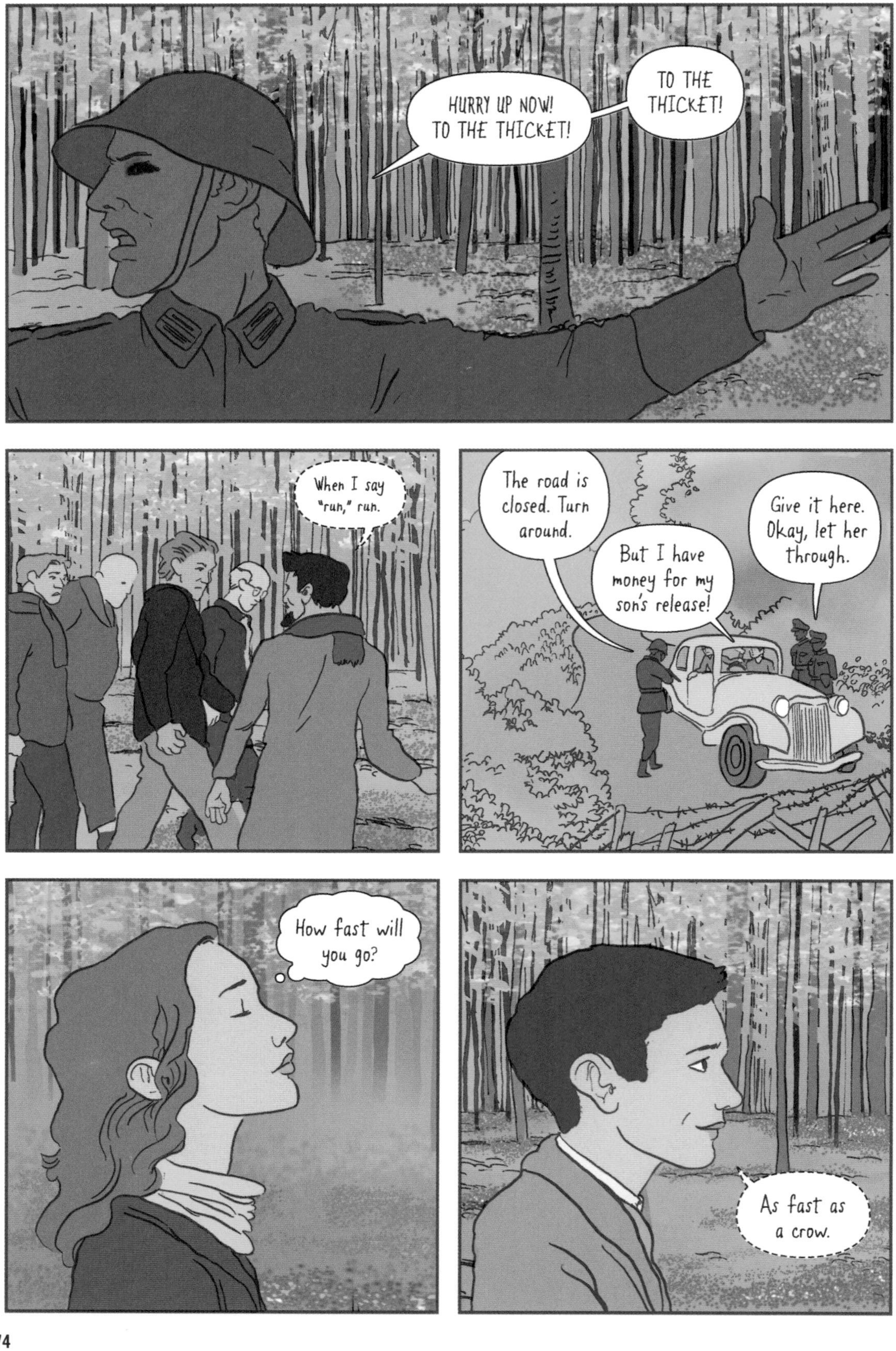
HURRY UP NOW! TO THE THICKET!
TO THE THICKET!
When I say "run," run.
The road is closed. Turn around.
But I have money for my son's release!
Give it here. Okay, let her through.
How fast will you go?
As fast as a crow.

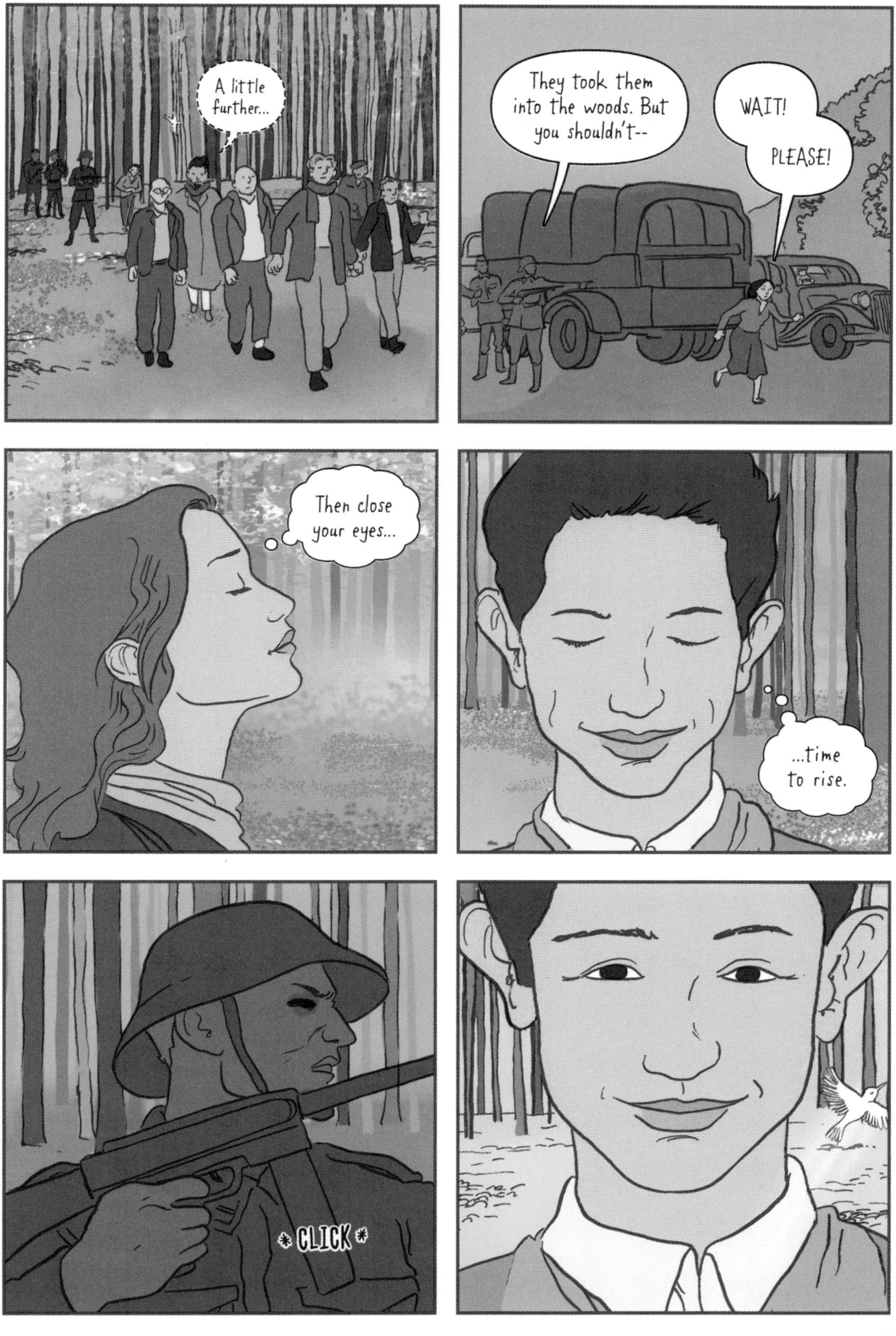
A little further...
They took them into the woods. But you shouldn't--
WAIT!
PLEASE!
Then close your eyes...
...time to rise.
* CLICK *

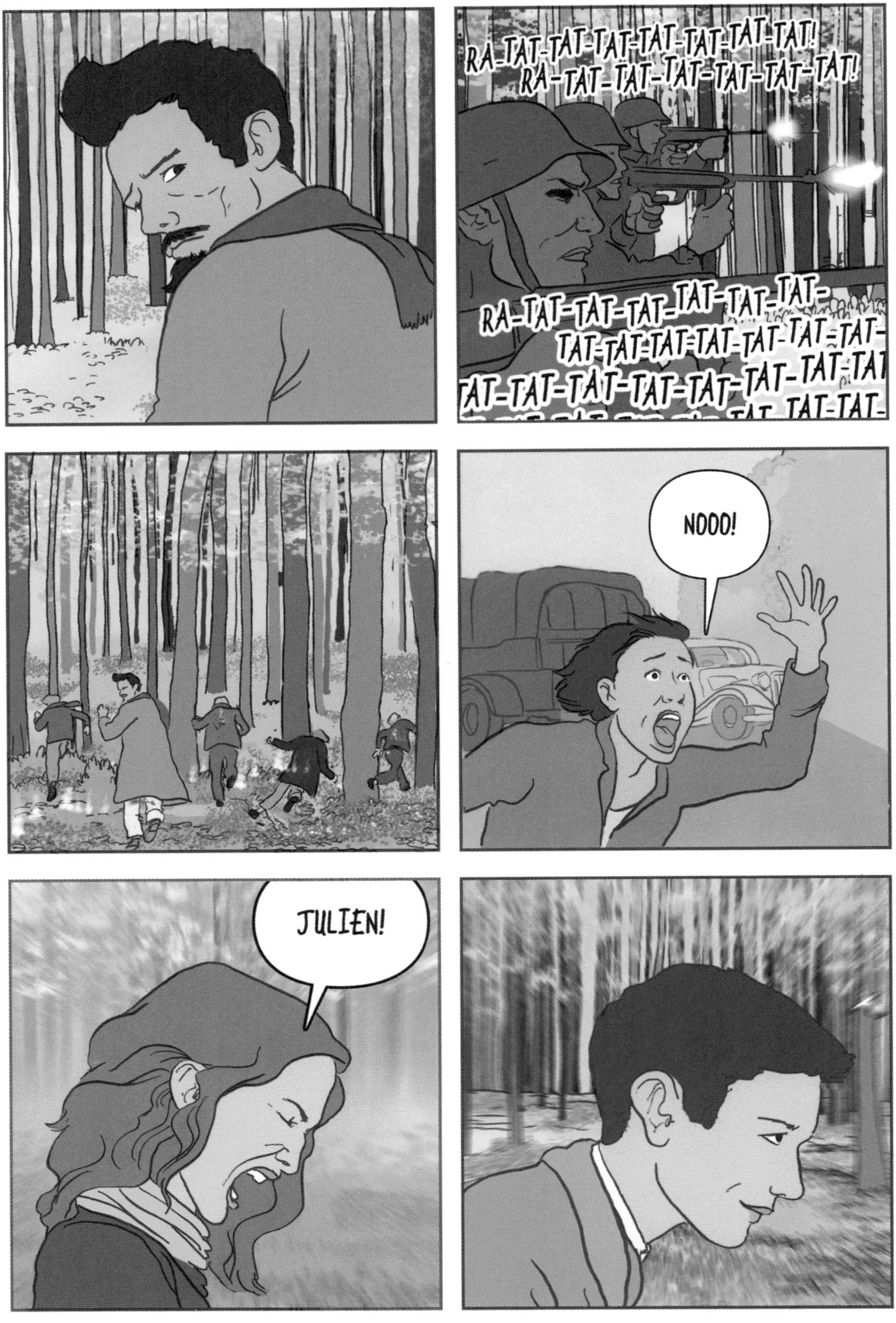
RA-TAT-TAT-TAT-TAT-TAT-TAT-TAT!
RA-TAT-TAT-TAT-TAT-TAT-TAT!
RA-TAT-TAT-TAT-TAT-TAT-TAT-
TAT-TAT-TAT-TAT-TAT-TAT-TAT-
TAT-TAT-TAT-TAT-TAT-TAT-TAT-TAT
NOOO!
JULIEN!

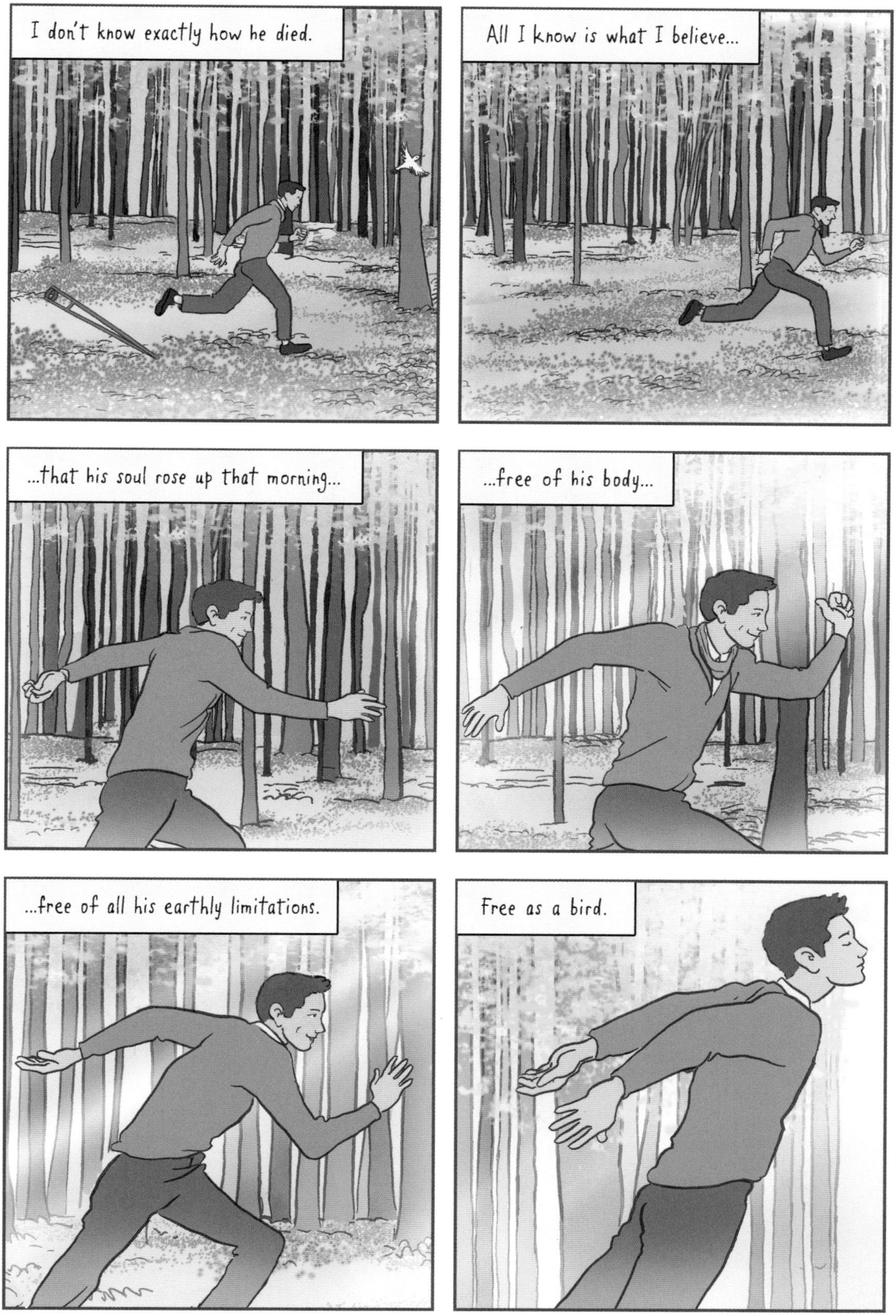
I don't know exactly how he died.
All I know is what I believe...
...that his soul rose up that morning...
...free of his body...
...free of all his earthly limitations.
Free as a bird.

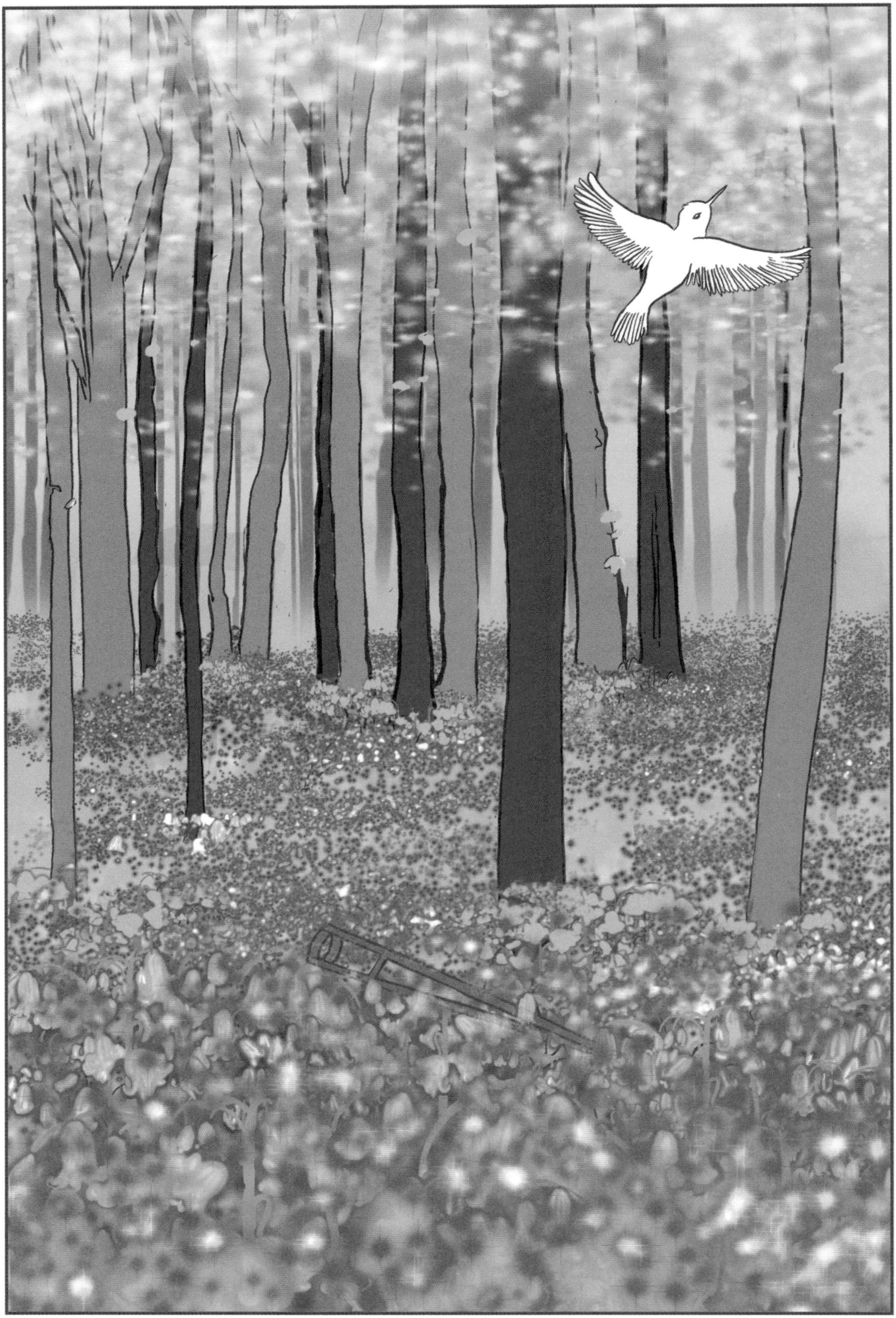

CHAPTER 5

THEY NEVER FOUND JULIEN'S BODY. WHETHER THAT WAS BECAUSE THE NAZIS COVERED UP THEIR DIRTY DEED OR THE FOREST BURIED ONE OF ITS OWN, WE'LL NEVER KNOW.

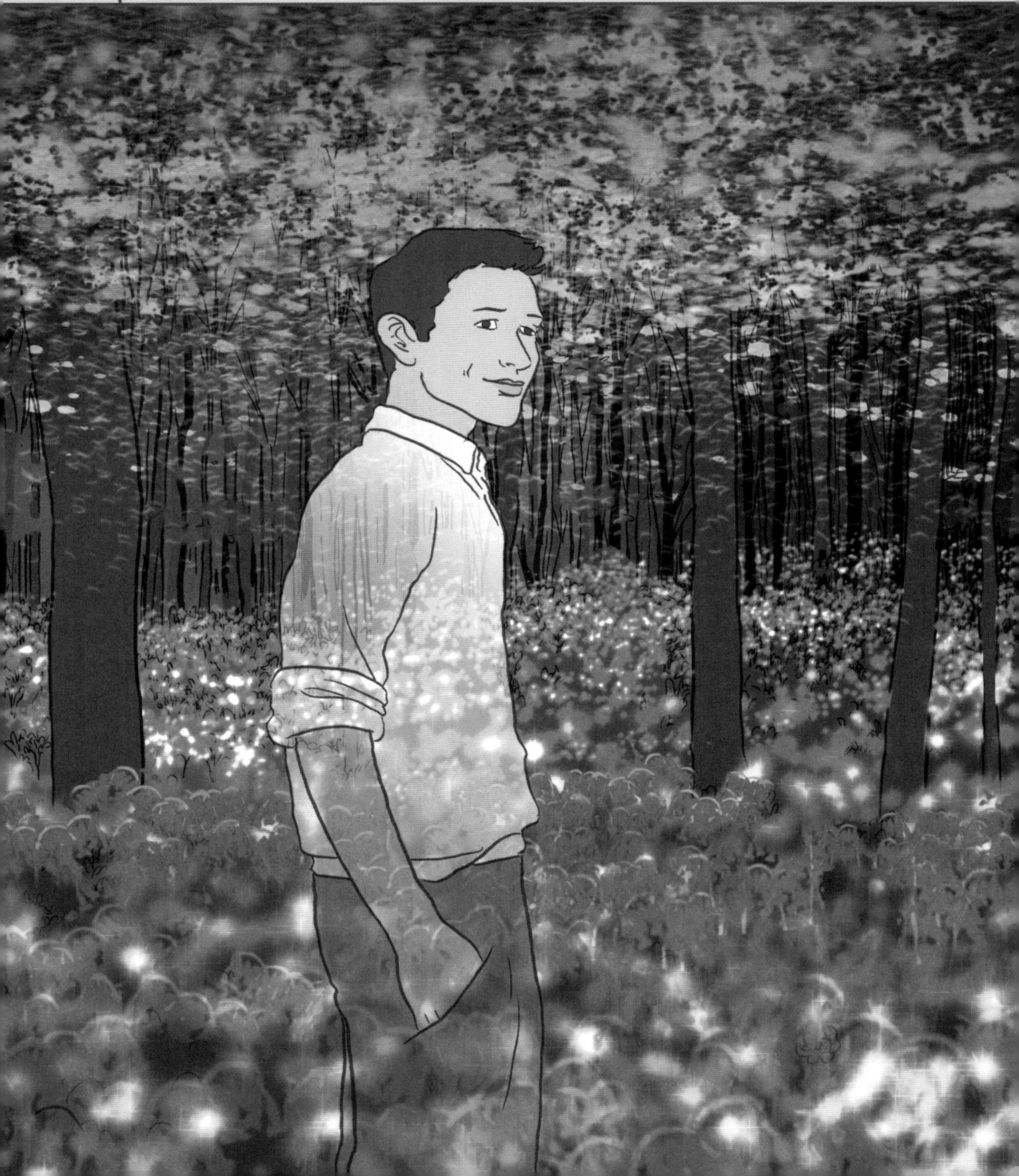

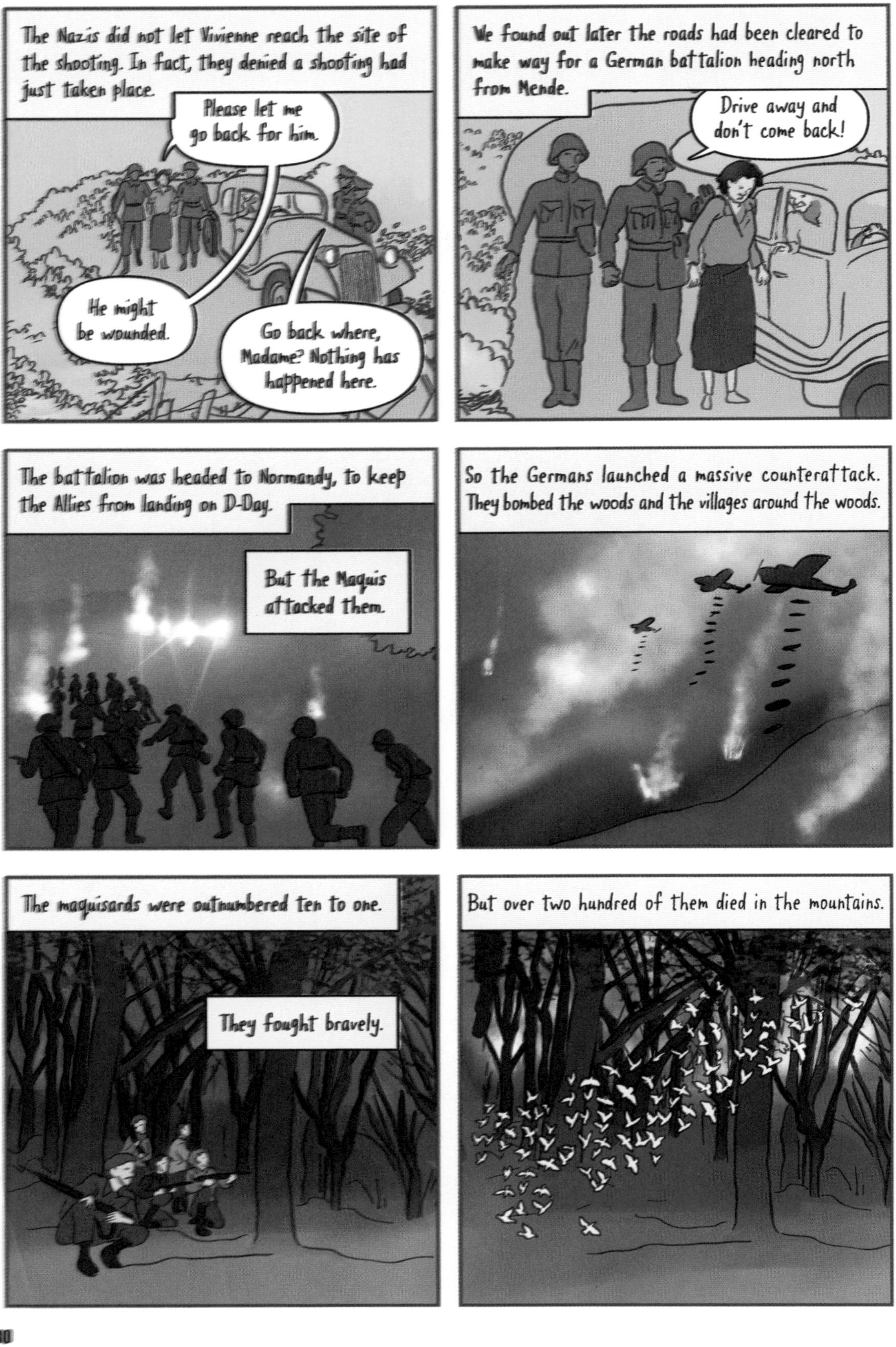

The Nazis did not let Vivienne reach the site of the shooting. In fact, they denied a shooting had just taken place.
Please let me go back for him.
He might be wounded.
Go back where, Madame? Nothing has happened here.
We found out later the roads had been cleared to make way for a German battalion heading north from Mende.
Drive away and don't come back!
The battalion was headed to Normandy, to keep the Allies from landing on D-Day.
But the Maquis attacked them.
So the Germans launched a massive counterattack. They bombed the woods and the villages around the woods.
The maquisards were outnumbered ten to one.
They fought bravely.
But over two hundred of them died in the mountains.

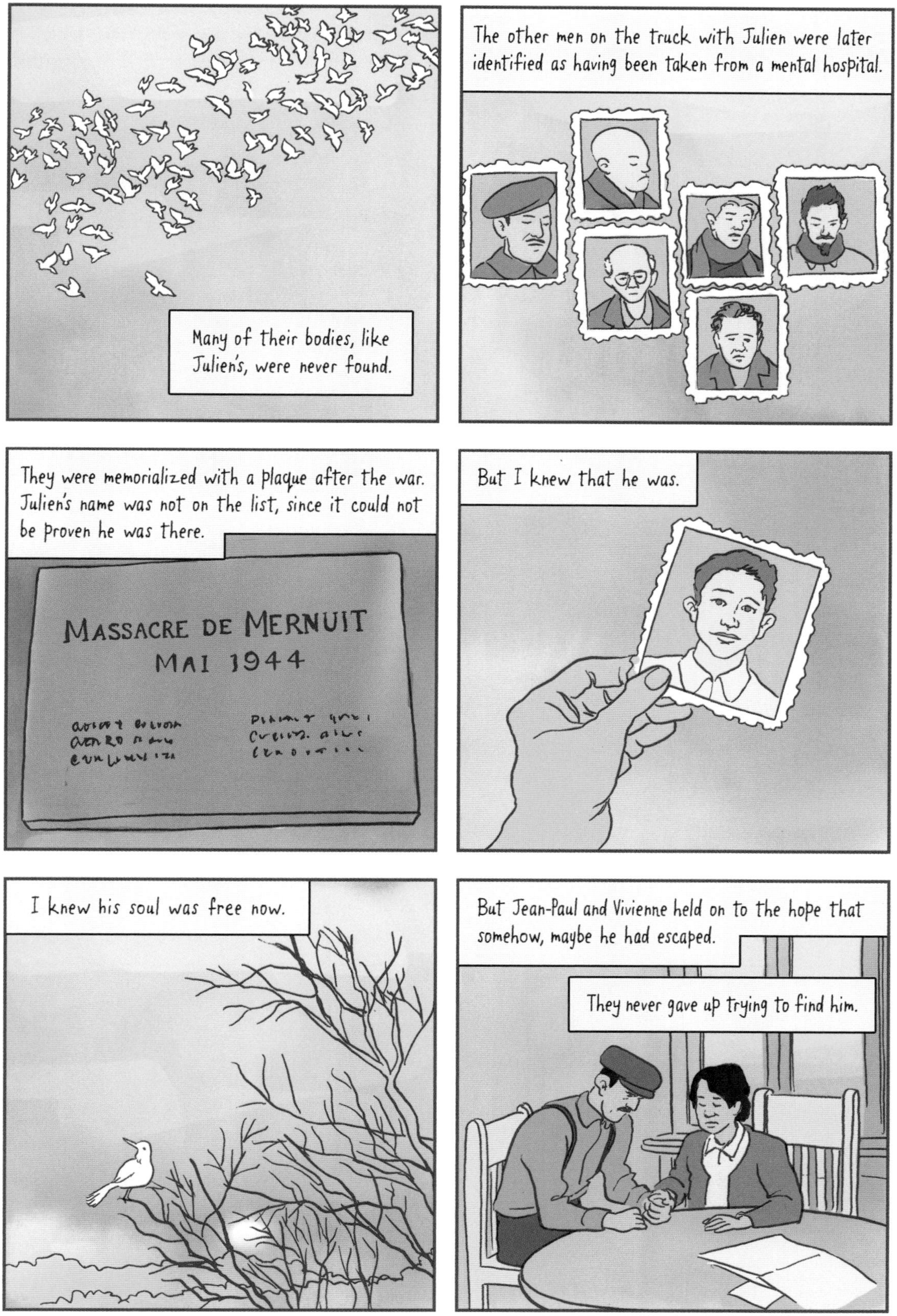
Many of their bodies, like Julien's, were never found.
The other men on the truck with Julien were later identified as having been taken from a mental hospital.
They were memorialized with a plaque after the war. Julien's name was not on the list, since it could not be proven he was there.
MASSACRE DE MERNUIT
MAI 1944
But I knew that he was.
I knew his soul was free now.
But Jean-Paul and Vivienne held on to the hope that somehow, maybe he had escaped.
They never gave up trying to find him.

I stayed with them for the duration of the war-- still hidden, of course.

We would listen to the news from Radio London at the Lafleurs' home.

When France was fully liberated in August of 1944, I was finally able to come out of hiding--but I still didn't go out.

Even after the war was over, it was not easy for me to face the world again...

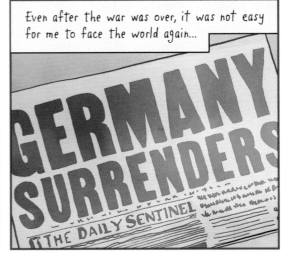

GERMANY SURRENDERS
THE DAILY SENTINEL

...though it was nice to see Marianne and Sophie when school started.

Still, everything felt different to me. I was different. I felt sad inside for a long time.

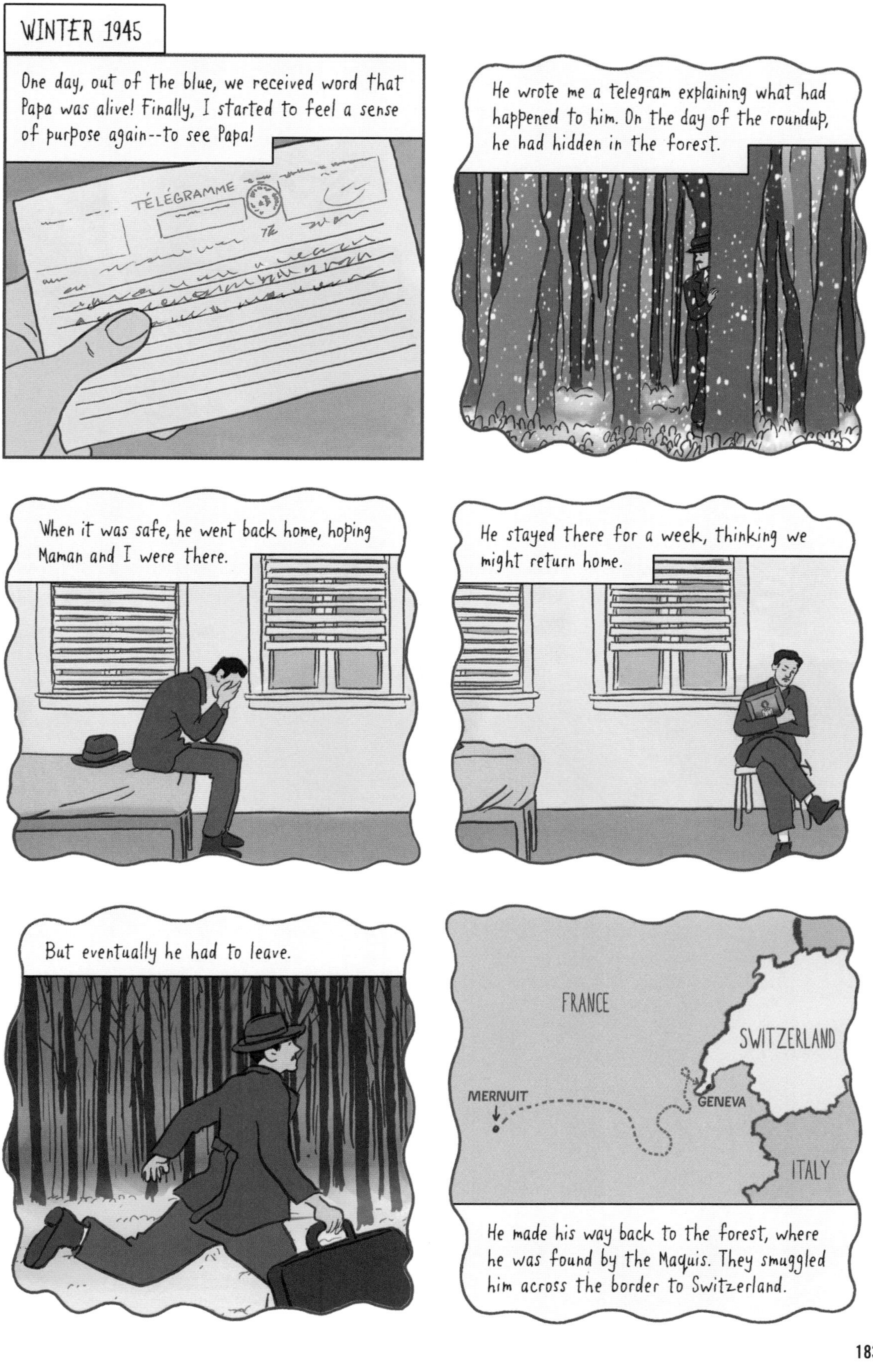
WINTER 1945
One day, out of the blue, we received word that Papa was alive! Finally, I started to feel a sense of purpose again--to see Papa!
TÉLÉGRAMME
He wrote me a telegram explaining what had happened to him. On the day of the roundup, he had hidden in the forest.
When it was safe, he went back home, hoping Maman and I were there.
He stayed there for a week, thinking we might return home.
But eventually he had to leave.
FRANCE
SWITZERLAND
MERNUIT
GENEVA
ITALY
He made his way back to the forest, where he was found by the Maquis. They smuggled him across the border to Switzerland.

After the war, he moved to Paris. He got a job at a hospital.

He spent all of his spare time trying to find me, looking through hundreds of lists.

So many names!

There was so much chaos in those days as Europe tried to heal from the war.

It was in those days that we learned the truth: six million Jews had been killed by the Nazis. Among them, Papa's cousins in France, my friends from the École Lafayette, and my beautiful maman.

Where are you, my little bird?

Then one day, the phone rang.

Hello? Yes?

We've found your daughter. She is alive and well, living in...

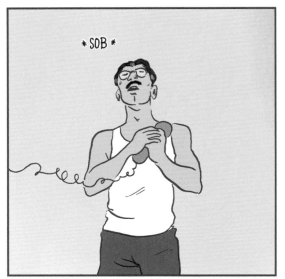

* SOB *

I cannot describe what it was like to be reunited with my father. Sometimes, there are no words.

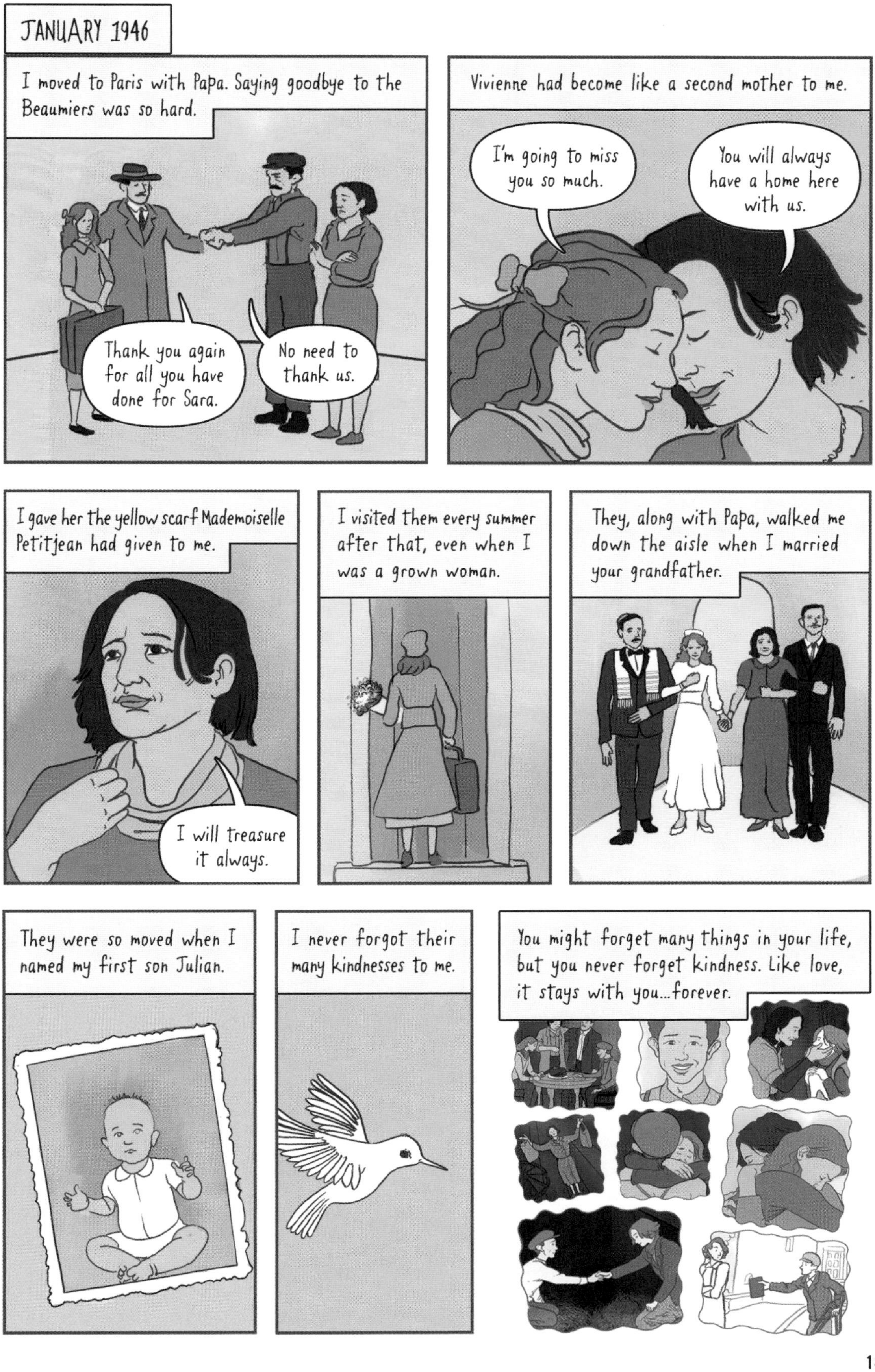
JANUARY 1946
I moved to Paris with Papa. Saying goodbye to the Beaumiers was so hard.
Thank you again for all you have done for Sara.
No need to thank us.
Vivienne had become like a second mother to me.
I'm going to miss you so much.
You will always have a home here with us.
I gave her the yellow scarf Mademoiselle Petitjean had given to me.
I will treasure it always.
I visited them every summer after that, even when I was a grown woman.
They, along with Papa, walked me down the aisle when I married your grandfather.
They were so moved when I named my first son Julian.
I never forgot their many kindnesses to me.
You might forget many things in your life, but you never forget kindness. Like love, it stays with you…forever.

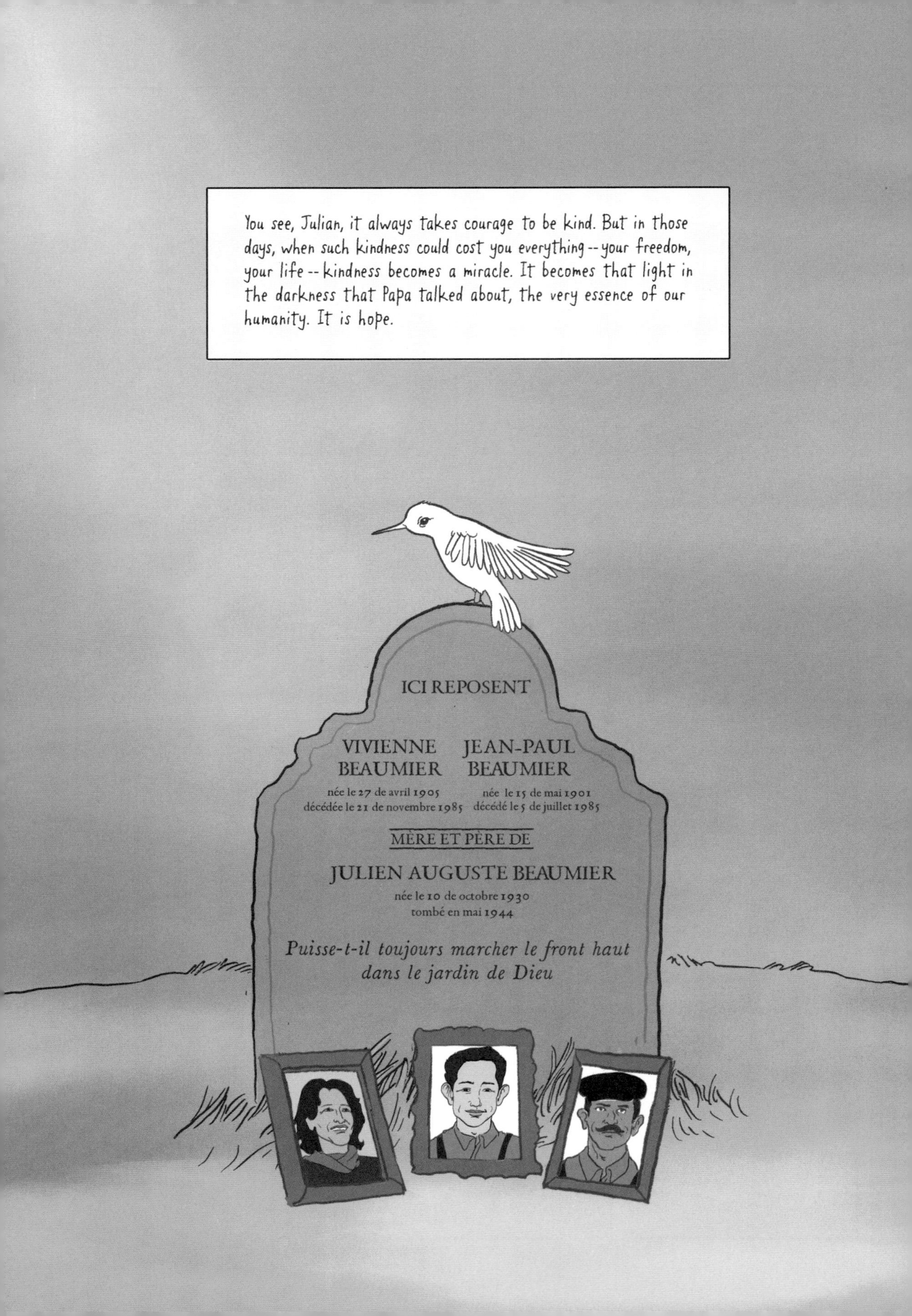
You see, Julian, it always takes courage to be kind. But in those days, when such kindness could cost you everything -- your freedom, your life -- kindness becomes a miracle. It becomes that light in the darkness that Papa talked about, the very essence of our humanity. It is hope.
ICI REPOSENT
VIVIENNE BEAUMIER
née le 27 de avril 1905
décédée le 21 de novembre 1985
JEAN-PAUL BEAUMIER
née le 15 de mai 1901
décédé le 5 de juillet 1985
MÈRE ET PÈRE DE
JULIEN AUGUSTE BEAUMIER
née le 10 de octobre 1930
tombé en mai 1944
Puisse-t-il toujours marcher le front haut dans le jardin de Dieu

EPILOGUE

What is done cannot be undone, but one
can prevent it from happening again.
-Anne Frank

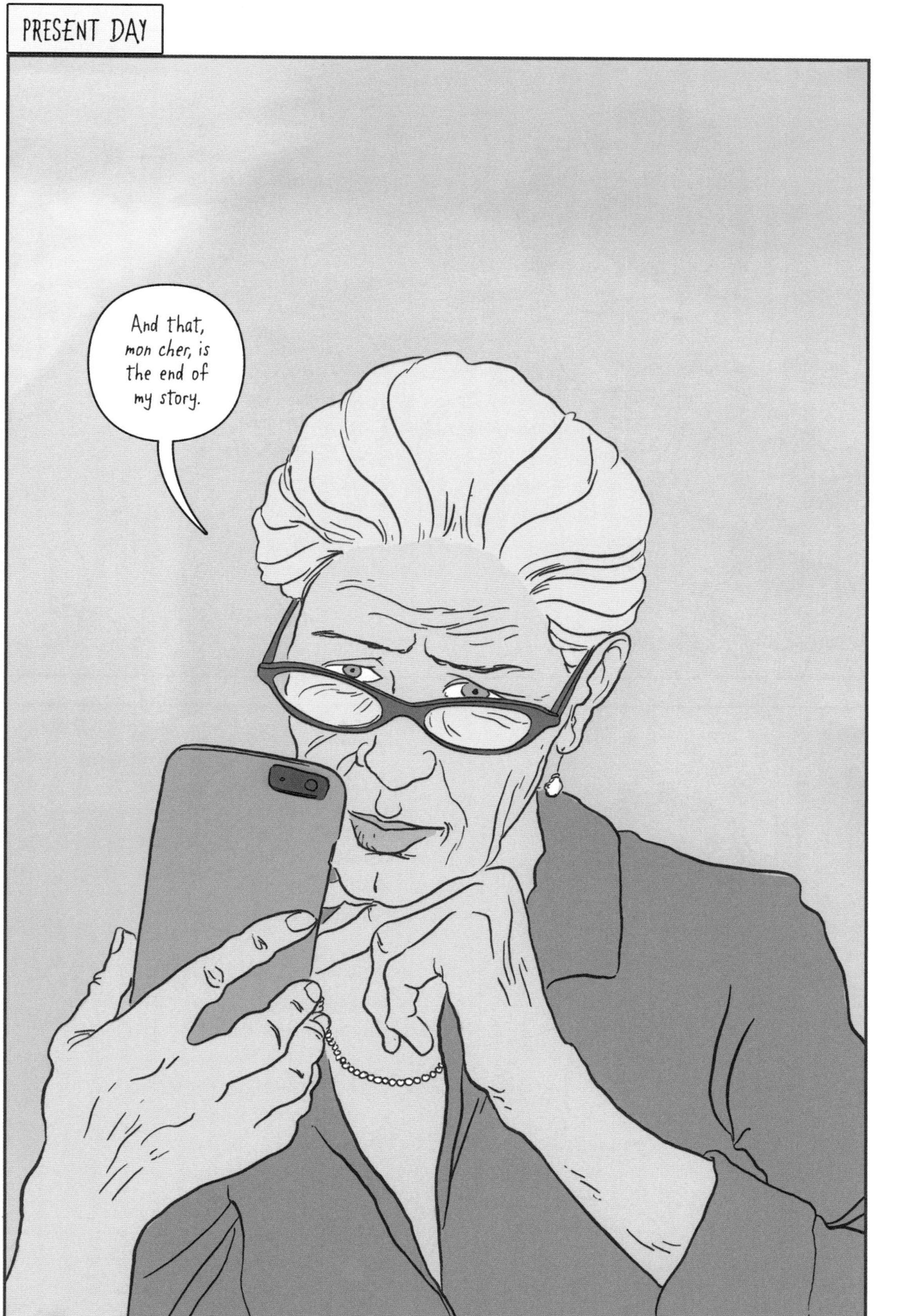
PRESENT DAY
And that, mon cher, is the end of my story.

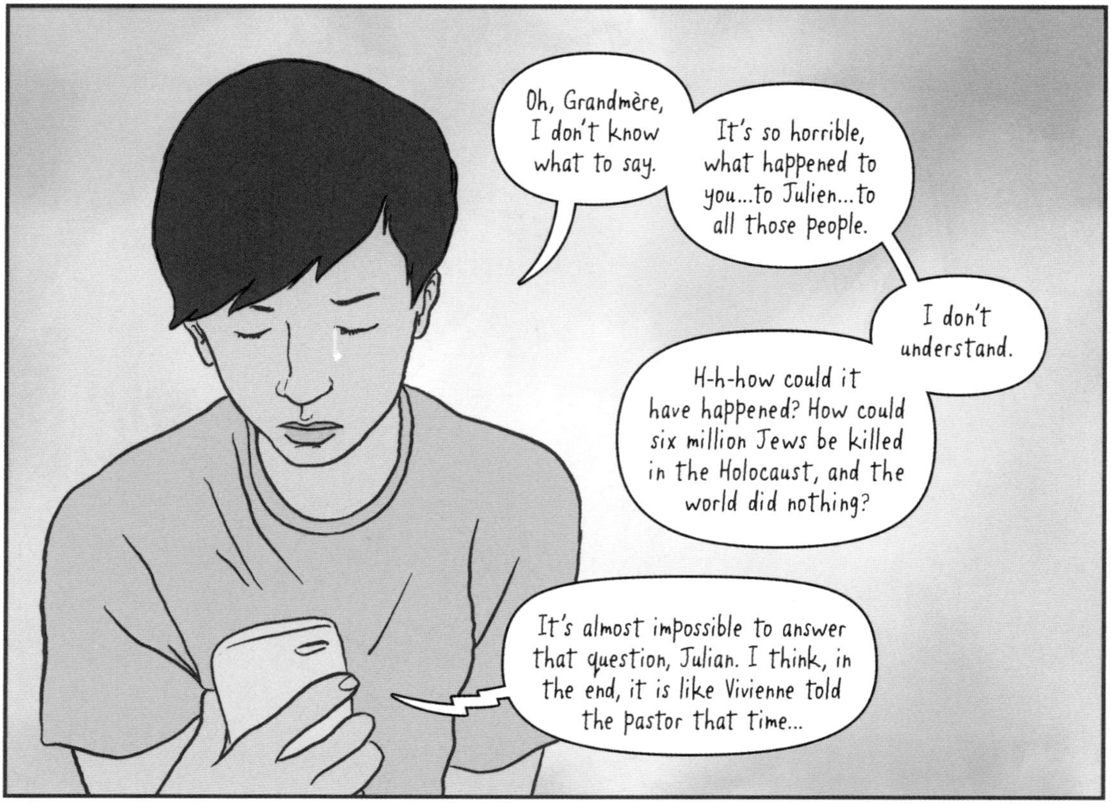
Oh, Grandmère, I don't know what to say.
It's so horrible, what happened to you...to Julien...to all those people.
I don't understand.
H-h-how could it have happened? How could six million Jews be killed in the Holocaust, and the world did nothing?
It's almost impossible to answer that question, Julian. I think, in the end, it is like Vivienne told the pastor that time...

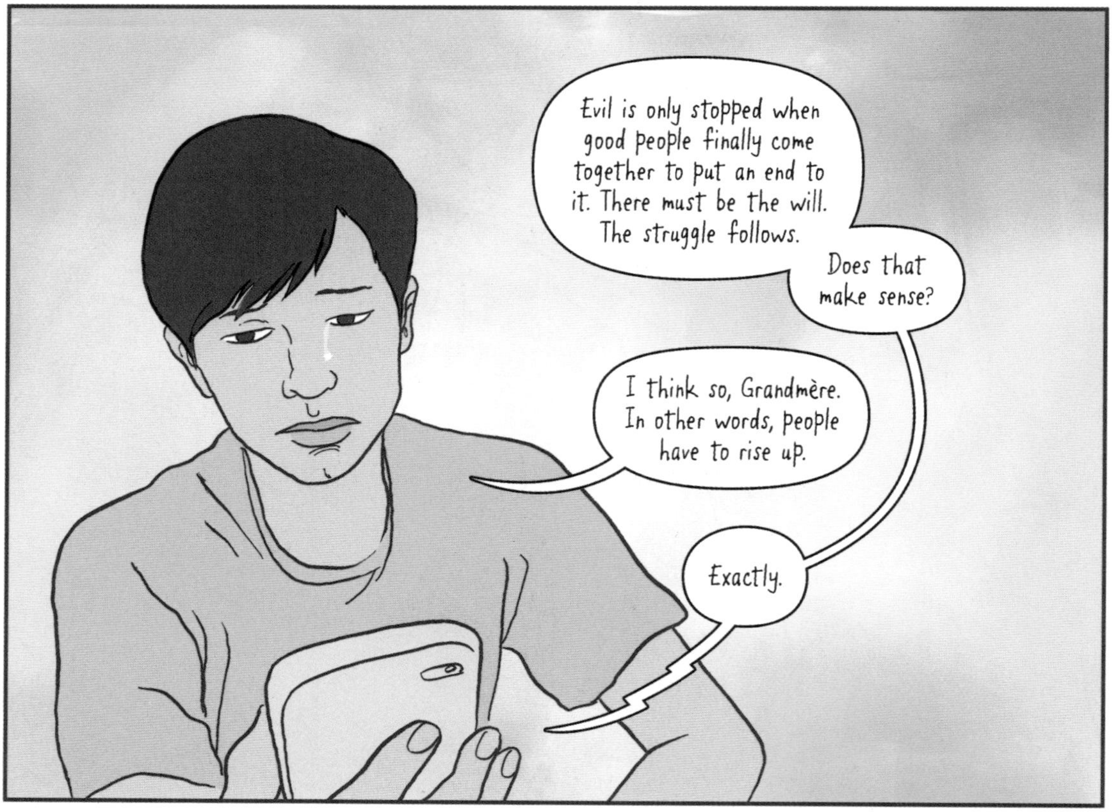
Evil is only stopped when good people finally come together to put an end to it. There must be the will. The struggle follows.
Does that make sense?
I think so, Grandmère. In other words, people have to rise up.
Exactly.

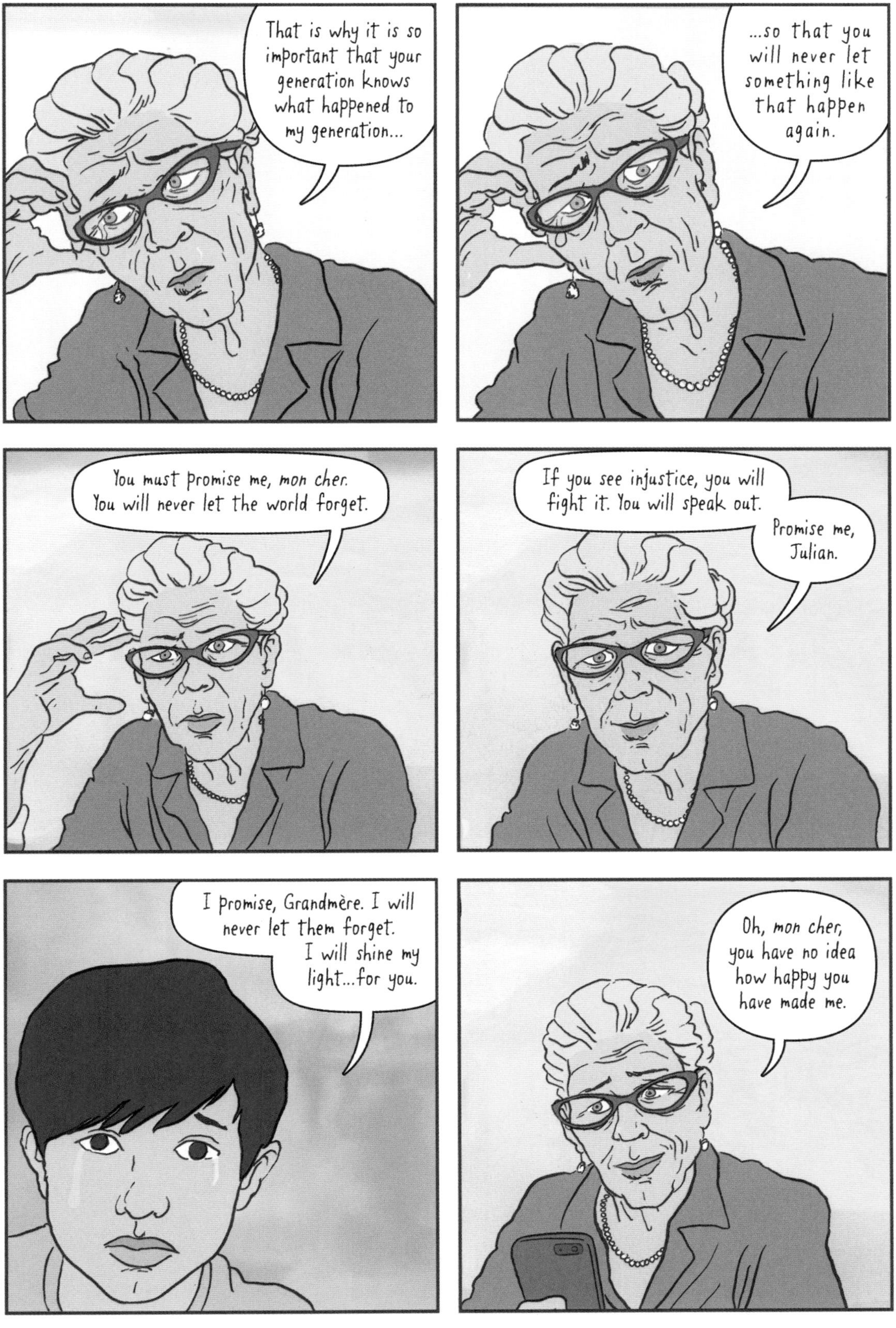
That is why it is so important that your generation knows what happened to my generation...
...so that you will never let something like that happen again.
You must promise me, mon cher. You will never let the world forget.
If you see injustice, you will fight it. You will speak out.
Promise me, Julian.
I promise, Grandmère. I will never let them forget.
I will shine my light...for you.
Oh, mon cher, you have no idea how happy you have made me.

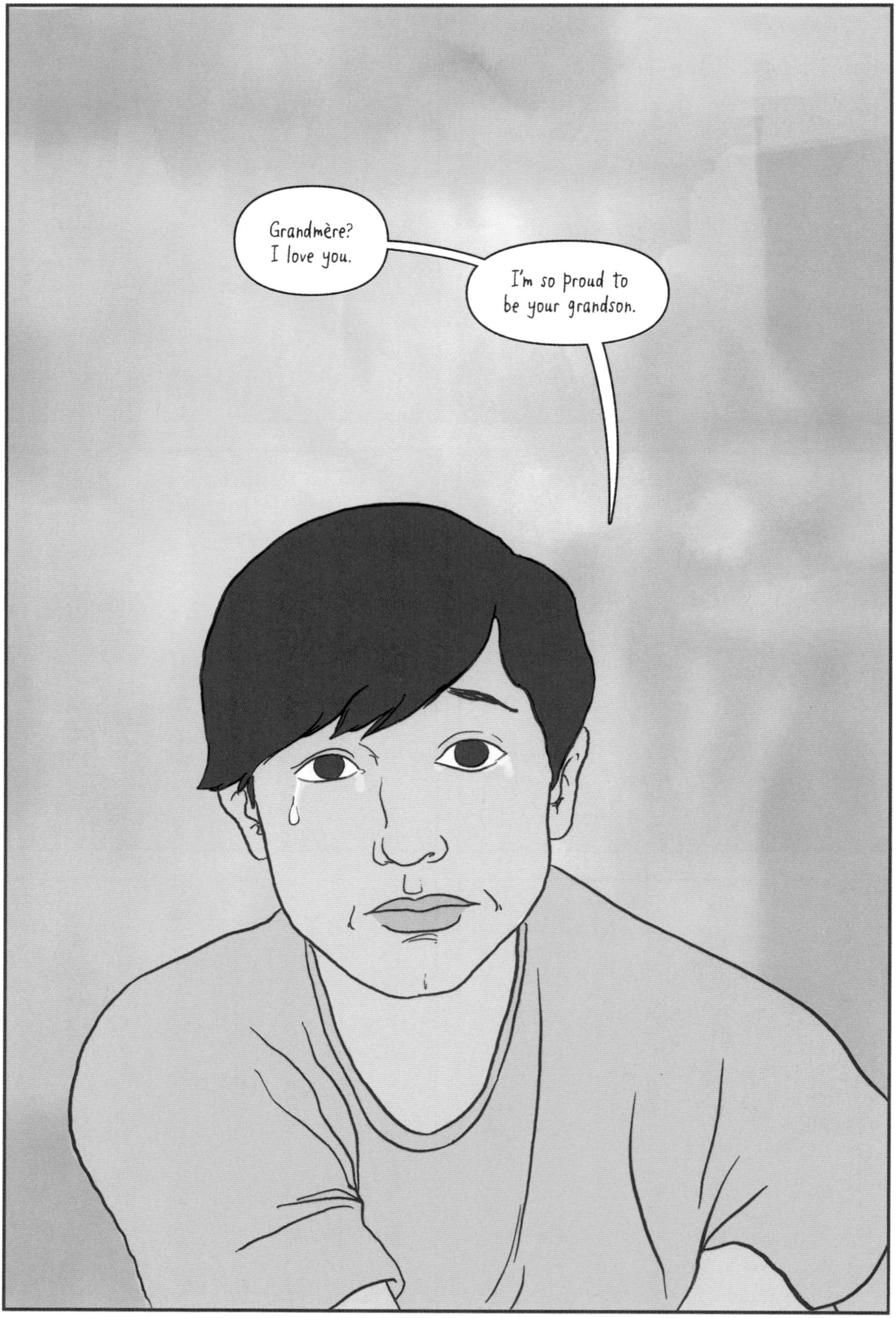
Grandmère? I love you.
I'm so proud to be your grandson.

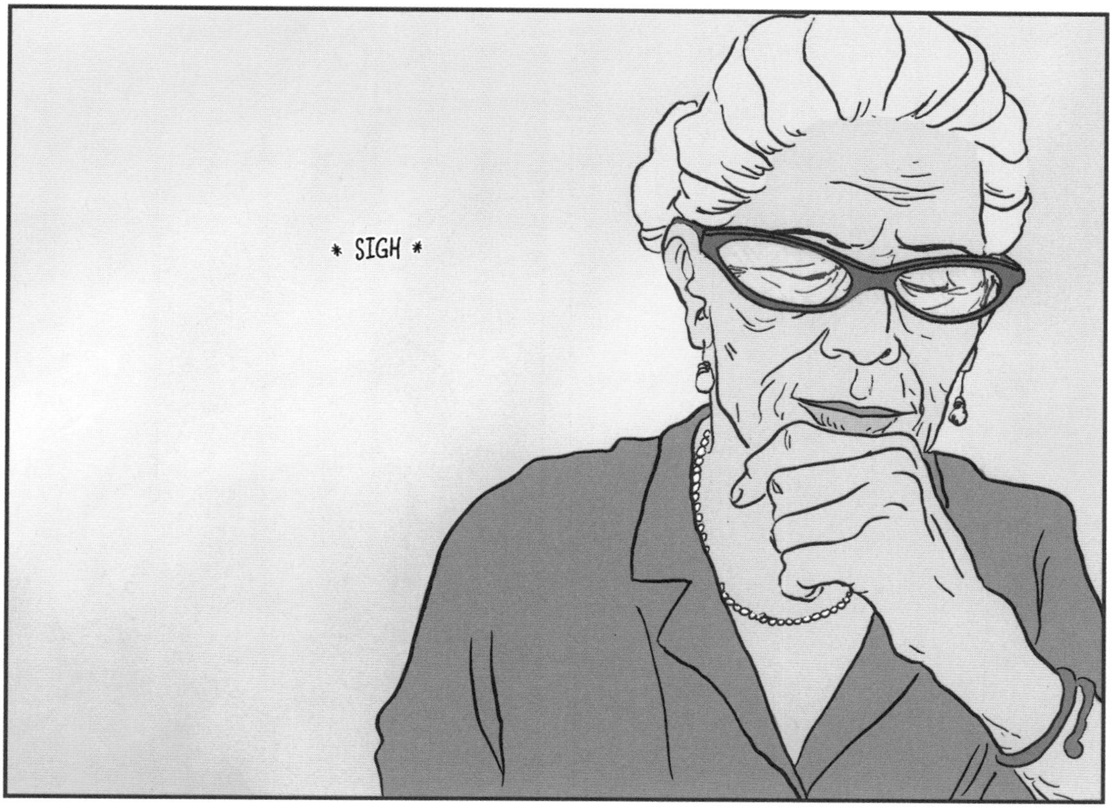
* SIGH *

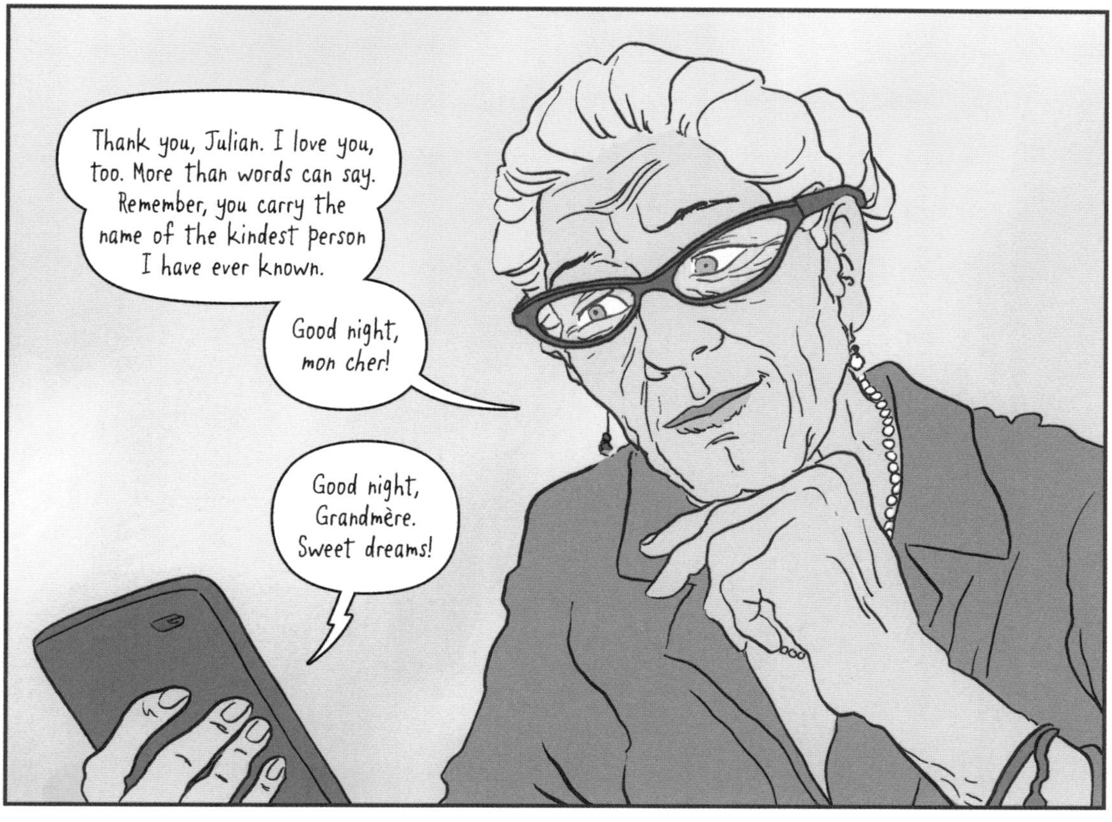
Thank you, Julian. I love you, too. More than words can say. Remember, you carry the name of the kindest person I have ever known.
Good night, mon cher!
Good night, Grandmère. Sweet dreams!

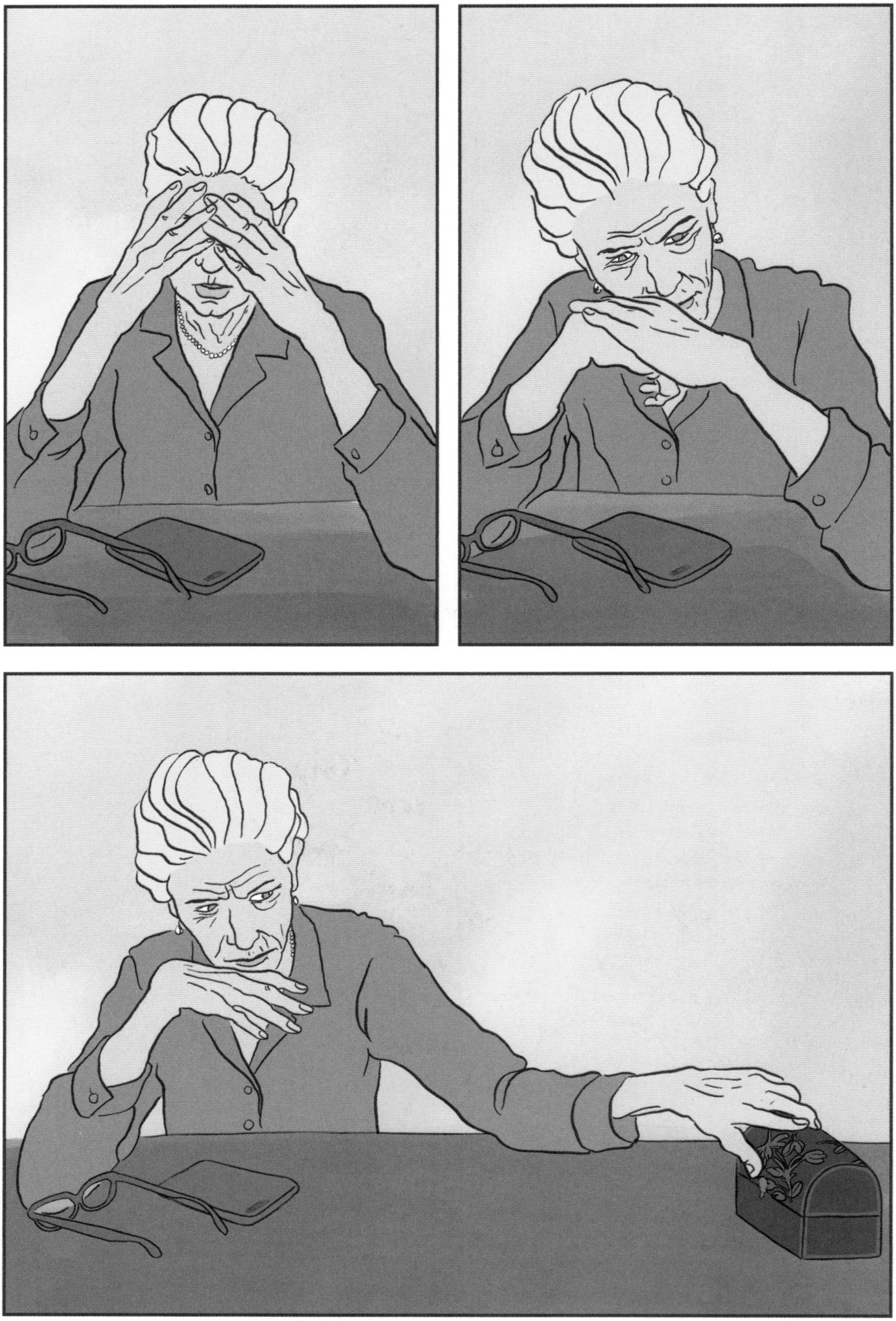

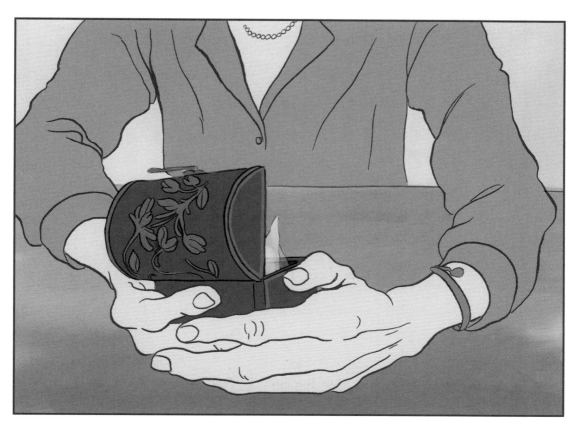

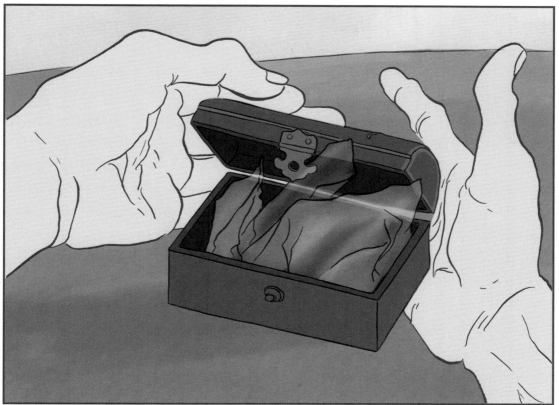

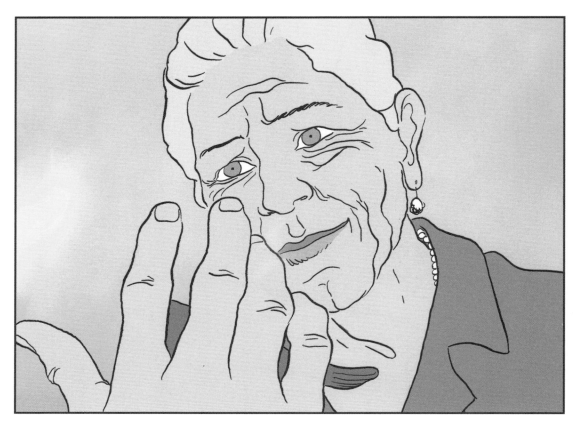

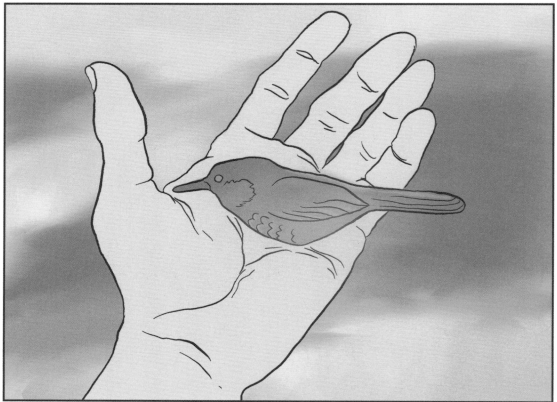

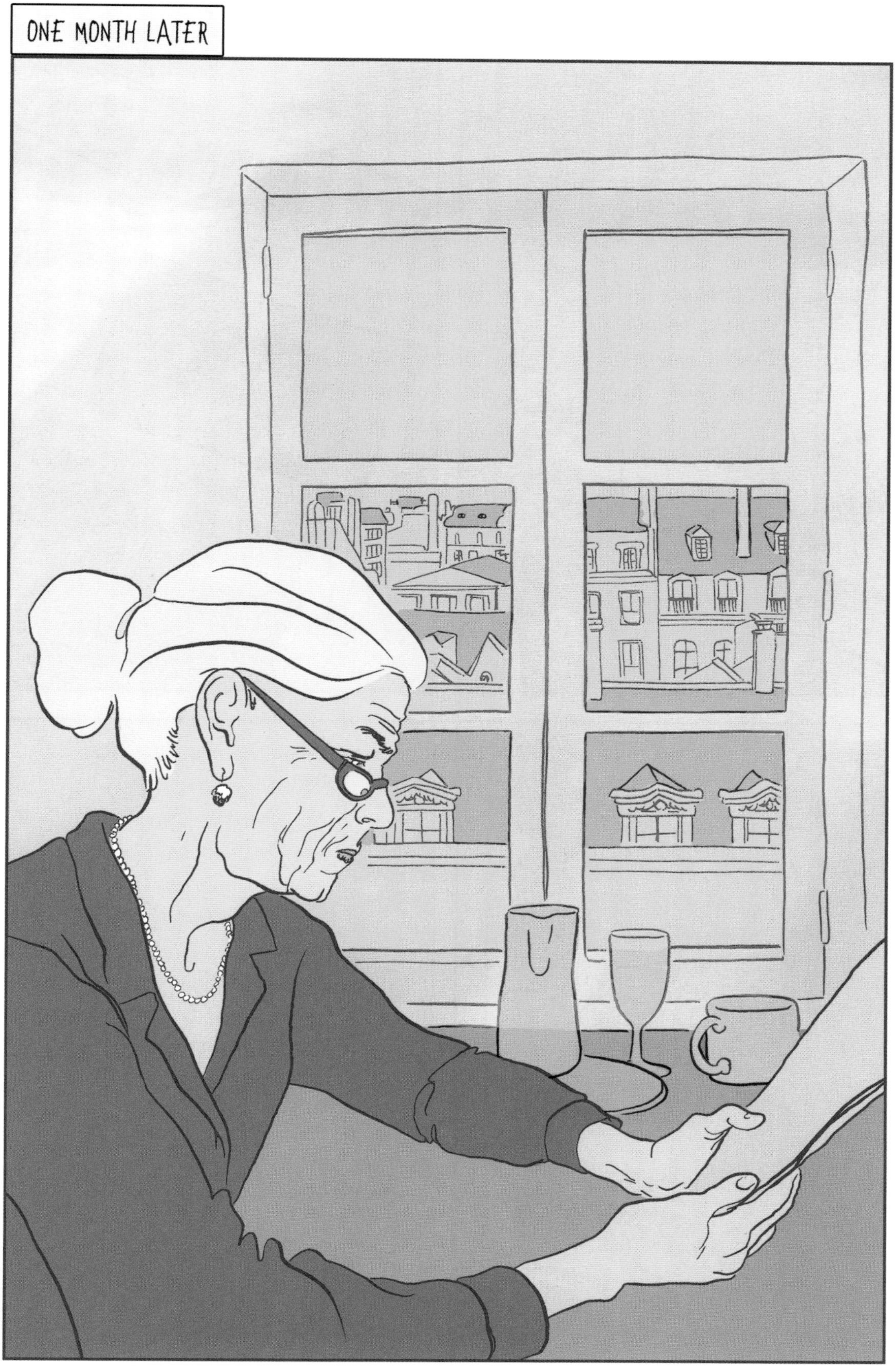
ONE MONTH LATER

No, no, no. It cannot be.
INTERNATIONAL NEWS
Rise in Anti-Semitism a
Islamophobia is Global
300 CHILDREN SEPARATED FROM PARENTS AS
PART OF TRUMP'S "ZERO TOLERANCE" POLICY
REFUGEES TURNED AWAY
WITH FEW OPTIONS LEFT
How? How can this be happening?
INTERNATIONAL
Have we learned nothing?

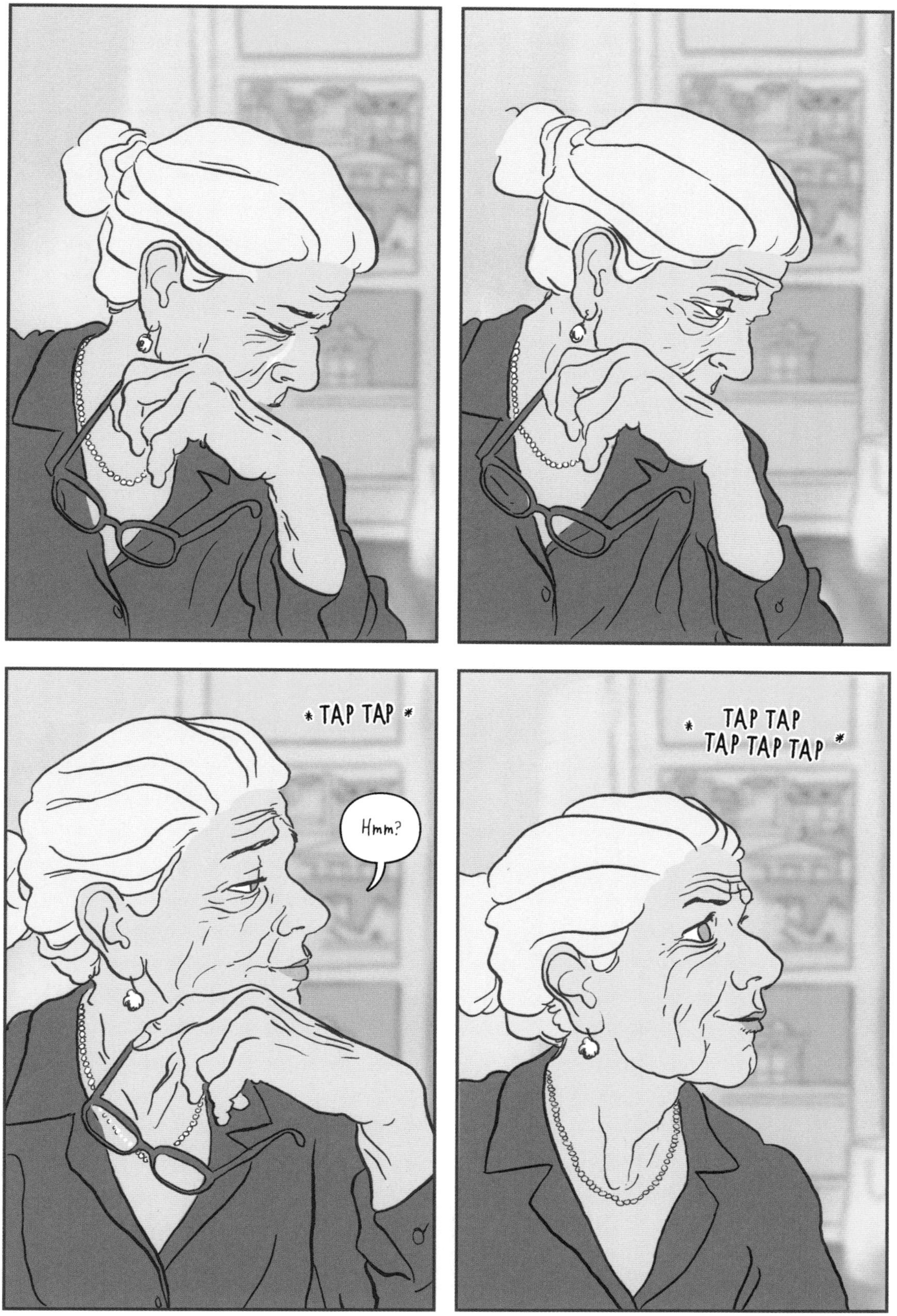
* TAP TAP *
Hmm?
* TAP TAP TAP TAP TAP *

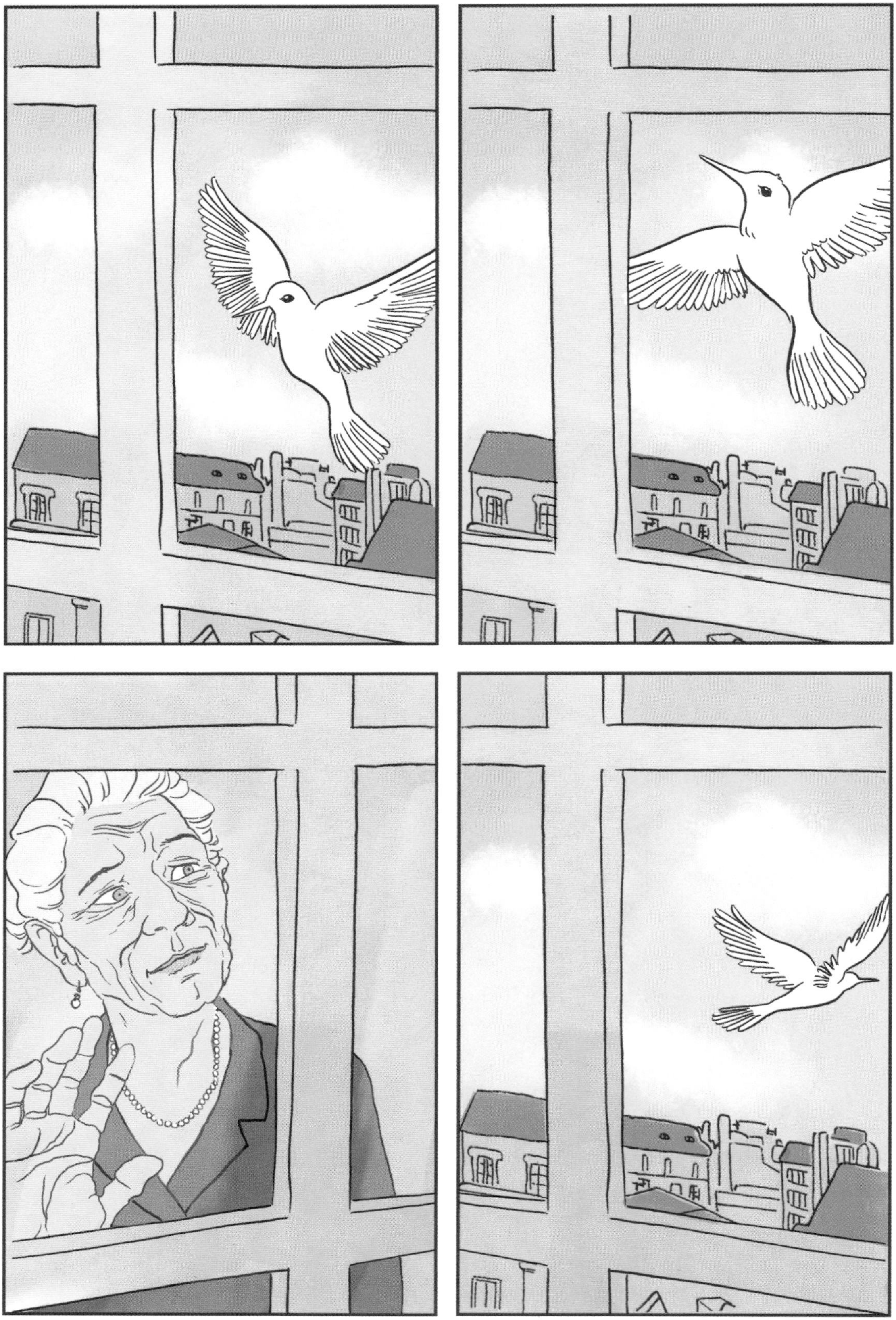

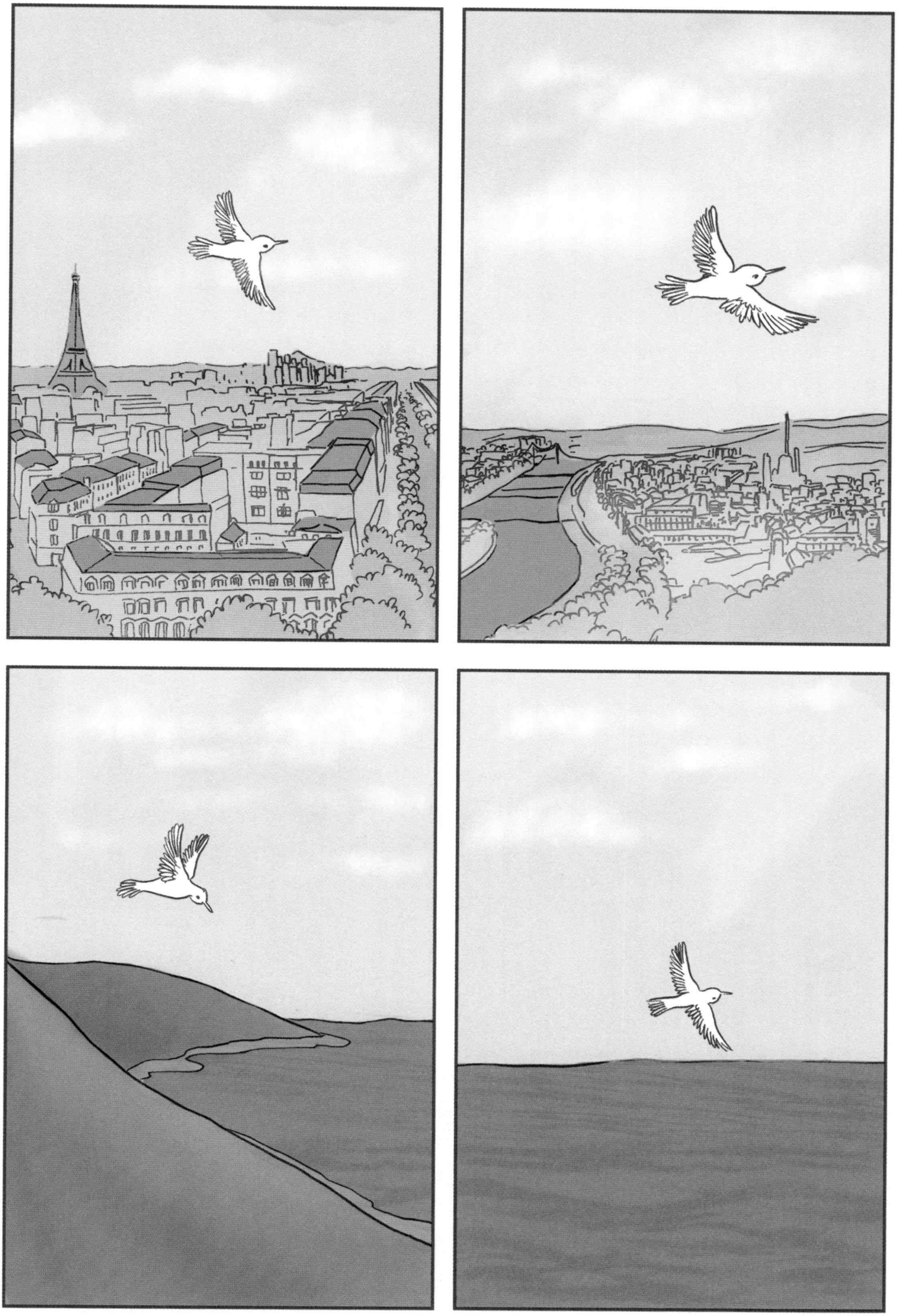

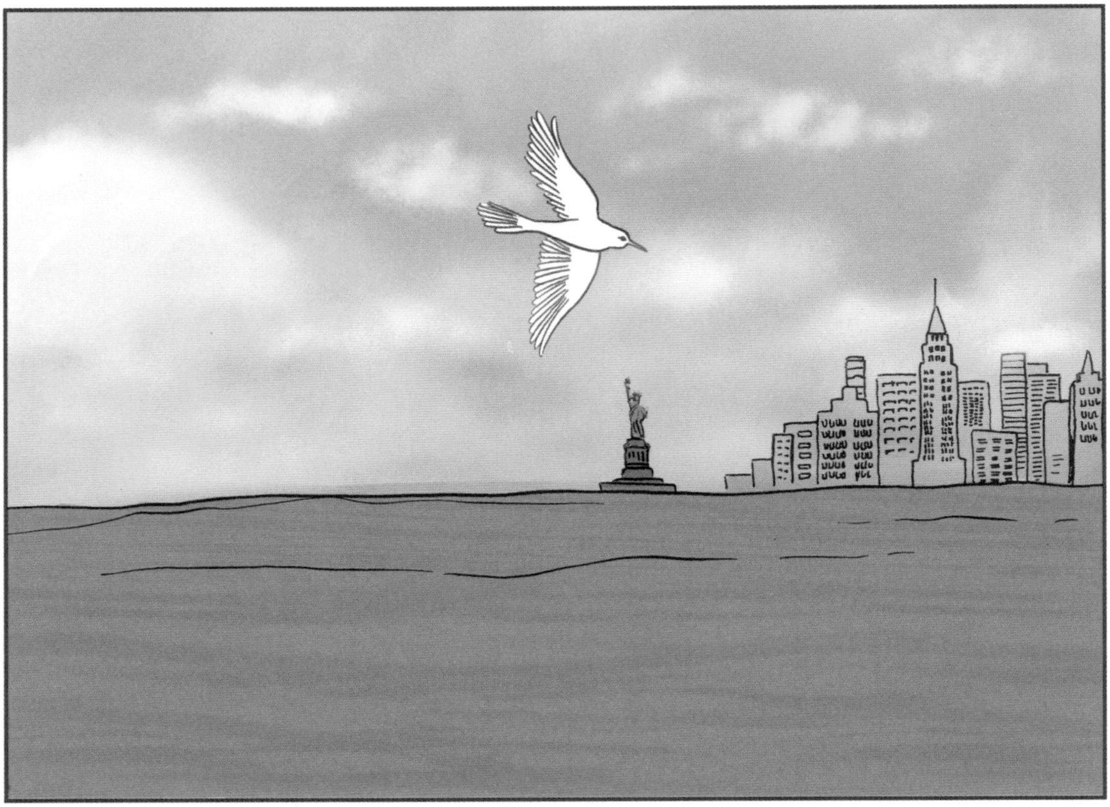

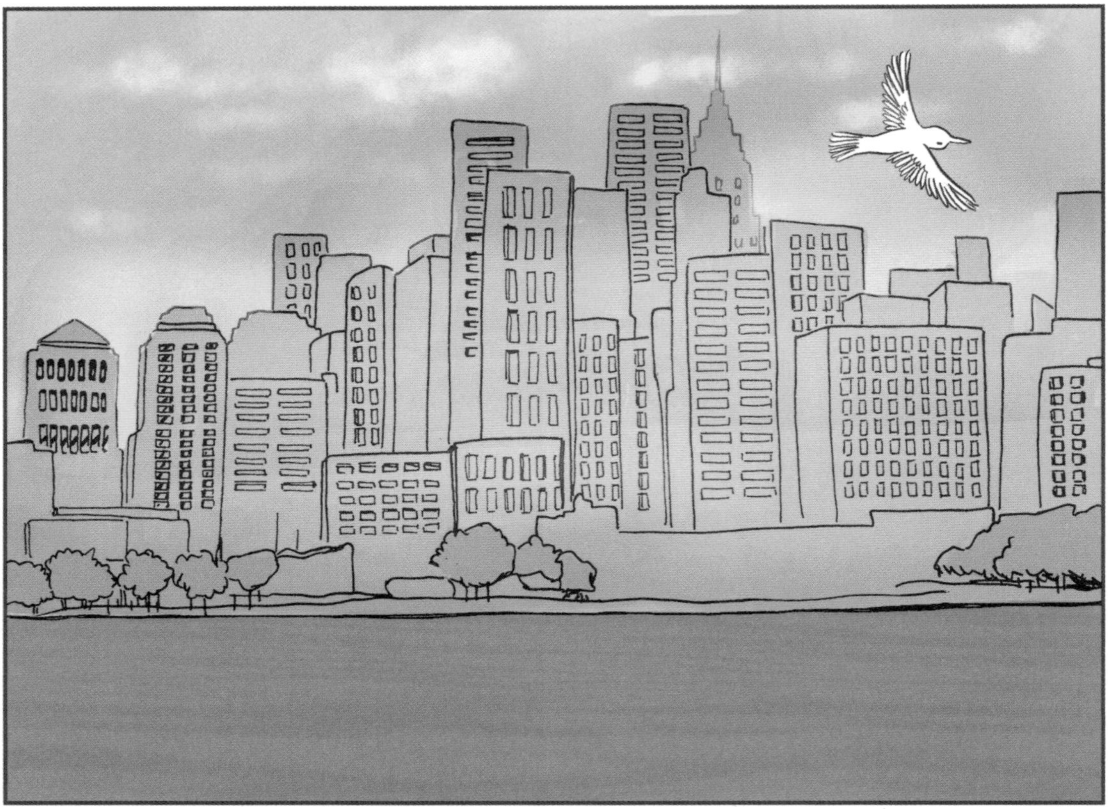

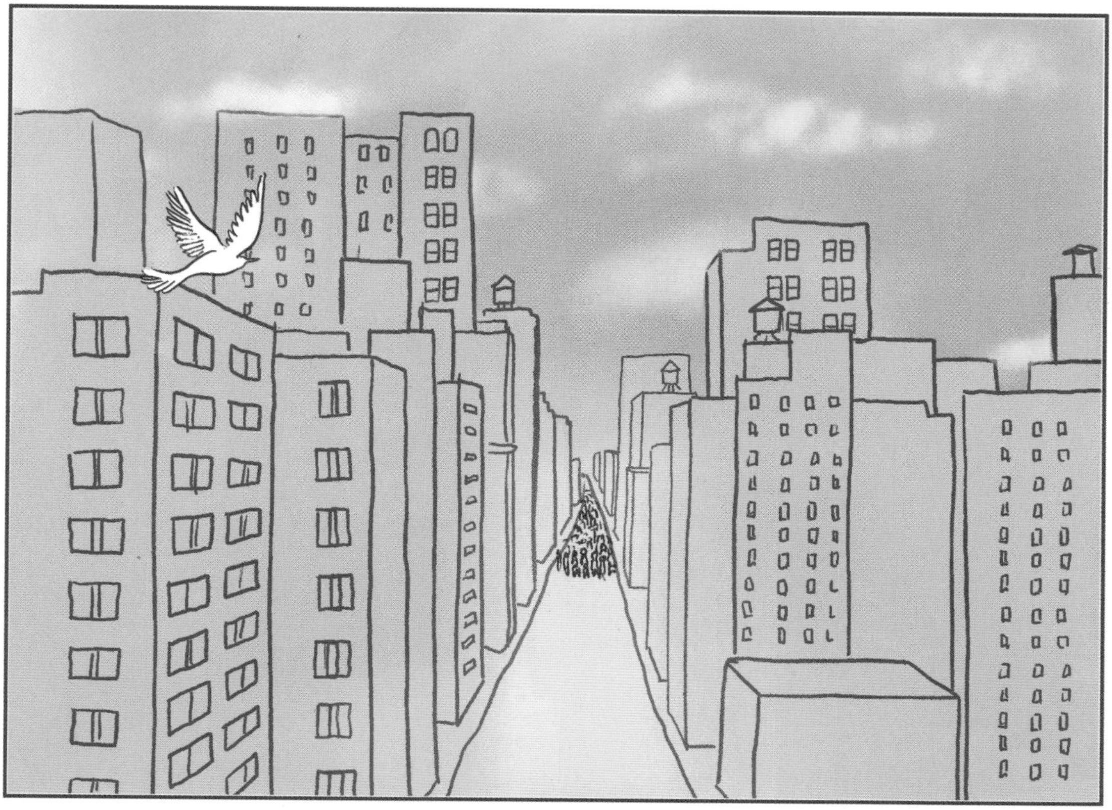

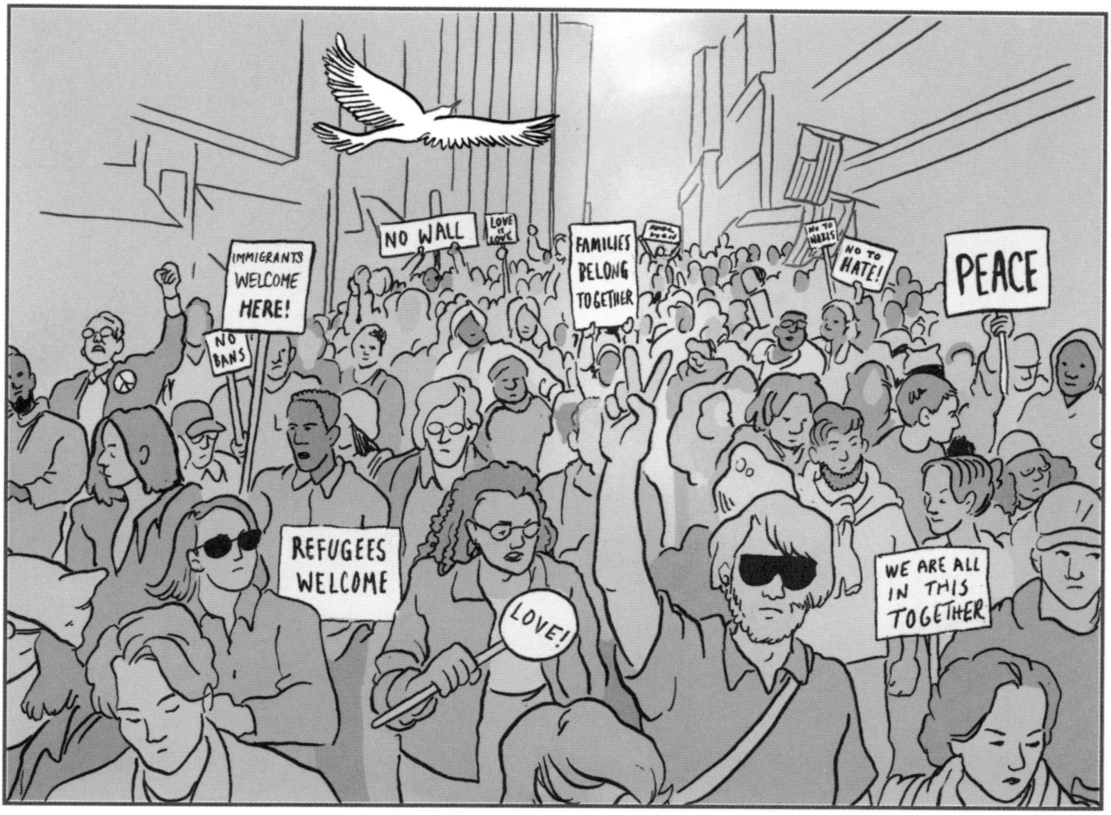
NO WALL
LOVE IS LOVE
IMMIGRANTS WELCOME HERE!
NO BANS
FAMILIES BELONG TOGETHER
NO TO NAZIS
NO TO HATE!
PEACE
REFUGEES WELCOME
LOVE!
WE ARE ALL IN THIS TOGETHER

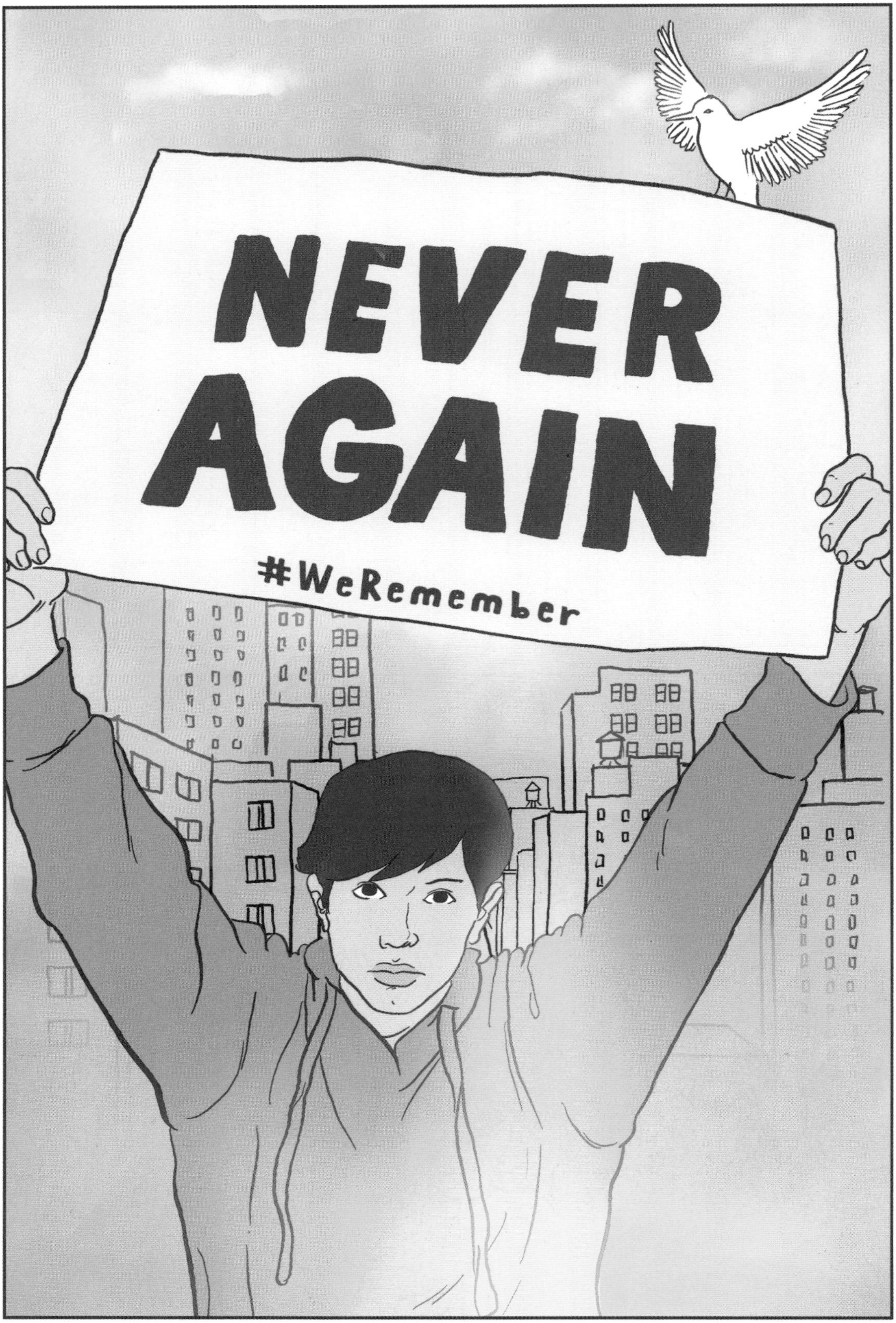
NEVER
AGAIN
#WeRemember

AFTERWORD

by Ruth Franklin

Most of *White Bird* takes place in France during World War II, but there's a scene early on that could happen in any school today. Sara, a budding artist who likes to doodle during class, has dropped her precious sketchbook. Her seatmate, who picks it up after class has let out, is a boy whose legs were twisted by polio; because of his sideways gait, their classmates call him by the cruel nickname *Tourteau,* or Crab. (His real name, as many readers will already know, is Julien.) Sara doesn't join in their teasing, but she also doesn't try to befriend him or speak up in his defense: she is a bystander. As he approaches her, balancing carefully on crutches, her friends start to whisper. "Eww. What does he want?" "I can smell him from here." (Julien's father is a sewer worker.) Sara thanks him for the sketchbook but doesn't object to her friends' cruelty. "I knew that I wasn't being very nice," she says later.

Anyone who has read "The Julian Chapter" in *Auggie & Me,* in which R. J. Palacio fleshes out the backstories of some characters from her groundbreaking novel *Wonder,* will remember this boy and the role he comes to play in the life of not only Sara but also her grandson Julian, his namesake. *White Bird* both continues and expands on that story, beginning—in a perfectly modern touch—with a FaceTime call in which the present-day Julian asks his grandmother to tell him more about her experience as a Jewish child in France during the war. Through her eyes, we see the Nazi menace as it gradually encroaches: the swastikas flying from the village buildings, the laws banning Jews from certain public places and requiring them to wear a yellow star, the first terrifying roundups and deportations. But for Sara, whose family lives in the Free Zone, life continues mostly as normal—until Nazis arrive at her school to round up all the Jewish children.

Like Lois Lowry's *Number the Stars, White Bird* is a fictional—though historically based—story of a child in hiding and the heroism of those who come to her aid. Notably, the book is not told from the point of view of the non-Jewish helpers, as is far more common in Holocaust literature for children and young adults, but from the perspective of the hidden child herself. *White Bird*'s message, too, is very much its own. "Evil will only be stopped when good people decide to put an end to it," says Vivienne, Julien's mother. For her part, Sara will come to understand—and deeply regret—her own moral crime in not standing up to her classmates as they bullied Julien.

When Sara apologizes to Julien, he consoles her: "The truth is, it doesn't matter how you used to be. It only matters how you are now." It's a message that everyone can relate to: Which of us has not, at some point, been a bystander to someone else's pain? The stakes in our own lives aren't usually as high as they are for Sara and Julien, but we never know when that might change. While we can't undo pain that we have caused, we *can* act differently in the future.

Holocaust survivor Elie Wiesel often quoted a line from Leviticus: "Do not stand idly by while your neighbor's blood is shed." Research has demonstrated that the Holocaust could not have taken place without the passive participation of millions of ordinary people who looked the other way as the Nazis exterminated their Jewish neighbors. But it's also true that the good deeds of those who saved the lives of their friends and fellow citizens—many of whom are honored by Yad Vashem, Israel's Holocaust memorial and research center, as "the Righteous Among the Nations"—are valuable beyond measure. Jewish tradition teaches that if someone saves a single life, it is as if they saved an entire world.

White Bird ends with a call to resist contemporary manifestations of prejudice and xenophobia. One needn't necessarily agree with the direct line the book draws from Nazi Germany to current events to be moved by its encouragement to stand up against tyranny and cruelty wherever we may find them, from the treatment of refugees to the tormenting of a disabled child in school. Sara's story has the power to transform her grandson from a bully into an ally. It might transform you, too.

Ruth Franklin is a book critic and the author of *A Thousand Darknesses: Lies and Truth in Holocaust Fiction* and *Shirley Jackson: A Rather Haunted Life.*

AUTHOR'S NOTE

Those who cannot remember the past are condemned to repeat it.
—George Santayana

The first time I heard this quote, which I use at the beginning of *White Bird,* was in my seventh-grade English class. We had just finished reading *The Diary of Anne Frank,* and my teacher, Ms. Waxelbaum, read the quote aloud as part of our discussion of the book. It has always stayed with me. So has the book. In fact, I would say that of all the books I've read in my life, *The Diary of Anne Frank* is the one that has had the greatest effect on me, not just as a writer, but as a person. *The Diary of Anne Frank* is one of the reasons I wrote this book.

Another reason—far more subtle—was a book I came across in a bookstore when I was nine years old. (It was actually the first "grown-up book" I ever purchased for myself.) It was called *The Best of LIFE,* and it was a large coffee-table book of photographs from the archives of *LIFE* magazine. *The Best of LIFE* was, in many ways, my introduction to the history of the world. It was from its pages of captioned photographs that I learned about the World Wars and the Vietnam War, the Cold War and the space race, Hiroshima and the atom bomb. I saw photographs of the civil rights movement, peaceful marches, hippies, famous people and ordinary citizens, visionary leaders and dictators. But the photographs I remember the most, too devastating to describe here, were of the concentration camps. Until then, I'd never heard of the Holocaust. Not at school. Not at home. All I knew about Nazis was from *The Sound of Music* and a TV show called *Hogan's Heroes*—which is to say I knew nothing.

That was not the case for my husband. He will tell you, as a Jewish man, that there was never a time in his life in which he did *not* know about the Holocaust. All of his mother's aunts, uncles, grandparents, and cousins had died in the Shoah (the Hebrew term for the Holocaust). It was an ever-present reality for her. It was an ever-present reality for almost every family in their predominantly Jewish neighborhood. It was taught in Hebrew school and Sunday school. It was discussed in temple. Just about everyone my husband grew up with had at least one relative—and sometimes an entire branch of the family—who had perished in the Holocaust.

In America today, there are children who may know a lot about the Holocaust, like my husband did, or very little, like I did. It's understandable that there would be a gap in what some kids know and some kids don't. The Holocaust, and the events leading up to the annihilation of six million Jewish people, is an extremely difficult subject to grapple with, whether you're an adult or a child. Most schools don't teach the subject until the seventh or eighth grade, if even then. This was explained to me by my husband's uncle Bernard, a New York City principal for many years, who was the first to suggest that the story of Grandmère, which I introduced in "The Julian Chapter," was the "perfect introduction"—his words—to the Holocaust. This is yet another reason why I wrote *White Bird.* (Thank you, Bernard!)

Although I did not know a lot about the Holocaust as a child, I've studied it a great deal as an adult, even before I wrote this book. It's a subject I think about often, which may seem odd to some people because, although I'm married to a Jewish man, I'm not Jewish myself. I know there may be some people who question whether I even have the right to tell this story, fictional as it is, because the Holocaust is not my story to tell. My feeling is that it should not fall solely on the victims of the Holocaust and their descendants to tell the story of the Holocaust. It should fall on everyone to remember, to teach, to mourn the loss. The millions of innocent people who died were the ultimate victims, but it was humanity itself—the very essence of who and what we are as human beings—that was attacked. It's not for Jewish people to stop anti-Semitism, after all—it's for the people who aren't Jewish to stop it in its tracks whenever they see it. That goes for any group that is discriminated against: the preservation of what is good and decent in our society falls on *all* of us.

That is what I believe, in any case, and why I made this book. To me, the heartbreak of a little girl, separated from her parents, forced to flee, living in fear of capture, is extraordinarily relevant at this moment in history. There are connections to be made between the past and the present. There are things we must always resist, wherever and however we can. I am a storyteller, so *White Bird* was my act of resistance for these times.

That the Holocaust took place, that people and nations let it happen, is something we should always struggle with, talk about, and learn from, so that we can make sure it never, ever happens again. Not on our watch.

A NOTE ABOUT THE DEDICATION

This book is dedicated to my mother-in-law, Mollie (Malka), whose parents, Max (Motel Chaim) and Rose (Rojza Ruchla), immigrated to America from Poland in 1921. Like hundreds of thousands of Jewish immigrants fleeing persecution and poverty in their homeland, Max and Rose settled on New York's Lower East Side, which is where Mollie grew up.

The rest of Max's and Rose's families—their parents, grandparents, siblings, aunts, uncles, cousins—all stayed behind in Poland. Max's family was from Maków Mazowiecki. Rose's lived not far away, in Wyszków. In 1939, when the Germans invaded Poland, that entire region was annexed by the Third Reich. Of the 3,000 Jews who lived in Maków before the war and the 9,000 Jews in Wyszków, none survived. We know this from archives that are carefully kept by organizations dedicated to preserving the names of the Jews who perished in the Holocaust. What we cannot know is the impact this must have had on Mollie's mother and father. But we can imagine.

We are, all of us, a collection of those who have come before. In my children, I see my husband. In my husband, I see his parents. In his parents, I see an infinite past. This book is for Mollie, a beautiful, kind woman, who loved to laugh and sing; for her ancestors, who I'm sure also loved to laugh and sing; and for her descendants, including my sons, who carry in them a lineage that goes back to the dawn of time, and a light that will never fade.

Mollie's high school graduation portrait.

GLOSSARY

This book is a work of fiction. It was not based on any one person's story, but was influenced by the many inspiring stories I've read over the years about children who went into hiding during the Holocaust and the ordinary citizens who helped them.

Some young readers, after reading *White Bird,* may decide they don't want to learn anything more about the Holocaust right now, which is totally okay. Some kids may wish to find out a little more. For these kids, I've provided a short glossary of some of the terms and events referred to in the book, as well as brief descriptions of the real-life inspiration for some of the characters and situations depicted in the book.

Anti-Semitism

Anti-Semitism is defined as the hatred of Jews as a group, be it religious or ethnic, which is often accompanied by hostile or passive discrimination against Jewish people. Anti-Semitism can be traced back to the Middle Ages in Europe, when Jewish communities were targeted for persecution. Examples of anti-Semitism: In Spain in 1492, Jews were expelled from all Spanish territories unless they converted to Christianity; in Russia, starting in the nineteenth century, pogroms were organized by local authorities to loot Jewish homes and businesses. The worst manifestation of anti-Semitism came in the twentieth century, when the Nazis committed genocide—the deliberate killing of six million Jewish people (see the Holocaust).

The Beast of Gévaudan

My inspiration for the wolf of Sara's nightmares came from the stories of the Beast of Gévaudan. This was a man-eating wolf that was purported to have roamed the forests of the Margeride mountains in the eighteenth century. Eyewitness accounts describe the beast as having enormous teeth and a gigantic tail. In a span of three years, from 1764 to 1767, it was said that the Beast of Gévaudan had attacked and killed over 100 people, including many children.

Although no one could prove that the victims had all been killed by the same wolf, or even by a pack of wolves, the legend became such a phenomenon throughout France that hunting parties were organized to find and kill the beast. This may have been the inspiration for numerous folktales and stories that have sprung up over the centuries involving a wolf-like beast living in the woods or the mountains, like *Beauty and the Beast,* the legend of the werewolves—*voirloups* in French—and even "Little Red Riding Hood." Recent forensic studies have led scientists to speculate that the true Beast of Gévaudan was, in fact, not a wolf but a lioness, an animal that eyewitnesses might not have even known existed in that part of the world.

An eighteenth-century engraving of the Beast of Gévaudan.

Concentration Camps

Concentration camps are detainment centers used to house large concentrations of people who have been imprisoned indefinitely, without legal cause or judicial oversight. During World War II, the Germans kept millions of captives inside concentration camps within both Germany and German-occupied territories. Some concentration camps were work camps, where captives were used as forced labor. Others were extermination camps, where large numbers of people were killed in gas chambers.

In *White Bird,* Mademoiselle Petitjean is last seen en route to the camp in Pithiviers after being turned away from the camp in Beaune-la-Rolande. These two were transit camps inside France in which prisoners were held before being deported to concentration camps farther east.

Sara's mother, Rose, is taken to the Drancy camp, which was another transit camp in France. From there, Rose was transferred to Auschwitz, the largest and most notorious of the concentration camps. Located in Poland, Auschwitz

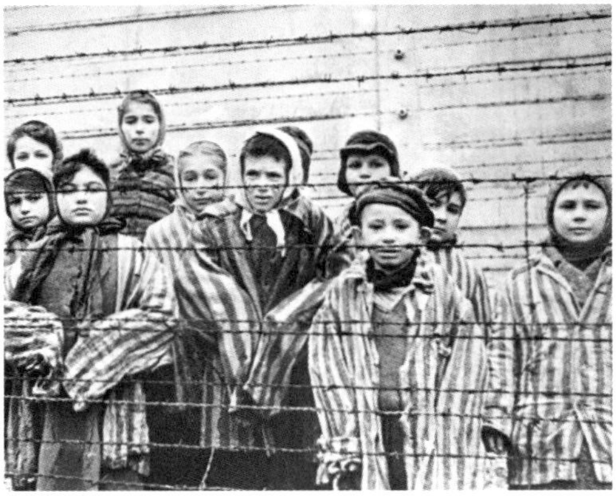

A group of child survivors at Auschwitz on the day of the concentration camp's liberation, January 27, 1945.

was both a labor camp and an extermination camp in which, historians estimate, over one million Jews were killed until its liberation in January 1945.

Deportations/Roundups in France

In *White Bird,* Sara's family stops receiving letters from their cousins in Paris after the roundup of Vel' d'Hiv.

The Vel' d'Hiv roundup occurred in May 1942. Over 13,000 Jews—including more than 4,000 children—were arrested and detained inside the Vélodrome d'Hiver stadium, and held without adequate food, water, or sanitation. From there, most were transported to concentration camps.

Although other roundups of foreign-born Jews had taken place in the Occupied Zone as part of the Vichy government's ongoing collaboration with Germany, the Vel' d'Hiv roundup is considered the worst for several reasons: 1. the number of people arrested; 2. its location in the heart of Paris; 3. it was the first time women and children were arrested along with men. By this time, the Vichy government had published its "Statute of the Jews," outlining the restrictions placed on Jews living in the Occupied Zone.

In *White Bird,* Max refers to the roundup of Marseille, which occurred in January 1943. This was notable because it took place in the Free Zone. Two thousand mostly foreign-born Jews were immediately deported to concentration camps, and over 30,000 Jews were forced to leave when the Germans set fire to that sector of the city.

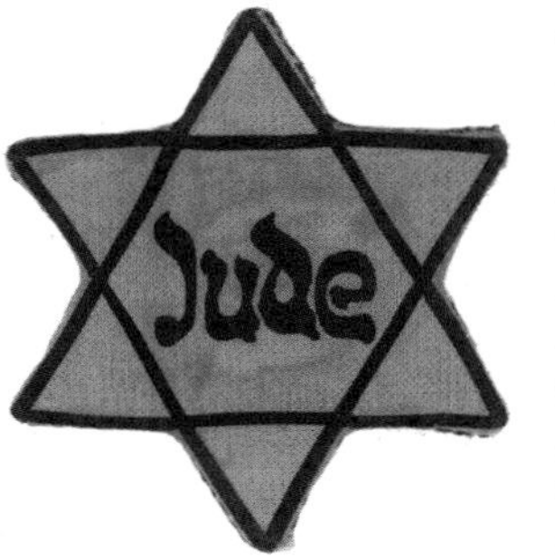
Jude

The yellow Star of David badge that Jews were required to wear. This one is from 1941.

The roundup depicted in *White Bird,* which results in the arrest of Sara's mother, is based on these well-documented roundups, as well as other, smaller ones that occurred after the Germans occupied the Free Zone in November 1942. Although the Vichy government never sanctioned the deportation of French-born Jews, it did allow the denaturalization of some Jews not born in France. Sara's parents, both born outside of France, may have ended up on a deportation list because of this.

The Diary of Anne Frank

Anne Frank was just ten years old when the Nazis invaded the Netherlands, where she lived with her parents and her older sister, Margot. As they did in every country they occupied, the Nazis began systematically oppressing the Jewish population. Anne's father, Otto, decided his family would hide behind his business to avoid the roundups he knew would come. With the help of his former employee Miep Gies, the Frank family, along with members of the Van Pels family, moved into the tiny quarters. The families had to stay very quiet during the day. They relied on Miep to bring them food. For the two years they were in hiding, Anne kept a diary, recording her thoughts and feelings and documenting the daily routines and drastic difficulties of being imprisoned inside a tiny room.

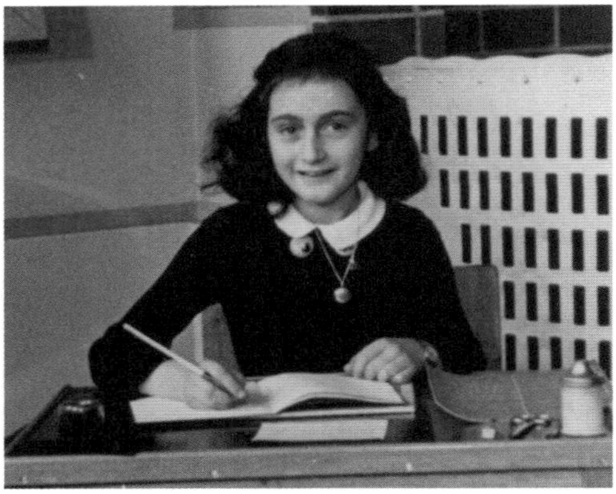

Anne Frank writing in a journal in 1940.

In August 1944, the police were tipped off and the secret annex was discovered. Everyone living in the secret annex was arrested and sent to concentration camps. Anne, her sister, and her mother were deported to the concentration camp Auschwitz, and then Bergen-Belsen. They did not survive. Neither did anyone else from the annex, except Anne's father.

After the war ended, Otto returned to Amsterdam, and Miep gave him Anne's diary, which she had kept hidden from the Nazis. *The Diary of Anne Frank* has been published in over seventy languages and has made a lasting impression on millions of people around the world.

The French Resistance

When Nazi forces invaded France in June 1940, the French government surrendered to Germany and signed an armistice, agreeing to split France in half. The Occupied Zone would be run by Germany. The Unoccupied Zone, or Free Zone, would be run by a German-approved French government located in a town called Vichy.

Shortly after, a French general named Charles de Gaulle gave a radio speech from London that called on French citizens to resist the occupation. By then, many small resistance groups, made up of men and women from all over the country and from all different social and economic backgrounds, including students, academics, artists, writers, doctors, housewives, and clergy from every denomination, had already formed secretly all over France, intent on fighting the Nazi occupation in whatever way they could. De Gaulle's speech became a clarion call for these resisters, whose actions—both great and small—were collectively known as the French Resistance. In the beginning, there was no central authority governing the French Resistance, but eventually it became a network of organized activity under the leadership of Jean Moulin, a civil servant, who parachuted into the heart of France to unite the various resistance factions under de Gaulle's Free French banner. Moulin was eventually captured and died in Nazi custody.

Different groups within the Resistance focused on different objectives. Some helped rescue, hide, or smuggle Jews and political prisoners to safety. Some sabotaged rail lines or blew up bridges to stop the advancement of the Nazi forces. Some established secret communications with the Allied forces outside France. Some were spies or double agents. Some published clandestine underground newspapers. Some, like the Maquis, were guerrilla soldiers (see the Maquis).

Members of the Maquis, a group within the French Resistance, study the mechanism and maintenance of weapons dropped by parachute into the Haute-Loire region in 1940.

Gendarmes

Gendarmes were officers of the French Armed Forces who served as policemen, especially in small towns and rural areas where the French National Police did not have a strong presence. Gendarmes were often sent to round up—or assist in the roundup of—foreign-born Jews and refugees across the country.

Grandmère

The character of Grandmère in *White Bird* is (like so many of the characters in my stories) a mash-up of different people I've known in my life. In the case of Grandmère, I had three people in mind as I was writing and developing the character. One was my mother-in-law, Mollie, who liked to tell long, detailed stories. The second was my friend Lisa, who served as my illustration model for Grandmère. The third was an old woman I never actually met myself, but kept envisioning as I was writing Grandmère.

This woman was someone I used to see when I was a student at the American University of Paris. I would ride the 92 bus line to my school on the avenue Bosquet, and almost every day she would get on at the Maréchal Juin stop. She was impossible not to notice; she had such an elegant, imperious air about her. And she was always—*always*—dressed to the nines. Such a fashionable lady! While she never acknowledged my existence (she coldly appraised my army jacket and clogs one day, which rendered me incapable of ever starting a conversation with her in my broken French), I do remember eavesdropping on her often. She had a striking voice and piercing gray eyes. One time, she got into a long conversation with another older woman, and she said: *"Moi, j'étais une fille frivole, mais quand les Allemands sont arrivés, tout a changé."* Translated, that means: "Me, I was a frivolous girl once, but when the Germans arrived, all that changed." Who knows why that one phrase has stuck with me all these years. Maybe it had to do with the sense of tragedy I felt inside those words, the endless possibilities of a story that I would never hear from her but could imagine for myself. But that one line, more than thirty years later, is what launched Grandmère for me.

The Holocaust

The Holocaust (from a Greek word meaning "burned whole") was the mass murder of six million Jewish people by the Nazis during World War II.

The Nazis were a political organization in Germany that started shortly after World War I. Their ideology, which was built on the premise of German superiority and a belief that people of the "Aryan race" (i.e., Northern European whites) were superior to other races, was not taken seriously at first. However, as national bitterness about the terms of Germany's surrender grew and the Nazi Party leader, Adolf

Hitler, rose in popularity, the Nazis acquired power. Hitler used the country's economic hardships to stoke deep-seated anti-Semitism in its citizenry, blaming Jewish people for all of Germany's problems.

When Hitler became Germany's chancellor in 1933, he launched a series of measures, including boycotting Jewish businesses, banning Jewish students from attending schools and universities, and expelling Jewish

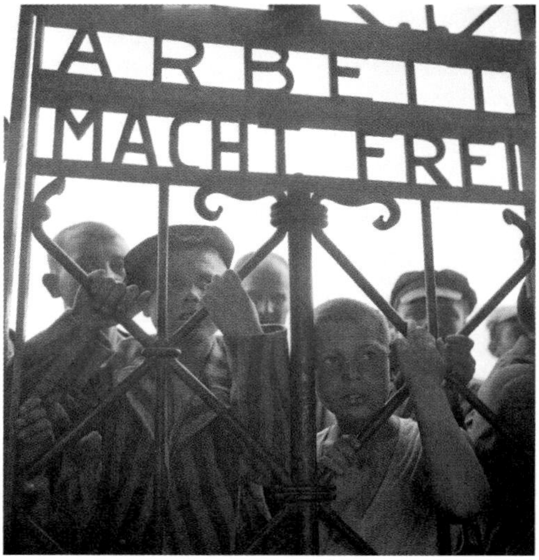
MACHT FREI

Children in the Dachau concentration camp on the day it was liberated, April 29, 1945, by U.S. troops.

officers from the army. In September 1935, he unveiled the Nuremberg Laws, which stated that only people of pure "German or kindred blood" could be citizens. This stripped Jews who had been born in Germany of all their rights as German citizens, making it easier for them to be persecuted.

In late 1941, German Jews who had not already fled were forced to live in ghettos, which were walled districts that separated Jews from the non-Jewish population. Eventually, the ghettos were liquidated and the Jews were deported to concentration camps (see Concentration Camps).

As the Nazi forces swept through the rest of Europe, the Jewish citizens in those occupied countries were also arrested and deported to concentration camps. As a result, millions of Jews from all over Europe were sent to concentration camps. The Nazis also targeted other groups, including the Romani people, persons with disabilities, and homosexuals.

By the time the Allied forces won the war in June 1945, six million Jews had been killed, or two out of every three Jews who had been living in Europe before the war. Also killed were an estimated 220,000 Romani, 200,000 people with disabilities, and an unknown number of the 5,000–15,000 homosexuals who had been imprisoned in concentration camps.

After the war, when the full extent of the horrors of the Holocaust became known, many Nazis were put on trial for crimes against humanity.

As for the survivors of the Holocaust, some returned to their homes and tried to rebuild their lives, as Max and Sara did in *White Bird.* Some survivors immigrated to the United States. And others went to Palestine, where, in 1948, the state of Israel was founded.

In 2005, the United Nations instituted an International Day of Commemoration to honor the victims of the Holocaust. They stated, "The Holocaust, which resulted in the murder of one-third of the Jewish people, along with countless members of other minorities, will forever be a warning to all people of the dangers of hatred, bigotry, racism and prejudice."

The Jewish Resistance

In *White Bird,* Rabbi Bernstein and his wife are smuggled out of Dannevilliers by the Armée Juive. This organization, founded in 1942 in the south of France, was a resistance group that helped Jews escape from France.

There were many underground resistance groups that formed all over Europe to fight the Nazis—either through insurrection within camps and ghettos or by joining armed groups like the Bielski partisans in Poland or the Maquis in France (see the Maquis).

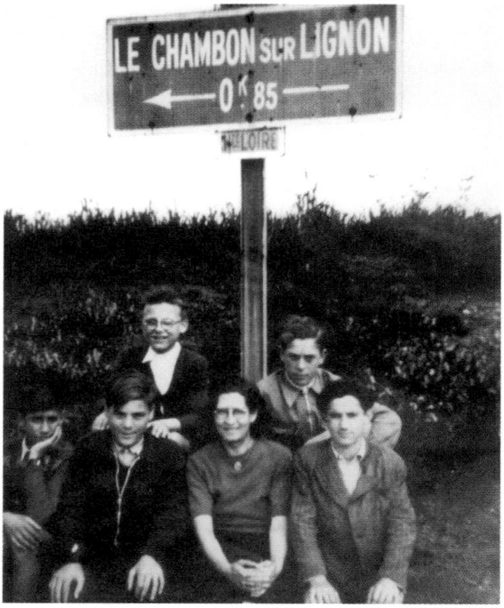
LE CHAMBON SUR LIGNON

Juliette Usach, a physician and the director of the La Guespy children's home, sits with five boys beneath a sign for Le Chambon-sur-Lignon in 1943.

The Maquis on a French mountain trail in 1944.

Le Chambon-sur-Lignon

In *White Bird,* Sara and Julien live in neighboring villages in the heart of the Haute-Loire region of France. Although Aubervilliers-aux-Bois and Dannevilliers are fictional, they are based on a village in France called Le Chambon-sur-Lignon, where thousands of Jews were hidden from the Nazis during the war. Its citizens provided shelter in their homes, schools, and churches, and even in barns, like the one Sara hid in. For their humanitarian efforts, they were collectively declared Righteous Among the Nations by Yad Vashem, the Holocaust memorial center in Israel.

The Maquis

In *White Bird,* a maquisard risks his life to help the Jewish children in the École Lafayette escape into the woods. Although this event is fictional, in real life the Maquis were Resistance fighters who lived deep in the the woods and mountains, where the Nazis could not find them. This is why they were called "Maquis," which means "thicket." An individual fighter was known as a maquisard.

Shortly before D-Day, word went out that the Maquis were gathering forces in Mont Mouchet, with the objective of delaying the Nazi troops en route to Normandy. It is estimated that 3,000 maquisards assembled in the Margeride mountains and began launching their guerrilla attacks against the German forces. The Germans, however, mounted a vicious counterattack, including bombardment by planes, tanks, and heavy artillery.

In the end, the few thousand maquisards gathered in Mont Mouchet were vastly outnumbered by the 22,000 German soldiers. About 300 maquisards were killed in the Battle of Mont Mouchet, although it's possible there were many more deaths unrecorded in the mountains.

The Milice

The Milice was a pro-Nazi militia group created by the Vichy government to help fight the French Resistance. They acted as a paramilitary police force and worked closely with the Nazis. After the war, many of them were executed in retaliation for their murderous efforts on behalf of the Germans.

Muriel Rukeyser

Muriel Rukeyser was a Jewish American poet (1913–1980) who wrote about the human struggle for love and equity in times of peace and war. An avowed pacifist, she wrote poetry as a form of protest, highlighting social injustice and inequity. The title *White Bird* is taken from Rukeyser's poem "Fourth Elegy: The Refugees," which I used as the epigraph of this book. It comes from her collection of poems *Out of Silence,* as do the quotes at the beginning of the first three parts.

"Never Again" and #WeRemember

"'Never again' becomes more than a slogan: It's a prayer, a promise, a vow … never again the glorification of base, ugly, dark violence." —Elie Wiesel

The phrase "Never again," which Julian has on his sign at a protest march at the end of *White Bird,* has been used by many Jewish institutions and organizations over the years, including the US Holocaust Memorial Museum, to remind the world about the genocide committed against the Jews during the Holocaust, and to guard against future genocides ever happening in the world.

#WeRemember is a hashtag that was developed as part of the #WeRemember campaign, the world's largest Holocaust remembrance event, which is pledged to fight racism and to end xenophobia (see Organizations and Resources).

Persecution of Persons with Disabilities

When Vincent accosts Julien in the barn, he says some things that reveal his knowledge of a Nazi-instigated euthanasia program called T4. This program's main imperative was to kill or sterilize people with disabilities, either physical or mental, who—in Nazi ideology—were deemed "inferior" or "unworthy of life." An estimated 200,000 people were killed in Germany as part of the T4 Program.

While there was no equivalent policy in France, an estimated 45,000 patients in several mental asylums and hospitals were known to have died of starvation and/or inadequate care during World War II. Whether this was part of a Vichy-sanctioned eugenics program or happened under the directive of highly unethical medical directors is still debated among historians and academics in France.

Polio

In *White Bird,* Julien walks with crutches because his legs were weakened from polio, which he contracted as a young child. Polio was a dreaded infectious disease that killed or paralyzed millions of people—mostly children—in the first half of the twentieth century. Families lived in fear of the disease, as children who caught polio were often quarantined, or separated from their families and sent to live in sanatoriums to recover. While some children made full recoveries, many were paralyzed.

Reverend André Trocmé with his wife, Magda (date unknown).

Bobby, a child suffering from polio, uses a cane and a brace in August 1947.

The identification card photo of Daniel Trocmé in 1938.

In the 1950s, Dr. Jonas Salk invented a vaccine to prevent the transmission of polio. Although the disease could be eradicated from the earth, it is still spread in certain areas of the world where children have no access to vaccines.

Reverend André Trocmé, Daniel Trocmé, and the École Nouvelle Cévenole

Even before the German occupation of France, Reverend André Trocmé had been using his pulpit to preach against Nazism to the townspeople of Le Chambon-sur-Lignon (see Le Chambon-sur-Lignon). The school he started with his wife, Magda, and another pastor named Édouard Theis was called the École Nouvelle Cévenole. It was a coeducational school founded on the principles of tolerance and equality, and was the inspiration for the École Lafayette in *White Bird.*

As Jewish refugees began fleeing south from the Occupied Zone, Reverend Trocmé and Magda, along with Pastor Theis and a schoolmaster named Roger Darcissac, helped organize the town's citizenry to hide the refugees from the Nazis and/or smuggle them to safety outside of France. For these efforts,

André, Édouard, and Roger were arrested and sent to an internment camp inside France, though they were eventually released.

Reverend Trocmé served as my inspiration for Pastor Luc.

The inspiration for Mademoiselle Petitjean was Reverend Trocmé's nephew, Daniel Trocmé, a schoolmaster at a nearby school called Maison des Roches. In June 1943, when his school was raided by the Nazis, Daniel Trocmé chose to accompany the eighteen Jewish students who had been arrested, although he himself had not been detained. This act of self-sacrifice ultimately landed him in the Majdanek concentration camp, where he died less than a year later.

For their heroism in saving at least 3,500 Jews, André, Magda, and Daniel Trocmé were recognized by Yad Vashem as Righteous Among the Nations.

Yad Vashem

Yad Vashem, the World Holocaust Remembrance Center, is an organization whose purpose is to document, commemorate, and research the Holocaust, as well as educate people around the world about the events of the Shoah. The Righteous Among the Nations is an honor bestowed by Yad Vashem upon non-Jews who saved Jews during the Holocaust.

SUGGESTED READING LIST

Dauvillier, Loïc, Marc Lizano, and Greg Salsedo. *Hidden: A Child's Story of the Holocaust.* New York: First Second Books, 2014.

DeSaix, Deborah Durland, and Karen Gray Ruelle. *Hidden on the Mountain: Stories of Children Sheltered from the Nazis in Le Chambon.* New York: Holiday House, 2006.

Feldman, Gisèle Naichouler. *Saved by the Spirit of Lafayette.* Northville, MI: Ferne Press, 2008.

Frank, Anne. *The Diary of a Young Girl.* New York: Bantam, 1993.

Gleitzman, Morris. *Then.* New York: Square Fish, 2008.

Gruenbaum, Michael. *Somewhere There Is Still a Sun: A Memoir of the Holocaust.* New York: Aladdin, 2015.

Kustanowitz, Esther. *The Hidden Children of the Holocaust: Teens Who Hid from the Nazis.* New York: Rosen Publishing Group, 1999.

Laskier, Rutka. *Rutka's Notebook: A Voice from the Holocaust.* New York: Yad Vashem and Time Inc., 2008.

Leyson, Leon. *The Boy on the Wooden Box.* New York: Atheneum Books for Young Readers, 2013.

LeZotte, Ann Clare. *T4: A Novel in Verse.* Boston: Houghton Mifflin Company, 2008.

Lowry, Lois. *Number the Stars.* New York: HMH Books for Young Readers, 2011.

Mazzeo, Tilar J. *Irena's Children: Young Readers Edition: A True Story of Courage.* Adapted by Mary Cronk Farrell. New York: Margaret K. McElderry Books, 2017.

Wieviorka, Annette. *Auschwitz Explained to My Child.* New York: Marlowe & Company, 2002.

Wiviott, Meg. *Paper Hearts.* New York: Margaret K. McElderry Books, 2016.

Zullo, Allan. *Survivors: True Stories of Children in the Holocaust.* New York: Scholastic Paperbacks, 2005.

ORGANIZATIONS AND RESOURCES

There are many wonderful organizations and institutions dedicated to Holocaust education and combating anti-Semitism and intolerance. These are just a few.

ANNE FRANK CENTER FOR MUTUAL RESPECT
annefrank.com

ANNE FRANK HOUSE MUSEUM
annefrank.org

THE ANTI-DEFAMATION LEAGUE
ADL.org

AUSCHWITZ MEMORIAL AND MUSEUM
auschwitz.org
Resources for teachers:
auschwitz.org/en/education

THE FOUNDATION FOR THE MEMORY OF THE SHOAH
fondationshoah.org

HOLOCAUST MEMORIAL & TOLERANCE CENTER OF NASSAU COUNTY
hmtcli.org

IWITNESS
Stronger Than Hate
iwitness.usc.edu

UCL CENTRE FOR HOLOCAUST EDUCATION
holocausteducation.org.uk

UNITED STATES HOLOCAUST MEMORIAL MUSEUM
ushmm.org
Resources for educators:
ushmm.org/educators
Resources for students:
encyclopedia.ushmm.org

USC SHOAH FOUNDATION
The Institute for Visual History and Education
sfi.usc.edu

BIBLIOGRAPHY

GENERAL HISTORY OF FRANCE, JEWS IN FRANCE, WORLD WAR II, AND THE GERMAN OCCUPATION

Gildea, Robert. *Marianne in Chains: Daily Life in the Heart of France During the German Occupation.* New York: Picador, 2004.

Lanzmann, Claude. *Shoah: The Complete Text of the Acclaimed Holocaust Film.* New York: Da Capo Press, 1995.

Marrus, Michael R., and Robert O. Paxton. *Vichy France and the Jews.* New York: Basic Books, 1981.

Rajsfus, Maurice. *The Vél d'Hiv Raid: The French Police at the Service of the Gestapo.* Translated by Levi Laub. Los Angeles: DoppelHouse Press, 2017.

Rosbottom, Ronald C. *When Paris Went Dark: The City of Light Under German Occupation, 1940–1944.* New York: Little, Brown and Company, 2014.

Vinen, Richard. *The Unfree French: Life Under the Occupation.* New Haven, CT: Yale University Press, 2006.

THE HOLOCAUST AND ANTI-SEMITISM

Gilbert, Martin. *The Holocaust: A History of the Jews of Europe During the Second World War.* New York: Henry Holt and Company, 1985.

Lazare, Lucien. *Rescue as Resistance: How Jewish Organizations Fought the Holocaust in France.* Translated by Jeffrey M. Green. New York: Columbia University Press, 1996.

BBC News. "Tel Aviv unveils first memorial to gay Holocaust victims." January 10, 2014. bbc.com/news/world-europe-25687190

Encyclopædia Britannica
britannica.com/event/Holocaust

Holocaust Encyclopedia
encyclopedia.ushmm.org/content/en/article/nazi-camps
encyclopedia.ushmm.org/content/en/article/introduction-to-the-holocaust
encyclopedia.ushmm.org/content/en/article/glossary

Montreal Holocaust Museum
museeholocauste.ca/en/history-holocaust

United States Holocaust Memorial Museum
ushmm.org

JEWS IN POLAND AND PERSONAL FAMILY HISTORY

Ancestry.com

JewishGen Inc. (affiliate of the Museum of Jewish Heritage, New York City)
jewishgen.org

Virtual Shtetl (POLIN Museum of the History of Polish Jews)
sztetl.org.pl/en

THE FRENCH RESISTANCE, THE MAQUIS, AND THE BATTLE OF MONT MOUCHET

Evans, Martin. "A History of the French Resistance: From de Gaulle's call to arms against Vichy France to Liberation four years later." *History Today* 68, no. 8 (August 2018). historytoday.com/reviews/history-french-resistance

Gildea, Robert. *Fighters in the Shadows: A New History of the French Resistance.* Cambridge, MA: Belknap Press, 2015.

Gueslin, André, ed. *De Vichy au Mont-Mouchet: L'Auvergne en guerre, 1939–1945.* Clermont-Ferrand, France: Institut d'Études du Massif Central, Université Blaise-Pascal, 1991.

Kedward, H. R. *In Search of the Maquis: Rural Resistance in Southern France, 1942–1944.* New York: Clarendon Press, 1993.

Sanitas, Jean. *Les tribulations d'un résistant auvergnat ordinaire: La 7e compagnie dans la bataille du Mont-Mouchet.* Paris: Éditions L'Harmattan, 1997.

Chemins de Mémoire: The Maquis du Mont Mouchet
cheminsdememoire.gouv.fr/en/maquis-du-mont-mouchet

Chemins de Mémoire: The Resistance and the Networks
cheminsdememoire.gouv.fr/en/resistance-and-networks

THE RIGHTEOUS AMONG THE NATIONS AND THE HIDING OF CHILDREN IN FRANCE

Bailly, Danielle, ed. *The Hidden Children of France, 1940–1945: Stories of Survival.* Albany, NY: State University of New York Press, 2010.

Flitterman-Lewis, Sandy. *Hidden Voices: Childhood, the Family, and Anti-Semitism in Occupation France.* Abondance, France: Éditions Ibex, 2004.

Gilbert, Martin. *The Righteous: The Unsung Heroes of the Holocaust.* New York: Henry Holt and Company, 2003.

Grose, Peter. *A Good Place to Hide: How One French Community Saved Thousands of Lives During World War II*. New York: Pegasus Books, 2015.

Jeruchim, Simon. *Hidden in France: A Boy's Journey Under the Nazi Occupation*. McKinleyville, CA: Fithian Press, 2001.

Klarsfeld, Serge. *The Children of Izieu: A Human Tragedy*. New York: Abrams, 1984.

Scheps Weinstein, Frida. *A Hidden Childhood: A Jewish Girl's Sanctuary in a French Convent, 1942–1945*. New York: Pegasus Books, 2015.

YAD VASHEM

Yad Vashem—The World Holocaust Remembrance Center
yadvashem.org/righteous/resources/righteous-among-the-nations-in-france.html
yadvashem.org/righteous/stories/trocme.html

swarthmore.edu/library/peace/DG100-150/dg107Trocme.htm

MURIEL RUKEYSER

Rukeyser, Muriel. *Out of Silence: Selected Poems*. Evanston, IL: Northwestern University Press, 1992.

THE BEAST OF GÉVAUDAN

Sánchez Romero, Gustavo, and S. R. Schwalb. *Beast: Werewolves, Serial Killers, and Man-Eaters: The Mystery of the Monsters of the Gévaudan*. New York: Skyhorse Publishing, 2016.

Smith, Jay M. *Monsters of the Gévaudan: The Making of a Beast*. Cambridge, MA: Harvard University Press, 2011.

Taake, Karl-Hans. "Solving the Mystery of the 18th-Century Killer 'Beast of Gévaudan.'" *National Geographic*. September 27, 2016.
blog.nationalgeographic.org/2016/09/27/solving-the-mystery-of-the-18th-century-killer-beast-of-gevaudan

FRENCH PSYCHIATRIC HOSPITALS IN WORLD WAR II

Lafont, Max. *L'Extermination douce*. Lormont, France: La Bord de l'Eau, 2000.

von Bueltzingsloewen, Isabelle. "The Mentally Ill Who Died of Starvation in French Psychiatric Hospitals During the German Occupation in World War II." *Vingtième Siècle: Revue d'histoire* 2002/4, no. 76.
cairn.info/article.php?ID_ARTICLE=VING_076_0099

IMAGE CREDITS

adoc-photos/Corbis via Getty Images: 214 left; Alexander Vorontsov/Galerie Bilderwelt/Getty Images: 212 top left; Anne Frank Fonds—Basel via Getty Images: 212 right; Galerie Bilderwelt/Getty Images: 212 bottom left; Hulton-Deutsch Collection/CORBIS/Corbis via Getty Images: 215, 216 left; Keystone/Getty Images: 213; PD-US: 211, 216 top right; R. J. Palacio: 210; United States Holocaust Memorial Museum, courtesy of Robert Trocmé: 216 bottom right; United States Holocaust Memorial Museum, courtesy of Rudy Appel: 214 right

ACKNOWLEDGMENTS

It takes a village to make a book. This is always true with any type of book that gets published, but it's especially true of a graphic novel—and especially, ESPECIALLY true of a graphic novel written and illustrated by someone who has never, ever done one before.

The first person I'd like to thank (and without whom this book could NOT have been made) is Kevin Czap. Thank you, Kevin, for taking my sketchy linework and turning it into beautiful, fluid, gorgeous line art. What a pleasure it's been working with you!

Thank you to Isabel Warren-Lynch and her wonderful design team, who guided me and shepherded this project from beginning to end. Thank you also to Carol Naughton, who helped us come up with this beautiful package.

Thank you to Lisa, Josey, Russell, Desi, Willa, Gayle, Denbele, Nick, and everyone who served as my illustration models. Whether you actually "recognize" yourselves in the final character renditions or not, please know your poses and acting were vital to the illustration process. Thank you to Helen Uffner for providing fantastic period-specific wardrobes for the characters.

Thank you to Apple for the iPad and iPad pencil, and the creators of Procreate, which made it possible for me to do this thing.

Thank you to Artie Bennett, who, once again, has proven to be the most amazing copy editor on the planet. He catches things like no one else! Thank you to my personal research team and fact-checkers (you know who you are). Thank you to Sarah Neilson for her careful review (and gentle critiques) of both the text and art. Your input was invaluable, and I, and Julien, are so grateful. Thank you to Dr. Elizabeth B. White and Edna Friedberg, PhD, from the United States Holocaust Memorial Museum, for their thorough examination of the historical events depicted in the book, and to Andrea Barchas for connecting us. The revisions made the work stronger in every way.

Thank you, as always, to Erin Clarke, *Madame Éditeur Extraordinaire,* for her endless patience, incredible instincts, and unshakable belief that this one needed to be put first in line. I thank my lucky stars we ended up together, Erin! And I know we both thank our lucky stars for Kelly Delaney, who bats cleanup for Team *Wonder* every time.

Thank you to my amazing publicist Jillian Vandall, to the WONDERFUL ship's captain, Barbara Marcus, and to the rest of my Random House family.

Thank you to Alyssa Eisner Henkin and the team at Trident Media. Alyssa, your wisdom in all matters means so much to me. So does your friendship!

Lastly, thank you to my husband, Russell, who is my partner in all things, and whose family I am so proud to be a part of. I know Mollie is looking down on you and smiling, Russell. And thank you to Caleb and Joseph, for reminding me every day that this world is worth fighting for.